HE WILL BE MY RUIN

ALSO BY K.A. TUCKER

Ten Tiny Breaths
One Tiny Lie
Four Seconds to Lose
Five Ways to Fall
In Her Wake
Burying Water
Becoming Rain
Chasing River
Surviving Ice

HE WILL BE MY RUIN

A Novel

K. A. TUCKER

ATRIA BOOKS

New York London Toronto Sydney New Delhi

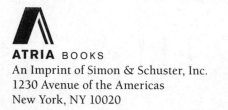

ATRIA BOOKS
An Imprint of Simon & Schuster, Inc.
1230 Avenue of the Americas
New York, NY 10020

This book is a work of fiction. Any references to historical events, real people, or real places are used fictitiously. Other names, characters, places, and events are products of the author's imagination, and any resemblance to actual events or places or persons, living or dead, is entirely coincidental.

First Atria Books hardcover edition February 2016

ATRIA BOOKS and colophon are trademarks of Simon & Schuster, Inc.

For information about special discounts for bulk purchases, please contact Simon & Schuster Special Sales at 1-866-506-1949 or business@simonandschuster.com.

The Simon & Schuster Speakers Bureau can bring authors to your live event. For more information or to book an event, contact the Simon & Schuster Speakers Bureau at 1-866-248-3049 or visit our website at www.simonspeakers.com.

Interior design by Paul Dippolito

Manufactured in the United States of America

10 9 8 7 6 5 4 3 2 1

Library of Congress Control Number: 2015033539

ISBN 978-1-5011-1207-2
ISBN 978-1-5011-1209-6 (ebook)

To Sarah Cantin—for your guiding words, your patient hand, and the magic you wield with an editor's pen.

HE WILL BE MY RUIN

PROLOGUE

Maggie

December 23, 2015

My wrists burn.

Hours of trying to break free of the rope that binds my hands behind my back have left them raw, the rough cord scrubbing away my skin and cutting into my flesh. I'm sure I'll have unsightly scars.

Not that it will matter when I'm dead.

I resigned myself to that reality around the time that I finally let go of my bladder. Now I simply lie here, in a pool of urine and vomit, my teeth numb from knocking with each bump in the road, my body frozen by the cold.

Trying to ignore the darkness as I fight against the panic that consumes me. I could suffocate from the anxiety alone.

He knows that.

Now he's exploiting it. That must be what he does—he uncovers your secrets, your fears, your flaws—and he uses them against you. He did it to Celine.

And now he's doing it to me.

That's why I'm in a cramped trunk, my lungs working overtime against a limited supply of oxygen while my imagination runs wild with what may be waiting for me at the end of this ride.

My racing heart ready to explode.

The car hits an especially deep pothole, rattling my bones. I've been trapped in here for so long. Hours. Days. I have no idea. Long enough to run through every mistake that I made.

How I trusted him, how I fell for his charm, how I believed his lies. How I made it so easy for him to do this to me.

How Celine made it so easy for him, by letting him get close.

Before he killed her.

Just like he's going to kill me.

CHAPTER 1

Maggie

November 30, 2015

The afternoon sun beams through the narrow window, casting a warm glow over Celine's floral comforter.

It would be inviting, only her body was found in this very bed just thirteen days ago.

"Maggie?"

"Yeah," I respond without actually turning around, my gaze taking in the cramped bedroom before me. I've never been a fan of New York City and all its overpriced boroughs. Too big, too busy, too pretentious. Take this Lower East Side apartment, for example, on the third floor of a drafty building built in the 1800s, with a ladder of shaky fire escapes facing the side alley and a kitschy gelato café downstairs. It costs more per month than the average American hands the bank in mortgage payments.

And Celine adored it.

"I'm in 410 if you just . . . want to come and find me."

I finally turn and acknowledge the building super—a chestnut-haired English guy around thirty by my guess, with a layer of scruff over his jawline and faded blue jeans—edging toward the door. Given the apartment is 475 square feet, it doesn't take him long to reach it.

I think he gave me his name but I wasn't listening. I've barely said two words since I met him in front of Celine's apartment, armed with a stack of cardboard flats and trash bags. An orchestra of clocks that softly tick away claim that that was nearly half an hour ago. I've simply stood here since then, feeling the brick-exposed walls—lined with floor-to-ceiling bookshelves and filled with the impressive collection of treasures that Celine had amassed over her twenty-eight years—closing in on me.

But now I feel the need to speak. "You were the one who let the police in?" Celine never missed work, never arrived late. That's why, after not showing up for two days and not answering her phone or her door, her coworker finally called the cops.

The super nods.

"You *saw* her?"

His eyes flicker to the thin wall that divides the bedroom from the rest of the apartment—its only purpose is to allow the building's owner to charge rent for a "one-bedroom" instead of a studio. There's not even enough room for a door. *Yes, he saw her body.* "She seemed really nice," he offers, his throat turning scratchy, shifting on his feet. He'd rather be unplugging a shit-filled toilet than be here right now. I don't blame him. "Uh . . . So you can just slide the key through the mail slot in my door when you're finished, if you want? I'll be home later tonight to grab it."

Under different circumstances, I'd find his accent charming. "I'll be staying here for a while."

He frowns. "You can't—"

"Yeah, I can," I snap, cutting his objection off. "We're on the hook with the lease until the end of January, right? So don't even think of telling me that I can't." I'm in no rush to empty this place out so some jackass landlord can rent it next month and pocket my money. Plus . . . My gaze drifts over the living room again. I just need to be in Celine's presence for a while, even if she's not here anymore.

"Of course. I'm just . . ." He bites his bottom lip as if to stall a snippy response. When he speaks again, his tone is back to soft. "The mattress, the bedding, it'll all need to be replaced. I would have already pitched it for you, but I figured that it wasn't my call to make. I pulled the blanket up to cover the mess and tried to air the place out, but . . ."

I sigh shakily, the tension making my body as taut as a wire. *I'm the only jackass around here.* "Right. I'm sorry." I inhale deeply. The linen air freshener can't completely mask the smell. Her body lay in that bed for two days.

Dead.

Decomposing.

"I'll be fine with the couch until I can get a new mattress delivered." It'll be more than fine, seeing as I've been sleeping on a thin bedroll on a dirt floor in Ethiopia for the past three months. At least there's running water here, and I'm not sharing the room with two other people. Or rats, hopefully.

"I can probably get a bloke in here to help me carry it out if you want," he offers, sliding hands into his pockets as he slowly shifts backward.

"Thank you." I couple my contrite voice with a smile and watch the young super exit, pulling the door shut behind him.

My gaze drifts back to the countless shelves. I haven't been to visit Celine in New York in over two years; we always met in California, the state where we grew up. "My, you've been busy," I whisper. Celine always did have a love for the old and discarded, and she had a real eye for it. She'd probably seen every last episode of *Antiques Roadshow* three times over. She was supposed to start school this past September to get her MA in art business, with plans to become an appraiser. She delayed enrollment, for some reason.

But she never told me that. I found out through her mother just last week.

Her apartment looks more like a bursting vintage shop than a place someone would live. It's well organized at least—all her trinkets grouped effectively. Entire shelves are dedicated to elaborate teacups, others to silver tea sets, genuine hand-cut crystal glassware, ornate clocks and watches, hand-painted tiles, and so on. Little side tables hold stained-glass lamps and more clocks and her seemingly endless collection of art history books. On the few walls not lined with shelves, an eclectic mix of artwork fills the space.

Very few things in here aren't antique or vintage. The bottles of Ketel One, Maker's Mark, and Jägermeister lined up on a polished brass bar cart. Her computer and a stack of hardcover books, sitting on a worn wooden desk that I'd expect to find in an old elementary schoolhouse. Even the two-foot-tall artificial Christmas tree has well-aged ornaments dangling from its branches.

I wander aimlessly, my hands beginning to touch and test. A slight pull of the desk drawer finds it locked, with no key anywhere, from what I can see. I run a finger along the spine of a leather-bound edition of *The Taming of the Shrew* on a shelf. Not a speck of dust. Celine couldn't stand disorder. Every single nutcracker faces out, equidistant from the next, shortest in front, tallest in back, as if she measured them with a ruler and placed them just so.

Being enclosed in this organized chaos makes me antsy. Or maybe that's my own ultra-minimalist preferences coming out.

I sigh and drop my purse onto the couch. My phone goes next, but not before I send a text to my personal assistant, Taryn, to ask that she arrange for a firm double mattress to be delivered to Celine's address. Then I power the phone off before she can respond with unnecessary questions. I've had it on silent since my plane landed in San Diego five days ago for the funeral. Even with two proficient assistants handling my organization's affairs while I'm dealing with my best friend's death, the stupid thing hasn't stopped vibrating.

They can all wait for me, while I figure out where to begin here.

I know I have a lot of paperwork to get to the lawyer. All estate proceeds will eventually go to Celine's mother, Rosa, but she doesn't want a dime. She's already demanded that I sell off anything I don't want to keep for myself and use the money for one of my humanitarian efforts in her daughter's name.

I could tell Rosa was still in shock, because she has always been a collector by nature—that's where Celine got it from—and it surprised me that she wouldn't want to keep at least some of her daughter's treasures for herself. But she was adamant and I was not going to argue. I'll just quietly pack a few things that I think would mean a lot to her and have them shipped to San Diego.

Seeing Celine's apartment now, though, I realize that selling is going to take forever. I'm half-tempted to dump everything into boxes for charity, guesstimate the value, and write a check. But that would belittle all the evenings and weekends that Celine devoted to hunting antique shops, garage sales, and ignorant sellers for her next perfect treasure.

My attention lands on the raw wood plank shelf that floats over a mauve suede couch, banked by silky curtains and covered with an eclectic mix of gilded frames filled with pictures from Celine's childhood. Most of them are of her and her mom. Some are of just her. Four include me.

I smile as I ease one down, of Celine and me at the San Diego Zoo. I was twelve, she was eleven. Even then she was striking, her olive skin tanned from a summer by the pool. Next to her, my pale Welsh skin always looked sickly.

I first met Celine when I was five. My mom had hired her mother, Rosa Gonzalez, as a housekeeper and nanny, offering room and board for both her and her four-year-old daughter. We had had a string of nannies come and go, my mother never satisfied with their work ethic. But Rosa came highly recommended. *It's so hard to find good help*, I remember overhearing my mother say to her friends once. They applauded her generosity with Rosa, that she was not only taking in a recent immigrant from Mexico, but her child as well.

The day Celine stepped into my parents' palatial house in La Jolla, she did so with wide brown eyes, her long hair the color of cola in braided pigtails and adorned in giant blue bows, her frilly blue-and-white dress and matching socks like something out of *The Wizard of Oz*. Celine would divulge to me later on that it was the only dress she owned, purchased from a thrift shop, just for this special occasion.

Rosa and Celine lived with us for ten years, and my daily routines quickly became Celine's daily routines. The chauffeur would drop Celine off at the curb in front of the local public school on our way to my private school campus. Though her school was far above average as public schools go, I begged and pleaded for my parents to pay for Celine to attend with me. I didn't quite understand the concept of money back then, but I knew we had a lot, and we could more than afford it.

They told me that's just not how the world works. Besides, as much as Rosa wanted the best for her child, she was too proud to ever accept that kind of generosity. Even giving Celine my hand-me-down clothes was a constant battle.

No matter where we spent the day, though, from the time we came home to the time we fell asleep, Celine and I were inseparable. I would return from piano lessons and teach Celine how to read music notes. She'd use the other side of my art easel to paint pictures with me of the ocean view from my bedroom window. She'd rate my dives and time my laps around our pool, and I'd do the same for her. We'd lounge beneath the palm trees on hot summer days, dreaming up plans for our future. In my eyes, it was a given that Celine would always be part of my life.

We were an odd match. From our looks to our social status to our polar-opposite personalities, we couldn't have been more different. I was captain of the debate squad and Celine played the romantic female lead in her school plays. I spearheaded a holiday charity campaign at the age of thirteen, while Celine sang in choirs for the local senior citizens. I read the *Wall Street Journal* and the *Los Angeles Times* religiously, while Celine would fall asleep with a Jane Austen novel resting across her chest.

And then one Saturday morning in July when I was fifteen, my parents announced that they had filed for divorce. I still remember the day well. They walked side-by-side toward where I lounged beside the pool, my dad dressed for a round of golf, my mom carrying a plate of Rosa's breakfast enchiladas. They'd technically separated months earlier, and I had no idea because seeing them together had always been rare to begin with.

The house in La Jolla was going up for sale. Dad was buying a condo close to the airport, to make traveling for work easier, while Mom would be moving to Chicago, where our family's company, Sparkes Energy, had their corporate headquarters. I'd stay wherever I wanted, when I wasn't at the *prestigious* boarding school in Massachusetts that they decided I should attend for my last three years of high school.

The worst of it was that Rosa and Celine would be going their own way.

Rosa, who was more a parent to me than either of my real parents had ever been.

Celine . . . my best friend, my sister.

Both of them, gone from my daily life with two weeks' notice.

They're just a phone call away, my mom reasoned. That's all I had, and so I took advantage. For years, I would call Celine and Rosa daily. I had a long-distance plan, but had I not, I still would have happily driven up my mom's phone bill, bitter with her for abandoning me for the company. I spent Christmases and Thanksgivings with Rosa and Celine instead of choosing to spend them with Melody or William Sparkes.

To be honest, it never was much of a choice.

Through boyfriends, college, jobs, and fronting a successful non-profit organization that has had me living all over Africa and Asia for the last six years, Celine and Rosa have remained permanent fixtures in my life.

Until thirteen days ago, when Rosa's sobs filled my ear in a village near Nekemte, Ethiopia, where I've been leading a water well project and building homes. After a long, arduous day in the hot sun, my hands covered with cuts from corrugated iron and my muscles sore from carrying burned bricks, it was jarring to hear Rosa's voice. California felt worlds away. At first I thought that I hadn't kept myself hydrated enough and I was hallucinating. But by the third time I heard her say, "Celine killed herself," it finally registered. It just didn't make sense.

It still doesn't.

Hollowness kept me company all the way back—first on buses, then a chartered flight, followed by several commercial airline connections—and into Rosa's modest home in the suburbs of San Diego. The hollowness held me together through the emotional visitation and funeral, Rosa's tightly knit Mexican community rocked by the news. It numbed me enough to face Rosa's eyes, bloodshot and rimmed with dark circles, as she insisted that I come to New York to handle the material remains of her only child.

The case is all but officially closed. The police are simply waiting for the final autopsy report to confirm that a lethal dose of Xanax—the pill bottle sitting open on her nightstand was from a prescription she filled only two days prior—combined with an unhealthy amount of vodka was what killed her. They see it as a quick open-and-shut suicide case, aided by a note in her handwriting that read *I'm sorry for everything*, found lying next to her.

The picture frame cracks within my tightening grasp as tears burn my cheeks, and I have the overwhelming urge to smash the entire shelf of happy memories.

This *just doesn't* seem possible. How could she do this to her mother? I shift my focus to the picture of Rosa—a petite brunette with a fierce heart, who gives hugs to strangers who look like they're having a bad day and spouts a string of passionate Spanish when anyone tries to leave the dinner table before every last bite is finished.

Before this past week, I hadn't seen Rosa since last Christmas. She still looks frail eleven months after the doctors told her that the double mastectomy, chemotherapy, and radiation had worked and she was considered in remission. It'll be a year in January since the day Celine phoned me to give me the good news: that Rosa had fought breast cancer hard. And had won.

So why the hell would Celine make her suffer so horribly now?

I roam aimlessly through the rest of the apartment, in a state of extreme exhaustion after days of travel and jet lag and tears, taking in everything that remains of my childhood friend.

But there are things here that surprise me, too—a closet full of designer-label dresses that Celine couldn't possibly have afforded on an administrative assistant's salary, a bathroom counter overflowing with bold red lipsticks and daringly dark eye shadows that I never saw touch her naturally beautiful face, not even in recent photos.

Knowing Celine, she bought those dresses at secondhand stores. And the makeup, well . . . She would have looked beautiful with red lipstick.

I smile, sweeping the bronzer brush across my palm to leave a dusting of sparkle against my skin. *I'm* supposed to be this girl—the one with the extravagant clothes and makeup, who puts time and stock into looks and money. As the fourth generation of one of the biggest energy companies in the world, I will one day inherit 51 percent of the corporation's shares. Though my parents don't *need* to work, they each run a division—my industrialist father managing the ugly face of coal burning while my mother distracts the world with a pretty mask of wind and solar energy farms, hiding the fact that we're slowly helping to destroy the world.

I grew up aware of the protests. I've read enough articles about the greed and the harm to the planet that comes with this industry. By the time I turned twenty-one, still young and idealistic and embroiled by the latest disgrace involving our company and an oil tanker spill off the coast of China, I wanted nothing to do with the enormous trust fund that my grandmother left me. In fact, I was one signature away from handing it all over to a charity foundation. My biggest mistake—and saving grace—was that I tried to do it through my lawyer, a loyal Sparkes Energy legal consultant. He, of course, informed my parents, who fought me on it. I wouldn't listen to them.

But I did listen to Celine. She was the one who persuaded me not to do it in the end, sending me link after link of scandal after scandal involving charity organizations. How so little of the money ever actually reaches those in need, how so much of the money lines the pockets of individuals. She used the worst-case scenarios to steer me away from my plan because she knew it would work. Then she suggested that I use the trust fund to lead my own humanitarian ventures. I could do bigger, better things if *I* controlled it.

That's when I began Villages United.

And Celine was right.

VU may only be six years old, but it has already become an internationally recognized nonprofit, focused on high-impact lending projects throughout the world geared toward building self-sustainable villages. We teach children to read and give them roofs to sleep under and clean water to drink and clothes to wear and books to read. Between my own money and the money that VU has raised, we have now left a lasting mark on thirty-six communities in countries around the world.

And I'm not just writing checks from my house in California. I'm right there in the trenches, witnessing the changes firsthand. Something my parents simply don't understand, though they've tried turning it into a Sparkes Energy PR venture on more than one occasion.

I've refused every single time.

Because, for the first time in a long time, I'm truly proud to be Maggie Sparkes.

I haven't even warned them about my newest endeavor—providing significant financial backing to companies that are developing viable and economical green energy solutions. VU was preparing to announce it to the media in the coming weeks. As much as I can't think about any of that right now, I'll have to soon. Too many people rely on me.

But for now . . . all I can focus on is Celine.

I wander into her bedroom, my back to another wall of collectibles as I stand at the foot of the ornate wrought-iron bed, the delicate bedding stretched out neatly, as if Celine made it this morning. As if she'll be back later to share a glass of wine and a laugh.

I yank the duvet back, just long enough to see the ugly proof beneath.

To remind me that that's never going to happen.

Edging along the side of her bed—I actually have to turn and shimmy to fit—I move toward a stack of vintage wooden food crates that serve as a nightstand. A wave of nostalgia washes over me as my finger traces the heavy latches and handmade, chunky gunmetal-gray body of the antique box sitting next to the lamp. The day that I spied it in an antique store while shopping for Celine's sixteenth birthday, it made me think of a medieval castle. The old man who sold it to me said it was actually an eighteenth-century lockbox.

Whatever it was, I knew Celine would love it.

I carry it over to the living room, where I can sit and open it up. Inside are sentimental scraps of Celine's life. Concert stubs and random papers, a dried rose, her grandmother's rosary that Rosa gave to her. Rosa is supremely religious, and Celine, the ever-devoted daughter, kept up appearances for her mother, though she admitted to me that she didn't find value in it.

I pull each item out, laying them on the trunk coffee table until I'm left with nothing but the smooth velvet floor of the box. I fumble with a small detail on the outside that acts as a lever—remembering my surprise when the man revealed the box's secret—until a click sounds, allowing me to pry open the false bottom.

Celine's shy, secretive eyes lit up when I first showed her the sizeable compartment. It was perfect for hiding treasures, like notes from boys, and the silver bracelet that her senior-year boyfriend bought her for Valentine's Day and she was afraid to wear in front of Rosa. While I love Rosa dearly, she could be suffocating sometimes.

My fingers wrap around the wad of money filling the small space as a deep frown creases my forehead. Mostly hundreds but plenty of fifties, too. I quickly count it. There's almost ten thousand dollars here.

Why wouldn't Celine deposit this into her bank account?

I pick up the ornate bronze key and a creased sheet of paper that also sits within. I'm guessing the key is for the desk. I'll test that out in a minute. I gingerly unfold the paper that's obviously been handled many times, judging by the crinkles in it.

My eyes widen.

A naked man fills one side. He's entrancingly handsome, with long lashes and golden-blond tousled hair and a shadow of peach scruff covering his hard jawline. He's lying on his back, one muscular arm disappearing into the pillow beneath his head, a white sheet tangled around his legs, not quite covering the goods, which from what I can see, are fairly impressive. I can't tell what color his eyes are because he's fast asleep.

"Well then . . ." I frown, taken aback.

I'm not surprised that Celine could attract the attention of a guy like this. She was a gorgeous young woman—her Mexican roots earning her lush locks, full lips, and voluptuous curves tied to the kind of tiny waist that all men seem to admire.

Nor am I surprised that he's blond. It has always been a running joke between us, her penchant for blonds. She's never dated anything but.

But I *am* surprised that she'd have the nerve to take—and print out to keep by her bed—a scandalous picture like this in the first place.

I wonder if she ever mentioned him to me. She always told me about her dates, utter failures or otherwise. Though it's been years since she was seeing anyone seriously, and she was *definitely* seeing this guy seriously if she was sleeping with him. Celine usually waited months before she gave that up to a guy. She didn't even lose her virginity until she was twenty-two, to a guy she had been dating for six months and hoped that she would one day marry. Who broke up with her shortly afterward.

So who the hell is this guy and why didn't I ever hear about him? And where is he now? When were they together last?

Does he know that she's dead?

Worrying my bottom lip between my teeth—it's a bad habit of mine—I slowly fold the paper back up. Celine's cursive scrawl decorates the back side in purple ink. Words I hadn't noticed before.

Words that make my heart stop now.

This man was once my salvation. Now he will be my ruin.

CHAPTER 2

Maggie

Celine was always more emotional than me. She had a love for flowery prose in literature and the kind of poetry that makes my eyes glaze over. She cried at movies and could sit and stare at a sculpture for hours. Her crushes were never *just* crushes.

It wasn't until her twentieth birthday that a doctor said the D word. He prescribed medication for low-grade depression and anxiety, and it seemed to work. She used to call them her "happy pills." They made her more levelheaded, less dramatic.

These words that I'm seeing now, though . . . What do they even mean? Is this an over-the-top profession of love for a guy she was sleeping with? A thread of poetry to express how much he meant to her? Knowing Celine, that's possible. But how was he supposed to save her? What would she need saving from? And did he end up breaking her heart?

Too many questions and I'm not sure who can answer them. Maybe this naked guy, but in a city of over eight million people, I wouldn't know quite where to begin.

If they were dating, there was surely a text-message chain with his name on it.

I root through the black leather purse that hangs on a hook by the door and find all the usual suspects—a full wallet, work ID badge, sunglasses, random toiletries.

But no phone.

I know she didn't have it on her when she died. The funeral

home arranged for all personal effects to be shipped along with the body when it was transported to San Diego. All that came were a pair of earrings and a watch.

Did it go missing somewhere along the way? Would someone be sick enough to steal a phone off a corpse? The last I remember, Celine raved about how great the camera was on her iPhone. I guess someone could make some money off of it. But her earrings were diamond, her watch a Michael Kors. Why steal a phone and not the jewelry? Missing earrings are less likely to be noticed than a cell phone . . .

I dial Celine's number with shaky fingers for the first time since her death. My throat tightens at the sound of her smooth, sultry recorded voice on the other side, telling me that she's not available. Her voicemail picked up immediately, so the battery must have died.

I hit redial and listen to Celine's voice four more times before forcing myself to move on.

Grabbing a sheet of paper and a pen from her desk, I begin my list of things I need to do tomorrow. The first one: ask the police about Celine's phone.

I run my thumb over the touch screen of my phone. It's both a godsend and a curse. I bring it along with me everywhere, even on those sweltering hot days when I'm elbow-deep in dirt and reception is spotty.

People's entire lives can be uncovered in phones.

Maybe someone took Celine's phone and it had nothing to do with making some easy cash. Maybe there was something on there that someone didn't want uncovered.

Or maybe I'm just tired and delirious.

I toss the pen aside and pick up the dried yellow rose that I found in the main compartment of the lockbox. Celine certainly couldn't have held on to it to preserve its beauty, I note, rubbing the shriveled brown-tinged petals between my fingers. There's still a hint of moisture in the base of the flower. It can't be that old.

I inspect each item pulled out of the box more closely now.

Ticket stubs to a Broadway show of *Romeo and Juliet*—Celine's favorite—from years ago. I remember her seeing this with "the love of her life" Bruce. The jackass who broke up with her one day with an "it's not you, it's me" excuse. A few weeks later she found out that the "it's me" part involved a redhead from her History class, which sent her into an emotional spiral.

It was the one and only time she has ever accepted a luxurious gift from me, in the form of an all-expenses-paid trip to Jamaica for the two of us. The only reason she agreed was because she was wallowing so deeply in misery that she couldn't think straight. Plus, it was already booked and nonrefundable.

I flick the ticket stub away with disdain, wondering why she'd keep it. That was Celine, though, ever the sentimentalist; even when the good memories were weighed down by the ugly aftereffects, she wanted to keep the evidence. A true glutton for punishment.

I find several tickets to memorable auctions, too. Attending the high-profile sales—witnessing the rich wave their money away with a paddle, one lucky winner walking off with a valuable piece of history—was like attending a gold medal game at the Olympics for Celine. Sometimes she'd call me afterward. It'd usually be the middle of the night on my side of the world, and I'd simply listen to her giddy voice, imagine her flushed cheeks, and I'd smile.

I find another card, from a Manhattan area florist, with a woman's handwriting in blue ink.

I still care very much about you. ~ J

If that doesn't smell of romance . . . and perhaps heartbreak . . .

On impulse, I turn my phone back on and punch in the number on the back of the card. A woman answers after the third ring.

"Hi, you delivered flowers to me recently and I wanted to thank the sender but I'm not entirely sure who they're from."

"Oh, well that's a little awkward, isn't it?" The soft-spoken woman chuckles. "Bear with me for a moment while I restart the computer. I was just about to leave for the day. Had the lights off and everything."

“I’m sorry.” If I were a more patient person, I would offer to call back tomorrow.

“That’s quite all right. We’re always happy to help our customers.” She hums softly. “We just opened two months ago and I’m still getting used to this system. So . . . what day did you say they arrived?”

“That’s the thing. I’m not exactly sure.”

“Oh?” There’s a hint of suspicion in her voice now, where there was only willingness before.

I quickly jump in with “I was away on vacation for several weeks and I came home to find them on my doorstep. If you’ll just check for delivery to . . .” I recite Celine’s address.

“And what is your name again?”

“Celine Gonzalez.”

“Well, it says here that you signed for them.”

I bite my bottom lip. “My neighbor must have signed for me. She was looking after my place while I was gone.”

“And she left them on your doorstep?” I grit my teeth with the long pause. “I’ll have to speak with the owner before I share any more information. We have privacy laws that we need to adhere to.”

I heave a sigh. “Look, Celine was actually my best friend. She passed away recently. I’d like to contact the person who sent these flowers to her and make sure they know what happened.”

There’s another long pause. “I’m sorry to hear that. Can I call you back tomorrow?”

“Sure.” I give her my number, doubting that I’ll hear from her again unless I go down there in person and bully the owner into giving me answers.

But I *have* learned one thing. Someone sent flowers to Celine within the last two months. Maybe it was the guy in the picture and maybe the rose in my hand was one of them, which would mean he was someone important to her, and she was someone important to him. And it sounds like maybe he screwed up.

I curl up with a blanket on the couch, listening to the soothing chorus of tick-tick-ticks from the shelf of clocks above, inhaling a hint of Celine's lavender perfume on the cushion as my exhausted and naturally suspicious mind spins.

A missing cell phone.

Flowers from a guy she never told me about.

A stack of money.

A picture of a naked man hidden away in her lockbox, with dramatic proclamations scrawled across the back.

A girl who I just can't believe would kill herself.

What if the police have it wrong?

When I drift off, my dreams are full of murder.

CHAPTER 3

Maggie

December 1, 2015

A crackling buzz startles me from a deep sleep and I lock gazes with twelve sets of eyes. Celine's porcelain dolls have been watching over me all night. I shudder, deciding that they'll be going into a box immediately after I have my morning coffee.

Another loud buzz sounds, followed by three shorter ones. It's the intercom and it's clearly what woke me up.

"Hold on," I grumble, giving my face a rub and my body a stretch before I check the collection of clocks to see that I just logged in fourteen hours of sleep. I can't remember the last time I slept that long.

I hold the chunky yellowed "answer" button down, surprised that this archaic system still works and hasn't been upgraded. "Hello?"

"Hey, it's me." A male voice fills Celine's apartment.

"Me who?"

"Hans. I'm here for the appraisal."

"What appraisal?"

"For the eggs!" His irritation hisses through the speaker. "This isn't funny, Celine. I don't do LES in the winter, and you know that."

Whoever he is, he hasn't heard the news yet. I could—and probably should—tell him to come back later, or not at all. But maybe he knows something that would be useful to me. Maybe he's important.

Maybe Hans is the mystery man.

"Where am I going again?" he asks.

"The stairs are on your left. Apartment 310." I buzz him in and rush to brush my teeth. At least I'm dressed, albeit in the same frayed jeans and rumpled flannel shirt that I flew to New York City in yesterday.

I throw the door open just as "Hans" reaches up to knock, and he lets out a squeal of surprise.

Hans is most certainly not the mystery man. Not unless the mystery man lost all muscle mass and dresses in a peacock-blue suit, complete with a fedora. And is now Asian.

He takes one quick head-to-toe review of me and then sneers. "You're not Celine." Bobbing his head up and down and around me, he asks, "Where is she?"

I sigh. "Come on in."

He pushes past me, dusting the snow off his coat, his boots tracking prints onto the worn parquet floor, his body bringing in a chill with him. With near-black eyes, he scans Celine's space with fascination, making me wonder if he's ever been here before.

I take a deep breath. "The thing is . . ."

Hans beelines for a shelf and, producing a magnifying glass and white gloves from his pocket, begins inspecting the fancy eggs sitting on stands, his attention riveted, oohing and ahhing to himself.

"So, how do you know Celine?" I finally ask, more curious than anything.

"We did our undergrad at NYU together. We've been friends for years." A pause. "How do *you* know Celine?" Again with that head-to-toe scan, like he completely disapproves of me and can't figure out what I could possibly have in common with her. Celine always did have an elegant style. One that didn't include torn jeans and wool work socks.

Now that I think about it, I remember Celine talking about a guy friend from school who was as into antiques as she was. "I grew up with her," I answer dismissively. "And you're here now because of those eggs?"

"My master's thesis was on Fabergé," Hans says matter-of-factly. "I work at Hollingsworth. She's been trying to get me here to do a formal appraisal for months so she can sell them. I just didn't have the time before."

Celine mentioned Hollingsworth to me enough times for me to know it's a well-established international art brokerage. Not only has it brokered some of the most significant sales in history through both public auctions and private deals, but it has an educational division—Hollingsworth's Institute of Art, where Celine had been accepted to attend. She planned on applying for a job as an appraiser at Hollingsworth after getting her MA.

But . . . "*Sell* them?"

"Yes. She figures the money from these will cover her storage fees." His black eyes take in the shelves. "At least for the first few months."

I frown. "Storage fees?" I realize I must sound like a complete idiot to Hans, with my two-word questions and clueless stare.

"It's a cruel world, isn't it? When a collector has to sell one of her children? Thank God I was able to talk her out of putting them up on that vile eBay." He spits out the name "eBay" and shudders.

Celine had an eBay store, where she sold the occasional vintage find. But she said she was building her "real" collection, so selling it all doesn't sound like something she'd do. "Did she say why she was doing that?"

He shrugs. "She needs the money, I guess."

I squeeze my eyes shut, my frustration at a boiling point. Between Celine and Rosa, I've never met two more obstinate people in my life when it comes to money. Rosa has always been too proud to take a dollar that she hasn't earned. Every check I have ever included in a Christmas gift or birthday gift has gone uncashed. Knowing Rosa, it was torn up immediately. When she was diagnosed with cancer and I flew back to stay with her, I had to resort to stealing her mail and paying her bills at the bank before she had a chance to.

Rosa taught her daughter to be just as proud and stubborn.

This must be about covering her tuition, and why she delayed starting her master's. I don't know how many times I offered to pay for it, but she refused.

"They're not *real* Fabergé, are they?" I ask. I don't know a lot about art history, but even *I* have heard about Fabergé. "Aren't those worth, like . . . *millions*?"

Hans laughs. It's one of those high-pitched, fake-sounding laughs that isn't actually fake. "No, of course they're not real. But even a well-made 'Fauxbergé' egg is worth something. Take this one, for example." He holds up a delicate blue egg with silver decoration. "Look at the punched-out detail and the enamel and . . ." He goes on, babbling about chasing and single-cut diamonds and color like I understand what he's saying. "She could get upwards of four thousand for this one. Can you believe that? She bought it for five bucks at a garage sale in the Bronx a year ago. Some clueless people clearing out their dead mother's attic."

"Wow."

He must sense my lack of excitement because his mouth flattens and that snooty tone reemerges. "Where is Celine?"

There's no great way to tell him. "You should probably put that egg back on the shelf."

He frowns but complies.

And then I tell him that Celine is dead.

Hans, the self-proclaimed Fabergé expert, crumples onto the couch and begins to sob uncontrollably. I don't really know what to do, so I simply sit down next to him and keep him company while he blubbers on. Outwardly emotional people and I have never meshed well.

Except for Celine, of course.

"But . . . but . . . *how*?" He peers at me in earnest. It's a fair question. It's the first question everyone asks. When it's an acquaintance who wants to know, I've found myself lying and saying she had a heart condition.

"Too much vodka. Too many pills."

Understanding fills his face. "You don't think she really meant to . . . ?"

My simple shrug is enough to send him into another fit of tears.

"She was such a beautiful, kind person. Never judgmental. She used to let me talk her ear off about everything. But then I got busy with work and I kept canceling on her." He blows his nose on a cloth handkerchief that he had tucked in his pocket. "I had no idea. I'm such a terrible person. She was truly one of my best friends."

"Yeah . . . mine, too," I say with a soft smile, adding quietly, "one of my only." It's only in the last few years that I've realized just how few people I've let get close to me, how short my list of must-call people when I'm back in America has become.

I've always done well with solitude.

"Wait, are you *that* friend of hers? You're . . ." He snaps his finger in my face as he points at me.

"Maggie Sparkes."

"Right." He nods slowly, and that gleam of harsh judgment has all but faded from his eyes. "She always talked about you." A long, awkward silence hangs between us as our gazes wander among the clutter. "I can't believe she's gone. What are you going to do with all of this stuff?"

"Good question." I tell him about Rosa's wishes.

"So you need to have everything appraised first. How are you planning on doing that?"

"I don't know yet. I was reading up on it and I think my best option is to find an online appraisal company that can take care of her entire collection. At like, ten bucks an item, that'll run me about . . . ," I cringe, "ten grand, give or take?" I'm guessing the appraisal will be worth more than the sum total of everything in here. Truthfully, I'll end up paying that out of pocket and padding the foundation generously in addition to it.

"Appraisals 'R' Us? Bite your tongue, woman!" Hans snaps. "Celine would be rolling in her grave if she heard you say that."

"I don't see any other options."

He takes a deep breath, swallowing hard as he looks at the shelves across from us with calculation in his eyes. "If you catalogue everything, I can make some calls. Yes . . ." He nods slowly, his jaw set with fresh determination as he dabs the tears from his cheeks. "I know plenty of people in the industry and *everyone* owes me a favor. We can do this. And I know good dealers, too, who might be willing to buy outright, or sell on consignment. Put them all in storage and we can take our time finding the right buyers."

"That's . . ." I exhale, feeling suddenly lighter now that I have some educated help. "Thank you. I don't know where to begin. Like, what do you mean by cataloguing?"

He mutters something in French. "Take pictures. Several, of different angles, including any markings. I can use them to help convince people to lend their expertise."

"Pictures. I can do that."

With his fingertip he traces the metal detail on the lockbox sitting on the coffee table. "Wow, eighteenth-century escutcheon."

"Sure." I smirk, though a part of me admires the guy for his vast knowledge. I can see why he and Celine were friends. They could geek out about art history in a way that she and I never could.

Hans absently picks up the picture of the naked mystery man, now lying on the floor by my feet, and unfolds it. His grief is temporarily suspended. "Well, hello . . . Who is this?"

The man who will be both Celine's salvation and ruin? Those words gnaw at my conscience. "I have no idea. I take it you don't know either?"

He frowns and shakes his head. "Why?"

"No reason. Just . . . curious." I pluck the picture from his fingertips and stuff it in my purse. I'll need it for the detective.

After a heartfelt hug and a few more quiet tears on his part, Hans and I exchange phone numbers and make plans to connect about Celine's collection over the next week, and then I say good-bye.

I've barely sunk back onto the couch when there's another knock on the door. I want to ignore it but I can't, because each knock may bring a new piece of information about Celine.

The super is back. "Hi, how's it going?" His gaze drifts over the pile of untouched cardboard flats, over the coffee table, covered with sentimental keepsakes. He shaved today, I notice, and made some effort with styling his hair.

"I got caught up in her things, and then obviously I fell asleep,"

I say, waving my hands over the exact same pair of jeans and flannel shirt I had on when I last saw him.

He nods. "When my brother died a few years ago, I spent an entire week lost in his stuff. It's overwhelming." His eyes—a pretty mixture of hazel and green—wander the space again. "And there wasn't nearly as much stuff to get lost in."

His casual words pluck at my heart, reminding me that everybody has lost somebody. I instantly feel less alone.

After a pause he says, "Listen, I'm just going to pull that mattress out of here and then leave you to it, okay?"

He was serious about doing that?

He nods his head to the side, and a burly man appears. "I brought the muscle with me."

I scan the super's arms—lean and cut—and can't help but smile, because he's obviously attempting a joke. It's all the more endearing, delivered with his light English accent.

"Okay." I turn my phone on to check for any messages—there are several, most work-related that I'll ignore, one about a mattress delivery for later today, and one from Rosa—while the two men pull the soiled mattress off the bed frame and turn it on its side to fit through the door, holding the duvet in place to hide the stains.

The super stops just outside the door. "Good luck in here, Maggie."

"Thank you . . . I'm sorry, I missed your name yesterday. I was a bit overwhelmed."

He smiles. "It's Grady."

"Well, thank you, Grady. And the muscle." They vanish down the hall with Celine's deathbed.

One second I'm alone in the narrow, dimly lit hallway outside Celine's apartment.

And then I lock the door and turn around to find a tiny, wrinkled woman standing no more than a foot away, smiling up at me.

She exclaims, "Hello, Maggie!" at the same time that I jump back and grab my chest.

"You're confused. Wondering how I know you, right?" she asks with a wide grin, showing a full set of dentures. She must be in her eighties, her white hair framing her face in perfectly set curls.

"Kind of." She made absolutely no noise coming out of her apartment. I'm guessing this encounter is no accident. She's probably been hovering just inside her door, the hearing aid tucked into her left ear turned up to full, waiting for me to emerge.

"I'm Ruby Cummings."

I frown. *Ruby Cummings* . . . I remember that name. "You sent flowers to the funeral home." I went through each arrangement, mentally noting the people who took the time out of their day for such a kind gesture. I knew most of them. I didn't recognize a Ruby Cummings, but I silently thanked her then.

Now I take her hand, the skin papery-thin but her grip surprisingly strong.

"I recognize you from the pictures on Celine's shelf. You're that rich one who does all those humanitarian things, right?" Cloudy green eyes survey me from behind glasses—my long caramel hair that is about six months late for a cut and pulled into a haphazard ponytail, my tanned skin in need of some moisturizer, my rough hands, the nails chewed and chipped. Perfectly acceptable while dragging building materials off wagons in a third world village. Basically, I'm the opposite of what you'd expect of someone with the size of bank account I have access to. "She was such a dear, sweet girl. Worked *so* hard, always off to the library or some garage sale when she wasn't at the office. Would you like to come in for tea or coffee? I've made shortbread. Celine always enjoyed those."

Clearly Ruby and Celine knew each other. There's no reason for me to be wary of a little old lady, even if she was waiting for me to emerge.

She gestures behind her, toward her apartment, from which the evidence of her baking wafts. I can't help but follow with my eyes, catching a glimpse of the inside. It makes Celine's apartment look minimalist. Shelves upon shelves of books line every visible wall.

Stacks of leather-bound spines sit in piles on the floor. Paperbacks rest on doily-covered tables. Hardcovers create obstacles everywhere, just waiting to teeter over and crush toes. I can see why she and Celine hit it off. It's a librarian's dream.

And a claustrophobic's nightmare.

My chest constricts at the sight of it.

Fortunately, I have an honest excuse for avoiding what would amount to an hour of difficulty breathing and possible blackouts. "Thanks for the offer, but I have to meet with the detective on Celine's case." I called before my shower to confirm that he's working today.

"Oh . . . ?" Curiosity flickers in her eyes. "About what?"

"Just want to clear up some questions I had." I smile. A smile that I hope conveys that this isn't to be gossiped about.

"Okay, dear. Well, you know where to find me. And if I can help with anything at all, don't hesitate."

"Thanks." I begin down the hall, but then stop. "Hey, quick question."

She nearly pounces. "Yes?"

"Did you ever see any of Celine's friends visit her?"

Her wrinkled face scrunches with thought. "Well, there's her coworker, the lovely Greek girl with those black ringlets. And then—"

I interrupt her. "What about men? Was she dating anyone?"

"No. Not that she mentioned to me. Odd, don't you think? She was such a beauty. I tell you, if I could turn back time and look like her, I'd have a parade lined up right here."

Dirty old bird. "Celine was a bit shy."

"Yes, I gathered that. She never brought a man home, not that I noticed anyway. And I'm *always* home. I would have heard or seen something." She drops her voice an octave. "I keep a watchful eye on the comings and goings around here."

I'll bet you do.

As tempted as I am to show her the picture of Celine's mystery man, I don't. It doesn't seem like that'll do anything but give her something to talk about with the neighbors. "See you around, Ruby."

CHAPTER 4

Maggie

"How much longer?"

"Detective Childs is out on a case and will be here just as soon as he can," the gray-haired clerk answers without looking up from her computer screen, her voice monotone, the line a standard dismissal.

"You said that two hours ago," I mumble, earning a leveled glare that makes me focus on the white Styrofoam cup I'm gripping, the grounds sticking to the rim. I helped myself to the precinct's coffeepot but haven't managed to choke down the muddy water.

At least I've been able to catch up on emails while sitting here, only mildly distracted by criminals and police officers alike milling about.

"Ahhh . . . well, there you are," the clerk calls out as footsteps approach from somewhere unseen to me. "This young lady has been waiting *so patiently* for your return."

"Well, how 'bout that." A man of average height and soft-bellied build appears and examines me through chocolate-brown eyes that match his skin. He shifts a grease-bottomed paper bag from his right to his left hand and then sticks his right hand out in greeting.

"Hi, I'm Maggie Sparkes. I'm here about Celine Gonzalez."

"Celine Gonzalez . . ." His heavy, untamed brow crinkles in thought, as if he has to filter through the various cases in his head to remember hers.

She only died two weeks ago. So far, I'm not impressed with Detective Chester Childs.

With a big meaty hand, he gestures me up and around the front desk.

I trail him down a narrow, poorly lit hallway that hasn't seen a coat of paint in far too long. It ends in a vast room of computers and desks in rows, with the low buzz of phones ringing throughout. He takes the third desk in. Dropping a heavy notepad next to the keyboard, he eases himself into the chair with a groan. "So, Celine Gonzalez." A few keystrokes on his keyboard has a file showing up on the monitor. "The pretty girl near Mott and Kenmare."

He's so casual about it. "Yeah." The pretty *dead* girl.

"Right. I spoke to her mother on the phone. Lovely lady. What can I do for you today, Miss Maggie Sparkes?"

I pull the picture out of my purse. "I found this in her apartment and I thought maybe it would be important."

Detective Childs peers first at me before pulling a pair of glasses from his front pocket and slipping them on. His short, curly hair is just beginning to gray. If I had to guess, I'd peg him in his early fifties. He reminds me of a younger Morgan Freeman, and I shudder, remembering *Se7en*. "Handsome man," he murmurs, appraising the picture.

I flip the picture over for him. "That's her handwriting there."

He pauses to read it. "And where did you say you found this again?"

"In a lockbox that I gave her years ago. It has a false bottom, for hiding things. I found almost ten thousand dollars in there with it."

"Hmm . . . and what exactly do you think this means, Miss Sparkes?"

"I don't know. *You're* the detective. But I think it's suspicious. Did you notice that her phone is missing?"

He refocuses his attention on the computer screen, too calm and collected for what I'm telling him. "Your friend had been taking antidepressants on and off for seven years. Treatment for depression and anxiety."

"*Mild* depression and anxiety. And who isn't?" It seemed like half the girls in college had a script for Prozac.

Dark eyes flash to me for a second before moving back to the screen. "She just renewed her prescription with her doctor and her dosage was increased. She said some things to her doctor that I can't reveal but are clear indicators."

I can only imagine. "Everyone says those things to get another prescription."

"The coworker who called the police gave a statement that your friend had seemed very down lately. She had found her crying in the bathroom on several occasions."

"Well . . . How recently? Because her mother was fighting cancer up until last January. I'd cry in the bathroom, too," I say snippily. I did cry once. I bawled my eyes out for a good hour in my bedroom one night, after witnessing an especially bad day for Rosa, sick from the chemo.

"Recently," Detective Childs confirms. "And we found a note with her body, in her handwriting, signed by her, saying that she was sorry."

"Maybe she was sorry she missed a meeting. Maybe she was sorry that she was late. Who knows what she was sorry for! If someone was trying to stage her death, that'd be a handy note to use, wouldn't it?"

"So that's why you're here." He smiles sadly to himself, leaning back in his chair until it protests under his weight. "The ol' murder theory."

He doesn't see what I'm getting at here. "I *know* Celine, Detective. She wouldn't kill herself."

"I've heard that a few times before. In my twenty-five years on the police force, I've never once seen it actually turn out to be the case."

"That doesn't mean it's not possible. We still don't even officially know what killed her, right? It's just some medical examiner's opinion."

"And we won't know for several more weeks." Detective Childs begins rifling through a stack of envelopes and file folders. He holds up a sealed envelope. "But I had the lab run some tests on the glass found next to Celine's body. Report came in this morning while I was out."

I watch him tear it open with leisurely fingers and scan through the page, humming to himself. I bite my lip until I can't anymore. "Well? What does it say?"

"It says that the glass contained traces of Xanax, OxyContin,

Ambien, and a wheat-based alcohol identical to the vodka found in her apartment. A bottle that she purchased early that day and drank half of, based on the receipt we also found. It's a deadly combination, especially if the Oxy was ground up."

"OxyContin? But that's . . ." I frown. "She didn't have a prescription for that, did she?"

"It's not a hard drug to find on the street."

I start to laugh at the absurdity of what he's suggesting. "Celine didn't do drugs." She lost a high school friend to an overdose. The one time she visited me in college, she got mad at me for smoking a joint. "Someone must have forced it into her."

"That's *a lot* of pills for someone to force into her, Maggie. And no signs of a struggle. No furniture knocked over. No abrasions on her palms, no blood under her fingernails." His tone tells me he's already dismissed any further objections I may make.

He taps the picture. "And what is his name?"

"I don't know. She never told me she was seeing anyone."

"Hmmm . . ."

His hemming and hawing is beginning to irritate me. "Look, I've known Celine since she was four years old, and something doesn't sit right with me. I just don't think she was capable of suicide. She had too many plans, too many good things going for her."

Detective Childs takes his time, folding his glasses and tucking them back in his shirt pocket. "Accepting that someone you love took their own life is very difficult. It's easier for our minds to look for other answers. I see it all the time."

He's choosing his words carefully here. A very political answer that tells me this is pointless. "So, that's it? You're not going to do *anything*?"

"This city sees an average of four hundred and seventy-five suicides per year. I'm sorry, Maggie, but we can't keep cases open unless there's a good reason. My investigation concluded that there were absolutely no signs of foul play and there was sufficient evidence to suggest intent to cause self-harm. The investigation is over. Consider your friend's case closed."

I throw an angry hand toward the picture I just showed him. "And you don't think this is a tad suspicious? You don't think it warrants a closer look?"

"It certainly makes me *curious*, but suspicious . . ." He shakes his head. "I overheard my twenty-one-year-old daughter talking to her friends just the other day about some guy making her ovaries explode." He chuckles. "My wife told me that means she finds him attractive. He's not *actually* going to make anything explode. For all you know, Celine didn't even know this guy. This could be some picture she found on the Internet and printed out."

"And her phone that mysteriously vanished?"

"Yes, I noticed that. Most people your age can't live without their phones. We questioned the neighbor and her coworker about it, and they both confirmed that Celine had a bad habit of misplacing her phone. Leaving it in coffee shops, at work. On the subway once."

I can't argue with him because I know that to be true. I think she lost a phone every year since college.

"She could easily have misplaced her phone earlier in the day and not bothered to do anything about it. All the other evidence was compelling enough to point to suicide that we chose not to pursue the question of the phone."

I fall back against the uncomfortable chair, equal parts angry and deflated. On the cab ride over, I had these visions of sirens going off and a flock of detectives jumping out of their chairs to go arrest someone once I handed them this smoking gun.

Now I realize how ridiculous that was.

And I'm smart enough to accept that Detective Childs could be right. The neighbor doesn't know about any boyfriend. Hans, her gay best friend, doesn't know about any boyfriend. *I* sure as hell don't know about any boyfriend. "What am I supposed to do?"

Detective Childs clicks a button that clears Celine's file from his monitor.

Case closed.

CHAPTER 5

Maggie

I've always preferred the real jungle to the urban jungles of New York and Chicago, where my mother still lives and I visit when obligation arises. But Celine . . . she was completely enamored with New York before she ever stepped foot in the city. I can't say I know another person who would gladly trade the beach and the laid-back West Coast lifestyle for a concrete horizon and cold climate.

Instead of staying in California, where I was enrolled in an Environmental Engineering program at Berkeley, Celine had her sights set on hopping on a plane for the Northeast and this mecca for museums and art. I think that had been her goal for years, probably since the day a seven-year-old Celine discovered my father's Gustav Klimt in the study, an original landscape portrait that had been passed down through generations. We weren't allowed to play in the study, and so I quickly chased her out before someone caught us.

But she kept venturing in, until one day my father came home to find her sitting cross-legged on the floor and staring up at it. My father has never been a cruel man, but he has always been abrupt and lacking patience. I expected him to discipline her but instead, he eased himself down on the floor and asked her what she liked about the painting.

I watched from the shadows of a corner, unseen, as the seven-year-old girl talked about the mix of bright colors and the flecks of gold. He, in turn, told her all about the painting, and about Klimt himself. He spent the next two hours telling her the stories behind all the sculptures and oil paintings and other pieces of art in his study.

An art history lover was born. Celine walked out of there that day and began making up elaborate stories for random objects she might find, until her voracious reading allowed her to refine her knowledge. I think that's around the time she realized that having a collection like my father's required *a lot* of money. She didn't let that dissuade her. At age eleven and with twenty dollars of allowance money in her pocket, Celine bought a silver tea set from a local garage sale that my dad believed was worth upwards of a thousand dollars.

That tea set currently sits on one of Celine's shelves.

Though Rosa would never guilt Celine into coming home, I think she secretly hoped that her daughter would move back after racking up four years of college debt, only slightly softened by Rosa's savings and a few small scholarships. But Celine had other plans.

She got a job.

I enter the same solid glass doors that she walked through every day for the last five years, wondering if Celine ever considered swallowing her pride and taking me up on my offer to pay for her graduate school tuition. She could have had her master's and been doing what she loved long ago, instead of filing papers and answering phones at an insurance brokerage firm.

It's a prestigious firm, fine, but still . . .

"Vanderpoel, please," I ask the security guard, my cold, stiff fingers self-consciously smoothing my ponytail as my eyes wander to the people speeding in and out of the lobby, cell phones ringing, heels clicking. Everyone's put together so well. I can now see why Celine had a closet full of dresses. Thankfully the chilly temperature outside has forced me into one of her winter coats and scarves, hiding my sweatshirt beneath. It's been so long since I've made a conscious effort with my appearance. Over in South Africa and Ethiopia or any of the countries I've spent the last six years living in, Gucci doesn't matter. Blush and mascara don't matter.

What does matter?

Clean water.

Malaria vaccinations.

HIV education.

And it's not that I suddenly care what others think here. I'd just rather not stick out; I've never been one for overt attention.

"Forty-second floor," the guy instructs with barely a glance before moving on, grinning broadly, to help an attractive woman with badge issues.

"Great," I mutter, shifting my focus past the giant silver-and-blue decorated Christmas tree to the long corridor where doors open and close in rapid succession and people pour out. At forty-two floors up, the stairs are out.

Thankfully the elevator I step into is nearly empty and it moves smooth and fast. Still, I bolt out of it the second the doors open, earning a high-browed stare from the receptionist who sits at a long marble desk. A wall of glass and security doors stretch behind her and VANDERPOEL is engraved on a sprawling metal plaque above. "Can I help you?"

I tuck the stray hairs from around my face behind my ear. "Yeah, I'm here to see Daniela Gallo." Human Resources told Rosa they could either courier Celine's personal belongings to San Diego or hold them for me. I opted to pick them up in person. It gives me an excuse to see more of Celine's recent life, plus it saves Rosa from the hard task of deciding what to do with her daughter's things.

The receptionist adjusts her headset. "Do you have an appointment?"

"Tell her it's Maggie Sparkes." I hesitate. "For Celine Gonzalez."

The layer of frost on the receptionist's face melts with a small, sympathetic smile. She must have known Celine. I'm sure she liked her. Everyone liked her. "Please, have a seat."

I'm not sitting for more than a minute before a striking woman around my age pushes through the door, her arms laden with a box, her three-inch heels echoing through the narrow corridor. She's dressed for the outside, her royal blue coat complementing her eyes.

I stand to meet her. "Daniela?"

"It's Dani." She drops the box down on the table and then envelops me in slender arms, like we've known each other for years, her soft, ebony-colored corkscrew curls brushing against my cheek. Even though I grew up with Rosa, a very affectionate woman, I find hugs from strangers awkward. But this is for Celine, so I grit my teeth and try not to stiffen when she touches me.

"How are you doing?" Bright, almond-shaped eyes, with flawless strokes of smokey shadow and smooth eyeliner, peer at me.

"Still in shock." I don't know how else to answer that.

She nods sympathetically. "So are we."

There's a moment of awkward silence as I trace Celine's writing on a piece of paper in the box and then Dani says, "I was just heading downstairs to grab a late lunch. I'll walk you down?"

Given it's nearly four p.m., it's a *very* late lunch. That could be my dismissal. I'll take it, wanting to get this elevator ride over with as soon as possible. I hold my breath as the doors close. If Dani notices my discomfort, she doesn't say anything. I normally hide my issue well.

"So, I packed up everything from her desk drawers that wasn't company-specific, and the few pictures on her desk. There wasn't much there, though, even after five years. She kept her space tidy."

I manage a tight "Thank you."

She nods. "How long will you be staying in New York?"

The doors open and I rush out, releasing a lung's worth of air and plenty of tension. "A couple of weeks, probably. It'll take me that long to sort out all of her things."

"Right. I remember her apartment being . . . full."

I follow her out the front doors and into the brisk December air. She leads me to a hot dog stand. "I wish he'd move his cart somewhere else, far away from my building. This is my second one this week. It's a sickness," she explains as she pays the vendor for a foot-long and dumps hot peppers and mayo over it. I don't know where she puts it. From what I saw beneath her previously open coat, she has the skinniest waist I've ever seen, accentuated by a fitted black dress. "Are you going to eat?"

The smell of it is actually tempting. I haven't had a solid meal in two weeks. But I shake my head and take a seat on a nearby bench in the courtyard, huddling against the chill. I'll never get used to this kind of cold.

"Celine told me about what you do. You know, your charity organization. It's pretty impressive. I don't know if I'd be brave enough to do it."

I smile. My first genuine smile today. "You'd be surprised how good it feels at the end of a long day." That's my party line. That's how I recruit most of my volunteers.

We kill the next fifteen minutes talking about life in Africa, about the kinds of initiatives I've funded—giving one village of children iPads to learn how to read, outfitting another with solar panels to generate electricity for every home, training locals to teach in the one-room schools that I built. The answers roll off my tongue as if I'm being questioned by the media. It's relaxing. It certainly helps distract me from other, darker thoughts.

"You sound like you miss it."

I pause to take in my surroundings. The horns blasting, the looming buildings casting shadows even when the sky is blue, the hordes of people rushing past like ants running for their hills, many weighed down by multiple shopping bags. Now that Thanksgiving has come and gone, people's thoughts are on Christmas. 'Tis the season to build credit card debt on material things. It's not me. "I can't wait to get back."

Dani purses her lips together, deep dimples forming in her cheeks. "I still can't believe she did it. I just talked to her earlier in the day that Sunday, too. She sounded down, but you know Celine, always putting up a brave front."

"On her phone? You called her on her cell phone that day?"

She frowns. "Yeah. Why?"

"No reason. I just haven't been able to find it. What time was that at?"

"I don't know . . . around noon, I think?"

So Celine had her phone up until noon that day, at least. While the delay in finding her body made it hard for the medical examiner to pinpoint time of death, he estimated that she died between eleven p.m. Sunday night and six a.m. Monday morning.

What happened to her phone between noon on Sunday and her death?

"Did she mention not feeling well? Or maybe that she had plans later?" I ask.

Dani's curls sway with her head shake. "She just didn't show up to work the next day, or the next, and I started to worry."

"Are you the one who called the police?"

Dani nods. "I know she was desperate to get to California, but she still had another week at work. We were even planning a farewell party for her that Friday."

I frown. "Farewell party? What are you talking about?"

She pauses, giving me a funny look. "She was leaving Vanderpoel and going back to San Diego."

Going back to San Diego? I don't know what to say. Finally, I mutter, "HR never said anything about that." *Did Rosa know?*

"She didn't want to lose any more time with her mom. Such a sad story. But Celine was still hopeful," Dani rushes to say, dabbing a napkin at a smear of mayo on her lip. "Not . . . *suicidal*."

Such a sad story?

"Vanderpoel was only willing to give her a three-month leave of absence, and she didn't know how long it would be before . . . *you know*. So she quit."

Blood rushes to my ears, blurring her words. *Lose any more time with her mom? You know? No, I don't know! What the hell is she talking about? Rosa is in remission!*

Isn't she?

"Are you feeling okay?" Dani leans in, scowling. "You're a little pale."

"Yeah." I clear my throat and stand, shifting the box in my arms. "I'm still fighting this jet lag. I should probably get going." So I can call Rosa and find out why this complete stranger knows things that I don't.

"And look, I don't know if Celine had mentioned me subletting her apartment from her, but I don't think I can do that now."

Now that Celine died in there.

She shrugs. "But I guess it doesn't really matter anymore. She's not coming back to New York."

Or San Diego. Or anywhere ever again. I swallow the lump in my throat. "It was nice to meet you, Dani."

"You too. And be careful. That's a heavy box."

"I'll grab a taxi. I'm fine," I mutter, rushing backward through the courtyard, toward the street, Dani on my heels. I make myself stop. "Thank you for caring enough about Celine to call the police when you did."

"Of course. If there's anything you need, *anything at all*, please call me." She pauses to blink away a sudden tear. "Celine and I started at Vanderpoel at the same time. She was a really good friend to me. A nice person."

I force a smile and nod, and in a fog over this latest news, I turn into the throng of people heading in every direction. I prepare myself to be bumped a dozen times before I reach the street.

Somehow I still spot him.

Taking long strides through the milling crowd, in his pinstripe suit, the perfectly tailored pant legs falling just right with each step. Mere feet away from me.

The guy whose naked photo sits tucked in my purse.

At least, I *think* that's him.

He slows as he passes, his eyes catching mine as I watch him climb the steps. Blue eyes the color of an early-morning sky capture me. The connection lasts mere seconds, but as I watch him disappear into Celine's building, time stands still.

"Maggie?"

By the look on Dani's face, she's been calling my name for a while. "Are you sure you're all right?"

"I'm fine. Do you know who that guy was?"

All it takes is one glance up the steps and she knows who I'm talking about. She smirks. "Every breathing female in our building knows who Jace Everett is."

Jace Everett.

He's real. He's not just an Internet picture, Detective Childs.

And Jace begins with the letter J. Like the "J" who sent flowers to Celine.

"He works with you?"

"Uh-uh. He's a hedge fund manager at Falcon Capital Management. A *really* successful one. His ego goes well with it, from what I've heard. He basically waltzed into a corner office with his Princeton degree and Tom Ford suit and started raking in the money, while everyone else is cutting their teeth at the bottom of the food chain. Most of his coworkers can't stand his privileged ass. As beautiful as it may be," she adds with a wry smile.

I look up at the building towering above us—all sixty-five stories of it, based on the elevator buttons. There must be thousands of people working in there. "You know an awful lot about him."

She shrugs. "I'm sort of friends with his assistant, so . . . you know how it goes. Office gossip makes the long, boring days more bearable." She pauses. "Celine always noticed when he was anywhere nearby. I think she had a thing for him."

No kidding. For the most part, Celine and I diverged in our taste in men. But this guy . . . I'd call him universally attractive. "Did they talk a lot?"

"Who? Celine and Jace?" She frowns. "No, not at all. He's too good for a lowly admin, the arrogant SOB."

"But she—" I cut myself off as I stare at the building. *This man was once my salvation. Now he will be my ruin.* "Are you sure?"

She chuckles. "If they knew each other, I would have heard about it. Trust me. He generally sticks to his rich bitches." She cringes. "No offense."

"None taken." You don't grow up in my shoes without forming

reptilian-thick skin. “See you later, Dani.” I hop into a cab and head home.

My thoughts are vaulting back and forth between Rosa’s failing health and the hedge fund manager who apparently wouldn’t give Celine the time of day.

But clearly must have.

CHAPTER 6

Maggie

I didn't need to drag the truth out of Rosa.

Celine's computer just gave it all to me.

Phone in one hand, a glass of Maker's Mark in the other, a hard soccer ball–sized mass sits in the pit of my stomach as I stare at the email. I hardly ever drink. But tonight, I pilfered the bourbon from Celine's brass bar cart, having looked for the first thing besides the half bottle of vodka that Celine *didn't* finish off the night she killed herself.

That half bottle, I dumped down the drain.

After returning from Vanderpoel, I spent a good hour digging through the box of Celine's work things. There wasn't much—a few framed pictures, including another one of her and me at Christmas on Coronado Island Beach when I was eighteen; a toothbrush, comb, lip gloss, moisturizer. Some personal paperwork files—her health insurance enrollment, a memo from HR regarding company holidays. A magazine.

So I decided to try her computer. It's password-protected, of course, but I know Celine well enough to know that while she'd make an effort to change her passwords frequently for security reasons, she'd also jot them down and hide them nearby. A big no-no in Security 101, but for Celine, who had a memory like a sieve, it would have been a necessity.

Sure enough, I spotted the sheet of paper tucked into a book on Roman Catholic relics sitting next to the keyboard. All of her latest computer passwords were listed there.

It took no time at all to get into her email, to find the message Celine sent to Rosa back in July, listing the questions she needed to ask her oncologist. Questions like:

How did they not catch this in the frequent checkups?

What treatment is most effective for cancer that has spread into the bones, the lymph nodes, the liver?

What does "terminal" and "one to two years to live" really mean?

When do we tell Maggie?

Rosa is dying.

I also found the draft email to me that Celine began back in September, sharing the devastating news and explaining that she was deferring school until "after." That she planned on working at Vanderpoel until December and then subletting her apartment to a friend until "after." As of Christmas, Celine would be living in San Diego, to be with her mother.

Rosa made Celine swear that she wouldn't tell me just yet. They planned on telling me together, when I came back to America for the holidays. Rosa didn't want me dropping everything and flying home to fuss over her, like I had done last time. I guess at some point while writing this message, Celine decided to not send it; to respect her mother's wishes.

Rosa picks up on the third ring.

Tears spring free the second I hear her melodic voice. "How could you not tell me?" I ask, my words shaky.

"Oh, *mijita*." She sighs. "Because there's nothing you can do."

"We can try!" We were in this exact same situation not even two years ago. Only, the prognosis didn't seem so bleak back then.

"No! Don't waste more money and time on trying to fix my diseased body."

I roll my eyes. "It's *not* a waste if it can save you."

"It can't, though. Not this time." I hear it in her voice. She's already made up her mind. I wonder if she was this resolute before losing her only daughter, if Celine was the only thing she was fighting for. She blows her nose. "I didn't want you to worry. You've already left everything to come and take care of me once. I couldn't let you do it again."

Stubborn, stubborn woman! "I do it because I can and because I want to. None of this other stuff matters."

"It *does* matter. It matters to all those poor people who you help. All those little children! You save lives. I can't bear the idea of children starving to death and miserable while you sit here and watch me die."

"Well, I'm coming back to California as soon as I'm finished here and I'm staying with you."

Normally, she would keep pushing, arguing with me. For such a small woman, Rosa has fire in her.

Rosa *had* fire in her.

She simply sighs. "Good night, *mijita*. Get some rest."

I listen to the dial tone for a long moment, swiping the tears away with my palms. I've dealt with plenty of death, doing what I do. Children who can't be saved from illness, adults who should have another forty years of life ahead of them, if not for the past forty years of hardship. I cry for them, but I avoid getting too close. This is different. Rosa and Celine were always more my family than my real family. And soon I will have lost them both.

If Celine's apparent suicide didn't make sense before, it *really* doesn't make sense now. Rosa is dying. That news would have hit Celine hard, but there's no way she would put her mother through this kind of pain, knowing what was to come. Celine would have stuck by her side until the end. That's the Celine that I knew.

Could she have changed so much?

Could Celine really have been *that* sick?

Sucking back a mouthful of bourbon to combat the rising emotional bitterness, I click through Celine's favorites bar, stopping on her blog. I smile at the header. *The Relics Hunter*. She's been running it for years. It was her way of sharing her growing knowledge and her creative mind. Even with a full-time job and all of her treasure-hunting, she was pretty religious about updating the blog with her latest finds, describing the items in detail, and her speculations about where they came from, and what they could mean. There are over seven hundred posts here, some featuring multiple items. That doesn't surprise me, given that there must be over a thousand collected pieces in this apartment.

I used to read every post. I can't remember when exactly I got too busy and stopped. We'd both grown busy over the years. What used to be daily phone calls became weekly ones. Then we started relying more on email and texts to keep up on the everyday stuff, and Christmastime to fill each other in on the things that really mattered, curling up with a blanket and a bowl of popcorn on Rosa's stiff, floral couch.

We could easily go weeks without talking to each other, because when we did talk, it was like no time had passed. I used to think that was great. Now I see that it just made it easier to take Celine's presence in my life for granted.

There hasn't been a blog post since August, around the same time she knew that her life was being put on hold.

Searching through her computer files, I find one entitled "Item Catalogue." Inside are more than three thousand images—multiple shots, at different angles, of each piece in her collection, capturing signatures and markings and particular details.

A wave of relief hits me. This is *exactly* what Hans needs. Which means *I* won't have to do it, thank God. This folder will save me *days*, I'm guessing. All I need is a large flash drive to copy the images and send them over.

Another thing to add to the list.

I fan through the stack of papers in Celine's work box haphazardly, my thoughts cycling through the events of the day. And to Jace Everett. On impulse, I type his name into Google and his face appears at the top of the search screen. I begin scrolling through each link, leading to articles about the thirty-one-year-old's remarkable success, including his education at Princeton that helped him secure a career at the New York branch of one of the largest investment management firms in the country.

A firm that his father helped start decades ago, before he stepped aside to become governor of Illinois.

"Well, that may explain a few things," I mutter through a sip of bourbon. Not that I can say too much against nepotism.

A magazine article shows up in the search, naming the governor's son as one of New York City's most eligible bachelors under thirty-five. It's a striking picture—a very typical business shot with Jace in a sharp blue pinstripe suit, perched on his desk, the formidable city skyline looming in the window behind him.

My eyes flash to the magazine among Celine's work things.

The cover matches the photo on the computer screen.

Flipping through it, I quickly find where Celine earmarked the page to identify the start of the article. Only the first paragraph talks about his career—with some extremely impressive stats. The rest focuses on Jace's interests—sailing, rock-climbing, and golf. Either he's the most unoriginal guy I've ever seen or he has genuinely been molded into the archetypal privileged offspring.

Apparently he's a budding collector of French fine art, as well, boasting a few pricey Henri Matisse and Edgar Degas paintings that were passed down to him from his maternal grandparents, people of old world wealth.

That would definitely grab Celine's attention.

Farther down are his qualifications for the "perfect woman"—confidence, attention to detail, an appreciation for honesty.

Aka—a hot, shallow trophy who doesn't mind being used for sex.

But what I'm most interested in are the photographs. Besides the desk shot, there is one with him, the family-oriented son, standing between the governor and his mother, who, with her upswept hair and pearl earrings and French manicure, appears to be every bit a politician's wife; a grand, historic home towers in the background, and each of them is in matching snow-white polo shirts and beige slacks.

I've met plenty of politicians and their families. I haven't trusted any of them. Maybe that's because they see my parents and me as nothing more than campaign donors. Maybe it's because I went to school with the children of congressmen who didn't like me because my parents didn't support their parents in whatever bill or scam they were trying to pass in the Senate. I'd bet money this eligible bachelor and I would ram heads like two mountain goats within five seconds flat.

The third picture . . . I'm guessing Jace Everett is somewhere near the Grand Canyon, based on the rusty cliffs. An evening sunset fills most of the picture, illuminating a powerful body as he scales a mountain.

Holding up Celine's secret picture of him, I compare the tattoos—an eagle perched on his shoulder. You don't find many guys like this marked by ink, but I guess it's patriotic enough that no one can complain too much.

My heart begins to race.

They're the same. Jace Everett is *definitely* the guy in the picture.

I'm on my feet, pacing the miniscule living room, my mind spinning. Celine *knew* this guy, but she was hiding it. From me, from Dani, from Hans. From the peculiar old lady next door. They worked in the same building, but they didn't work for the same company, so it couldn't be a case of office politics. But I'm almost positive Celine was sleeping with one of New York City's most eligible bachelors.

And there doesn't seem to be any proof of it, except my gut, a flower delivery card from someone named "J," and an eight-and-a-half-by-eleven sheet of paper with a picture printed on it.

"Ow!" I howl as something sharp digs into my foot. I pick up the loose screw and launch it across the apartment. The tiny, cramped apartment, whose walls are suddenly closing in on me. I need out.

I yank on my boots, coat, and hat, grab my keys, and throw open the door.

And yelp when I find Ruby standing there, wrapped in a colorful afghan, her white hair set in rollers for the night, a small tin in her hand.

"Is everything all right, dear? I heard you yell. Would you like to come inside?"

I fight the shudder that comes with thoughts of all those books.

Right now, I'd suffocate in there. "I just . . ." I heave a sigh and fall against the doorjamb with frustration. "I need some fresh air."

She smiles like she has a secret, her cloudy eyes magnified behind thick lenses. Pointing a gnarly finger toward the forest-green door marked EXIT at the end of the hall, she says, "Take those stairs *all* the way up. You'll find your fresh air there. And take these cookies." She hands me the tin. "You'll need them as bribery."

I frown, my panic and frustration giving way to curiosity. "Thanks, Ruby. Have a good night."

Without looking back, I head for the stairwell, a narrow and dark, musty space that forces me to hold my breath and climb steps two-at-a-time in my rush to reach the top, my vision beginning to tunnel. Barreling through the cracked door with closed eyes, I exhale in relief as fresh cold air hits my cheeks.

I'm on the roof. I expect to find snow-coated concrete and utility meters and pigeon poop up here. Instead, a wooden fence door stands about ten feet away, with lattice-screen walls on either side, a bramble of dead vines weaving through the gaps, blocking the view beyond. I don't hesitate to seize the metal handle and yank it open.

Inside hides a garden of twinkling white Christmas lights snaking around potted shrubbery and urns that overflow with evergreen branches. To my left sits a small teak table with only one folding chair; to my right, a raised flower bed, lined by stone and filled with decorative markers that show where plants grew in the summer months. Lanterns flicker throughout.

And Grady is lying stretched out in a giant hammock ahead, sandwiched between layers of blankets, one arm tucked beneath his head. A sizeable enclosed fire pit—no doubt a hazard—burns next to him.

I inhale deeply. Growing up on the West Coast and spending the last few years in the developing world, my nose can always pick up on the faintest scent of marijuana, even when entangled in the smell of burning wood.

I step past the vine-covered arbor and into the rooftop garden, working at my coat's buttons with my one free hand. "Hey. I'm sorry. Am I intruding?"

He simply eyes me from his spot. Until I'm pretty sure he's looking for a polite way to say *Fuck off. I want to get high in peace.* But I'm not ready to fuck off, and this place . . .

This is quite the little paradise.

Suddenly, Ruby's words make sense. I hold up the tin. "Ruby gave me these. In exchange for safe haven."

Finally, a small smile touches his lips. "Well in that case . . ." he drawls in that charming English accent, gesturing toward the only chair.

I choose to wander instead, having never been good at sitting still. "This is amazing." I peer over the edge and down to the street below, still busy for a Tuesday night at eleven.

"I like it." He sounds so relaxed, I envy him. It must be the pot. I haven't smoked anything since I was twenty and revolting against all forms of authority. Tonight, I think I want to revolt against reality. I could get high as a fucking kite and let my mind fly away. Maybe I'd find the truth somewhere up in the clouds.

Picking a sprig of sage that's shriveled and brown but still intact, I hold the leaf to my nose, breathing in the delicious scent. "Did you do all this?"

"Yup."

"Even that?" I point at the sturdy-looking pergola that canopies him. The hammock he lies in is self-supported, with an impressive curved wooden frame to hold the corners up.

I sense his heavy gaze on me. "Even that."

"A guy who can garden and build." *I could use him in Ethiopia.* "Can tenants come up here?"

He eases himself upright until he's sitting within the hammock, his brown suede slippers planted firmly on the cedar platform below. The blanket falls to reveal the long-sleeved cotton shirt that clings to his body. It's nowhere near warm enough for twenty-degree weather. "They can come to the roof, sure."

I survey the arbor gate behind me again, and the wooden lattice fence that stretches all the way around, framing this little garden. "But not into here."

He kicks off, somehow managing to balance himself while the hammock sways. "It's one of the few perks that comes with my job."

"And the building owner really doesn't care? Because I feel like this would be a code infraction or something. What if there's a fire and the tenants have to come up to get to the fire escape?" I'm rambling, but if I keep talking then it can't get awkward and I won't be forced back inside.

"My experience is people travel down when there's a fire." He chuckles as if that's the silliest idea, his English accent making me smile. "But if they come up here, then I guess they'll have a nice place to sit while the building burns."

"Fair enough." I pause. "Did Celine ever come up here?"

A shadow flickers over his face. "No. I didn't see much of her at all, really."

I'm not surprised. She was afraid of heights.

Silence hangs between us and I figure I have nothing to lose. I edge toward him with the tin. "Trade you . . . One of these for a hit of what you're smoking."

At first Grady meets my question with a blank stare, and I think I've overstepped my bounds. But then he grins, a handsome boyish grin that I never noticed before. One that makes him all the more attractive. "How do I say no to that?" He accepts the tin of cookies and then eases back into his hammock, stretching a long, toned arm out to fetch the hidden joint from a planter. "It's big enough for two," he offers, gesturing beside him.

Normally, I would never think of climbing into a hammock with a guy I barely know, but there's something oddly familiar about Grady and the way he offers it. No leery glances, no winks. Nothing overtly sexual beyond his natural presence.

And I'm too drained to care about any of that right now anyway.

"This could go disastrously wrong," I warn, stepping onto the wooden platform. In answer, Grady drops his leg on the far side to stabilize us. He lifts the blankets and I climb in, resting my head on the pillow while trying not to roll on top of him. With smooth movements, he adjusts himself on my right, until we're balanced perfectly, my shivering body pressed against his surprisingly warm one.

"Come on, it's not *that* cold." He stretches the wool blankets over me, tucking them around the far side of me, the faint scent of his soap making me inhale.

"It is when you're coming from eighty-degree weather."

He pulls out a grill lighter. "San Diego you said, right?"

"And before that, Ethiopia."

That earns a raised brow.

"A humanitarian thing I'm working on," I explain vaguely.

"Humanitarian. *Interesting.*" I can't tell if he's being sincere. Holding the joint between a set of nicely shaped lips, he lights the end.

I watch, fascinated, as he closes his eyes with his inhale, holds for a few seconds, and then opens his mouth to release a puff of smoke into the quiet night. We're in the heart of Manhattan, but besides the occasional horn blaring, you'd never know.

"So, how's it going with the cleanup?"

I sigh. "Okay. It'll take weeks to clear through everything. But I have some time." Now that I know the truth about Rosa, I'll only be leaving here to stay with her in San Diego toward the end, whether she likes it or not.

He chuckles softly, passing the joint to me, and our fingertips graze in the exchange. His skin is rough from manual labor, but I can see that he maintains tidy nails. "I've never seen someone so excited by bookshelves. When I first showed her the apartment and offered to rip them out for her, she actually started crying, she was so upset. Then, two weeks after she moved in, I saw her standing outside the front door with *more* shelves, which she had salvaged from a teardown site. They were tossing them and she wanted them. Don't ask me how she got them here, but I dragged them in for her and screwed them to the wall."

I take a long haul off the joint and feel the burn as the smoke fills my lungs. I smother the cough threatening and hold it in until my limbs sink into the canvas. Relaxation slithers into my body. By the time I've exhaled, a nice buzz has taken over my senses. "Yeah. Lots of creepy dolls and breakable shit."

"I'd be lying if I told you I wasn't happy you're here. I was afraid *I* was going to have to deal with those creepy dolls and breakable shit."

"According to her appraisal friend, some of it is pretty valuable."

"Really?" He sounds skeptical.

I take another hit and then stare at the night sky as smoke sails up. And let my body press further against Grady's.

I sense his gaze on me as he murmurs, "I've never seen a dead body like that. You know, not already in a casket."

I close my eyes.

"Do you know why she did it?" he asks.

"A guy," I say, before I can stop myself.

There's a pause. "Seriously?"

"Yes. No. Maybe." Our fingers brush against each other again as I hand him the joint and sigh. "I don't know. I really hope not."

"And what does this guy have to say about it?"

"I have no idea. She never even told me about him." Not me, not her closest coworker, not her gay best friend, nobody. Not even the nosy neighbor. "I don't know if he even realizes she's dead." I pause. "Why am I even telling you this?"

He doesn't answer, inhaling more from the joint before passing it back to me.

Because I need to talk about it out loud, that's why. On impulse, I ask, "You never saw her with anyone, did you?"

"Nope." Opening the tin, he shoves a shortbread into his mouth.

"I'm sorry. You probably don't want to talk about it."

"No, it's okay. I'm just . . ." He holds another cookie up. "These are *so* damn tasty and I'm really fucking hungry now." He eats another one and moans, "God, that Ruby and her shortbread."

"You just moaned the old lady's name."

"Oh, God! Ruby!" he moans again with exaggeration.

I can't help but laugh. It helps me let go of a bit of the anger I've been holding inside. "What's the story with her, anyway? How can she even afford a place like this at her age? She can't be making very much." How could Celine afford it, for that matter? I found a raise letter in her work documents, announcing that she was getting bumped to forty thousand dollars a year. At $40K, she'd have little money for anything *but* rent in this neighborhood. I guess that would be another reason for her to start selling her prized possessions.

He slips the joint from my fingertips with a wink. "It's called 'rent control.' Ruby moved into her apartment in the seventies." Rings of smoke float up into the night sky as Grady's jaw works to puff them out. "If people around here knew how little she was paying, they'd revolt. But don't say anything because these cookies are fucking dynamite and we won't have anything to eat while we get high up here if she cuts us off."

I chuckle. "Don't get ahead of yourself. This is a once-in-a-blue-moon kind of night for me."

"Of course. Same here." He smirks, like he doesn't believe me. "They'll never taste better than they will right now."

I grab one and take a bite. And moan just like Grady, as the buttery cookie melts in my mouth, hints of curry and parmesan sparking my taste buds.

He nudges my leg with his. "See?"

"You're right, this is the best damn shortbread I've ever had. And it's not just because I'm high."

"She makes a batch every week. Right around the time that her kitchen drain gets clogged or a screw *somehow* goes missing from her cabinet hinges."

"You think it's a ploy to get the strapping young super into her apartment?"

He smiles, scratching at the light stubble along his jawline. "The screwdriver she uses to take them out is usually sitting on the counter."

For some reason—because I'm high—I find that hysterically funny and I burst out in a fit of giggles.

"You have a nice laugh," Grady says through his own chuckles. "Did she tell you what she used to do for a living?"

"No, but if I had to guess, I'd say part-time librarian, full-time hoarder."

"Close. Ask her next time you see her." His eyes twinkle with mischief. "It's pretty cool."

I roll my head to face him. "You know, *you're* pretty cool, Grady."

Golden eyes, more hazel than green and richer than before, stare back at me from only inches away. "This is out," he finally says, taking one last haul off the roach until the tiny spark dies. Leaning over until his upper body weight presses against my chest, he flicks the evidence into the fire.

I hold my breath as he shifts back to lie next to me, adjusting the thick wool blanket that traps our body heat as if he has no intention of going anywhere anytime soon. "Warm enough?"

"Warm enough." Staring up at the sky where I know stars blanket us, though I can't see them beyond the city lights, I silently thank the little old lady for steering me to the roof tonight. I needed this escape. And some human connection.

The question is, what should I do tomorrow? What *can* I do besides sell a thousand-plus antiques and slowly dismantle all that was Celine's life?

I know what I'm inevitably *going* to do. Dwell on the tiny voice in the back of my mind that tells me something isn't right here.

If Celine was dating Jace Everett, why keep it secret?

Maybe it's like Dani said—maybe Jace didn't want to bring a lowly administrative assistant home to meet his governor dad. Or maybe the issue wasn't her day job. Maybe it was something else. Something he won't want to admit to.

"I need some advice, Grady, and I have no one else to ask."

"Shoot."

"If you needed answers and the only person to give those to you was a person you didn't know, had never met, and who might not like the questions you have to ask, what would you do?"

He twists his lips in thought. "I'd create a situation to meet this person and make it hard for them to refuse me."

Simple in theory . . . "But how?"

He exhales heavily, his warm breath grazing my cheek telling me that he's facing me. "Find common ground. A location, a purpose, an acquaintance. Force the meet and then work your questions around the real ones that you want to ask. You can get a lot of information out of a person just by treading too close to what they don't want to talk about. The look in their eye, their facial expressions, the way they react to the mention of a name, or a place."

Grady seems more intelligent than what I'd expect of a pot-smoking building super. "You sound like you've been in my situation before."

"Once or twice. Maybe." I hear the smile in his voice.

Find common ground. Force the meet. The only common ground I have with this guy is now six feet underground in a San Diego cemetery.

Unless . . .

There *is* something that we're both *very* familiar with.

I pull out my phone and scroll through my emails to find the one with her phone number. I know this is beyond inappropriate, but once I get something in my head, there's no dislodging it. Plus, I'm high.

"Hello?"

"Hey Dani. It's Maggie Sparkes."

"Hi . . . Is everything okay?" She definitely sounds shocked to hear from me.

Grady watches me quietly. "I'm sorry to be calling so late. You know how you offered help with anything I needed? Well, I need a favor." I hesitate. "I need a meeting with Jace Everett."

CHAPTER 7

Maggie

December 2, 2015

I step into the building, taking a second to smooth the skirt down over my hips once more.

"Wow. You look . . ." Dani's sapphire eyes skim me from head to toe, stalling first on my freshly cut and styled hair and then on the coating of mascara and liner rimming my eyes. ". . . different."

I *do* look different from yesterday. Almost unrecognizable, actually. That was my full intention when I finagled an eight a.m. appointment with my mother's New York stylist—after a call from my mother to him at midnight, while I was still curled up next to Grady—and told them to make me look good.

What Dani doesn't remark on—and I'm thankful for it—is the fact that I'm wearing one of Celine's dresses. It's fitted, with a plunging neckline and black-and-white stripes that run diagonally along the entire length. It's one of those dresses that Celine could wear once and no one would ever forget.

I chose it intentionally.

Our heels click against the marble in tandem as we stroll toward the elevator. Dani agreed to meet me in the lobby so we could ride up together.

"How much time do I have?" I ask as she hits the button for the top floor and the doors slide shut. My heart rate begins to climb.

"Twenty minutes, which isn't enough time for a new client, but his calendar is completely packed for the next month." She's talking a mile a minute. "Natasha had to bump another client and juggle a bunch of things around. I'm still surprised that she agreed to this."

"Reservations are already made, for two at eight p.m. this Friday, with the bill going directly to my family's account there." We needed a carrot to dangle in front of Jace's assistant, and Dani suggested dinner at Per Se for her and her boyfriend.

"He doesn't take new clients unless they meet a certain minimum threshold, and there's a screening process and everything that you haven't gone through." Dani frowns with worry.

"I'll meet the threshold."

"Do you even know what it is?"

I smirk. "It doesn't matter. I'll meet it." Celine told Dani who I am, so she should realize that I have a lot of money. I assume that's the only reason she agreed, albeit reluctantly, to go along with this plan in the first place. The woman who came in yesterday, in her hiking boots and jeans, would not have been able to pull these kinds of strings otherwise.

That's the power of money.

"You didn't tell her that I was a friend of Celine's, right?"

"Nope."

"Good." I need to watch his face when I say Celine Gonzalez's name.

"Natasha could get into trouble for this if Jace starts digging into why he has no files on you." Dani worries her mouth. "You really are going to invest a lot of money with him, right?"

"If he impresses me."

If Dani's smart, she's wondering if this has anything to do with yesterday's run-in—if this is more about wanting to sleep with the handsome asshole than investing my money with him. She's definitely wondering if I'm going to railroad her friend and make her look like an idiot. I feel only slightly guilty about using her for this "forced meet" as Grady calls it. But it's the only way I'm going to get the answers that I need about Celine.

My ears pop with the quick ascent, the high altitude weighing on my lungs. I don't know how people handle being up here, nearly in the clouds.

"Marnie," Dani calls the second we step out. She begins rushing through floor-to-ceiling mahogany, crystal chandeliers, and white Italian leather, toward two women sitting behind the mammoth front desk, her heels speeding up as they click against the travertine.

If the lobby of Falcon Capital Management is meant to make a statement, it's that FCM has made an obscene amount of money at the hands of its investors.

The woman on the left—a narrow-faced girl with mousy brown hair and a long pointy nose—stands, yanking her headset off. Round, doubtful eyes that are too close together appraise me. "Margaret Sparkes?"

"Yes." No one refers to me by my given name. Not even the media. That's why I asked Dani to use it. I assume that if Jace even notices me tucked into his calendar, he won't put two and two together. An heiress to an energy fortune would already have an investment firm to manage the family money. And I do.

"This way." Marnie's floral perfume wafts as she leads me away.

"Thank you for your help." I wave to Dani, dismissing her. I'm sure she'd love to be a fly on the wall, but I'm not having any of that.

I'm forced to pick up the pace to follow Marnie's lithe body down a long hallway of small fishbowl offices where people mill about and phones ring and a low chatter buzzes. As we weave farther back, I see the distinct separation between the general office environment and what I'm guessing is the executive space, complete with solid doors and frosted glass and plenty of space for everyone.

"Natasha, this is Miss Sparkes, for that eleven thirty with Jace."

Natasha, an attractive Scandinavian-looking blonde with high cheekbones, a severe updo, and an even more severe face, looks up from her desk. Sharp eyes size me up from head to toe, the flash of shock so fast I nearly miss it. She glares at Marnie. Dani said that the three of them—and Celine—were somewhat of a group, occasionally connecting for lunch or morning coffee. I wonder how much of a friend Natasha truly was to Celine. "Have a seat, please."

Marnie nods at me once and then takes off abruptly as male voices approach from behind the glass door. As if she doesn't want to be anywhere near this side of the floor.

"All right. I'll see you next month. Say hi to your dad for me. And make me some more money." A silver-haired man exits with a chuckle, winking at both Natasha and me before disappearing down the hall.

I'm not normally a nervous person, and yet I can't keep from tapping my fingers against the cold metal armrest. A moment later, a deep male voice hollers, "Natasha! Come in here!"

With a full breath, she stands and stalks forward, her tall, leggy frame accentuated by a short skirt. "Yes?" The harsh edge in her voice falls off to make room for a soft coo. All I hear is "Where is this person's file?" before the door shuts behind her.

My stomach instantly tightens. This seemed like a brilliant idea last night. When I was stoned. I'm fighting the urge to get up and leave but . . . No, I need to confront him, I decide. There's something here. I don't know what exactly—and it may not prove to be anything except that Jace Everett didn't want his secret fling with the Mexican secretary from downstairs out in the open—but it'll drive me insane until I find out.

Natasha reappears, her face a shade paler than it was and looking chastised. "I'm sorry, but we'll need to reschedule."

"Why?"

She gives me a pointed stare but then explains in a fake, polite voice, loud enough for her boss to hear, I presume, "We're awfully sorry but there's been some sort of glitch with the investment questionnaire you completed for Mr. Everett, and he'd feel much more comfortable locating it for perusal before continuing."

"So he doesn't want my money?" This is a first.

"His time—and your time—is valuable. He wants to have the most productive meeting possible. As soon as I can locate the files,

I will give you a call and we can reschedule. Again, we're *very* sorry about this." She doesn't sound sorry at all as she scans my dress again. If I didn't know any better, I'd say she's happy this played out as it has.

What I do know is that this is my best and likely only shot at getting information out of Jace Everett.

With a deep breath, I get up and straighten my skirt. And then I stalk forward and push through the door, because I didn't get where I am today by playing by other people's rules.

It's the scene from the magazine photo. Same walnut desk, same daunting city view. Even the same blue pinstripe suit.

The only difference is that Jace Everett isn't posed on the edge of the desk with a brash smile. He's sitting in his chair, a stack of papers in his hands, a phone pressed to his ear. His blue eyes are full of irritation as he watches me stalk into his office, Natasha on my heels.

"I'm sorry, I told her," she blurts out.

I ignore her and approach his desk with all the confidence I can muster as my heart pounds against my breastbone. "Hi, I'm Maggie Sparkes of Sparkes Energy." I've never used my family's status so blatantly before. I've also never used my looks like this before. I push the icky feeling away. There's no way he hasn't heard of Sparkes Energy. We're traded on NASDAQ for fuck's sake.

And there it is. The realization in his eyes. "I'll call you back," he murmurs, hanging up. He stands, adjusting his tie as he rounds his desk. "Miss Sparkes. I'm so sorry we're starting off on the wrong foot." I take his proffered hand, keeping my eyes on his face, unable to shake the thought that I have a naked picture of him tucked in my purse. I wonder what he's going to say about that.

"I'd like to see what you can do for me," I say instead, clearing my voice because I'm sounding too unsteady for my liking. "Though I'm beginning to wonder if this firm is too disorganized to help me."

"We've never had an issue like this before." His eyes flash past me, and I apologize quietly for throwing his assistant under the bus, even if she is a bitch. A flicker of amusement touches his expression. "But I'm feeling quite confident that we can have a good conversation despite the missing paperwork. Thank you, Natasha." His look is as much a dismissal as anything I've ever seen.

She shuts the door on her way out, leaving us alone. "So . . . Sparkes Energy." He pulls out a chair for me and I take it, feeling his gaze rake over my body. Does he recognize the dress as Celine's? I study his perfectly coiffed blond hair as his back is to me. Does he know that Celine is dead? Does he care? When did he talk to her last?

This man was once my salvation. Now he will be my ruin.

"I would have thought that your family already has a firm to manage your investments."

"They do. And I do. But I like to venture out every once in a while. I have money to do that with, with the right person."

"I'm sure I'm that person." His chemically whitened teeth gleam as he begins to laugh. "How'd you come across my name?"

I had a feeling he'd ask me this. I can't go throwing around names of his other clients, because I don't know any. I briefly consider hurling Celine's name at him to see how he'll react, but it's too soon, too abrupt. So I reach into my purse and pull out the magazine, tossing it on his desk. "It says that you're *very* good."

He regards the cover with a smirk. But I notice that his cheeks don't flush. He's not embarrassed by the attention. I can't relate, and my pinpricks of distrust grow stronger. When a prominent environmental magazine did a full exposé on me last year and people started pulling out their copies with big grins on their faces, it was all I could do not to crawl under nearby tables. I didn't even want to do the stupid profile to begin with. Celine is the one who convinced me I should, to get the attention of both investors and activists.

Maybe Jace really is the cocky SOB that Dani claims. But why the hell would Celine have been with a guy like this? She was too shy, too sweet for him.

"I don't recall them talking very much about my professional career in here." Letting the magazine fall to the desk, he leans back in his chair and settles amused eyes on me. He must think I'm more interested in his skills as an eligible bachelor.

Whatever works.

"I'm at a loss here, Maggie Sparkes. Normally I like to do my due diligence, learn about the client—their goals, their financial situation. I've had no time to prepare. I don't know what you have in mind."

I pick up a pen and scribble down a figure on my business card that I know will blast through any "minimums" he may have. I slide it forward. "You're the expert. You tell me how we can make this grow."

His shoulders lift with a sizeable inhale, and when he raises his gaze, his long lashes bat. They fucking *bat*. "We have plenty of options."

I figured as much.

"What market sector are you interested in? If I had to guess . . ." He looks at the business card again. "Health care?"

"You read my mind." Clifton Banks, our family's aptly named financial planner, normally guides me in this area, and I'm happy to let him do so. I have other people who manage the nitty-gritty details of fund management as it relates to the foundation, the kind of things that make me want to scratch my eyes out when I'm forced to listen for too long.

Luckily I can pretend to be either enthralled or knowledgeable when I must.

We spend forty minutes—double my allotted meeting time—going over hedge fund strategies, Jace explaining risk and return profiles, instruments and diversification; things that are beyond my basic understanding but prove to me that either he's a complete bullshitter or he knows what he's talking about. He seems meticulous in his notes, jotting down my risk thresholds with tidy handwriting, plying me with just enough charm to hold my attention, without any opportunity to be accused of inappropriateness for a first meeting.

His eyes only occasionally wander to the deep V dip of this dress, when he thinks my attention is busy reviewing documents that he's handed me to sign.

I watch and wait, searching for a good opportunity to bring up Celine. I know there will definitely be no good opportunity to whip out the naked picture of him from my purse.

Before I know it, he's leading me to the door. "So, you don't live in New York?"

His hand grazes the small of my back and I try not to stiffen. "No, I actually hate this city. I'm leaving for San Diego as soon as possible."

He chuckles and I somehow feel it in my chest. His hand rests on the door handle, but he doesn't open it, simply standing there, just on the edge of my personal space, gazing down at me. He's tall; a good five inches taller than me when I'm not in heels, I'm guessing. His eyes flicker to my blood-red lips oh so quickly before shifting back up to my eyes.

There is certainly a reason why every woman in this building knows who Jace Everett is.

"How long do you expect to be in New York?"

I sense a proposition coming on. Drinks, to discuss business. Dinner, to discuss my organization.

A nightcap, to discuss favorite positions.

I need to end whatever is happening right now. "Just until I sort out a friend's estate. She died recently." I peer up at him, seeing my chance, my heart pounding. "She actually used to work in this building, on the forty-second floor. Celine Gonzalez. Maybe you knew her?"

A flicker of surprise catches his eye that I can't quite read but know I didn't imagine. His brow furrows slightly. "There are so many people in this building . . . I'm sorry for your loss."

That's all. Grady promised I'd learn something by his body language, but this tells me nothing, except that Jace either truly doesn't know Celine or he's a phenomenal actor. Which is it?

I reach into my purse, pinching the edges of the paper between my fingers, preparing to blindside him so I can gauge his reaction.

The door opens with a knock, forcing Jace back a step. "I'm sorry to interrupt. Hey, Jace. I mean, Mr. Everett. I grabbed your lunch for you," Natasha offers, holding up a container of salad.

More than a hint of adoration shines from her eyes as she stares at him.

"Thank you," he says politely, all traces of the asshole from earlier gone, but barely giving her a glance. His attention is fully on me, his business card magically appearing, held up between two manicured fingers. "Let me get on this right away so we can finalize the rest of the paperwork while you're still in the city."

I know that he doesn't really need to see me in person. It's nothing a printer and a FedEx delivery service can't solve. People arrange for these sorts of investments without meeting all the time. But this gives me another chance to see him face-to-face, to hopefully get answers. So, I nod.

"Make arrangements for Maggie to come in on Friday, Natasha."

"Your calendar's full," she says, lips pursed.

"Then bump someone." He fires a sharp glare at his assistant before warm eyes shift back to me. "We'll be in touch soon."

I pull my hand out of my purse to accept his card, noting a third handwritten number scribbled on it, marked "personal cell." I'm guessing he doesn't give that out to just anyone. "Great. Thank you for your time."

I stroll down the hallway, feeling two sets of eyes on my back.

"So how did it go?" Dani steps into the elevator ahead of me and hits the "L" button. I wasn't expecting her to be waiting in the FCM lobby for me.

I rest my head against the wall and close my eyes, trying to ignore the fact that I'm trapped inside this little metal box again as it stalls at what feels like every floor. It's lunch hour, and we're sixty-five floors up. Unfortunately there is no express trip down.

"Fine." I'm not really sure what to do next. The longer I keep up this charade, the more awkward it's going to get. And I don't think I want to piss Jace Everett off after handing him a pile of my money to play with.

"Was he nice to you?"

"Yes, he was." More so than I had expected, actually. I pause. "His assistant, on the other hand . . ."

"I should have warned you." She drops her voice. "She's more Marnie's friend than mine."

"How long has he been screwing her?"

Dani's eyes widen with shock. The seven other passengers suddenly stand taller, their ears perking up.

"I don't care," I quickly clarify. "I just want to know if I'm going to be dealing with a possessive bitch."

"She wouldn't risk getting fired by pissing off his clients and losing money for him. She loves her job. And she does *everything* for him. Grabs his lunch, picks up his dry cleaning, books all his reservations."

"Why am I not surprised?" He seems like the kind of guy who would expect a woman to take care of all his personal needs.

We ride the elevator the rest of the way down in silence. It's not until we're outside and away from prying ears that Dani speaks again. "It happened back in October. As far as I know, it was just the once and they were drunk. But please don't even hint that you know because Natasha would probably get fired and I don't want to be the cause of someone getting fired, even if she's not all that pleasant."

"Wouldn't his job be on the line, too?" A lot of companies don't condone relationships in the workplace, let alone bosses sleeping with their assistants.

"Doubt it," she mutters. "Rumor has it Jace had a short and steamy affair with a married coworker that turned ugly. He's still there and the coworker isn't."

"Because it was his daddy's firm."

Her eyebrows rise knowingly.

"So, by the daggers she was shooting at me, I take it Natasha wishes it was more than just the once?" Despite the fact that she has a boyfriend, it would seem.

Dani chuckles. "The second you went into that office, she called Marnie and chewed her out. Then Marnie called and chewed *me* out. I guess they weren't expecting you to look the way you do."

Because you told them I was nothing Jace Everett would be interested in, based on how I showed up yesterday. I guess showing up like an aid worker who's barely run a brush through her hair was a good idea after all. Natasha never would have agreed to smuggle me into the calendar otherwise.

"Hot dog?" she asks, handing the vendor a twenty and collecting her lunch, dumping streams of condiments on it like a pro.

"No, thanks. And you can let Natasha know that her boss is not my type, so she has nothing to worry about." As appealing as he may look, I'm not attracted to arrogant men. I just want to know how he knew Celine and move on.

Dani takes a giant bite and then dabs at the mayo on her lip with a napkin. When she pulls her hand away, there's a secretive smile there. I see a decision made in her twinkling eyes. "You sure? Because you might be interested after you see this." Punching her password into her phone, her crimson-painted thumb scrolls through her pictures. "You can't *ever* let anyone know that I have this," she cautions, hiding the screen, completely serious. Only when I nod does she hand me her phone. "It was a big work party. Celebrating someone's retirement, or something. They got loaded and went back to his place. She took this the next morning. Before he woke up, realized that he had banged his assistant, and kicked her out."

My jaw drops open when I see the picture on the screen. Jace Everett, sleeping peacefully on his back, tangled in white sheets that don't quite cover his nakedness.

"How'd you get this?"

"Natasha sent it to Marnie and, well . . ." Dani rolls her eyes. "Marnie thought Celine and I would appreciate it."

I stare at the picture that matches the one in my purse. Dani giggles, assuming that I'm enthralled. But really, my mind is three thousand miles away, back in California, on a Berkeley friend who dated a guy for a short period of time. He liked to text her random dick pics. For months after the relationship fizzled, he kept sending them. He must have thought they would win her back. It was a big topic of discussion one night among a few friends, and she forwarded one of these pictures to all of us in our group messenger chat, to settle a debate.

Well, one of my other friends in the group chat was married and the picture automatically downloaded to her photo album and her husband saw the pic on her phone and . . .

This is how misunderstandings happen.

This guy, who Celine privately professed would be her salvation and her ruin, was screwing his assistant.

"What did Celine say when she saw this pic?"

"Um . . . not much from what I remember." Dani's eyes are squinted, like she's thinking back to that day. She winces. "Oh, well Celine was having a hard time that day. I found her in the lady's restroom, bawling her eyes out."

"Over the picture?"

"No! Over her mom. She said her mom had the flu and she wished she could be there to take care of her. Given how sick she already was, Celine was worried that it might put her in the hospital."

Would Celine have used Rosa's health as an excuse to explain away her tears over a man? "So she wasn't upset by it at all?"

Dani frowns. "I don't see why she would be. She'd be jealous, if anything. Hell, I am! Look at him!"

"Yeah." *I've spent plenty of time looking at that picture.*

My stomach sinks as the flimsy theories I've been clinging to for the last few days drown in improbability. While I still have some questions—about her phone and who sent her flowers and how she'd become so infatuated with a guy she might not have had a connection with at all—I'm beginning to wonder if Detective Childs was right. Maybe this was nothing nefarious. Nothing sensational.

Just a mentally unstable woman who killed herself over a broken heart.

CHAPTER 8

Maggie

"Did you get the files?"

"I did. Almost crashed my computer," Hans announces, his voice a song in my ear. "And I, of course, have a *brilliant* idea!"

"Okay, I'll bite." I'm smiling as I listen to him. His excitement is palpable.

"Well, Celine was somewhat of a regular at Hollingsworth. So I spoke to the director and, as long as all of the costs are covered and I organize this on my own time, they are willing to let us hold a special exhibit and silent auction in her name in their gallery."

Warmth fills my chest. "Oh my God, Hans. That would have been Celine's dream."

"Oh, I know," he says, matter-of-factly.

"Seriously, Hans. This is amazing. Thank you."

"You're welcome. So, you'll just have to write me a big, fat check."

I roll my eyes but laugh. "Story of my life. No problem. When do you think we can do this?"

"There's an opening on December twenty-second. It's not the greatest time for an auction, with Christmas and all, but that's why they're willing to give us space."

December 22. So I definitely need to stay in New York until then. "Sounds great. And then whatever we don't sell, I'll stick in storage and give you the key so you can pull things out after I'm gone."

"Perfect. And I've already shown pictures of Celine's clock collection to my clock expert."

I snort. "Your *clock* expert?"

He ignores me. "He said there's nothing remarkable, but we can probably get about two grand for all of them."

"That's not bad." Celine really did have an eye for treasures.

"You're using the gloves I couriered over, right?"

"As soon as I start packing, I will." The ones that will ensure I don't leave my "dirty, oily fingerprints" on anything.

"And plenty of foam peanuts and newsprint paper. Not actual newspaper."

"Yup."

"And those instructions that I sent you on how to package antiques?"

"Memorized." I haven't so much as scanned them. I've had no time!

He huffs into the phone. "I'm serious, Maggie. You can't just throw these things into a box. Even the creepy dolls. I'm pretty sure there's a French Bisque Poupee in there. That one alone could fetch anywhere from fifteen hundred dollars to twenty-five hundred, depending on the shape of it."

My eye drifts to the boxes in the corner, where I dropped the dolls in a pile. "Yup. They're *all* individually wrapped."

"Why don't I believe you?"

"You can come by and check. *And* help me pack all thousand-plus items. In which case, I'll love you forever."

"Venture to the LES again?" He heaves a dramatic sigh. "I suppose I could."

I decide that I both like and trust Hans. He's unlike anyone in my world and he genuinely seems to want to help me, with no benefit other than for Celine. If he were straight, I'd think he were in love with her.

"Hey, Hans?"

"Yes?"

"Is your name really Hans?"

There's a long pause. "It's Francis," he admits sullenly. "But Hans sounds way more cool and artsy. Don't *ever* call me by my real name in front of anyone."

"No one is as they seem, are they?"

"Where's the fun in that?" He laughs. "Don't worry. We'll get this packed up so you can go back to saving the jungle, or whatever it is you do."

"You want to come with me when I go?"

"Oh, hells no."

"Come on. I'm sure there are some unique finds down there." I use my best singsong voice to entice him.

"You can mail them to me."

I chuckle. "That's okay. You wouldn't survive a day there anyway."

"Are you kidding? I wouldn't last ten minutes there, and I'm okay with that."

We hang up, my heart temporarily lightened. Talking to Hans was a hundred times more pleasant than the phone call I had with my financial advisor, Clifton, an hour ago, in which he berated me for the forms he received via fax today. Forms from an investment manager in New York, requesting the release of a significant amount of money. Forms that I'd already signed. I'm supposed to discuss all of these decisions with him *before* I go signing any papers.

I told him not to file anything through the bank yet. That I haven't decided what I'm going to do. I'm on the fence, between backing out or letting Jace invest my money, mainly because I feel guilty for wasting his time earlier today on my wild goose chase. The problem is, if I invest with him, I'll just be dragging out the aftermath of Celine's death. Keeping a tie to a part of her.

And I *need* to just get this over with.

I drop a box in front of a shelf. I fully intend on filling it today. But first, I promised my accountant that I'd courier Celine's paperwork to him so he could begin to prepare her taxes. Even the dead have to file, he had assured me.

Celine already had a folder in the back of her desk marked "2015 taxes." I begin flipping through it, expecting that this is going to be pretty straightforward. And it is, at first. Right down to photocopies of rent checks and interest on student loans and her meager pay stubs, neatly organized by month.

Then I come across several folders' worth of blue notebooks—like the ones they use in primary schools, and the ones I supply to the missionaries to distribute to village children. The first one is marked "Antiques." In it, Celine has catalogued each and every item she has picked up and from where, as well as pictures that she has printed, cut out, and pasted in.

The folder is filled with books like this, itemizing every last antiques purchase she made through the years. I can already hear Hans's squeal when he sees these. I set them aside and continue on.

The next folder isn't a catalogue of purchases. I frown, trying to decipher the columns of numbers in the little blue book.

Dates beginning back in 2012, followed by dollar amounts and an "hours worked" column, and 2013 has its own pages, as does 2014, and 2015.

Did Celine have another job? It would appear so, and I assume it paid cash. I calculate the hourly rate and my eyebrows jump. That's a lot of money. It must have something to do with antiques, perhaps? An envelope sits tucked in the back of the book. Inside is a stack of receipts. I begin flipping through them.

And my mouth drops open.

Apparently Celine has purchased *a lot* of condoms. And lube. And lingerie. She's racked up waxing bills from an aesthetician. She's also rented several costumes from some place in Chelsea. There are drink receipts in here, too, from three hotel bars. High-end hotel bars, which she seemed to frequent mainly on Friday and Saturday nights, based on her handwritten notes next to the recorded dates.

Next to the names of men.

A sinking suspicion has me racing to her closet, the tears burning my eyes, making my vision blurry. I had only leafed through her clothing before, grabbing the bold striped dress because it made such a statement. But now I focus more closely. The deeper I go, the shorter, the tighter, the more risqué the dresses become.

My stomach churns as I throw her dresser drawer open and begin rifling through her private things. Basic cotton and white lace panties and bras spill out onto the floor as I dig down. It isn't until the second drawer that I find the black and red lace, the G-strings and garters, adorned with bows and tassels.

Celine wouldn't step inside a church without pulling a cardigan on to cover her bare arms, even in ninety-degree heat; and while her curvy figure always made it hard for her to dress modestly, I never saw her in a skirt that didn't reach at least halfway to her knees. I just can't imagine her buying these for herself.

It's when I rummage through the bottom drawers and find her collection of condoms, varying in size and brand, that my dread begins to mount.

I open a metal case sitting on the right-hand side. "Oh my God . . . ," I groan, slamming it shut to hide all the sex toys that I don't want to see—or even think about touching.

These are Celine's most private things. No one was ever supposed to find them.

With slightly shaky hands, I shift my focus to the bottom of the closet, where shoe boxes and storage containers are stacked in tidy piles. I toss them about, rooting through the contents, anxious over what I might find.

Until I come to a decorative box of dangly necklaces and bracelets, made from giant stones. An uneducated person might mistake them for costume jewelry, but I know that the diamonds are real. I can tell by their sparkle. Several receipts sit at the bottom of the box, indicating a pawnshop where it looks like Celine had already sold some pieces.

I crawl on my hands and knees to check under the bed. Nothing but a single dust bunny—the soul survivor of Celine's excessive cleaning regimen—hides there.

I toss the lamp onto the recently delivered and freshly made bed—the silk white shade bends but I don't care—and pull apart the makeshift end table, yanking the long and narrow crates apart to hit the hardwood in a loud clatter.

Books spill out everywhere.

The crates are full of little books, ranging from pink journals with unicorns to leather-bound diaries with locks. No keys included.

I didn't know Celine kept a diary. But of course she did. She liked keeping track of everything. It only makes sense that she would keep track of her life.

I gather every last one and spread them out across the bed. Hoping that somewhere in here I'll find a reasonable answer for all the racy lingerie and slutty outfits and paraphernalia.

Dreading the truth.

CHAPTER 9

Maggie

December 3, 2015

"I'm not sure what's wrong. I'll call my advisor when I have a chance," I lie, my voice hollow.

"Mr. Everett has prioritized you as a client and he would like this all sorted out quickly. He fit you into his extremely busy schedule for a follow-up meeting tomorrow morning. *I* fit you in," Natasha snaps.

"Looking forward to your dinner at Per Se?" I throw back and then sigh. I don't have the energy to outwit anyone. I wonder if Jace is feeding her these words or if she actually cares whether I come back or not. "Look, I'm just . . ." I stare at my reflection in the mirror, my eyes lined with bags, my skin sallow, my hair matted. I look like someone who sat in bed for twenty-four hours, eating cold pizza from the box I had delivered last night and polishing off a bottle of vodka, all while reading the deepest and darkest thoughts from the last fifteen years of Celine Gonzalez's life. Discovering things that I could have happily gone the rest of my life without knowing.

Which is exactly what I've done.

I can barely keep my eyes open and yet I know that sleep will not grant me a reprieve. "I'm dealing with a few private matters."

"Well, I can't guarantee that I'll be able to fit you in when *you* decide that you're ready."

"You will, because your boss wants my money." I hang up before I hear her snippy answer and stare at the journal in my hands.

I was torn between starting from the latest diary first and easing myself in with the oldest one, afraid that I wasn't ready for what might lie within those last pages. That I wasn't ready to witness just how Celine had lost herself.

And then I picked up a pink book with butterflies on it—the earliest dated journal—and read a thirteen-year-old Celine recount her major crush on my boyfriend at the time: a tall, gangly guy named Jordan who kissed her behind our house one day while I was changing into my bathing suit upstairs. She felt so guilty, she couldn't sleep for a week. Through tears, I laughed—because I hadn't even given that guy a moment's thought in years—and I knew then that starting at the beginning of Celine's story was the only way to do this.

And so I did, living the past fifteen years through Celine's eyes, since the days she and Rosa still lived with me. It wasn't hard to follow along. She dated every single entry. Some days she didn't have a lot to say. Other days she'd fill an entire page, even writing along the margin. She seemed to follow a simple rule as the years progressed: one page per day, no more.

So many days.

So many confessions.

So many things that made my heart swell.

And so many that made my heart bleed with pain.

Some of them were about me.

It's only natural, of course. No one is perfect, nor does anyone have a perfect life. And those closest—the people we love the most—are the ones most likely to spot these flaws. To judge them. Maybe through an understanding, accepting lens. Maybe, sometimes, with more than a twinge of hostility. But they bury the critical thoughts, the thoughts that could hurt us, and they continue to smile at us, to laugh with us, to offer their support. To love us.

And apparently some of them then divulge those most inner thoughts on paper.

Celine saw me as I saw her—as family, as a forever friend. As the person she could always call up, who would drop everything to help.

Who adored her mother as much as she did. Who shared her childhood.

But she pitied me. I had so much and Celine had so little and yet *she* pitied *me*.

And rightfully so.

She saw that I had two parents who didn't really know me, who put Sparkes Energy and the legacy of the family name before *their* legacy, their daughter. Who expected straight-A's from me but never expressed how proud they were, who would throw lavish birthday parties but had no idea what my friends' names were. Sometimes they weren't even there. They were clueless that I was bullied as a freshman at the posh high school they paid so much money for me to attend. They didn't understand why I kept leaving newspaper article clippings of environmental issues caused by energy companies like ours on the kitchen table, on their nightstand. Anywhere that they might take notice of them, and of their budding ideologist's concerns.

Celine only had one parent to my two, and yet Rosa was so much more to both of us than my distracted parents ever could be. Perhaps that's unfair, given that Rosa was paid, and paid well, to lavish attention on me. But it's true.

As hard as it is to recognize Celine's pity for me, I can handle it. Hell, I've pitied myself sometimes, too.

What I can't handle—what I would never in a million years have believed if I weren't looking at it in purple ink—is the resentment.

Celine resented me for my money.

For everything I had at my fingertips that I turned my nose up at. For all the ways that my life would always be easy, while she would always struggle. For the ways I'd continuously throw my money at her—for tuition, vacations, clothes—knowing full well that she could never accept it without gravely offending her mother and everything that Rosa did to give her the life she had. As proud as Celine was, she so desperately wanted to take what I was offering.

She never admitted any of this to me. But she wrote plenty about it. About what she would do with that kind of money, how she wished she had been born to wealthy parents instead of a poor Mexican woman, her father's whereabouts unknown. How she wished I'd realize how lucky I was.

She wasn't *always* so focused on the money. Those diary entries started around the time that we moved and Rosa had to find another job. She decided not to get another nanny job because it wasn't good for Celine, being surrounded by such wealth and greed. It skewed reality for her. Rosa's words, as quoted in one entry.

Though Rosa had always been strict with Celine about earning her own way, about not accepting extravagant gifts, this was Celine's first taste of "real" reality, as she was too young to remember what life had been like before coming to La Jolla. Rosa must have saved every last penny she earned while under employ with us, because she had enough to buy one of those prefab homes in Chula Vista, a working-class suburb of San Diego. She got a job in Walmart making minimum wage and Celine went to a local public school.

She hated it.

There are five diaries dedicated to how much she hated it. How the kids found out that she grew up in La Jolla and she instantly became pegged as "the Mexican Princess," though she was far from that. How the girls ganged up on her, spreading rumors about her, all because she spoke more eloquently, and seemed more cultured, and carried herself with grace.

They even attacked her behind the school once, leaving her with a swollen eye and a split lip before a teacher broke it up.

The guys weren't much better. She discovered there was a running bet to see who could steal the Mexican Princess's virginity. At the one and only party she ever went to in high school, at age seventeen, someone slipped something into her drink. Had it not been for the help of one of her few friends, she would have very likely been raped that night.

And she never told me.

Never uttered a single word, except to say how perfect things were, how happy she and Rosa were. How everything was just fine.

While I bitched about how small my private school room was and how cold it was in Massachusetts, how the technology was three years behind and the girls there sucked, Celine listened and offered apologies for what wasn't her fault and never once mentioned the Peeping Tom that the police caught sitting outside her window, watching her change. Or the gang shooting two blocks over.

Or how Rosa was robbed at knifepoint late one night, walking home from the bus stop after a twelve-hour shift.

Celine was miserable, having lost her relatively privileged life. She didn't want to be the girl who used to live in La Jolla and now lived in a glorified mobile home. She wanted to be far away from all of it.

That's why she chose New York. She would take the money that Rosa saved for her college degree, she'd apply for every scholarship she could, and she'd make something of herself. She'd take her passion and talent and knowledge of antiques and make a real, comfortable life for herself where it might be most appreciated.

She would not be kicked out of her home ever again, and she would stop wishing that she had *my* money.

The diary entry a few days before my twenty-first birthday is especially scathing.

April 17, 2007

There are two kinds of rich people in this world: materialistic and idealistic. If she has to be one of the two, I guess the latter is more bearable. I just wish she was REALISTIC. She's never had to live like the rest of us, and here she is, ready to just sign all that money over to some "foundation." Money she didn't earn, from someone who gave her everything that she has today. Meanwhile I'm begging for thousand-dollar grants just to finish an undergrad that's useless on its own. Her mom phoned me last night and asked me to try and persuade her not to do it. The selfish, vindictive part of me wants her to. Wouldn't that be a cold slap in the face, the day she finds herself looking at bills and wondering how she's going to pay them? I know it'll never come to that. But wouldn't it be nice for her to walk in my shoes for a year. Maybe then she'll climb down off that self-righteous, ignorant horse she's been riding all this time.

She may as well have smeared "I hate Maggie" in blood, as cutting as that particular entry was. In later journal entries, Celine rarely ever refers to anyone by name. They are simply "he" or "she." Once in a while she references someone with an initial, but that's as far as she ever goes. It's like she was protecting herself in case anyone ever read these. I'm not surprised. Celine was never the type to talk badly about anyone, so it would make sense that she felt guilty about doing it even in the privacy of her journals.

I had to take a break not long after reading that entry, chug a glass of vodka, and calm my scorned heart before I moved on. Thankfully, it seemed that my decision to keep the money and start Villages United appeased Celine somewhat. I was finally getting a grip on reality, according to her. Doing something real instead of being that "holier-than-thou person who bites the hand that feeds her."

I wonder, had my family's money come from organized crime, would she have said the same? Does no one see the criminality of what Sparkes Energy and other companies like ours do to the world, even if it's not deemed "illegal" by government standards? Sure . . . there are tax incentives and propaganda and "investments" being made in renewable resources, but not nearly enough for a six-trillion-dollar global industry. There isn't a day that goes by without seeing what some people more ideological than me consider environmental murder: entire forests being cut down, glaciers melting away, poisoned water from coal ash and radioactive leaks. Everyone knows what's happening and yet we continue to gobble up the world's resources like hungry little puppies. And I sit on a pile of wealth borne from it.

Over the next several diaries—I broke an antique screwdriver while trying to pop the lock on one of them (I'm hoping the screwdriver isn't valuable, or Hans will have my head)—Celine seems more focused on school, her fledgling eBay business, her new antiquing blog, and dating than on me and my life choices. She's still struggling, eating ramen noodles and canned tuna, but she's doing what she wants and she sounds happier.

More hopeful.

I skim through the pages about her ex-boyfriend Bruce because I already know how that story ends and seeing how infatuated she was with him makes me want to throw the diary at the wall.

She talks about graduating and moving from NYU's residence to share a one-bedroom apartment in Brooklyn with a friend from school, paying for her share with a waitressing job until, nine months later, she finally lands an admin job at Vanderpoel. An insurance company and nothing glamorous, but she knows that with a bachelor's in art history, she's lucky they looked twice at her application. Plus, she figures working at an insurance company is good on her résumé, down the road. Of course she would have rather gone straight to her MA, but New York is expensive and she just can't afford tuition. She has her future mapped out, though. She knows she wants to apply to Hollingsworth and that, based on what her brilliant friend, Hans, told her, they look more closely at graduates of Hollingsworth Institute of Art in their hiring process. I guess it doesn't take a genius to figure that out.

So, she just needs to save sixty-eight thousand dollars for tuition fees. Or borrow it.

From a bank.

Not from her wealthy friend.

Up until this point, I've read her diary entries with an eager heart, though heavy at times.

But *this* diary, with its black, soft suede engraved letter C . . .

I need to stop now. To catch a breath, calm my shaking hands.

CHAPTER 10

Celine

July 12, 2012

I awake to a banshee's screech.

"Not again," I groan, stumbling as my legs get caught up in my sheet. I grab my winter boot on my way out to the living room. "Which way did it go?"

Patty points to the far corner of our kitchen, but makes no move to climb down from the piano stool wobbling beneath her weight.

I toss the shoe to the doormat, knowing it'll be useless. The cockroach has sought refuge within the crack in the wall.

"That's the third time this week. I've had it!" Patty cries out.

Last year we battled a mouse infestation. Now roaches. Between the two of us, I've somehow become the assigned vermin killer. I still haven't figured out how that happened; I'm no less skittish. "You should get down off that stool before you break your neck." I salvaged the claw-footed antique from someone's trash a few weeks ago and replaced the missing screws, but it's far from "good as new."

She complies, wiping the light sheen off her brow with her forearm. We've been living in a constant state of sweat for the past three weeks, thanks to a scorching summer and a broken air-conditioning unit in our sixth-floor bedroom window. Our landlord said he'd take a look at it.

He also told us he'd get exterminators in, back in May.

"Hey Celine . . ." Patty bats her full lashes at me from her new spot, curled up on our couch—a corduroy hand-me-down from her older brother Gus that's splitting along the seams and has no doubt seen college guy things we don't ever want to know about.

Heaving a mock sigh, I drag my feet toward the kitchen.

"You're the best!"

"I know." Patty and I have been roommates for almost four years. Long enough to know that she gets up once a night between the hours of one and three for an ice-cold glass of milk, without fail.

"How am I going to survive in London without you?" she wails, accepting her drink.

"You won't." I flop down next to her. "So don't go. Please." I give her my best sad face.

"I have to. I can't turn down an opportunity like this. It's what I've been working toward."

I pick at a loose thread in one of the cushions. We first met in college. She had a job lined up before she even graduated, at one of those up-and-coming advertising agencies. The kind that bounces your meager paycheck every once in a while and works you to the bone. But in just a few short years, and with Patty's help, that ad agency landed enough key clients to make a real name for themselves. She's been promoted to a director's role and asked to relocate to London to help the fledgling office over there get their bearings.

While I'm ecstatic for her, I'm going to miss her terribly. The likelihood that we will drift apart when she's gone is high. Patty lives for the moment and strives for the future; she's never been good with keeping connections to her past.

"So come with me!"

My head flops back. We've had this conversation at least half a dozen times. "I've got a job at Vanderpoel."

"As a gopher."

"And plans for my master's."

"You can rack up seventy grand in debt getting a piece of paper over in England. They have schools there, too."

Just hearing her say that number makes me cringe. I've been setting aside money every paycheck for over a year now and I barely have enough to buy textbooks. If I manage to squirrel away even half of that by the time I'm thirty, I'll be surprised. "But Hollingsworth wants Hollingsworth Institute graduates."

"That's what Hans told you. You *hope* he's right. Just like you *hope* he can actually get you a job." I feel her knowing glare boring into the side of my face. Sometimes Hans likes to paint himself in a very fair light, to the point that you'd think people bow in his very presence. In this case, I hope he's not stringing me along and that he can actually get me a job at one of the world's top auction houses. They gave *him* one because he graduated at the top of his class, with impossibly high grades. He's an actual genius on paper. It probably doesn't hurt that his uncle is a renowned curator who currently works for the Guggenheim, and he comes from a long line of archaeologists and historians.

"I belong here. In New York City. In the same country as my mother." Rosa Gonzalez would lose her mind if her twenty-five-year-old daughter moved across the ocean. It's bad enough that I'm on the opposite side of the country, but she knows how much I love it here, so she doesn't guilt me about it. Too much.

Patty doesn't have any rebuttal for that, as I expected. "Yeah . . . I guess." She pauses. "Have you decided what you're going to do about this place? We have to give notice next week if you're not staying."

"I'm not sure yet." I can't afford the rent on my own. It's almost my entire month's take-home salary. And I'm not going to find a cheaper one-bedroom, or even a studio, unless I leave the city completely. It already takes fifty-five minutes each way from this shitty apartment in Brooklyn to my office in Manhattan as it is.

"I can ask around. See who might be looking for a roommate," Patty offers.

"Thanks." I eye the one bedroom. I hope I don't have to resort to sharing it with a complete stranger.

"Or . . ."

I turn to find her watching me with *that* look. "I can't."

"How many times do I have to tell you that it's not that bad. Honestly!"

"I can't." The conviction I had in my voice the first time she suggested it eight months ago has faded. I'm afraid that desperation may finally be winning over.

"Yes, you can! Celine! Wouldn't it be nice to *not* worry about how you're going to pay bills? Wouldn't it be nice to *not* go into major debt, just for school?"

"Yes, but . . ."

"Okay, look." She shifts until she's facing me head-on, her hair a mess of tendrils from the top knot she didn't bother to take out earlier. "All I've ever had to do is wear a beautiful dress, eat delicious food, and drink martinis. You don't even have to talk, really. You're just arm candy, and then they drop you off in a town car at your door with a pile of cash. *Nothing* more. Nothing that you don't want to do. I promise!"

How I ended up with a roommate and friend with such loose morals, I'll never be able to explain. She started going on these "dates" almost two years ago now, an opportunity that arose after she ran into an old college friend who was putting herself through law school with these same "dates." Patty wasn't doing it to pay tuition, though. She just wanted to cover her bills and shop for clothes way above her pay grade, until her career in advertising took off. I told her she was crazy, but who am I to argue whether she needs a five-hundred-dollar purse when I spent my week's grocery money on an antique china doll.

"You remember Carrie Seltzer from Human Psych?"

I frown. "She had ginger hair?"

Patty nods. "Doin' it to pay for medical school."

"Really?"

"Remember Sorcha Jackson?"

"The newspaper's editor?"

"Columbia Journalism graduate now."

I sigh. Patty knows how to work away at my defenses. "I just . . . can't."

She pouts. "I hate that I'm leaving you in the lurch like this."

"Honestly, it's okay. And you're not." I reach out and settle a hand on my friend's knee. "You could have afforded to move to a much better apartment years ago and you stayed, because of me."

She hasn't given up on persuading me just yet. "At least try it once, this Saturday night, and see if you can handle it."

"*This* Saturday?" As in two days from now?

"Yeah. Why? What big plans do you have? I mean, I know that *Antiques Roadshow* is on . . ."

I grin sheepishly. She knows me too well.

"Seriously. I have something lined up with a really nice guy. I'll tell him I'm sick and you can go in my place. He won't care."

"I don't know."

"One date a week and you could have this palace all to yourself when I leave."

We each scan the dumpy, five-hundred-square-foot roach-infested apartment before our eyes meet again.

We double over in laughter.

"I can't believe you talked me into this." I smooth the black silk over my abdomen. It's one of Patty's more subdued cocktail dresses, which she reserves for one of the many agency entertainment functions she has to attend throughout the year. We're the same size, only my curves are much more pronounced, making this dress hover on the brink of scandalous.

"You look great," she murmurs, catching a loose strand of hair with a shot of hairspray. "Just don't eat too much or you might pop out of it."

My laugh sounds wobbly, thanks to my nerves. "I'll be lucky to keep anything down."

"Well, try not to puke either. These guys pay a lot of money. They expect a certain pedigree. One that doesn't puke all over them."

The buzzer sounds, and I'm hit with the overwhelming urge to pee.

"You'll be fine. Come on." Answering the buzzer with "We'll be right down!" she grabs her keys and leads me out the door in her signature flip-flops, tank top, and baggy shorts. "I went out with Raymond when he was in New York last time. He's *really* nice. And filthy rich. Big-time into the oil business."

Oil business. I wonder if the Sparkes would know him.

God, Maggie would literally fly all the way over from Africa and murder me if she knew I was doing this. Definitely one of those secrets I'll take to my grave.

The archaic, musty-smelling elevator creaks and groans down six stories while Patty fills me in on sixty-nine-year-old oil tycoon Raymond Easton from Dallas, Texas, who lost his wife ten years ago to cancer and hasn't remarried. "Don't bring her up unless he does, but if he does . . ." Her face turns sad-puppy. "It's so sweet, Celine. Oh my God! You can tell how much he loved her and misses her." Her slender arms tense with the strength needed to open the old lobby doors. "Just be yourself and he'll adore you. And, for God's sake," she gives me a little push toward the town car waiting to drive me to Manhattan, "make sure you smile!"

I climb the cracked concrete steps to the front door. Our building looks even shabbier now, in comparison to the travertine-and-glass venue I just spent the last four hours at, eating delectable food I couldn't refuse despite my nerves and my binding dress, pacing my martinis to avoid getting drunk, and listening to industry chatter that made no sense to me.

Luckily, it didn't matter that it made no sense because, as Patty promised, I wasn't there for more than polite chitchat and arm decoration. I did exactly what she told me to do: follow his lead, answer his questions, and above all else, smile wide. The first hour, those things proved difficult, but I managed, and Raymond didn't seem to mind. I admitted later that this was my first "companion outing" as he calls it.

I waited for him in the hotel lobby, at a private table under his name. And when a weathered man with white hair, a rotund belly, and a bulbous red nose approached, I was sure I'd made a terrible mistake. I was sure I couldn't go through with it.

But he shook my hand and sat down, and just started rambling. He talked about his children—two sons—and his four grandchildren, and their latest report cards. He talked about his five-hundred-acre ranch and his seventeen horses and his three dogs. He talked about his business and about how he's thinking of retiring.

He talked to me like he hadn't had anyone to talk to in a long time.

Once we left for the event—an industry meet and greet of sorts—he gave me his arm and led me around. I watched and listened quietly as all kinds of guys in suits introduced themselves to him, lavishing him with compliments. In between, he'd lean in and tell me what they wanted from him. Invariably, it was always money. The question was only how much.

And when he walked me to the town car and bid me good night, he kissed my hand, told me my payment was waiting for me in the car, and asked if I'd consider another "companion outing" in a month's time.

I smiled. And agreed.

Now I rush to my apartment, a war of relief, guilt, and curiosity swirling within me. Relieved that the night is over, guilty that this would kill my mother if she ever found out, and curious about the contents of the Tiffany-blue gift bag that was waiting for me in the car. I didn't dare open it under the driver's watchful eye.

I hope Raymond didn't rip me off.

"How was it?" Patty exclaims as I push through the door and kick off those painful stilettos. She's sitting on the floor, a series of storyboards sprawled around her, and what I know to be a homemade extra dirty martini at her lips.

"Okay. I guess." I head straight for the bedroom to peel off the dress and replace it with a tank top and boxers, tossing the bag on my bed. When I've washed my face and brushed my teeth and delayed the inevitable for as long as possible, I finally hazard a look into the bag. Inside, I find the cash that was promised—five hundred bucks—plus an extra three hundred, plus a diamond necklace that's got to be worth . . . I have no idea.

"Did he give you a little extra?" Patty hollers. "He usually does."

"Uh . . ." I stare at the sparkles wordlessly. *Is this okay? Is this appropriate? I mean, I guess some could argue that none of tonight was appropriate but . . .*

"Let's see!" Patty appears at my side. "Wow! Nice!" The smile on her face tells me she's not entirely surprised. "He likes to buy jewelry. You know that rose-gold bracelet I wear out sometimes? Raymond gave me that."

"This is just . . ." Four hours of hanging off his arm, eating, drinking, and looking like a queen, earns me eight hundred dollars and diamond jewelry?

She shrugs. "These guys have a lot of money and they like to spend it. This is nothing to Raymond, but he knows that it's life-changing to you."

I look at the pile of cash with a twisted sense of hope. Three nights like that a month and I could easily afford to stay here by myself. "So now what?"

"Now you pay twenty percent to the house. Of the original fee, of course. The rest is yours to keep. Just don't say anything about it." She winks. "I'll give you the address to her place. You can drop it off tomorrow and see about getting added to the regular call list." She wanders back to her work.

Leaving me to stare at a dozen sparkling diamonds.

And consider new possibilities.

CHAPTER 11

Maggie

December 3, 2015

My chest tightens as I flip the pages.

She said yes.

Some rich, lonely old geezer with an oversized nose plied her with martinis and diamonds, and an invitation for another function in a month's time, and she said yes.

Why did she have too much pride to accept my money but not too much to sell herself? Several unread journals lie in front of me. My stomach twists at the thought of what they will reveal: that there's enough evidence in this shoe box–sized apartment to suggest that Celine had many nights with rich, old geezers who only wanted arm candy.

As well as nights when someone may have wanted more.

And Celine may have agreed.

Taking a deep breath, I turn the page.

December 4, 2015

Streetlights cast a glow behind the gauzy curtain. A quick time check shows that it's now two in the morning. I must have succumbed to exhaustion. Or vodka, based on my throbbing head.

It definitely wasn't the reading material that put me to sleep.

Sure, it started out innocent enough. A date with an older gentleman, a bag of diamonds and money. More social functions hanging off his arm. Then the arm of another wealthy older man, who paid even more and liked to send her to Bergdorf ahead of time, to pick out dresses and charge them to his account. And then another, until she had several wealthy men taking her on "companion outings" each month. This went on for a year-and-a-half, blurring her boundaries and building her confidence, as well as a nice little education nest egg. It also allowed her to move from her dingy apartment in Brooklyn to this one on the trendy Lower East Side of Manhattan in early 2014. Making as much as she was, she figured she'd have enough saved to pay her full tuition in another nine months, right in time for the start of the program. Of course, there was still the issue of supporting herself during the fifteen-month-long full-time program, because she'd have to quit her job at Vanderpoel. But she figured it was nothing a few "dates" a week couldn't solve.

And Celine was so happy. Finally feeling like she was in control of her life and her future, and that lack of money would no longer hinder her from doing what she was meant to do, what she loved.

She was halfway through the Hollingsworth application paperwork when Rosa was diagnosed with breast cancer. Everything changed. The extra flights home, Rosa's living expenses and medical bills—the ones that I didn't find out about so I could pay them—quickly depleted Celine's nest egg, leaving her back at her starting point instead of starting school last fall. Only she had missed so many weekends with her regular gentlemen over those months that they were forced to move on to new "companions."

It was last year, in October, that "L" suggested a new guy. A guy who "L" sold as "younger and will pay double" but . . . there was a catch.

There's always a catch.

The new guy wanted a happy ending.

I don't know who this "L" person is, but she better hope I never find her.

Celine, nervous and conflicted and not knowing how she'd keep her apartment let alone save enough for tuition to start school the following year, invested in some slinky lingerie and a bottle of Grey Goose. Because God forbid she ask for some help from her wealthy friend, who would jump on a plane and fly over and personally kill her if she ever knew what she had been doing for money.

I flip through page after page of journal entries, overwhelmed with relief on the days when Celine was focused on the latest antique she had scavenged, or a fun night with Dani, out for Thai food. Smiling as I read about the day Rosa was declared "in remission" and the day that Celine finally submitted her application to Hollingsworth Institute of Art, to begin her MA if they accepted her. Which they did.

But there are many days when her "dates" continue, thanks to "L's" seemingly endless clientele list. With time, gentle coaxing, and the lure of big paydays, soon there doesn't seem to be much that Celine won't do, because for the first time she's not worried about how she's going to pay tuition or her rent, and she can do it all on her own. In fact, with the kind of money she's making now, she's already replenished her lost savings and then some. She'll have enough to cover the first semester within months, assuming her mother is still in remission by then.

And she tells herself over and over again that it's okay. A lot of girls do it to get through school. "L" did it, too.

No one will ever know.

I have to force myself to read those days—the days when Celine has to sneak a few shots of hard liquor in the client's hotel bathroom before she returns to the bedroom, or the times that she will do the coke or Oxy offered to her, because it all makes the night easier to get through and, later, forget.

Especially if it involves strange and perverted requests, things she usually complied with because they meant extra cash.

I grit my teeth as I read every last one of those entries, looking for some bit of valuable information.

It's in one dated mid-July that I think I've found something.

July 16, 2015

New York City is big but this industry is intimate. That's what L said when she warned me that this day would come. That I would find myself in a horrible predicament, face-to-face with someone I know. I was hoping I'd be out of this racket long before that might happen. I guess not . . . Of all the people to find waiting for me on the other side of a hotel room door.

And I just spoke with him at the office earlier today.

What if he tells someone what I've been doing to make money? I need that job! I can't handle doing this full-time. Plus, I don't want anyone knowing about this!

I'm still not entirely sure that I didn't do the wrong thing by going along with it. He introduced himself to me as Jay and asked if I was Maggie (M would strangle me if she knew I used her name with clients). I was afraid not to go along with it. Afraid that if I refused, he'd tell people what I was doing.

He must have known how nervous I was, my hand shaking when he handed me that glass of vodka and watched me down it in one gulp. He even laughed and promised that this would be just between us and told me to relax, as he opened his wallet and pulled out a stack of bills, fanning it out on the coffee table so I could easily count it.

If I didn't know better, I'd think he were an old pro at hiring escorts, the way he settled into the couch, loosening his tie with a casual tug, calling me by my fake name, that disarming smile of his aimed at me, reaching a hand out to me.

Beckoning me.

It worked because I felt my body relaxing and reacting and believing that I might actually enjoy this.

We did it right there on the couch, with all the lights shining down on us. And it was the best I've ever had, client or otherwise. For a while after, when he just stared up at me, it even felt "real."

The extra $250 in cash that he handed to me at the end put a small damper on that, but then I did the math in my head and my spirits lifted again. L expects a cut when the tip is over 20 percent but I need this money more than she does. She'll get her cut off the grand and we'll be square.

Did he really mean what he said when he kissed me goodnight and asked if I'd like to do this again sometime soon, "Maggie"? He winked at me when he used that name.

My heart is racing by the end of this entry. The guy paying for an escort *has to be* Jace Everett. He works in her building; he knows enough to recognize that she was using a fake name. *My* name. It sounds like he had this all planned out.

Which means Jace lied to me about knowing Celine. Maybe because he doesn't want anyone knowing that he has sex with escorts.

But this entry was from July, and it's the last one in this journal. Did they ever connect again?

I flip through the first page of every diary scattered around me to see that I've already read through them all. I search the crates, behind the crates. I squeeze my body between the wall and mattress and press my cheek to the floor to check beneath the bed once again, using my phone as a flashlight.

There are no more diaries to be found.

The diary that contains the last four months of Celine's life—and any proof of what may have led to her death—is gone.

CHAPTER 12

Maggie

My boot catches the corner of a planter and I stumble, catching myself seconds before going face-first into the asphalt. "Fuck!" I hiss, yanking my blanket, caught on something. I hear a loud rip before it breaks free, sending me on another three-step tumble before I regain my balance.

No twinkling Christmas lights illuminate Grady's rooftop oasis, nor would I expect them to at four a.m. I wonder what he'd say about me invading his private space. The light coating of snow on the ground will expose my tracks. Hopefully the snowflakes still falling—large, fluffy white flakes that melt when they land on my skin—will cover up the evidence soon enough.

I make quick work of the tidy pile of logs that sit beside the fire pit, warming my hands in front of flames within minutes. That's a definite benefit to living in the developing world for the last five years; I've learned how to start a fire, and fast.

With that going, I locate the main power source, and soon I'm cocooned within my blanket and lying in Grady's hammock, my side warmed by the flames, thinking about my best friend.

Celine wrote something every single day of her life for the last fifteen years, and on the rare occasion that she missed a day, she'd make specific mention of it in the next entry. It was clearly an obsessive practice. People don't just quit obsessive practices cold turkey, for no reason.

But there are no more diaries anywhere in Celine's apartment. I spent the last two hours searching. Not in her desk, not in her dresser, not even tucked in with the other books on the shelves. I have to believe that she kept the current one in her bedroom. Maybe on top of that crate of boxes, where she could easily reach over to grab it, already changed into her pajamas and curled within her sheets, ready to fill the page with her curly purple-inked scrawl. It was likely the very last thing she did before switching off her lamp.

There *must* be a diary somewhere that will tell me what happened between July 16 and the night in November that Celine died. Specifically, what happened with "Jay."

And, if it's not in her apartment, then it must be because someone stole it.

Perhaps because something in it would incriminate them.

A soft creak sounds from behind the gate, making the hairs on the back of my neck spike. It's the door into the building. At four in the morning, I can't see why anyone would be coming up to the roof. Anyone other than me, that is.

The padlock clicks and the wooden door swings open. Grady strolls through in a pair of flannel pants and a jacket and slippers, his wool blanket tucked under his arm, not stopping until he's standing over me. Judging by the sleepy look in his eyes, he just woke up.

"I've had a really bad few days and I thought I might feel better up here."

He still says nothing, his gaze rolling over me, over the fire, over the lights that I've plugged in. Finally, I get a slight nod. "You climbed over the fence?"

"I impressed myself, actually." I may have kicked a hole through the lattice, but I'm not going to bring that up right now.

After stoking the fire with another log, Grady walks around to the other side of the hammock and eases himself in, tugging on my blanket until he has enough to wrap around himself, before layering his thicker, heavier one over both of us. "That *is* quite impressive."

"How did you know I was up here?"

He leans in until his temple touches mine and then stretches an arm out, pointing to a corner of the fence, the tip of his finger helping guide my line of sight. A tiny red speck of light catches my eye. "Motion-activated camera. An alarm goes off in my apartment if someone comes in here."

Seriously? "Paranoid much?"

He shrugs. "I just like my space to be . . . mine."

"And here I am, invading it."

He chuckles.

"Were you coming up here to kick me out?" I'm guessing not, seeing as he came with a blanket. I feel his gaze on me, but I keep my eyes focused upward, enjoying the added warmth that his body is providing me. I wandered up here fresh from a shower, my hair still damp. It now crunches against the hammock, frozen.

"No. But you should tell me, Maggie . . . why have your days been so bad that you've resorted to breaking and entering?"

I smile despite my bad mood, because I love the way my name sounds with his accent. But it slips just as easily. "I found Celine's diaries."

He doesn't say anything for a long moment. "And I take it you found things in there that you didn't know about?"

"Yeah, you could say that." I haven't had enough time to process all this, to decide who—if anyone—I'm going to tell. Or who I should tell. And yet for some reason I have the urge to tell Grady. Maybe because he knew Celine but didn't *really* know her. Maybe because I doubt he's the type to run off and tell everyone he knows. He's a quiet guy. Private, most definitely, if the security camera up here tells me anything. Maybe because we've already lounged up here once, and he didn't try anything on me, didn't seem to want anything from me. He was content to simply *be* with me.

Or maybe just because I'm still too shocked to think straight. "Celine had been moonlighting as an escort to make extra money."

Grady lets out a low whistle. "I didn't see that coming."

"I know, neither did I." I shake my head. "It's like I didn't even know her. The girl I grew up with would never have had the nerve to do that, not for all the money in the world." I turn to look at him, his rich hazel eyes muted in the darkness. "I have money, Grady! I have so much fucking money that I don't even know what to do with it. I would have paid for everything—her rent, her tuition, *everything*—but she would never accept it!" A hot tear rolls down my cheek.

"Some people don't want to be charity cases."

"I don't care. I should have made her take it. I should have been here more for her, paid more attention. Called her more. Flown to New York to see her more. I should have gone straight to that admissions office and paid for her tuition and made her go. I should have come here and handed you twelve rent checks and made you tear hers up whenever she tried to pay. Then she never would have felt forced into it."

He frowns, his mouth opening but hesitating.

"What?" I snap, unintentionally.

"From what I hear, some girls . . . *enjoy* that line of work."

"Celine didn't. I know she didn't. I *read* about how much she didn't. For the most part," I add quietly, because that last diary entry with "Jay" would suggest otherwise. "She enjoyed having money, that's what she enjoyed. To not have to worry about how she would pay her bills, and instead live out her dreams."

He sighs, lifting his arm to fit beneath my head and pull me into his chest. "Money is a tantalizing whore, isn't she?" I tense and he immediately apologizes. "Sorry, poor choice of words. I just meant that people will find themselves doing things they never expected to just to get their hands on it. Sometimes it's for a good cause; sometimes it's not. I hate money for that reason."

I can't relate. But can Grady? "And what disgraceful things have you done for money?"

He smirks. "I'm a simple man, who appreciates the simple things in life."

"Like fixing old ladies' sinks?"

"Like fixing old ladies' sinks." He chuckles, reaching up to swipe my tears away. "And enjoying the great outdoors with a beautiful woman."

His compliment—however undeserved it may be, after my thirty-six-hour diary-reading marathon has left me with dark bags under my eyes and sallow skin—warms my heart slightly. I sigh. Yes, having someone to talk to about this helps. "I just don't know what to tell her mother."

Grady frowns. "Why on earth would you tell her mother? There are some things that parents just shouldn't know about." He adds quietly, "Let that secret die with Celine."

"It's not that simple. I think one of Celine's diaries is missing. The latest one. It's nowhere in the apartment, and diaries aren't something you simply misplace. If it's missing, it's because someone took it. And I can only think of one reason why someone would take it."

He thinks for a moment. "Because maybe she was servicing someone she shouldn't have been with?"

"Exactly." Like the governor of Illinois's son.

"But that would mean that the guy had to be in her apartment. What are you saying? That you don't think she killed herself?"

Yes, that's exactly what I'm saying. "It's just strange, is all," I say, backpedaling, realizing that perhaps I've shared too much. "It's a loose end, and I don't like loose ends."

He nods slowly. "Did you ask Ruby? If someone walks down that hall and she's awake, she knows about it."

"I did. She never noticed any men visiting. Ever."

"Did Celine mention names or anything like that in the diaries you did find?"

"Nothing to clearly identify anyone."

Grady heaves a sigh. "I don't know, Maggie. That's some theory."

"I knew you wouldn't believe me." I need someone to believe me. I can't be alone in this.

"It's not that. It's just . . . When my brother OD'd, it took me months to come to terms with it. I wasted so much time trying to prove that the drugs were laced with poison, even though no poison was found in the toxicology report. I even tracked down the guy who sold them to him and threatened to kill him if he didn't confess. You can imagine how well that went over, threatening a drug dealer." The sound of his chuckle reverberates against my ear, sending a tingle through my limbs.

"Finally, I just had to accept it: My brother was a drug user who mixed things he shouldn't have mixed." His deeply accented voice cracks with emotion.

"I guess Celine's case must bring back some hard memories for you."

"Yeah, kind of," he says softly. "I hadn't thought about it for a while, actually. After he died, I jumped on a plane for America. It was supposed to be a vacation, but I stayed."

"So you're an illegal," I say to tease him, partly because I need to break up the cloud that's formed over this happy little place, but also because I'm interested in learning more about Grady.

A brief smile flashes across his face. "Dual citizenship. My mum is from Seattle. She met my dad while on vacation in London and married him right away. The family business was over there—just outside of Ipswich—and so that's where they stayed. And that's where I grew up."

"And what kind of business is your family in?"

"Sheep farming."

"*Sheep* farming?"

He nods, chuckling. "Glamorous, right?"

"Almost as glamorous as fixing toilets and replacing screws."

He smirks, but then his face grows serious. "It's easy work and my rent is paid. I never have to worry about where I'm going to live. Plus, my interests lie elsewhere, besides sheep."

"Oh yeah? Where?"

"At the moment, right here." He's watching me, his long dark lashes fluttering as his eyes drift over my features, settling on my mouth more than once.

I know what's supposed to happen now, and I find myself wanting it to happen, and yet I hesitate. I haven't made time for a guy in my life since my senior year of college. That guy was an environmental engineering major, like me. Three months into the relationship, I found him snooping through my desk drawer, flipping through my files. Apparently he had his sights set on my money. That's usually the case, I've found. This enormous trust fund doesn't come without a cost. Namely, a genuine love life. My choices are kind of simple: date privileged assholes who have plenty of their own money, or lay low.

I've chosen to lay low. It hasn't been hard, letting my time be consumed by work as I hop from country to country, as I focus my attention and energy on people who need it.

But Grady's actually the kind of man I would be attracted to. Aside from the obvious physical chemistry, he's laid-back and easy to talk to; he clearly enjoys the outdoors and is good with his hands; he seems to be generous. Perhaps most importantly, he doesn't seem to be money-hungry.

He doesn't seem very ambitious, though, and I do appreciate *some* ambition.

It's not that I want to date Grady—or anyone—right now. But after so long, it's hard not to wonder what he would feel like, especially when we're sandwiched together in this hammock, already sharing our body heat, with a fire nearby and the strings of twinkling Christmas lights above.

So when he leans in and skates soft, wet lips against mine tentatively, I make a firm commitment and press my mouth against his. He tastes like minty toothpaste. He must have stopped to brush his teeth on his way up to confront the trespasser.

He's no longer hesitant, reaching up to cradle the back of my head and pull me closer into him, forcing my mouth wider as his tongue slides against mine in a long, sensual kiss.

I haven't been kissed like this in forever.

I forget about our current predicament—being in a hammock, next to a fire, in December—until Grady's leg nudges mine, working his way to fit his body in between my legs, and we start to swing. "Is this a good idea? I mean, aren't we going to tumble out of here?"

He chuckles against my neck, where his mouth has now ventured, his short beard scratching against my skin. "Well, I'm not a pro with this exact situation, but I think we'll be okay. Just no sudden movements." His fingers begin weaving along the buttons of the flannel shirt I threw on, unfastening them slowly. I never bothered to put a bra on, something he discovers quickly enough. He pauses to stare at my naked breasts—I'm suddenly feeling self-conscious; I haven't been intimate with a man in years—but when I shiver against the frigid air, he quickly smothers my body with his, and his mouth is back on mine.

No sudden movements is exactly the philosophy Grady's operating under, pressing his erection into me with a painstakingly slow rhythm until my panties cling to my body from moisture; his fingers coiled within my hair, my lips growing plump and raw with his attention to them. The air is frigid, and yet within these blankets we've created a degree of heat that is actually making both of us sweat, my fingers against his hard body feeling how hot and damp his skin is.

"Do you want to move to your apartment? Or mine?" I ask, hoping that my question is clear enough to him.

He reaches down between us in response. "Straighten your legs," he whispers, and I obey without question, allowing him to tug my sweatpants and panties down until they're past my hips, my thighs, my knees. From there, the farther I stretch my legs apart, the lower they slide, until my feet are tangled up in material and two of Grady's fingers are sliding into me, eliciting my moan, and his murmur of approval.

I guess this is happening here.

"Condom?" I whisper against his mouth.

"Left pocket."

"Awfully presumptuous," I joke, digging into his pocket to retrieve the foil packet. As soon as I have it within my grasp, I push his pajama bottoms down and wrap my fist around him, appreciating his size. Something else I didn't realize how much I've missed.

Grady takes the foil packet from my fingers and tears at it with his teeth until it comes apart. I slide the condom on for him, and the second I'm done, he thrusts into me.

It's easy to forget that we're outside, on a rooftop in Manhattan in winter, as our breath and tongues tangle, and our bodies grind against each other with a new fervor, not at all the slow and steady pace from before.

True to Grady's word, we don't topple out in some embarrassing half-sexed heap on the cold tar roof. He keeps us centered as he pushes into me, hiking one leg up with a hand under my thigh, getting impossibly deep. What I thought would last two minutes goes on much longer, and he grinds expertly against me until I feel my body finally relenting, my own need building slowly in my lower belly, tingling along my spine.

I come a few seconds before Grady does, the sound of my moans quickly echoed by his own. We lie there in comfortable, satisfied silence for a stretch of time, watching the flames burn bright, then shrink to embers, until we have no choice but to either stoke the fire or go inside to avoid freezing.

With hasty movements, we tug our clothes back on and scoop up the blankets.

Grady walks me to the third-floor entrance from the stairwell. "You okay from here?" he whispers.

I smirk. "You afraid that Ruby will find out?"

He checks his watch. "She *is* awake at unpredictable hours."

I stifle my laugh and stretch to my tiptoes to lay a kiss against his scruffy cheek. "Thank you, for tonight." I quickly clarify: "For lending me your ear."

He grins and dips down to steal one last deep, intense kiss that could easily spark round two. "Thanks for lending me your other body parts." He takes off, climbing the steps two at a time, back to the fourth floor.

It's too late to go back to sleep now. Back in Celine's apartment, I box all of her diaries back up. Except for the latest few. Those, Detective Childs needs to see.

CHAPTER 13

Maggie

"Enjoying the cold?" Detective Childs drags a piece of toast through the runny egg yolk coating his plate.

I slide into the booth seat across from him, shrugging the hood back off my head. The sun streaming in through the window is deceptive. The temperature has dropped at least ten degrees since earlier this morning. "Not especially." I gaze around at the strings of tinsel and sprigs of mistletoe that hang from the ceiling. The elderly man sitting near the door was waiting with puckered lips and a big grin when I walked in. I might have humored him with a kiss on the cheek, had I not just had sex on a rooftop with a near-stranger only hours ago.

I think I've filled my kissing quota for the day.

Still, I'm happy that Detective Childs suggested meeting at this fifties diner—with its big windows and delicious smells and jukebox charm—instead of the stuffy precinct. "Thanks for making time for me."

"Well, you're much better company than the fella I just left over there," he murmurs, nodding toward the caution tape wrapped around a convenience store across the street.

"Not a big talker, was he?"

"Not anymore." His smile is easy, like he didn't just leave a crime scene with a dead body. "What is it you needed to talk to me about so urgently? You look tired."

"Yeah. Late night." I set Celine's latest diary on the table, the entries outlining her "dating" exploits marked with Post-its.

He takes his time wiping his hands on his napkin—Detective Childs doesn't seem to be in much of a rush to do anything—and then, slipping his glasses on, he flips through the pages, running his index finger along the side as he speed-reads Celine's most private thoughts. He gets through four of the marked pages before handing the diary back to me. "So she was a working girl." Not even a hint of shock in his voice.

"Yeah. And I had no idea."

"Family and friends usually don't. Most of these girls are *very* discreet."

"She wrote a diary entry almost *every single day* since she was thirteen, and yet the last book ends in July."

"Hmm . . ."

Oh fuck. Here we go again with the hemming and hawing. "It doesn't make sense. There has to be a current one. Was there a diary in her bedroom when you arrived? Maybe by her bedside?"

"I can't recall offhand."

"No wonder people get away with murder in this city," I mutter, earning a flat smile in return. I roll my eyes, more at myself. I'm not going to get help from him by being an asshole. "She *did* know the guy in the picture, by the way. His name's Jace Everett. He paid her for sex. See? Right here." I open up to the last page.

"Where does it say Jace Everett here?"

"Well, it says Jay. That's short for Jace. And I just . . . He's an investment manager who works in her building, and here she is referencing him talking to people at work. His father is the governor of Illinois. What do you think his dad would say if he knew his son paid prostitutes?" Based on what I read up on Governor Dale Everett this morning, he has taken a very vocal stance against the sex trade industry in the past, going so far as to call it the downfall of family values and an industry that must be dismantled. If he decides to run in the next election, this would be one hell of a missile for his opponents to lob against him.

"Did this Jace Everett admit all of this to you?"

"No! That's the thing! He lied and told me that he didn't know her."

Detective Childs sighs and leans back in the booth. "You're connecting a lot of widespread dots to paint a picture that you're desperate to see."

"Can't you just look into him?"

"Why? Because you think he paid for sex and doesn't want anyone to know about it? There's no prior history of this guy harming or threatening your friend, or even knowing her. We don't have the resources to chase down hunches."

I was afraid he'd say that. "Okay. How do I get something compelling enough for you then?"

He hesitates, offering a "Thank you, Tiffany" to the waitress who sweeps in to clear his plate. "You could hire a private detective and have him look into it. Maybe that would get you the answers you need. But I have to warn you that most PIs are overpriced and lousy at anything but catching cheating spouses."

"Would you happen to know of one who is good at more than catching cheating spouses?"

He sighs, and then, digging into his wallet, he pulls out a business card and tosses it on the table. "Call for an appointment and drop my name. He's one of the better guys. Honest. Well connected. But he's not cheap. Not that I imagine that matters much to you. Just don't tell him that."

So the good detective looked into *me*. I wonder if he's getting a referral rate for this.

I stand. "So, if I hire this . . . ," I read the card, "Douglas Murphy, and he finds compelling evidence, you'll reopen the case?"

"I'd definitely have something to bring to my superiors. But keep in mind, Miss Sparkes . . ." Kind, weary eyes settle on me. "Dougie can't find something that doesn't exist."

My nose is assaulted by a mixture of cigarette smoke, musky perfume, and floral air freshener the second I push through the door.

"Mista Murphy will be with you in a moment," the woman behind a chunky old metal desk announces, her Brooklyn accent thick and nasally. She gestures with neon-orange painted claws toward the plum-colored armchair across from her before picking up the phone and punching in a button. "Yeah. She's here." Chomping on a piece of gum, twirling a strand of long, shiny black hair between her fingertips, she's exactly how I pictured her when I called earlier to make the appointment. Right down to the faux fur shrug. "'kay."

Her nails click away at the keyboard at a furious tempo while I sit and survey the interior of the Brooklyn brownstone where PI Douglas Murphy keeps office. A few cracks run along the plaster on the ceiling, but otherwise it's in decent shape. The old oak floors look like they've recently been sanded down and revarnished, and an eclectic mix of office furniture gives the space a trendy feel.

The office is in a relatively quiet residential area not far from the Brooklyn Bridge. No signs are posted out front, no stickers on the window. Nothing that would indicate that a business operates here. I wonder if that's for privacy reasons or because of zoning issues.

Heavy footsteps sound, first above my head, then moving quickly down a set of stairs, as if running. The bell rings and a short, bald man—no more than five-foot-four—shoves through the door. "Miss Sparkes?" He sticks a hand out and I take it, wincing as he squeezes too hard. "Come in, come in," he urges, already moving toward a small office off to the side.

I'm barely in before he kicks the door shut, the translucent glass pane rattling with the force. "So, Chester sent you?"

It takes me a moment to realize that he's talking about Detective Childs. "Yes. He said you may be able to help me. Thanks for seeing me so quickly."

"All right, lay it on me." He practically jumps into his chair, but not before I catch him doing a lightning-quick once-over of me—of my jeans and one of Celine's nicer sweaters, of my short but tidy red nails, of my leather boots and Celine's Kate Spade purse. I did my best to dress "average"—not like I had enough money to get taken for a ride, but not like he'd have to worry about getting paid.

I spend the next fifteen minutes walking him through Celine's "suicide" and the bits and pieces that I've discovered so far, while he madly scribbles notes down that are beyond illegible to the common eye. It makes me think of my meeting with Jace and how efficient but calm and composed and neat he was, compared to this frantic little man in front of me.

"So you think she didn't kill herself." His accent isn't Brooklyn-strong like his receptionist's, but there's no doubt he's a born-and-bred New Yorker.

"I realize it may seem a little far-fetched, but if you knew Celine, you'd understand." Though I'm beginning to wonder how much I really knew her. Or who she had become, anyway.

"And you want me to look into this guy?" He holds up the picture of Jace.

"Into him, into this 'L' person. Into Celine. Anything that can help me understand exactly what happened and why. There's more to this than the police think. I'm sure of it, Mr. Murphy."

"Call me Doug." He tosses the pen against the desk. "Okay, my rates are as follows . . ." He flies through a list of costs—surveillance and monitoring costs, mileage, background checks, GPS checks, special equipment costs, extra costs if he needs to hire additional experts—and ends with his retainer fee, which, as Detective Childs warned, requires a lot of zeros. No 40K-a-year average American could afford to hire him without taking out a loan.

He sticks a hand out. "The diary? The florist card?"

With slight hesitation, I dig through my purse and hand them to him.

"I'm working on three other cases right now, but I'll get started on this as soon as the check clears. I'll need a number where I can access you at all times for questions and check-ins."

"Good, because I insist on getting very regular updates."

"And give me her cell number, too."

I scribble the numbers down on a piece of paper instead of handing him my business card. The less he knows about me, the better.

"Did she have a desktop or laptop?"

"Desktop. I could bring the tower—"

He cuts me off with "I'll swing by the apartment. Donna!" He hollers.

Heels click across the oak floor outside at a rapid tempo and the door pushes open. "Yeah, hun?"

He holds up my check. "Be a doll and take this down to the corner so we can clear it and get started."

She plucks it from his fingertips with a wink and then leaves, her electric-blue pleather pants and waggling ass capturing Doug's attention until she's gone. "Okay!" He drums his desk with open palms. "Expect my call later today or tomorrow, latest. Are you talking to this guy anytime soon?"

"Later today. I have an appointment at his office." Natasha left another brash message on my voice mail. I called back and agreed to meet him at six.

"'kay. Don't let on that you know anything about him and your friend. That'll make him paranoid, and that makes it harder for me to do my job."

"Should I just cut off all communication?" It wouldn't be hard. I could tell him that I've changed my mind about the investments.

Doug frowns. "No, keep it up. It's harmless and you may learn something else." He smiles, the first smile I've seen from him. "Which makes it *easier* for me to do my job."

"Would you like to come in for some tea? I just made a pot," Ruby says, her glasses magnifying her eyes to cartoonish proportion as she stands in her doorway. "And I baked a fresh batch of shortbread, too. You liked those, right?"

My gaze wanders over her head and into her open apartment. It's a tomb of books. The afternoon sun highlights the dust particles floating through the air in there. My lungs are clogging just at the sight. "I'd love to, but . . . I'm behind on packing up Celine's things. I really need to get started on that."

"Of course, dear. I understand. Well, I'm here, any time you'd like to come by."

Shame overtakes me. The old lady is obviously lonely and I can't make even an hour for her. I open my mouth, about to tell her that I've changed my mind—even though an hour in there may put me in a mental ward—when the clang of metal and an Englishman's voice stalls me. "All set, Ruby."

I feel an unexpected spike of excitement, knowing that Grady's in there. Even with my focus on Celine, he's crossed my mind more than a few times today. I can't help but think I let things go too far with him. I'm so upside down over Celine right now, I can't see straight. I hope he realizes that.

Ruby peers over her shoulder with a big smile. To me, she shakes her head. "I'm always jamming that darned sink. Thank goodness for this wonderful young man."

I press my lips together to keep from laughing. Grady suddenly appears at the door in a pair of jeans and a worn T-shirt. "Hey, Maggie." He has an impish grin on his face as he runs a hand through his dark hair, sending it into sexy disarray. He still hasn't shaved that scruff either.

Memories of last night hit me and I feel my cheeks flush. "Hey, Grady."

"You coming in for tea?"

"I wish I could, but I have a bunch of work to do around here and then I'm heading down to Celine's office for something."

"Really?" He checks his watch and I can almost read his mind. It's already three o'clock on a Friday. He probably thinks I'm avoiding him. "Okay, well I'll try to save you some shortbread. Can't promise anything, though." He grins wide again, so relaxed. Maybe what happened last night didn't faze him. Maybe he lied and he has sex with women up there all the time.

I squash the spike of jealousy that erupts in me with that thought, because I have a missing diary and an investigation into Celine's death to focus on.

CHAPTER 14

Maggie

It's a quarter to six by the time I push through the heavy glass doors of Celine's building.

Jace's building.

The lobby is filled with people heading home for the day. Far too crowded for my liking, but I didn't think about that when I agreed to this meeting. I'm forced to press my back against a wall and wait for the rush pouring out of the last elevator before stepping in, hoping that the time of day will make the ascent up sixty-five floors extra quick.

The doors have begun to close when an arm shoots in to stop them.

"I thought that was you." Jace steps in, out of breath as if he was running.

I check my watch. Still fifteen minutes to go before our meeting, which means he didn't need to run. Unless he was intentionally running to catch me.

"Natasha said you had some personal issues come up?"

I nod, my eyes focused on the reflection of Jace in the shiny metal doors ahead.

Jay?

"Well, I'm glad we were able to get you in today."

"Yes, that worked out." I need to act normal. I don't know if I can pull this off.

He checks his hair in the reflection as the elevator begins to move. We're the only two in here. Just me and my new investment manager—the guy who likely paid Celine to have sex with him.

"You okay? You seem . . . worried." I look up into curious blue eyes, his gaze dipping down to catch the top of my red-and-white polka-dot dress for a fleeting second. Another flirty dress of Celine's that I intentionally wore because polka dots are *always* memorable and I'm still fishing for obvious signs of recognition.

Just not right now, because all I can think about is getting out of this metal death trap.

"I'm not a fan of elevators. I usually take the stairs," I answer truthfully, stepping back to lean against the wall and wrap my hands around the brass rail at hip level.

"I guess me being on the sixty-fifth floor throws a wrench into that." He smiles easily. "It moves quickly, at least. Don't worry. We'll be up in no time."

The second the words are out of his mouth, the elevator comes to a jarring halt, the red digital number flashing "49."

We're suspended forty-nine floors up and not moving.

Jace stands taller, his eyes surveying the ceiling, where the lights blink on and off.

My heart rate climbs with each flicker.

"That's weird," he murmurs, pressing the button to his floor several times with his thumb.

We wait . . . and wait . . . and wait . . .

An automated male voice sounds over the speaker, telling us that the elevator will be returning to the lobby shortly and to please remain calm.

"Probably just a power outage. Don't worry, these elevators are programmed to move down to the lobby in these cases. We'll be out of here soon."

"Yeah." It comes out in a pant, as I feel my lungs closing up. I hold my breath and we listen in silence. I'm expecting to hear the mechanics kick in, to feel us start to move.

And then the lights cut out, throwing us into complete darkness.

"Oh my God . . ." The narrow walls that I can't even see begin to close in, sucking the air out of the space.

A harsh light floods the cramped space as Jace shines his phone on the control panel, jabbing the emergency call button. He waits five seconds before pressing it again several times. "Shit. I think the backup power is gone." He pauses, looks back at me, his face just visible within the glow. "Can that even happen?"

I close my eyes as dizziness sets in and my body breaks into a sweat.

"Hey, are you going to be okay?"

"Claustrophobia," I manage to force out. I rarely ever admit that to anyone. It makes me feel weak and vulnerable, two things I hate. Plus, most people think it's some benign condition, that it's "all in your head." It is, technically. It just has overwhelming physical side effects to go along with it.

"Well, don't worry, it'll get fixed soon. We'll just have to hang out here until it does."

Hang. Visions of the suspension and brake system failing next and us plummeting to the ground take over all my rational thoughts. I shrug off my winter coat and unwrap the scarf that threatens to strangle me, then drop to the floor before I pass out.

"Good idea." Jace takes his time, easing his coat off and folding it neatly before laying it down. He sits, so close that his shoulder rubs against mine. I don't pull away because right now he isn't all of those other things I suspect him of being. He's just a living, breathing human who's trapped in here with me. My senses—already operating on overload—absorb the smell of his spicy cologne and his minty breath, the sound of his sigh, the warmth of his body heat. It helps ease the rising panic, but only a touch.

Jace shuts his phone's flashlight off and, after punching a few numbers, holds his cell to his ear. I curl my arms around my chest and listen to him give the 9-1-1 dispatcher our details in a very calm and businesslike manner—the building's address, number of occupants. State of health.

It's pitch-black and I still somehow feel his eyes on me. "My fellow rider is claustrophobic so this isn't the best situation for her." He listens quietly and answers questions sporadically. I can imagine what he's being asked. "Yes . . . she sounds like she's short of breath. Yes . . . she's trembling. Yes . . . I'm pretty sure she's having a panic attack."

I close my eyes and begin counting to twenty inside my head. That sometimes helps.

"Listen, my phone is going to die any second," I hear Jace tell the operator. "Okay . . . Yup. I can do— Hello? . . . Hello? . . . Shit." I hear rather than see his hand drop to his lap. "End of the day. Of course my phone needs a charge. Do you have yours?"

"No." I do, but I don't get reception in elevators, and explaining that to him will take too much effort. I startle as fingers graze my elbow, my forearm, until they find my shaking hand and coil around it, squeezing lightly.

"You don't need to panic. We're going to be just fine."

"That's not . . ." People just don't get it.

"Just take deep breaths, calm down . . . you're overreacting."

I grit my teeth against my rising annoyance. "Did the dispatcher tell you to say these things?"

There's a moment's pause, like he's deciding what he should admit to. "Yeah. Why?"

"Do me a favor? If you talk to her again, tell her she's an idiot. You don't tell someone who's having a panic attack to calm down. It only makes them feel crazy, which makes everything worse." My words shoot out of my mouth in rapid fire, soaked in bitterness.

A finger grazes over the fleshy part of my thumb. "Okay, what should I do?"

"Just talk."

"About?"

"I don't care! Anything. Your job . . . college . . . your dog . . ." I'm scrambling, my words choppy, my breaths ragged. "Just talk about yourself." I mutter under my breath, "You shouldn't have a problem doing that."

He exhales and I think he's getting ready to tell me to fuck off after that jab. I'd deserve it. Before he has a chance, I throw out, "So, your father's a governor?"

"Yup."

"What's that like?"

"Fine, I guess."

The seconds tick by, every single one taking far too long because I'm stuck inside this elevator and apparently my companion doesn't know how to carry on a conversation unless he's earning money from it.

"Does the media ever hound you?"

"They've had their moments, but I think I lucked out in that regard."

"How so?"

He sighs. Uninterested in the topic. "Well . . . campaigns can be tough on kids. When your parents are in politics, stupid moves will always come back to bite you in the ass somewhere down the line. Luckily, I was smart enough to keep my nose clean over the years."

Except for those escorts you pay to have sex, right? Having that conversation would definitely distract me from this hanging coffin we're trapped in.

"He's already talking about running again, isn't he?"

"You've been doing your research."

"Of course I have. I'm no idiot."

"No, I definitely don't take you for one." A light chuckle and then a pause. "So, what's it like to be an energy empire heiress?"

"It's a dream come true."

"Right. That's why you were arrested for protesting one of your family's plants?"

"*You've* been doing *your* research."

"Of course I have." I hear the smile in his voice. "I'm no idiot."

Touché. "I was eighteen . . . I *was* an idiot back then." I figured that in a crowd of two thousand people, I would be invisible. I wasn't.

I made the headlines that week, feeding the critics more ammunition against Sparkes Energy.

"And now you spend your time playing Mother Teresa."

"You should try it sometime, if you can stop counting your money for more than a second, Scrooge."

"At least I've earned my money," he throws back without missing a beat.

"My, has Jace Everett lost his charm so quickly?"

His body tenses next to me. "I'm sorry, that was rude of me."

"What's wrong, afraid I'll take my funds away before you get to play?"

He clears his throat. "Clearly this situation is stressful for you. I doubt you're normally such a—"

A fire alarm sounds somewhere in the building.

And suddenly I don't even hear what Jace is saying because all I can think about is flames tearing through this skyscraper and cooking us alive. I'm going to die in this little box before they find us, which could be in forty hours, like that recent story on the news about that woman who was stuck in an elevator all weekend, but no we won't be because Jace called 9-1-1 so they know we're in here, but if the building is burning down, they won't be able to get to us and—

"Maggie!" I'm only faintly aware of two strong hands gripping my shoulders. "You're hyperventilating. You need to slow your breathing down."

"Like it's that easy!" I hiss, my chest ready to cave in from the pressure. I've never had an attack like this before.

"Tell me what to do."

I'm shaking my head, the fire alarm a torturous repetitive echo pounding inside my head. "I don't know. I can't remember. I can't . . ." There are techniques—all kinds of techniques—but I'm too panicked to remember any of them right now. "We're going to die in—"

Grabbing either side of my head, he yanks my face into his, covering my mouth with his until I'm punching his chest repeatedly to break free.

"What the hell are you doing?" I scream.

"Limiting your air intake. And shutting you up." Hot puffs of his breath skate over my face a moment before he seals my lips against his once again, forcing me to breathe in through my nose to get air, and curbing the amount that I can exhale. He's right, I realize, as the pressure in my lungs eases and my heart rate slows and I'm calm enough to become conscious of the fact that I'm basically kissing Jace Everett.

At that precise moment, when the air around us hangs hot and wet and tension streams through my body like a live electric current, his tongue slides against mine.

And then whatever good Samaritan act on Jace's part this was quickly morphs into lips smashing and tongues tangling and teeth nipping and aggressive hands yanking at hair. I'm hungrily stealing Jace's air now, tasting the residual spearmint gum flavor, absorbing his body heat and his confidence. Strong hands move feverishly over my legs, under my dress, until he has a good grip around the backs of my thighs. He pulls me onto his lap to straddle him, crushing our chests against each other until my knees are jammed against the cold metal wall, hard enough to bruise, and I can feel his speeding heart beat against mine and his erection digging into me.

And I find myself wanting it.

He's arrogant and condescending, his morals likely reprehensible, and yet I press myself further against him. He groans as my fist curls around his tie, roping it tight until I can't be sure that I'm not choking him. And I don't care, because there's something about Jace that makes me forget all manners and consideration. There's something that makes me want to take control.

He doesn't seem willing to relinquish it, though, his hands fumbling in the dark to find my plunging neckline and the loosely draped material of this wrap-style dress. With a quick tug against it and my lace bra, cold air hits my bare chest a second before his tongue finds a nipple.

I can hear him working his belt buckle and zipper in haste, as if he's afraid to run out of time. Warm hands find my inner thighs and I hiss in pain as he pinches my skin in his attempt to grab hold of my pantyhose. Before the sting has faded, I feel the pull, hear the tear, sense his fingers pushing past my panties and sliding into me without shame.

"I knew it," his whispers against my neck, his hand pushing my hips from behind and into him, until the end of his cock is sliding against me.

Lights flicker and then flood into the elevator like a cold bath to whatever insanity just took over my senses, illuminating this mess I've gotten myself into. Eyes the color of cool water stare back at me, a question in them. Forceful hands pulling my body closer, slowly inching him into me, tell me that Jace is too far gone to stop now.

And then the elevator jolts, beginning its rapid descent.

Snapping me out of his spell.

I scramble off Jace's lap, and rush to fix my bra and smooth my dress as best I can. I have my coat on and pulled tight just as the doors open on the lobby level, a wall of firefighters in full gear standing at the lobby entrance. I push through them, my face burning.

Plenty of other bewildered and relieved people wander around. People trickle out of the stairwell, red-faced and rubbing their thighs from the long descent.

"Ma'am! Are you the one suffering from claustrophobia?" a heavyset paramedic calls out. After lying to her—thankfully there's too much chaos in the lobby to take up more than a few seconds of anyone's attention—I edge my way out of the circus.

From the snippets of conversation that I hear, apparently there was a serious malfunction with the elevator system, leaving all six elevators and their passengers stranded at various spots in the building. When the backup system didn't kick in, a security guard triggered the fire alarm to get emergency response here, fearing the worst.

I'm sure the news crews are on their way. I don't want to be anywhere near them.

I'm twenty feet from the doors when a firm hand grabs my arm. I shake it off, turning to glare at Jace.

There isn't even an ounce of apology in his eyes. My eyes veer to his mouth without warning. I can't believe that just happened. I can't believe I just *let* that happen.

He steps in front of me, blocking my path a second before I move to leave. "I still need you to sign the last bit of paperwork." A bitter laugh escapes me and he grins. "I'm serious. Let's grab dinner and you can sign everything there. I know a great place nearby. Ground-floor dining. No elevators. I just need to get your paperwork, so let me see how long they think it's going to be before the elevators are back up and running. We could always just have a few drinks while we wait. Just stay here for a few minutes. Please."

I watch him head toward the security guys standing near the elevators.

And then I duck out with the crowd, feeling every bit the heathen.

CHAPTER 15

Maggie

"And that is why I hate elevators," I mutter, balancing the glass of merlot on my stomach, the heat from the fire next to me chasing the cold winter air away.

"I don't think I've ever heard anything like that happen before. Have I?" Grady's face twists in thought as he peels a chestnut he's been roasting over the flame for the past half hour. "Nope. Can't say I have."

"And yet it happened to a severe claustrophobic." I didn't mention what actually happened in the elevator. Namely, Jace. I'm still shaken up by it, having never been one to lose control over a guy—a guy I don't even particularly like, though I'll admit I do feel a "thing" between us. Some connection that now brings with it deep shame.

Grady's arm tightens around me, reminding me of the last time I was lying in this hammock with him. And that leaves me severely perplexed. A part of me—a big part—could easily allow that to happen again. If for nothing else but to help shake my discomfort.

When I got home from that disaster, I immediately climbed into a nice hot shower. I stood under that stream of water until all the old sweat from my panic attack dissolved. Unfortunately the dirty feeling from my moment of weakness didn't wash away so easily.

There was no question that I was going to come up here tonight, regardless. I enjoy the peaceful space and the company, a damn deal more than I do sitting in Celine's belongings. And I hoped that an hour with a guy who actually doesn't make me feel vile—who I'm growing more and more fond of each day—would make the rest of my day fade away.

It hasn't. And for now, I think I need a break from male companionship, under duress or otherwise.

"Should you maybe answer that?" he asks as my cell phone goes off for the third time.

I've already ignored two calls from Jace. This caller, though, is unknown, and I'm thinking it could be Doug.

I'm right.

"Hey, Doug."

"I'm coming by tomorrow at nine a.m. for a site visit."

Site visit. "Okay."

"Great." The phone clicks without another word and I shake my head.

"Who's that?"

"A very strange little man." I sigh. "There are a few loose ends about Celine that I want tied up before I leave. He's going to help me with them."

Grady frowns. "What is he . . . an investigator?"

"Yeah. That's exactly what he is. Supposed to be good. I guess we'll find out."

"Huh. That's cool." The guy is always so even and relaxed. I'd say it might be because he's always high, but I actually haven't seen him smoke anything since that first night up here. "What's he gonna do for you?"

"Just look into a few people. Dig a little into Celine's past."

He tosses the chestnut peels over me and into the fire. "How much does one of those guys cost? I'd think they're expensive."

Unless Ruby's told Grady who I am, then I have to assume he has no idea whose thigh he's pressing his erection against right now. I'd prefer to keep it that way. Yeah, in my emotional fit the other night, I told him that I have lots of money. But it's still more than he can imagine. "I've given him a check. I guess he'll keep working until I get my answers or I stop paying him, whichever comes first."

His hand settles on my abdomen beneath the blanket. "I'm in the wrong racket."

I place my hand on top of it and press down, stopping him just as his fingers attempt a slip under the waistband of my sweatpants. "You think you could make a good private eye?"

He coils his fingers around mine, like he's gotten the hint. "No, probably not." He smiles at me, his gaze drifting down to my lips. And then he kisses me so softly, as if he knows that's what I need.

Frustration begins growing within my body. If I don't leave now, I know exactly where this is going to lead again and I will hate myself for it, after what just happened in the elevator. I have an unwritten rule against two dicks in one day. It's a new rule, because the opportunity has never arisen before, but it's one I'm feeling committed to. "I think I need to get some sleep. Today has been overwhelming."

I feel his mouth pull into a smile against mine. "Okay." With one last kiss, he shifts back, relaxing his grip on me, making no move to leave his spot. Not until I'm near the gate does he call out, "Hey, I forgot to tell you. I have a potential renter for the apartment. She could take it by January first and the landlord will give you the last month's rent back. Let me know if that's something you'd be interested in."

That would give me about three weeks to pack everything up and get it out before flying to San Diego for Christmas. I think I can manage that, but what about all of my unanswered questions? What will Doug have discovered by then? I guess I could always just stay at a hotel, if I need to fly back to New York again. "Can I let you know in a few days?"

"Of course. She wants to come by and see the place next weekend, if you're up for it. But only if you're up to it. No pressure, seriously."

He really is a nice guy. "Thanks, Grady. Good night."

CHAPTER 16

Maggie

December 5, 2015

"What's that show called again?" Doug edges around the box of silver spoons I just finished wrapping.

"*Antiques Roadshow*?"

"No . . . *Hoarders*." I trail him wordlessly as his eyes scan the space at lightning speed. "This is where it happened?" He points to the bed, digging out and opening a folder from the inside of his bomber jacket.

It's not difficult to see over his shoulder. "How did you get a copy of Celine's case?"

He slaps the cover shut before I can get a good look at the photocopied picture and sticks it back into its hiding place. "Chester had prints taken the night of. Nothing but hers turned up."

"I'm surprised they bothered," I grumble.

"The shitty ones don't. They take one look at the body and start the suicide report. But Chester's a good detective. He covered his bases." He hops up onto the bed—his boots leaving prints on the bedding I just purchased—to fiddle with the locking mechanism on the window. He blows on it, and tiny wood shavings lift off, floating through the air. "This was replaced recently."

I frown. "What does that mean?"

He jumps down. "It means that someone replaced this recently. These old windows are notorious for being easy to break into."

I feel my face pale. "Are you saying someone broke in?" Someone who may have stolen her diary? Someone who may have hurt her?

"No. I just always like to test locks for my clients." He shrugs. "It's New York City. You can never be too careful, especially when a fire escape leads to your apartment from an alleyway. It's too easy to yank the ladder down to ground level if you know what you're doing. I did a check of this building. The last reported break-in was twenty-two years ago, so I don't think you should worry too much. But you should ask the super about it. Find out when it was fixed. I need Celine's computer and those passwords. Can I use this?" Doug dips down to take one of the antique wood crates.

"Uh . . ." I follow him to her desk, where he grabs the sheet of passwords I set out, and then he yanks cables out of the back of the computer tower and sets it inside the crate.

He holds out a hand. "And the phone?"

"Still nowhere."

"You sure you checked everything? Her purses? Dresser drawers?"

"Yup."

"Pockets?" He's sticking his free hand in the coat draped over the couch arm as he asks, dumping tissues and receipts out.

"That's *my* coat, and yes, I've checked every pocket."

His lips pucker in thought and then finally he taps the computer tower. "Well, if she backed it up, we should be able to pull information off of here. Otherwise, my tech guy, Zac, will see if he can get into her phone records."

I cross my mental fingers, hoping that Celine would know to back up her phone. She was never the most technologically astute person.

"By the way, the flowers were sent in October, but otherwise it's a dead end. The sender paid cash and left no personal information. The person behind the register was on her second day of the job and wasn't going to push."

I chew on my lip. Is Jace the kind of guy to go into a flower shop and order flowers himself? Or would he get his assistant to do it, calling in the order with his credit card?

I'm thinking the latter, which means maybe they weren't from him at all . . . "Listen, about that hedge fund manager—"

"Keep up appearances with him. I'll call you soon." And then he's testing the dead bolt on my door before charging out, leaving the door swinging open and me stunned.

"My, he was in a rush." Ruby stands in the hallway between our doors, watching him go.

"I think that's just how he is." As opposed to Detective Childs, Doug Murphy seems to operate on fast-forward at all times. I don't know how he catches anything important as he speeds past. "Did you need something?" I notice the tray with a tea set within her trembling grasp.

"I used to have tea with Celine sometimes, when she wasn't working," Ruby says timidly, shifting on her feet, just outside my threshold.

I finally clue in. Hans is coming by in half an hour to collect a few boxes, but I have a lonely old woman on my doorstep, waiting for an invitation, and I've blown her off too many times. "Would you like to come in and have tea with me, Ruby?" When was the last time I even drank tea?

Her face instantly lightens and she nods, shuffling in to set the tray down on the trunk coffee table, as I'm guessing she's done many times before. "Would you be a dear and bring that over?" She points out a weathered teak folding chair leaning against a wall. "If I get into that couch, I'll never get out."

Holding the top of the teapot with one hand, she carefully pours steaming hot tea into one of the matching teacups. She even has the creamer and sugar pot, and a set of tiny silver tongs at the ready for a sugar cube. "Celine got me this set last Christmas. It's a Crown Staffordshire from 1938 that she found at a garage sale."

"It's lovely," I murmur, passing on the sugar and milk, picking up the cup to study the delicate burgundy-and-pink floral pattern. "Do you have children, Ruby?"

She chuckles. "No. No children. No husband . . . I've always marched to my own drummer. Never could find a man who could handle marching along with it." She sighs. "I really enjoyed having Celine next door." Her clouded eyes wander over the half-empty shelves, countless boxes already marked and stacked on one side of the living room. "Things look different since I was here last."

"And when was that?"

"Just the day before she passed." She takes a dainty bite of a cookie. "What are you going to do with her collection?"

"Sell them and then start a foundation in her name. That's what her mother wants."

She nods slowly, chewing. "She was such a good girl."

I avoid answering by taking a sip of my tea. I don't know what I think anymore. Was Celine still a good person, despite what she did for money? Yes, I believe so. And yet my memory of her has been tainted. No wonder she never told me. I've never been in a position where I felt that my best option to survive would be to sell what I was born with—myself—to get ahead. I've never pined for money. I've never felt the frustration of not being able to buy something that I wanted or needed.

I could argue that I face limits, too. I can't afford to buy all the things I'd like for every child in every poor village across the world.

But if we're being honest, I can't possibly understand what it's like to feel trapped. To have to decide between paying my rent on time or flying across the country to care for my terminally ill mother, my only living relative.

I was so quick to judge.

I'm trying to understand now, to be more open-minded. To accept that perhaps Celine was fundamentally a different person from me.

Or that perhaps, faced with the same limitations, I might have found myself doing the exact same thing.

Look what I've been willing to do to get information from Jace! Keeping up these business pretenses, handing over more money than most people will see in their lifetime.

And what has keeping up these pretenses gotten me so far? Besides trapped and almost screwed in an elevator . . .

"Who was that man earlier, taking Celine's computer?" Ruby asks.

"Just a guy doing some research for me."

She leans closer, like what she's about to say shouldn't be overheard. "You don't think it was suicide either, do you?"

She said "either."

I set my teacup down carefully, afraid I'm going to break it, as my heart pumps a rush of blood through my body. "You don't? I mean . . . why don't you?"

She smiles softly. "When you've been alive as long as I have, you know when a person has no plans on dying. That girl was ambitious. The only plans she was making were for living."

That's always how I'd seen Celine, too. "You don't think that maybe she wasn't in the right frame of mind at that particular moment?"

"She'd seemed down lately, true. More emotional than usual. But I'd talked to her earlier that day, in the hallway. She had just come back from one of her little treasure hunts, with an antique rosary for her mother. She was so excited to give it to her for Christmas."

My eyes veer to a box in which I had wrapped up a set of crucifixes and other ornate church paraphernalia, and I remember the very rosary Ruby is talking about. I was going to donate that box to the local missionaries in the town I'm currently working in. I'll have to fish the rosary out and wrap it up. Rosa will love it, even if it makes her sad.

"I found an email confirmation for a one-way plane ticket to California. She was supposed to fly home at the beginning of December," I say. Who books a plane ticket home and then washes down a bunch of pills with vodka before she gets there? It just doesn't make sense.

Ruby pushes."So, the research that that little man is doing for you . . ."

"Doug's a private investigator, recommended by the detective who closed this case," I finally admit. "He's going to look into a few people Celine associated with. And into her. Into her daily activities and such."

Ruby quietly sets her teacup down on the saucer. Astute eyes settle on me. "And what do you think you'll find out? About Celine."

I'm kicking myself for not sitting down with Ruby for tea the first day she invited me into her apartment. The old woman clearly has a good grasp of the situation. "So you know?"

A sad smile touches her creased lips. "I've suspected for some time, though I never asked her. I didn't want her to shy away from me, or worry that I would think less of her. I myself did some things in my twenties that I wasn't proud of, just to get by." She pauses to shift and straighten the china on the tray. "I saw Celine leaving at night sometimes, and she didn't look like the Celine who shared tea with me. Of course, I rarely saw what she was wearing because she'd cover herself in a long black coat, but those heels were enough."

"Why didn't you say anything to the police?"

She settles a pensive look on me. "Hold on just a moment." She shuffles out of my apartment, only to return thirty seconds later with a paperback clutched between her fingers. She hands it to me, allowing me time to study the mediocre cover of the murder-mystery novel.

"I don't get it."

Ruby taps the author's name.

"R. J. Cummings," I read out loud, frowning. And then it hits me. "R is for Ruby? You're a writer?"

She offers a small smile. "I published my first murder mystery when I was forty-two. Just a small press, but I was awfully proud."

I look at the tiny little woman in a new light. "You write crime books?"

"I used to. It's been twenty years since my last one was released. I live off of my royalties now, which is just enough for the simple things in life, thanks to my rent control. My point is that I'm the daft old lady across the hall who thrives on conspiracy theories and solving mysteries. Nobody would believe me if I said Celine was murdered. And as for the other thing, well . . . I figured she'd want to keep that secret to herself."

"But it may be that secret that got her killed in the first place. I don't know. I don't know anything about it, other than what I read in her diaries, because she never told me." What else might Ruby know? "Did she ever talk about a friend whose name started with an L?" I hesitate using the word "friend."

Ruby's wrinkled face creases further with her frown. "No. I'm sorry. That doesn't ring a bell."

"What about a guy named Jace? Or Jay?" Her frown makes me prompt further. "He worked in her building."

Her eyes narrow in thought. "Yes . . . I seem to remember her mentioning someone from work. Just once or twice, though. In passing."

"Did it sound like they were together?"

"Like I said, she never told me much about her 'dates.' But I do know that it's difficult to keep a relationship with that kind of profession on the side." She offers a sheepish smile. "I tried. Failed miserably."

The door buzzer goes off. We'll have to pick up on this conversation later. "That's Hans. Have you met him?"

She shakes her head.

I hit the front door release button and flip open the dead bolt. "He's eccentric, but I think you'll like him." Though I don't know if I have the energy to deal with him right now. "Just, please, do me a favor and don't mention anything about the investigation and what we suspect about Celine?"

"There's no benefit to getting others involved just yet," she agrees as she pours another cup of tea for herself and tops mine off.

A few moments later a knock sounds. "It's open!" I holler and a creak sounds.

"Ruby, this is—" I turn to greet Hans.

Only it's not Hans.

"What are you doing here?" I blurt out as Jace stands in my doorway, his golden-blond hair speckled with large snowflakes, a charcoal-gray wool coat shielding his pricey clothes from the elements, the collar curled up stylishly.

"Maggie . . ." Ruby sets her teacup down, and using the coffee table to support her as she stands, she walks over and offers a wrinkly hand. "My name is Ruby and I live next door."

He flashes a thousand-watt grin that I'm guessing he reserves for the elderly during his father's political campaign. It works on Ruby, earning her wide smile. "I'm Jace Everett. It's a pleasure to meet you."

"Jace." She's so old and stiff, she needs to turn her entire body to look at me, her knowing eyes twinkling. "We were just talking about you."

"No we weren't!" My cheeks flush.

She ignores me. "Would you like some tea?"

"Uh . . ." His gaze drifts over our setup. "I would love some tea. Thank you for *your* hospitality, Ruby." He shoots a reprimanding look my way.

She pats his arm like a grandmother would her grandson's. "Make yourself comfortable. I'll be back in a moment."

Ruby shuffles away as Jace kicks off his wet shoes. His eyes scan over the shelves and boxes. "So you weren't abducted the other night. That's good to know."

"How did you find me?"

Shaking his coat off, he drapes it neatly over the couch's arm and then takes a seat next to me. "You gave the address to Natasha, to have the papers couriered over, remember?"

Right. I did do that. I was so relieved when I saw the email request this morning, I answered quickly. While I could just cancel all plans for letting Jace have my money, I don't want to risk any part of Doug's investigation by closing an open door. But after what happened in the elevator yesterday, I definitely didn't want to see him again in person.

And now here he is.

"So you thought it'd be appropriate to just show up. On a Saturday."

He slides an envelope out from the inside pocket of his jacket. "I thought I'd deliver them to you in person."

"You really want my money badly, don't you?"

He sighs, a hint of irritation flickering in his eyes as they settle on me. "Are you always so cynical? Or have I done something to offend you?"

"I don't know. Have you?" I ask pointedly.

He holds his hands up in surrender. "Look, yesterday was . . . unprofessional of me. I get it, and I'm sorry. It wasn't my intention. I didn't know what else to do, though. I don't sing or dance and I couldn't think of any stories. You sounded like you were going to die." He smiles, and has the grace to look somewhat sheepish. "It worked."

It did. Too well.

Unprofessionalism. That could be my excuse for tearing up these forms. Then again, I'm equally to blame. And I've been ordered to keep up appearances.

I hold a reluctant hand out. "Where do I have to sign?"

He smiles. "Already marked with flags."

"I'm assuming these are the exact documents that my advisor approved?"

"They are, but I'm in no rush. You should read through before you sign."

"No thanks," I grumble, scribbling my signature over and over. *I'm* in a rush. To get rid of him.

"There's a lot of stuff in here," he muses, scoping out Celine's apartment. "Are you going to have a garage sale or something?"

"Oh, hell no! She's having Celine's brilliant and talented friend work his buns off to sell this valuable collection at a silent auction in the esteemed Hollingsworth showroom," a petulant-sounding male voice announces. Hans stomps his heavy boots on the doormat. "Someone took pity and let me in downstairs. My delicate skin was not made for this weather!" he whines, unwinding the red plaid scarf hiding half his face. It's just barely below thirty degrees Fahrenheit out there and yet he's dressed for a trek through Alaska.

"Oh, goodie! More people," Ruby says with a smile, sneaking up behind him as he peels off a bulky fur-lined coat. "You must be Hans. I'm the neighbor across the hall, Ruby. Celine and Maggie both told me so much about you. You look like you could use some tea." She holds up a cup in her hand.

"Crown Staffordshire?"

"1938."

Hans nods with approval. "*Very* nice."

Ruby grins at us with excitement. For a lonely old woman, this is now a full-fledged party. "I'll be back in a moment with another cup."

After disrobing from his winter gear, Hans gets his first good look at Jace. His eyes widen and flash to me. Yes, he recognizes him from the picture.

I do quick, begrudging introductions. Thankfully Ruby quickly reappears with a fourth cup and another plate of shortbread. She insists on pouring for the men and I watch, thinking how bizarre this all is. In the apartment of a dead girl, the friend helping me sell off her life's work on my left, the guy who paid for her sexual services but pretends not to know her on my right, and the old crime fiction novelist who thinks this stinks of murder across from me.

Having tea.

All we need is Grady here, smoking a joint.

"Are these the catalogues you were telling me about?" Hans picks up the five journals sitting on the coffee table, so full that none of them close completely.

"Yup."

He inhales, his eyes lighting up as he fans the pages and colored pictures flash past. "I'll bet she has a page for every single item she ever bought. Talk about OCD, but I love that girl. Cuts our work in half, at least." He sticks them into his leather satchel.

I sit quietly sandwiched between the two men on the couch while

Hans chatters incessantly and Ruby watches like a hawk perched on its post. I would expect nothing less from a writer.

"So, what are you doing here, Jace?" Hans's bony elbow digs into my ribs, making me jump.

"Maggie needed to sign some paperwork for the investments she's making through me," Jace explains politely.

"Are you investing the money we make off Celine's collection?"

"No, I'm not going to risk losing that," I mutter. "It's going directly toward a local project."

"Hey . . ." Jace's hand lands on my knee. "I don't lose my clients' money. I thought you trusted me."

I want to slap his hand away. And in the time that I consider it, Grady appears in my doorway. It takes all of two seconds for his eyes to zero in on Jace's hand.

"Hi, Grady." I stand quickly, moving a few steps toward him. "What's up?"

He smiles—a tight smile—and holds up a drill. "Ruby just called me down, about a kitchen cabinet hinge needing fixing?"

"Oh, that's right. I did." Ruby's eyes twinkle. "But why don't you come in for some tea first?" She produces a fifth cup from somewhere, as if she anticipated this. I'm sure that's why she also left Celine's apartment door open.

Grady's work boots, unlaced, clomp against the floor as he saunters in, the late-day scruff along his jawline reminding me of the other night. In his dark faded jeans and Black Sabbath T-shirt, he's about as polar-opposite to Jace as a guy could get.

And I'm becoming that much more attracted to him because of it.

I feel myself blush and duck my head as Ruby introduces Grady to everyone—because I clearly have no manners anymore.

When I dare look up again, Jace is sizing up Grady, and Grady is glaring daggers at Jace, and neither Ruby nor I miss the exchange. The only one who seems oblivious is Hans, too busy stuck in a hot-guy haze to stop smiling. "So what local project were you talking about, Maggie?"

I turn to level Jace with a gaze. "Helping steer women away from prostitution."

Jace coughs against his mouthful of tea. "Is that something your friend was passionate about?"

"It was definitely something on her mind."

"That's a great idea, Maggie," Grady offers softly, close enough to reach out to me, his fingers giving my elbow a light squeeze. Making me smile and wish that it was the evening already and I was curled up with him under the lights of the rooftop garden.

"Well . . ." Jace sets his cup on its saucer. "That sounds like a commendable charity then." He clears his throat and stands. "Thank you for the tea, Ruby. I should get going now."

"So soon?" Hans says with a pout.

Jace collects the signed papers from the table and heads for the door, his eyes landing on Grady. He stops abruptly. "You know, I have an idea." Pulling his coat on slowly, he says, "I'm going to give you the first three months of my earnings—after overhead to the firm—and you can add that to this charity fund." His gaze rolls over the apartment, ending on the bed. "For your friend."

My heart speeds up. "That's very generous of you. Why would you do something like that?" *Feeling guilty?*

His eyes flicker to my mouth. "I figure I owe you." He pauses. "And you seem so hell-bent on believing that I'm an asshole, maybe this will change your mind."

"Don't forget, December twenty-second. Hollingsworth Gallery. Eight o'clock. Silent auction for Celine!" Hans chirps, his eyes glued to Jace's smooth strides.

But the second the door shuts behind him, Hans's undivided attention turns to Grady. "So . . . We have some heavy boxes to lift, and you look strong."

———

"My back hurts a little," Grady admits with a chuckle.

"I can't for the life of me figure out why." I giggle into his chest.

Hans seemed to enjoy ordering Grady around, telling him where to stack boxes, only to make him move them repeatedly because of weight concerns or height concerns or, maybe, just because the lively antiques appraiser liked watching the rugged building superintendent's muscles strain. "I think Hans has a crush on you."

Grady shifts his body until we're pressed against each other from noses to toes in the hammock, my back to the fire. "I think I have a crush on you," he whispers.

I exhale as nervous flutters fill my stomach. Is that what's happening to me, too? Am I crushing on Grady? We hardly know each other, and yet I feel more comfortable with him than I have with any guy in recent memory. Too bad he lives worlds away.

He must be able to read my mind. "So, where is home for you, Maggie Sparkes?"

"San Diego." I pause, hesitant to go on. It's nice, the feeling that someone doesn't know—or doesn't care—how much money you have. I figure it's one or the other for Grady, seeing he hasn't brought it up since I let it slip. "Ethiopia . . . Kenya . . . Malawi . . . South Africa."

He leans in, the tip of his frosty nose touching the tip of mine. "So you like warm climates."

I laugh. "Yes, in fact, I do."

He smiles. "Well, I'll be thinking about you in February, when I'm digging my hammock and fire pit out of a foot of snow."

I know this "thing" that we have is temporary, so I'm mostly joking when I say, "Or you could come down and help me build a house. If I'm back down there by then," I add quickly, remembering Rosa, a bitter twinge sliding into my spine.

"What . . . and leave this paradise?"

"You could build another one. Of course, you'd have to build a windmill if you want electricity for the little lights."

"A windmill. That sounds complicated."

"A fourteen-year-old boy in Malawi built one using only wood, a bicycle, and tractor blades. Look it up. You seem handy. You could build me a few of those, right? Until I get the solar panels up and running?"

"I'd have to do some research, but I doubt I'm as smart as that fourteen-year-old boy."

I lean in to steal a kiss, our half-naked bodies pressed up against each other. The temperatures have dropped even further tonight, to the point that we've more pushed clothing aside rather than undressed, even under layers of wool covers, which are pulled right to our chins.

I know it's all talk, but a small part of me wonders if it would be possible. Is there a chance that I could be doing exactly this, with Grady, under the warm skies of Kenya or Ethiopia, in a year's time? He's the first guy I've been with in years who I could see fitting into my world.

What does he have to hold him back here? No career aspirations, by the sounds of it.

A call from Doug—I've assigned him his own ringtone now, to save me from screening—breaks apart this intimate moment.

"Her computer has back doors in it."

Doug's words quickly pull me back to my purpose for being in New York City. "Okay? What does that mean?"

"Someone may have hacked into her computer, remotely."

I sit up abruptly, the cold, the snow, my state of dress, *everything* else forgotten. "What do you mean? Could that mean something important?"

"Can't say for sure, yet. Stay tuned. Also, we went through Jace Everett's school records. He's a smart guy, based on his grades. Stayed out of trouble for the most part."

"The most part?"

"Well, he had some issues with fighting at his prep school when he was around thirteen. He had a temper, from the sounds of it."

"How bad of a temper?" At thirteen, most boys are acting out. At least that's what I remember of my private school. If they weren't pushing and shoving each other around, they were trying to cop a feel of the more developed girls to give them something besides their mom's Victoria Secret catalogues to jerk off to in their sheets at night.

"The report is vague, but that doesn't surprise me. His dad is a big donor to the school. I'm sure that bought the right to keep specifics out of the paperwork."

I sigh with frustration.

"I do have some good news, though. We found her phone's backup in her computer."

"So you mean—"

" 'L' stands for Larissa Savoy. It's the only L in there. Thirty-one years old, single, a real estate lawyer at Delong and Quaid, lives on East 30th Street. We've got a string of texts between her and Celine. All carefully worded." He snorts into my ear. "But I've got names of clients. Some phone numbers. You want more information on them?"

"Sure." Though I don't know that I'll do anything with it. Yet. "Is there a Jay in her contacts list?"

"No, but there *is* a Jace Everett."

My heart leaps with anticipation. "Are there any texts between them?"

"Quite a few, from August to October."

I smile, though I'm far from happy. Vindication at last. That lying asshole. "What did they say?"

"They were definitely meeting, but it's not clear for what, or where. That's not abnormal though. Any john paying for sex isn't going to spell it out in a text. Half of these numbers probably aren't even their normal phones. These guys tend to get prepaids for their hookers."

I scowl at his choice of words.

"Don't get too excited yet. Maybe he only knew her as 'Maggie.' "

"But her diary made it sound—"

"*You* want it to sound like he knows Celine."

I roll my eyes. "That's what Detective Childs would say."

"Something else I noticed—her journal log shows that she stopped with the escort services in late July."

"Really?" I missed that part. I sigh. Too many questions still. "What about Larissa? When was their last text?"

"July as well. Celine didn't text much to begin with, from the looks of it. Mainly just to Larissa, you . . . a few to someone named Grady."

My eyes dart to the man lying next to me, who's now sliding off the condom and tugging up his track pants. An edge of distrust pricks me. He said he never talked to her. "About what?"

"Her oven element being out . . . Her fridge wasn't cold . . . toilet . . . Oh, here, she mentioned the window lock seeming a bit too loose. She was worried. That was only a few weeks ago."

"Okay, that all makes sense." He's the building super. She was asking him to come by and fix things.

Grady wraps the blanket around my shoulders, covering me against the cold winter's night as my teeth start to chatter.

"Zac is going to search out the phone records to see what more we can find and how many calls were exchanged between Jace and Celine. I can pay Larissa a visit tomorrow and feel her out, but I doubt she'll talk to me."

"No. I'll go." An angry thrill shoots through my chilled body. I want to look into this woman's eyes when she explains to me how she lured Celine down this ugly path.

CHAPTER 17

Celine

July 28, 2015

"Hey, do you have a few minutes?"

"For you? Always," Larissa purrs into my ear, though I can hear her heels clicking frantically against tile in the background. On her way to court or a meeting, or whatever it is that real estate lawyers do.

Suddenly, I'm nervous. "Okay, so here's the thing: I'm not sure I can do this anymore." I don't need to spell it out; she knows what I'm talking about.

"Is this about what happened the other night? Because that issue has been dealt with, I promise. He and the people who gave him references are on my shit list now."

I shudder. "I'm not comfortable going back. Not right now anyway."

"Okay." She doesn't hide the disappointment in her voice. I've made Larissa a lot of money over the last three years, after all. "But how are you going to afford to do this?"

I don't know. "I'll manage. I should have enough savings to get me through until I move back to San Diego in December, to be with my mom." I'm not really even sure how much her meds are going to cost.

In reality, my savings could be wiped out in two months.

"Well, you know where to find me if you change your mind. Maybe all you need is a break?"

"Yeah. Maybe. Thanks for being so understanding."

"Take care, sweetie. Gotta go."

I hang up, anxiety gnawing away at my stomach.

CHAPTER 18

Maggie

December 6, 2015

I smile at the security guard as he sits unmoving, watching me saunter toward the front desk. "I'm here to see Larissa Savoy, please." I tried her cell earlier this morning—twice—but she didn't answer. I decided I couldn't wait.

He picks up the phone and dials, while I study the glitzy lobby of this prewar boutique condo in the heart of Midtown south. Larissa has clearly done very well for herself.

I wonder just how much of it is on account of her career as a lawyer.

"Your name, miss?" he asks.

"My name is Maggie Sparkes. I'm a friend of Celine Gonzalez."

I watch the middle-aged man repeat my words and listen to the speaker on the other end of the line. I'm expecting to be turned away, preparing exactly what I'll say to convince her that she needs to meet with me—now—when he waves me toward the elevators.

Fantastic.

Luckily, I'm more apprehensive about this meeting than about my own mental issues in the elevator at the moment.

The second I lay eyes on Larissa Savoy, I can tell that she's both a lawyer and a whore. Okay, maybe "whore" is too judgmental. But we started off on the wrong foot long before she ever opened her mahogany door.

"Miss Sparkes?" She pushes a hand through a thick, shoulder-length mane of auburn hair. Equally wary eyes—pretty, deep amber, and almond-shaped—survey the simple pants-and-blouse outfit I pulled from Celine's closet this morning, partially hidden under a winter white coat. Also Celine's.

"Yes."

Her slippered feet slide back several steps to allow room for me. "Has something happened to Celine? I haven't spoken to her in a few months."

Since the end of July, if the cell phone records are accurate. "Yes." My gaze wanders around the corner unit, the view of the Empire State Building spectacular. "She killed herself." While I'm not convinced of that, no one else besides Ruby, Doug, and Detective Childs needs to know that yet.

Larissa's hands fly to her mouth to cover her gasp. It's one of those gasps that makes me suspicious. Then again, everything makes me suspicious lately. It's not a far distance to her couch, and she somewhat staggers over to take a seat, her dark complexion ashen.

I'll admit, it's hard to fake that reaction.

Finally, she manages a ragged, "How?"

"A mixture of medication and alcohol."

"Was it . . . ," she struggles for the words, a few tears slip out, "accidental? I mean, could she have made a mistake?"

"The police have ruled it a suicide."

She nods to herself. "Thank you for telling me. I've known Celine for a few years now and considered her a friend. I met her through a mutual acquaintance several years ago, way back when I was still in law school."

"I'm sure you've come a long way since being a student." My eyes scan the condo again. It's nice, modern, clean. Doug said this unit sold for 1.3 million last June. "And so quickly."

As if pulling on a mask of composure, she sits taller. "I suppose I chose the right profession."

I'm guessing her second career isn't one she broadcasts widely. It probably wouldn't be great for her professional reputation at Delong and Quaid. I'm having a hard time biting back the cynicism, leveling my gaze at her harshly. "Yes, I'm sure you're *very* good at what you do."

Her eyes narrow for just a flash, so quick that I almost think I imagined it. "I'm surprised you thought to track me down."

I can tell she's mentally playing out a conversation, trying to figure out exactly what I know and how I know it. I save her the trouble. "I know that you were the one setting Celine up with 'companions.'" I air quote that word.

She clears her throat. "She told you?" I hear her add in a low mumble, "I didn't think she would."

"She wrote about it all in her diaries."

Larissa's color returns, her cheeks flushing suddenly. "She was a friend who needed to make money to pay for school. I simply introduced her to a few older gentlemen who I know like to take pretty, young women to social events. That's all I did and there's nothing illegal about that. Unless of course she didn't claim the income for tax purposes. I warned her to."

I highly doubt most of these girls working under Larissa file taxes for sex work. It's free cash on the side. Scanning Celine's tax files, it appeared that she started out honest, including a secondary income amount in her yearly income when she was serving strictly as a companion. But, based on my quick scan of last year's filing, she wasn't claiming everything that was in her notebook. "I'm still sorting through that. What I do know is that some of these men paid for an awful lot more than a social event."

She shrugs, seemingly more relaxed. "I specifically told her that getting paid for sexual favors is illegal. Anything in those diaries that indicates I said otherwise won't stand in court."

"Right. If she decided to make a little extra money, that was on her. Not you. Because you were very careful about what was ever recorded. So tell me . . . do you claim that 'twenty percent referral rate' that you make your girls pay you?"

Larissa's initial shock over Celine's death has quickly given way to a cold exterior, rank with self-preservation. She presses her lips shut tightly. When she speaks again, it's with a smile. "You're obviously mistaken about that. I realize that you're looking for people to blame for what Celine chose to do with her life. But might I remind you that making accusations without solid proof will only harm you and Celine's memory. Any pot you'd like to stir will end with her mother finding out what she was doing. Do you really want that? I think the poor woman has been through enough, don't you? From what Celine told me of her, that kind of news would kill her."

Well played, Larissa. I grit my teeth against the urge to scream at her. Scream and reach out to wrap my fingers around her spindly neck and shake her until her head topples off. She's right. It would kill Rosa to know. And the truth is, I don't have any solid evidence. A diary with a person by the name of "L" gives me nothing.

I won't get anywhere with this woman by threatening her. "Did she ever mention that one of her 'clients' "—I roll my eyes—"was a man who worked in her building?"

"No, I don't recall anything about that," Larissa answers quickly, dismissively, checking her fingernails. She's lying. I know she is. She's protecting herself. But I've got no way of proving it.

I exhale heavily, preparing to use the power that I try so hard never to wield. "I have a private detective on retainer and an inexhaustible amount of money to spend digging up every last piece of information I want, if I so choose. So please . . . don't piss me off. I need to know about the client who worked in her office building. He would have gone by Jay, or Jace." Would he have used his real name at some point with Larissa? How thorough was she, really, when she set Celine up on "dates"? Real escort agencies would have background checks and a paper trail, however well concealed. I'm getting the impression that this operation of Larissa's was extremely "off the books."

We simply sit and stare at each other, each weighing the threat that the other may pose. I hold my back rigid, my legs crossed, my face coolly collected, just as I imagine the most astute femme fatale might in an interrogation.

Finally, Larissa relents. "A guy called. He told me that one of my regulars had referred him and he asked for a young, pretty Hispanic companion. Obviously, I thought of Celine. I arranged for a meeting between the two of them."

"Where?"

"A hotel. I can't recall which one. But it was for drinks," she quickly adds. "I never met him, I don't know what he looked like. He introduced himself to me as 'Jay.'"

"And this regular of yours—"

"Is too valuable for me to lose, as are all of my regulars, so go and waste your money trying to find the name if you want, because I won't give it to you willingly," she snaps, the stubborn set of her jaw telling me that she's not bluffing.

"Did Celine ever see this 'Jay' again?"

She folds her arms over her chest, and I read that as a sign that the information vault is officially closed. "You tell me. She's the one who wrote about her exploits in her diary, right?"

If Larissa doesn't know, then it's either because Celine only saw Jace that one time, or because Celine decided to pocket Larissa's cut and not tell her.

"Celine stopped taking client calls through me after the incident, so if she was meeting with men after that, I had no involvement."

"*Incident*? What incident?"

"A new client whose tastes are very particular, and not something that Celine wanted to be involved with."

"What does that mean, exactly?" Forced sex? Bondage? How bad could it be that it would make her stop?

"Check her diary. Maybe she wrote about it."

Maybe she did.

And maybe that's why that diary is missing.

No, I need to focus on Jace right now. Jace holds the secret here, I'm sure of it. But I file the other possibility away in my mind. I'll flag it to Doug, just in case.

Larissa stands and begins walking to the door, signaling the end of the conversation. I follow, admiring her firm, curvy profile. I can see why men would buy her. I just can't understand why she—already a successful woman—would sell herself. But I guess it's like Celine said about me: I'll never have a good grip on reality because I've never wanted for anything. Not financially, anyway.

"Why are you so interested in this 'Jay' anyway?" she asks.

"Because I think he was very important to Celine."

She folds her arms over her chest. There's a hint of concern in her eyes, which makes me think she's not just a money-hungry bitch. "How important?"

"Too important, maybe."

Larissa opens the door. "So, are we square here?"

She means: Am I going to drag her name through the mud, forcing her to do the same to Celine?

"I have no interest in Rosa ever finding out what her daughter was involved in."

She offers a tight, satisfied smile. "Good."

CHAPTER 19

Maggie

December 9, 2015

The intercom begins buzzing in rapid succesion, as if someone's pounding on the button over and over again, until I'm rushing out of the bathroom to shut it up, with Celine's hot rollers in my hair and one eye finished with mascara. "Let me in!" Hans screams.

I have just enough time to throw on the satin robe that hangs from a hook in the bathroom before the sound of feet pounding up the stairs and down the hall has me opening the front door. "Where is it!" Hans screams, his winter clothes in disarray.

"Where is what?"

He pushes past me just as Ruby's door creaks open and she sticks out her head. We exchange shrugs.

"The twin! My voice mail!"

I glance over at my phone, plugged in and on "Do Not Disturb" so I can get ready for lunch with my mother, in town for business and the Sparkes-sponsored charity gala this coming Sunday.

"The missing twin! Where is the twin?" Ruby now joins me in a salmon-colored terry-cloth robe that could be pushing thirty years old, to watch Hans as he crouches and frantically scans the handwritten labels on the boxes stacked against the wall.

"What are you talking about?"

"The missing twin!" I've never seen his eyes so wide, heard his voice so shrill. He whips out one of Celine's journals where she catalogued everything she ever bought and shoves the opened page in my face. "The eighteenth-century Qing Dynasty porcelain vase that is worth *millions*!"

I study the picture—a tall, thin vase with a golden yellow base, decorated by colorful floral detail around the neck and a red dragon on the body. "I don't remember packing this one."

"But you *did*, right? You had to!" Spotting the box of vases, he lifts it as if it's laced with C-4 explosives and places it on the ground ever so gently. "So help me God, if you didn't wrap it properly . . ."

"Let me see that." Ruby slides her glasses down onto the bridge of her nose and reaches for the journal. I watch her study it, her gaze darting back and forth between the picture and the top shelf where Celine's collection of porcelain vases used to sit. "Ah, yes." She smiles. "I thought something looked different when I was here last. It was almost too tall for the space. Oh, Celine was so excited about this vase."

Hans prattles on as he unwraps each fragile piece, his voice shaky with nerves. "I can't believe Celine would have had this and not phoned me right away! It's a well-known story. The seventh emperor of the Qing Dynasty—the last Chinese dynasty before the Republic of China was formed—commissioned two such bone china vases to be added to his imperial collection, in honor of his firstborn, a set of twins who died three days after their birth. They were exact replicas of each other, made using the bone ash from the children's bodies."

I cringe at the thought.

"I know. Creepy. And to use red, which is considered a celebratory color in my culture, was just tacky. Anyway," he dismisses that with a wave, "one had a red phoenix to represent the girl, and one"—he stabs the picture of the vase with his index finger—"had a red dragon, to represent the boy prince."

"So, this is a knockoff." I'm sure there were plenty made.

Hans isn't listening to me. "When the palaces were pillaged by Anglo-French troops in the Second Opium Wars, both vases were taken by people who clearly didn't understand the significance of keeping them together. The vase with the phoenix—the emperor's twin daughter—was recovered in the early 1900s in an attic in London during an estate clean out. It went for almost a hundred thousand pounds to a private collector in France—an exorbitant amount for Chinese art at that time. That estate held on to it until 1996 and then sold it to a collector in Beijing for the equivalent of thirteen million dollars."

"That's some serious inflation!" Ruby exclaims.

"Yeah, well the heirs of that French collector are probably ready to hang themselves now. Had they just held on for a few more years . . ." Hans tsks. "The Chinese art market has exploded over the past decade. They could get double for it. Triple! I can't even be sure! And that is for the daughter's vase. I don't have to tell you how much the Chinese value their sons, do I? *Especially* in the dynasty era."

"And you think *Celine* had this twin?" I start to laugh.

"If I could just see the official period seal . . ."

"That I'm sure anyone could Google and copy," I rationalize.

"Not a seal written in *kaishu*!"

"Hans . . ." Sometimes I wonder if he truly forgets that normal people don't know what the hell he's talking about, or if he just likes being questioned so he can share his vast, impractical wealth of knowledge in that condescending tone he gets when he's talking about antiques.

He heaves an exasperated sigh. "It's handwritten, which means it's that much harder to copy. It'll match the seal on the twin vase."

Ruby and I watch Hans dismantle a day's worth of packing work, handling each vase as if it might shatter under the weight of his fingertips.

As hard as it is to believe that his hunch could actually pan out, I have to remind myself that this entire investigation of Doug's is based on a hunch, too. My belief that Celine didn't kill herself.

I kneel down beside Hans and begin helping him unwrap. "So, you said this could be worth millions?"

"Chinese collectors are paying record-setting money for imperial work to preserve their history. Another Qing Dynasty vase went up for auction six years ago. They appraised it at over a million pounds at a UK house. And do you know how much it went for when the auction actually opened?" I wait for him to answer as he pauses to glare at me. "Equivalent to eighty-five million dollars!"

Ruby lets out a low whistle.

"And that was an ordinary vase, by comparison. Of course there are nonpayment issues because of a fee disagreement between the buyer and the auctioneer. Some people are accusing the Chinese government of sabotaging the sale because they believe the vase was stolen and therefore still rightfully theirs, but—"

"Okay, calm down, Hans. You're not even breathing." He's talking a mile a minute.

"Don't you see? Everyone assumed the male twin vase had been destroyed and was lost forever. Can you imagine what this would mean?" He stops to stare at me, his eyes full of wonder. "An artifact with actual emperor DNA in it! Celine would have made a *monumental* discovery. And she had a keen eye. She wouldn't have mistaken a fraud easily. I really think she might have had something here."

It's time for a reality check. "And what are the chances that Celine found this missing twin vase for"—I check the journal record that sits beside me—"fifteen dollars at a garage sale in Queens?"

"The guy who bought that vase six years ago paid twenty for his," he shoots back. "If I can just find it and check the markings, then I'll know if it's worth taking to my director. We'll need multiple appraisals, of course, and testing, and—"

"What about the pictures I sent you? Didn't she take all the angles?" From what I saw, if there were any signatures, Celine had made sure to capture them.

"That's the thing! There *weren't* any pictures of this vase on that jump drive, period. It's a complete fluke that I even saw that page in her notebook, to be honest. I was flipping through, looking for something else. It's her last purchase, from the looks of it."

"That doesn't make sense. She was always so meticulous. Why include it in this book but not in her other cataloguing?" I frown, eying the now empty desk, where her desktop used to sit. Could someone have erased the pictures of this vase? Her passwords were sitting right there.

I stop asking questions and help Hans unwrap Celine's entire collection from the box, until a row of fragile vases sits before us.

Not one of them matches the twin dragon vase in Celine's journal.

A sinking suspicion fills my gut. I peer up, first at Hans, then at Ruby. "You know what this means, right?"

CHAPTER 20

Celine

November 11, 2015

The romantic and complex notes of Piano Concerto no. 25 fill my apartment and my heart. Mozart has always been my medicine after a long, miserable day. And I've had a bunch of them. The entire last month has been miserable.

A year ago, when I decided I wanted to write my thesis on Chinese art—the market is booming, the history is rich, and Hans said that Hollingsworth salivates over North American appraisers with this type of expertise—I realized that I would need to start educating myself long before I even began my master's. For as well versed as I am in European and British art, the farther east I go, the more ignorant I become.

So I began reading everything I could in my spare time, studying the politics of China and its surrounding countries, the customs. Even traditional Chinese calligraphy. That alone—the origins of the characters, the very specific pen strokes required, where markings must begin and end—could be the bulk of my thesis.

I've only just started acquainting myself with the actual art history aspect, so I'm still unfamiliar.

Downing the rest of my vodka—it's become a nightly habit as of late, to help me drift off after I've cried myself empty—I pick up the appraisal certificate and scan it again with a hopeful smile. I swung by the local antiques shop a few blocks away in Chinatown earlier this week and asked the dealer, Ling, to give me an appraisal. She's very knowledgeable and has become a friend over the last year. I needed proof, before I offered this bowl up on a silver platter.

I was right. It *is* a Ming Dynasty lotus bowl from the Xuande period—the cobalt-blue lines crisp from the addition of manganese. It's likely worth anywhere between four and seven thousand dollars. I paid thirty-five for it, plus the appraisal fees, which I can't really afford, but it was necessary this time.

It'll make a nice gift for her. And hopefully it'll be a suitable peace offering.

My gaze shifts to the vase and my heart rate jumps. Finding the bowl was one thing, but this vase . . .

I still won't let myself believe it. I'm still in shock.

I wasn't supposed to be buying for myself when I strolled into the driveway of a lovely elderly German couple in Queens, who were selling off their things to move into a retirement home together. I found the vase sharing a box with an archaic two-slice metal toaster and manufactured china dinnerware. I at first wrote it off as just another beautiful mass-produced knockoff. When I picked it up, though, and wiped off the thick coat of dust to study the artwork lines that show wear from age, I began to wonder.

And then I turned it over and saw the markings.

And I had to buy it.

Using my iPhone—which has made cataloguing all of my finds *so* much easier—I carefully turn the vase over now and take a picture of the seal. The strikes are light and flowing, instead of heavy and thick. Judging by the slight curve in one of the letters, I'm pretty sure it's handwritten, and not a computer-generated font meant to look handwritten. The blue paint matches the rich blue hues used in the detailed floral artwork. And I'm also quite sure that the blue-tinged glaze that coats the seal is uniform to the glaze that coats the rest of the beautiful and meticulous design.

And this red dragon . . .

I could have just spent fifteen dollars on something that came off an assembly line and that five thousand other people have sitting on their mantel. But I would hope that by now I can tell the difference, otherwise I probably shouldn't bother pursuing this career path of mine.

And if I'm right, if this vase is what I think it is . . .

But everyone in the industry has written the twin vase off as lost. Destroyed. There have been enough false discoveries of it over the hundreds of years since its disappearance that to say you have found the long-lost twin vase is like crying wolf.

Nobody believes you.

I considered bringing it to Ling, but given she's a Chinese art dealer, I'd feel obligated to sell through her. There's no way I want to sell something as worthwhile as this may prove to be to some rinky-dink Chinatown dealer. This is a find for the likes of Hollingsworth, somewhere where I can make a name for myself in the industry.

Besides, I'll need a slew of experts to assess the vase—I'm guessing, given the value of this antique, that they'll want to use thermoluminescence testing to be sure of its age—before I'm able to ever claim its authenticity and auction it off. I've done all that my naked, semi-educated eye can.

I need to talk to Hans. He was supposed to come tomorrow night to check out the Fauxbergé but he bailed on me, *again*. He promised he'd come in a few weeks. I almost feel stupid even suggesting the authenticity to him. I'd rather just show it to him and see what he says.

Turning the vase right-side-up again, I carefully set it back into the cardboard box on the floor next to me. I send the picture of the vase's front—the dragon—to my little inkjet printer, so I have something to add to my hard copy catalogue. Call me obsessive, but I like the ability to touch my records.

While that's printing, I type out the headline for a new *Relics Hunter* blog post: "Discovery of a Lifetime?".

CHAPTER 21

Maggie

December 9, 2015

"Has Rosa told you yet?"

"Yes. Just last week." I watch Melody Sparkes, nee Roswell, smooth the cloth napkin over her champagne-colored pants, her elegant, fluent tone sounding the same as it did ten years ago. The funeral was the first time I'd seen her in close to a year, since I was last in San Diego to take care of Rosa. Between hectic work schedules and time zone conflicts, we're lucky if we catch each other on the phone once a month. Our relationship mostly exists through email.

The woman has so far defied age, her complexion glowing, her features sharp. No doubt some of that is thanks to judicious Botox injections and laser treatments, but nothing over-the-top. She's always been a classic beauty, her honey-blond hair kept long and layered, her makeup simple but effective, her wardrobe heavily geared toward traditional wool suits in pastel colors and pearls. It's a rather deceptive front, given her reputation as a fierce businesswoman in boardrooms full of egotistical men in a male-dominated industry.

It's that energy that first attracted my father to her, or so he said. I wonder, had he married a compliant country club debutante like all the Sparkes men before him, instead of a career woman, would they still be married today?

"I wish there was something we could do. She's already been through so much," my mom says through a glass of Perrier. I hear the sadness in her words, her voice, and that brings me some comfort. I like knowing that Rosa and Celine meant something to her, too. It's not that Melody Sparkes is an uncaring woman. She's just never been one to put her emotions on display for others.

"I'm heading back to San Diego as soon as I'm done here, to stay with her until . . ." My throat begins to close with a sizeable lump. "Until she doesn't need me anymore."

"You know, I come to New York so often. I wish I had made more of an effort to reach out. To visit Celine. I hadn't seen her since . . . I don't know when I saw her last. It puts things into perspective, doesn't it?" She blinks several times. It's the closest I've ever seen to her crying since her mother's funeral, when I was ten. Clearing her throat, she asks, "How is handling the estate going?"

I sigh. "Slow, but I'm making progress. You wouldn't believe how many antiques she crammed into that tiny apartment."

"And how are you doing with that? Rosa said you're actually staying there?" My parents have known about my claustrophobia since I was seven, when they took me to see a specialist. Up until that point, they had just attributed my getting upset about being in a car too long to being a fussy child; my refusal to walk through crowds or step into small rooms, and my need to search out exits, to being "difficult."

When I accidentally locked myself inside the bathroom and Rosa found me curled into a little ball, drenched in sweat, my heart pounding in my chest, screaming at the top of my lungs, they decided to have me assessed. The diagnosis came back, and they sent me to a world-renowned therapist in L.A., who helped me learn to cope, to talk myself down from my panic attacks, should that ever happen again.

While my parents haven't always been there for me, they always ensured I had the best of everything, I'll give them that.

I shrug. "It's manageable." The waiter comes by with fresh drinks just as Doug's ringtone chimes from my pocket, cutting into our conversation. "I'm sorry, I need to take this."

She waves me away, pulling her own phone out as I stand.

I answer with "Hey, what's up?"

"You're right. Four pictures of that vase were deleted from the computer."

A nervous flutter explodes in my stomach. It's odd, how the sensation of being right about something so wrong can inspire excitement. "How do you know?"

"Zac found them. Whoever did it either didn't care to delete them permanently or isn't smart enough to make sure they were gone. Or was in too much of a rush. And guess what night they were deleted on?"

"November fifteenth," I whisper. That date will forever be a dark day for me. The night Celine died.

"Someone also went into her blog account and deleted a blog post she had been working on for days. Guess which one?"

"The one about the vase."

"Bingo."

"What does this mean, Doug?"

"Could mean a whole lot of things. Maybe your friend deleted the pictures and the blog post. She may have decided it was risky to have that out on the Internet before she confirmed the vase's authenticity. Or, it could mean someone hacked into her account and deleted it. It definitely means you're going to need to cut me another check."

I walk back to the table, dread and excitement competing within me. Tiny bread crumbs are trailing in, important nuggets that I don't yet fully understand. What if Celine's death has nothing to do with her side profession? What if I've been chasing the wrong rabbit this entire time?

I do my best to carry on a normal conversation through the rest of lunch, as my mom asks what plans I have coming up with my organization that she should be aware of, so she doesn't look like an idiot to the reporters when they ask. Not that she ever does, because no matter what I'm up to, she stands in front of cameras with a smile and makes the same generic statement: "Sparkes Energy is proud of Maggie's ongoing work in developing countries. We will always support her philanthropic efforts."

Not until an eggnog cheesecake with two spoons is placed between us—compliments of the chef, because the Waldorf Astoria knows the Sparkes Energy matriarch well—does she inadvertently bring Jace Everett up. "So Clifton Banks mentioned that you're investing some funds with the New York branch of Governor Everett's investment firm. Not that it's *his* firm anymore, per se."

I roll my eyes as I slide a sliver of cake into my mouth. Clifton has not yet grasped the concept that "confidential" includes other members of the Sparkes family. The good thing is that it doesn't sound like she's going to try to dissuade me. We've come a long way over the years. I honestly think that my parents just didn't know what to do with a child. It wasn't until I began college that it seemed like we could relate on a human level.

"Yes, I am. Long story . . . ," that I'll never try to explain to her, "but I figured I'd diversify. His son came highly recommended."

"His son?" The sparkle in her eye hints at her curiosity.

"Yes, his son who is arrogant, privileged, and money-hungry." *And paid Celine to have sex with him.*

"Some might say the same about you . . ." She pops her fork into her mouth with a knowing smirk. "That's too bad. I was hoping you'd bring a date to the gala this weekend. The money *is* going to your organization, after all."

"I would not invite Jace Everett to a charity event." I wouldn't even invite Grady, and I'd actually enjoy bringing him. But I can already tell that a night of Cristal and duck confit is not his kind of thing.

"But you're coming, right?"

"I *am*. And I'm bringing Celine's neighbor from across the hall." The only time I ever enjoy being a part of a Sparkes Energy social event is when it's for charity. If there's one thing my family's company does right, it's this. When I was little, it was a chance to get dressed up and walk down a gold carpet and into a wonderland of delicious food and elegant surroundings. Now I simply enjoy seeing the final tally at the end of the night, of thousand-dollar-per-head tickets sold and additional donations received, knowing that a large percentage of that amount will go to a cause of my choosing. Lately, it's been the foundation that I built from the ground up.

I haven't actually attended one of these events since I was twenty-two.

"Well, I hope these investments work out for you. Dale Everett is a nice man."

Of course my mother would know the governor of Illinois. Given that Sparkes Energy headquarters is just outside Chicago and they're always tied up in one political mess or another, it makes sense she'd be on a first-name basis with him. Why hadn't I thought of that before? "How well do you know him?"

"Well enough. Almost seven years now, since he started campaigning for his first term. Actually, I was just at a holiday event at his home last weekend. You should see this house, Maggie!" She goes on and on, describing the governor's English-style Tudor home on the bluff overlooking Lake Michigan, paid for not through his elected position but decades of success at his firm, coupled with the "old money" that came with his wife, Eleanor Everett, nee O'Neill, a political debutante. Apparently the governor's mansion wasn't appealing to her.

My mom pulls out her phone and begins scrolling through her pictures with me, showing me the expansive backyard of the Everett estate, filled with people mingling under a white tent set with heaters and twinkling lights, the view of the water beyond spectacular.

"If you should ever have a chance to tour their house, take it," she says excitedly. My mother has always had a penchant for historic homes, even though she chooses to live in a Trump Towers condo in downtown Chicago. She hands me the phone. "Look at this library. Isn't it beautiful? All custom-made walnut cabinetry, and it must be more than a thousand square feet."

"Celine would have loved that," I murmur, studying the home magazine–worthy picture of peaked ceilings and shelving, skillfully lined with books and sculptures.

"You're right, she would have. Dale and Eleanor are huge art collectors, in fact. They've bought and sold several rare pieces over the years. Eleanor claims herself to be somewhat of an aficionada. She spends a lot of time educating herself."

Celine would have *really* loved dating a guy whose mother shared her passion, I'll bet. Though Celine's real thrill was always in identifying the treasures and paying very little for them, rather than handing over thousands—if not more—to someone else who had done the legwork.

I expand the screen, getting a closer look at one of the shelves, at the vases and plates and other ceramics on display.

"What's the matter, Magpie?" my mom asks. "If you scowl like that, you'll get wrinkles."

I zoom in on another shelf.

And another.

And I can feel my scowl deepening.

I can't tell her what I'm thinking.

But this is all just too coincidental to be ignored.

"I need you to find out everything you can about Governor Dale Everett and his wife, Eleanor," I demand, bracing myself as my taxi driver blasts his horn and swerves around a stopped car while people climb out of it, skates slung over their shoulders, smiling and laughing and oblivious. No doubt on their way to the rink at Rockefeller Center.

"His parents. What for?" Doug asks.

I tell him what I learned over lunch, specifically about the vast collection of Asian antiques that Jace's parents have amassed—the many, *many* decorative vases that line Eleanor's shelves.

"So you're thinking . . ." Doug sounds skeptical.

"I'm thinking that if his mother is the expert that she claims to be, then she might have heard the story of the twin vases." *And Jace might have heard it, too.* "We need more information. Just find out what they've bought and where. Hans has tons of contacts in the industry if you need any ins. I'm going to text you a few pictures." I forwarded the pictures of Eleanor Everett's library to myself from my mom's phone. I figured Hans can also help in identifying what's on those shelves.

"You know this is going to cost—"

"So I'll write you another check!" I snap, hanging up on him.

CHAPTER 22

Maggie

December 10, 2015

"This is why I love the holidays." Detective Childs helps himself to three more of Ruby's shortbreads while she simply holds the tin open with a grin, pleased with another satisfied customer.

Maybe I shouldn't have brought her to the precinct with me. I wanted her here to corroborate the facts, but I need Childs's undivided attention and the cookies are stealing the show. "Ruby saw the vase on the shelf *the day* before Celine's death." I refuse to refer to it as suicide anymore. Any lingering doubts I might have had that perhaps Celine killed herself have disappeared. "And now it's gone. This is what it looks like." I smooth the creases in the pictures that Doug printed out for me, recovered from Celine's hard drive. "Someone deleted these from her computer, *the same night* that she died."

Detective Childs lifts the top sheet with mild interest. "So, let me get this straight. On November eighth of this year, Celine bought this vase at a garage sale for fifteen dollars, based on these records. Ms. Ruby Cummings here"—he smiles kindly at her, but I know exactly what's going on inside his head, that my eyewitness is an eighty-one-year-old with cataracts and a hearing aid—"insists that she noticed *this* vase on the shelf, along with the thousand other items that fill Celine's collection, only the day before. This friend of Celine's who is helping with appraisals tells you that he thinks it's an eighteenth-century . . ."

"Qing Dynasty," I fill in, seeing his eyes squint as he struggles with the name.

"Thank you. Qing Dynasty vase, worth millions—"

"Potentially. And based on these pictures, he thinks it could be real. And it's not just any vase. It's the missing twin, fired with the emperor's son's bone ash."

"Okay. Potentially. *You* think that someone who knew what this was worth killed Celine and took the vase, and that Jace Everett—who *may* have been paying Celine for sexual services—is the culprit because his mother and father, the governor of Illinois, have an appreciation for Chinese antiques."

"And he deleted the original pictures and a draft blog post, don't forget that."

"Right."

"See? I didn't even have to connect the dots for you."

"I see what you want me to see, Miss Sparkes." He sounds tired today. "Tell me, why wouldn't the person just steal the vase and leave? Why would they add murder to theft?"

"I don't know." That's a good question. One I hadn't thought to ask. "Maybe because . . . well, she definitely would have noticed it missing right away. Celine was extremely particular." When we were younger, Rosa was sure her daughter had OCD, always lining up her dolls and stuffed animals in rows. She didn't have any of the other peculiarities that come along with such a diagnosis, though. It turned out that she just loved order and patterns.

Childs's attention moves to his computer screen, where he's opened up screenshots of the blog post that Zac recovered and emailed, entitled "Discovery of a Lifetime?". The one that was deleted the night that Celine died, describing—in detail—the history of the deceased twins and the creation of the matching vases in their honor. His finger drags along the screen as he reads her words. "'The markings bear a striking resemblance to its twin, and the glaze appears uniform and well aged. But is it even possible? Could I be lucky enough to find such a treasure? I'll continue to do my research, but I'm excited to think that we may have a winner here.'"

"This was in the stack of books on her coffee table." I hold up another piece of evidence that I discovered when I got home—a Chinese history book, with a bookmark tucked into the section on the Qing Dynasty. "She was reading up on it."

"And yet she said nothing to anyone? Not even to her friend who was an appraiser?"

I can only shrug in response. Celine would be the type to educate herself more before getting too excited over such a monumental find.

Detective Childs finally smiles. "I'll get one of the officers to help you file a theft report. But, remember, without an appraisal certificate, you can't claim that a vase worth millions was stolen. If she has property insurance, I'd recommend contacting them and filing a claim there as well, to leave a complete paper trail."

"And then what?

"Keep Murphy and his guy on it."

I feel my cheeks begin to burn. "You can't tell me that this isn't compelling enough to warrant further investigation into her *murder*."

"I'm sorry, but no. It's not." He sighs, rubbing his brow with a hand. "We're just weeks before Christmas and everyone's trying to close cases before they take off for the holidays."

"Yes. Clearly." I look around at the vast room—phones ringing, feet up on desks, people chattering, people laughing—and feel the urge to scream.

Thankfully Ruby is there to pat me on the knee. "Let's let the detective go so he can catch those bad guys. Okay?" Easing herself out of the chair, she leaves the cookies on Childs's desk and begins shuffling away.

"If you ever feel like actually doing something useful . . . ," I add, not bothering to hide the bitterness from my voice as I fish the manila envelope out of my purse and drop it on his desk. "There's the name and address of a female lawyer in the city who is running a prostitution ring, along with a dozen names and phone numbers of men who made full use of the service through Celine. Just do me a favor—seeing as I'm handing you a case on a silver platter—keep Celine's name out of it. At least until after her mother is gone."

He taps the envelope. "Where'd you get this information?"

"From Celine's phone."

"So you found her phone?"

"Nope." I turn and march out, before he has a chance to tell me that they can't use any of that evidence to build a case either.

"If someone asks for an appraisal on this vase, it's going to cause one heck of a commotion. I'll hear about it." Hans paces back and forth, his long, slender legs weaving around the boxes with surprising skill.

"Unless they go through a private dealer."

"They would still need it authenticated by several reputable appraisers, which means I'll hear about it," Hans argues, his voice turning snippy.

"Now, who would like some tea?" Ruby settles her afternoon tea tray on the old trunk.

I'm watching and listening to all of this from my spot on Celine's couch. But I'm not really watching or listening because I'm too busy wondering whether it's better that Rosa dies believing her daughter took her own life or that she was murdered over a valuable antique, by a man who had previously paid to have sex with her.

So far, Hans has confirmed that Eleanor Everett's collection is highly Asian-inspired and predominantly Ming Dynasty, though he sees a few pieces from other reigns.

Including the Qing Dynasty. It's too hard for him to discern value from the pictures, though.

Doug's tech expert, Zac, has been able to shed a little more light, finding records of Chicago, New York, and Hong Kong auction house purchases by the Everetts, dating back twenty-five years. One of those prizes cost them a hundred and twenty thousand dollars. Not exactly in the league of "major" art collectors, but Zac was also able to confirm that the Everetts' entire art collection is insured for 1.2 million dollars.

That's considerable.

It also means that the rest of their collection—or at least a good portion of it—had to have been purchased through private dealers, and neither Hans nor Zac has any visibility on that.

It *also* means that Jace Everett was raised by a woman who would know the story of the twin vases. Who would appreciate the missing one for its monumental value.

But would that appreciation translate to murder?

I don't trust Jace. That's all I know at this point.

"We need to figure out why Celine had an IP camera shoved in her desk and wasn't using it," Doug says, holding up the small white rectangular device, studying it closely.

"I wonder if the police reviewed the footage from the lobby camera," Ruby offers, her small silver spoon clanging against her china cup as she stirs three cubes of sugar into her tea. The woman seems to survive on nothing but sugar and shortbread. How she's not diabetic, I can't understand.

"You mean that giant dinosaur that was put up in the seventies and never turned on? There *is* no footage. That's just a decoy to scare intruders and give tenants a false sense of safety," Doug mutters, a hint of irritation in his tone, as if he's annoyed that he's even being questioned. "And besides, the police investigation wouldn't have even gotten that far. Everything in this apartment pointed to suicide."

"Oh, not the one by the door. The *other* one."

Doug pauses, looks at her. "What other one?"

"The little black one that's tucked into the corner as you step through the door. It's kind of hard to see. I'm not surprised that you missed it."

Doug takes off out the door, leaving it wide open, the sound of his heavy footfalls echoing.

"Where did you say you found this private investigator?" Ruby asks through a small sip, a triumphant smile on her face.

Moments later, Doug returns. "How long has that been there?" His jaw is tight. I wonder what bothers him more—that he missed it, or that the old lady didn't. To be fair, I never noticed it either.

"I can't say for sure, but ask Grady. He knows everything that goes on in this building."

The mention of Grady's name makes my heart skip a beat. I haven't seen him since Tuesday night, in our usual spot up on the roof. Another welcomed night of intimate distraction for me.

"And which apartment is Grady's?" Doug demands.

"Four ten." She smiles and points that spoon to the ceiling. "Right above us."

"Thank you, Ruby," I say with a wink, following Doug out the door. "What am I paying you for again?"

"He's in there. I hear him," Doug insists as we wait outside Grady's door. I've never been in his apartment. I'm curious to see what it looks like, and if it's anything like the rooftop paradise he's created.

Finally, someone begins fumbling with a chain on the inside. The door opens a crack and a sleepy-eyed Grady pokes his head out.

"You know Maggie Sparkes. I'm investigating Celine Gonzalez's death. What do you know about that camera down in the lobby? Not the fake one. The real one," Doug demands.

"Uh . . ." Grady runs a hand through his hair, sending it further into disarray. The bewildered look as his eyes pan between Doug and me makes me want to apologize for my PI's lack of finesse. The fact that he's wearing nothing but a pair of checkered pajama pants that hang provocatively low on his waist makes me want to shove Doug out of the way and lock myself in Grady's apartment with him.

But now is not the time for that.

"I convinced Dean that he should—"

"Who's Dean?"

"The building owner," Grady answers coolly. "I convinced him that he should get a proper security system and he agreed."

"And who oversees it?"

Grady shrugs. "Some security company."

"Which one?"

"I couldn't tell you. I can ask Dean the next time I'm in touch with him. He's in the Caymans for the next three months so his response time is a bit slow."

He's acting differently today, as if we don't know each other. It could be just a reaction to Doug, who might not bring out the best in people. But no, there's something else there. I feel him closing off to me.

As if he doesn't really want to help with my investigation.

Or . . .

Grady glances over his shoulder quickly. He's blocking the door from the inside with his knee, keeping it from opening too wide. "If there's nothing else . . ."

Why is he being so secretive? Unless . . .

Oh my God. Does Grady have a woman in there?

Jealousy burns deep inside me as I eye his state of dress—or lack thereof—again.

"Yeah, you do that please," Doug answers gruffly. Grady's eyes meet mine for a split second before he shuts and locks his door. I'm left with no other choice but to trail Doug down the stairs, taking the steps two at a time, passing the third-floor exit and continuing on. He has his phone pressed to his ear.

"Hey Zac? I need you to tap into this building's surveillance system." I follow him to the lobby. Sure enough, there's a small camera tucked into the overhang, hidden from casual notice. "Yup, standard."

"Do you think Zac can get in?" I ask when he finally hangs up.

"Any good hacker can get into this if it feeds into a network. Too bad there aren't any on the fire escape or the back of the building." He freezes, then snaps his fingers at me, a smile on his face. He has his phone out again in seconds. "Also, look for any deleted video feed files on Miss Gonzalez's computer."

CHAPTER 23

Maggie

December 11, 2015

"You sure you saw him come in *here*?" I hiss, navigating my way around the shop.

"He didn't just come in here," Doug mutters, sucking back an extra-large coffee from the greasy diner down the street, exceedingly grouchy after spending the last fourteen hours in his car, monitoring Jace. "He walked in with a cardboard box in his hands and spent half an hour in that office back there, with the store owner, Ling Zhang."

Hans sniffs his displeasure as he touches the vintage white ceramic cuff links resting on the shelf next to him. The handwritten price tag claims one hundred and twenty-nine dollars. "Only an idiot would take a priceless vase like that to this place. I'll bet he googled 'Chinatown appraisers' and walked into the first place that Yelp listed."

Hans and I were busy wrapping Celine's collection of handblown glass when Doug called, only a few blocks away. Hans offered to come with me. Maybe I should have declined. The last thing I need is him making a memorable stink in here. "It doesn't seem that bad." Crisp white walls give the Mott Street shop a clean, modern feeling, especially as compared to the retailers in the area—a ragtag mix of gift and dress shops, as well as several businesses I can't even identify thanks to the anti-theft metal screens and lack of English signage.

Plenty of shiny metals and sparkly crystals vie for my attention as I scope out the wares. Everything is neatly arranged and beautifully displayed on thin dark-wood shelves.

"And she's a certified appraiser," I add.

Hans shakes his head. "Anyone can open a shop like this and call themselves an appraiser. This Bone Lady probably registered for a two-day course, and voilà, she's now part of a certified appraiser's guild." His eyes narrow on a petite middle-aged Asian woman with a bob cut and thick-rimmed glasses, talking to an older couple near the back. "I'll guarantee you she undervalued every last item in here so she could buy them and sell for an inflated profit. That's how these private dealers work."

I frown. "Bone Lady?"

"That's what the sign out front says." He pauses. "I do speak Mandarin, you know. I'm guessing she specializes in porcelain art. What's ridiculous is that calling herself 'the Bone Lady' makes it sounds like her expertise lies in bone china." He leans in to hiss, "Bone china wasn't created by the Chinese. Thomas Frye invented it in 1748 in East London. He used animal bone ash from slaughterhouses and cattle farms in his formulation."

Every conversation with Hans is beginning to feel like a history lesson. "But I guess you could argue that, if this emperor used his children's bone ash in his vases, then the Chinese *did* invent it." The more I think about it, the more morbid the legend of these vases seems.

"No. You absolutely cannot argue that. Not bone ash in such trace quantities."

I shrug. He takes this stuff *very* seriously. "Either way, she'd be a good person to bring a porcelain vase to."

I get an exasperated stare in return. "Have you not listened to a word I've been saying about her so-called expertise?"

"You two finished?" Doug mutters under his breath as "the Bone Lady" closes the distance with a smile.

"Can I help you find something?" Her voice is a faint whisper, her accent worn from years of life in America, I'm guessing.

"Yes, my wife and I are looking for a unique piece for our foyer," Doug says, looping his arm through mine, a lively lilt in his voice. I can't help but glance down at him. He's a good five inches shorter than me. Thank God I'm not wearing heels because I'd never be able to pull this off with a straight face.

A sharp elbow to my ribs gets me talking. "Yes, I was thinking that a pretty vase would look good on our foyer table." Oddly enough, that's exactly what we had in the entranceway of our La Jolla home, though it was a vibrant terra-cotta piece from Mexico.

"Ah, yes. Maybe something like this?" She leads us over to a glass cabinet, where several colorful vases of different sizes sit.

"These are nice." I lean in, pretending to be studying the patterns. "Do you have any in a lighter color? Maybe something with gold tones?"

"With a red dragon on it," Doug pipes in.

I shoot him a sideways warning glance, because that wasn't subtle at all. "Yeah. My husband is really on this dragon kick lately." I watch her closely to see if there's any reaction, if she may have just sat in a room for half an hour with a man trying to sell a valuable vase by that very description.

I see nothing.

"This one is lovely." She reaches in and pulls out a burgundy one with birds. "Nice, yes?"

"Yes." I nod in agreement, fighting my disappointment.

"Not birds. Dragons," Doug reiterates, losing patience. "Do you know of anywhere we could find what my wife has described to you?"

The Bone Lady is already shaking her head and smiling, her inky black eyes seeking out other customers in the shop. Closing off, now that she realizes she's not getting a sale. "No. Just birds."

We leave the store and head down Mott Street, weaving through throngs of pedestrians and around the endless trash bags and piled-up cardboard boxes. "It doesn't make sense that he'd bring a vase like that here," Doug says, biting into a peanut shell that he just mysteriously produced, and tossing the empty shell to the ground. Noticing our stares, he pats his coat pocket and shrugs. "What? I do a lot of long hours. I need to keep snacks handy."

"You think he'd take it to an auction house if he stole it?" I ask, dismissing Doug's rather unseemly habit.

"I guess not." He pauses. "Unless he thinks he has covered his tracks. He may wait awhile, though, just to be sure he's going to get away with it. He doesn't know that you hired me to root through her computer, right?"

"Right." The only people who know about Doug are Hans, Ruby, and Grady. "So we need to connect with anyone his parents might use."

"I'll call the auction houses they've bought through in the past," Hans offers.

"Will they talk to you? I mean, aren't you a competitor?"

Hans mocks my concern with a laugh. "Oh, they'll talk to *me*. Anyway, I've already flagged it at all the big houses in the city. They know that this vase has been reported stolen to the police."

"What'd the cops say, Maggie?" Doug asks, breaking open another peanut.

"That unless they find Celine's fingerprints on it or the thief confesses to stealing it, it's going to be hard to prove that it was hers." After I stormed out of the precinct with Ruby in tow, Detective Childs was kind enough to send a police officer over to the apartment to file the necessary paperwork to report the theft.

Doug nods. "Of course. I wonder if he'd be dumb enough to exchange emails about it with someone. I'll get Zac to try and get into FCM's email system."

"He knows how to do that, too?" Who exactly *is* this Zac guy that I'm paying a lot of money to do illegal things?

"There's not much he can't do. The firewalls will be tight, but it's a big network and all you need is one person to open the wrong email."

"What about Jace's home computer?"

"A little tougher. Jace'd have to open an email with a backdoor program." His feet slow, and when he turns to look at me, I see the idea taking form. "You know, you should get into Jace's condo."

"My B and E skills are less than stellar." I can't even break into a rooftop garden without getting caught.

"No B and E. Get invited. Tell him you want to know more about the market and that you might have more money to spend with him. Say . . . your advisor sent some investment plans through that you aren't a hundred percent excited about, and you'd like Jace to look at them, for a second opinion."

"But why would he agree to that?" I counter.

Doug dismisses my concern with a hasty wave. "Because it's an in for him to convince you to invest more with him. Trust me, he'll take it. And Zac'll load up an email with some financial bullshit and a back door, and you forward it to his personal email. He'll have to open it on his home computer."

Doug's grasping for straws here. "That's the kind of thing we'd do in his office, though."

"You're too busy during the day. It has to be at night."

"I don't know if he'll—"

"If he's making house calls to the LES to get you to sign his papers, I'm guessing there isn't much he won't do to get his hands on your money." His eyes dart over my frame. "Put one of your friend's pretty dresses on. I'm guessing that's been working well on him, too."

"How do you know—" I cut myself off. I don't want to know. "Don't you think that's dangerous? You know, if . . ." I let my voice trail. It's enough that Hans thinks Jace may have stolen Celine's vase. I don't want him to know what I suspect about Celine's death.

"No. If he thinks you're there to see *him*, it'll be fine. He won't suspect a thing. Just dangle all that money in front of him and get a good look around."

Doug's basically sending me on a date with Jace. In his apartment, alone. I remember what happened the last time I was alone with Jace, not that I'm too worried about a repeat. "I'll think about it."

"Hey." I glare at my reflection in the mirror. I lasted all of two hours after my conversation with Doug on the streets of Chinatown, distracting my thoughts with packing tape and bubble wrap and two boxes of rare first edition books, before dialing the personal cell number on Jace's business card.

"Maggie? Just give me a sec—" I hear his muffled voice say to someone, "I'm sorry, just give me five minutes and I'll be back with you. Why don't you review this plan I've laid out while I'm gone." A door clicks. "Hey. What's up?"

"I need to bounce some investment ideas off you."

"Really?" The surprise in his voice is unmistakable.

"Yes. I have more money to invest and I want a second opinion on my advisor's recommendations. Can we talk about it? In person." I practiced that line for ten minutes before picking up my phone, afraid he'd hear the duplicity in my voice otherwise.

"Okay." He's smiling, I can tell. "I'll have Natasha make room for you in my calendar and you can come in—"

"I'm not getting in those elevators again." That's an even better excuse than simply being busy. He witnessed firsthand how crazy I got.

His chuckle tickles my ear in a way that I love, before I remember just who this guy is. "Fair enough. How about we meet over dinner? I know a great Italian place over in Chelsea."

"How about your place. Tonight?"

There's a long pause, and I bite my lip, afraid that even Jace Everett might find that a bit too forward. "You have a pen handy?"

"What am I doing, Ruby!" I pace around the boxes as the shriveled little woman sits and watches from her folding chair, the tea set steaming from its place on the brass tray. Before coming to New York City, I could count on my hand the number of times I'd had tea in the last year. Now she's showing up at my door every afternoon—since that first visit—turning me into a habitual tea drinker. And I'm glad for it. She's become the ear I so desperately need. "Is this insane?"

"I think it's exciting." Her old eyes crinkle with her smile. "Do you think he actually has the vase in his house?"

Would he be that stupid? "I have no idea. That's what we're hoping to find out. But I don't know if I can do this."

A very grandmotherly chuckle escapes her. "If you can handle all those powerful tycoons trying to weasel your money from you, you can handle one handsome fool."

"Who may have had something to do with Celine's death, remember."

"Celine was a very sweet girl. Sometimes too sweet, I think." She smiles sadly at the cup within her gnarly fingers. "Just don't drink anything that you haven't seen him pour or eat anything you haven't seen him plate."

Her warning catches me off-guard, though it's surprisingly shrewd. "Is that the crime novelist's official advice?"

"Just basic survival skills, my dear. Oh! Just a moment." She's off, heading toward her apartment.

I take that time to ransack Celine's closet, looking for a suitable dress to wear. Something in between professional and seductive.

"Oh, that's a smart choice," Ruby says on her return, eying the simple black sheath with a deep V top. "Sexy but not overt. Here." She holds out her hand. "Ambien. I use them to help me sleep. They work well for some people, and not for others, but it's worth a shot, in case he gets too frisky and you need to tire him out. It should buy you some time to search for the vase, too. Just crush two into his wine."

A lump forms in my throat as the cylinder of pills rolls within my grasp, my gaze veering to the bed.

"Oh, dear." Ruby's face falls. "I'm so sorry. I forgot. How could I forget? I didn't mean . . . What a terrible thing for me to suggest." She's suddenly flustered, putting her hand against the wall to gain some support.

"It's okay, really." I offer her a soft smile, before I study the bottle now resting in the palm of my hand.

If Jace had something to do with Celine's death, then he had something to do with all the drugs that were found in her body.

This isn't nearly as terrible as that. And I don't have to use it.

"The sommelier promised me that this was a good one." I press the bottle of Bordeaux into Jace's hands, not wanting him to see the shake in mine as I stand at his threshold, pill bottle in pocket and ulterior motives firmly in place.

"You braved the elevator." He smiles and steps back to let me into his palatial apartment in the heart of TriBeCa. Doug already gave me the rundown of the building—nineteenth-century, converted and fully restored. Originally purchased by Jace's parents for investment purposes and given to him as a college graduation gift. Though, based on the kind of money I can guess he makes at his job, he could probably have afforded it anyway.

"Yeah, well . . . this one hasn't failed me yet." And at seventeen floors up, I didn't have much choice. I'm already feeling faint from the rash of nerves flooding me. Am I actually going to do this?

"Dinner will be ready in an hour." He gestures around him. "Do you want a tour?"

"Yes. I do." It comes out like an announcement and way too serious, so I add quickly, "It'll be nice to see what making money off of *my* money can afford you."

"You know what I like about you, Maggie?" He slips Celine's winter coat—hell, my coat, now that I've basically appropriated her wardrobe—off my shoulders, his fingers sliding down the length of my arms. "No bullshit."

I follow behind him, noting that he's exchanged his typical suit for a cashmere sweater and dress pants that hug his form. Filthy pig who pays for sex or not, he dresses well. I just don't understand why he'd pay for it, when he has an assistant like Natasha, on her knees and waiting. "Really? I would have thought you liked the prim and proper debutante."

"I've had my share of those. At this point in my life, I like a woman with a bit of fire in her." He flashes that bright-white smile at me, dropping his gaze to my outfit for just a moment. Given the need for pockets, I rehung the sheath dress and opted for a pair of dress pants and a fitted blouse.

He leads me through a spacious living room that overlooks Manhattan's Financial District and pushes through a frosted white door on the far side. The sound of a pot lid clattering beyond tells me that it's the kitchen.

A lady in her mid-fifties with the same short chestnut hair and plump figure as Rosa stands at the island, peeling parsnips.

"Everything okay, Carla?" Jace asks with a chuckle.

"*Sí*, Mr. Everett. You scared me."

"I'm so sorry. I'm just giving my client a quick tour. This is Maggie Sparkes," Jace says to introduce me, settling a hand on the small of my back.

I take a deep breath and then force myself to relax into it.

Carla's coffee-colored eyes flash to me and she nods, smiling politely.

To me, Jace says, "And this is the kitchen, which Carla uses more than I do."

"It's a nice kitchen," she says and laughs, her thick accent stirring a pang in my chest for Rosa.

I float through the rest of the apartment—a substantial place with four bedrooms tastefully decorated in white linens and vibrant, oversized oil and watercolor paintings. I don't know enough about fine art to appraise their value, but if that magazine article is true, then I'm guessing they're worth a lot.

Jace's bedroom is at the very back. I immediately recognize it from the picture, sans naked man wrapped in the sheets. The overall décor is modern minimalist—white walls with chrome and glass details.

And not a single piece of porcelain art in sight.

He guides me into his home office next, a traditional man cave of custom wood cabinetry and dark chocolate leather chairs, and more oil-on-canvas artwork. I immediately spot a cardboard box sitting on the shelf behind him, and my heart starts racing. Is that the same one he brought to the Bone Lady today?

I struggle not to dive for it.

"Have a seat." He seems to be taking every opportunity he can to touch me, his hand now on my shoulder.

"What's all this?" I force my attention away from the box and survey his desk, noticing that it's covered in opened folders.

"You said you were considering investing more money with me."

"No . . . Actually I said I wanted your opinion on what my advisor is recommending I do," I correct, and quietly scold myself. I can't be confrontational with him if this is going to work.

A small, cocky smile touches his lips. "Sure." He hits the space bar and his screen saver clears to show a convoluted graph with a dozen different colored lines. "Let me walk you through what *I* can do with that money. I'll be better, I promise."

"You don't even know what he's recommending."

"Doesn't matter."

Doug was right. Which means I have Jace exactly where I want him. I clear my voice, trying to shift into stealth mode, afraid I'm going to somehow fuck this all up. "Fine. But we're going to review the plans from my advisor first." I can't give in too easily, after all. That's just not me.

"Sure. Where are they?" He thinks he's already won.

"It's all in an email. I try to go paperless as much as possible. You know, for the environment." I glare pointedly at the stacks of printouts he obviously prepared for this meeting. Or had Natasha prepare.

He chuckles. "Of course you do."

I pull out my phone, steady my shaky hand, my heart pounding in my stomach. "Which email address should I send it to?"

He drops into his chair, turning the monitor on. "Just send it here, so we can look at it together. It's . . ."

I type Jace's home address into the email that Zac prepared for me. Doug promised that this would slip past firewalls unnoticed. That I wouldn't be standing face-to-face with Jace, trying to explain why his security system just flagged a virus.

I hit "send," and I hold my breath.

A few awkward moments pass, and I watch his long fingers tap over the keys, his dazzling blue eyes dance over the screen.

"Yeah, I'm glad you came to me. I would never recommend these investments and here's why . . ."

I let the sigh of relief ease out of me as quietly as possible. "Time out. Are you pouring the wine?"

Because I'm going to need lots to get through tonight.

"So you actually *live* like the locals do. Sleeping in huts for weeks at a time."

"Sometimes months." I devour the last bite of roasted squash. When I sat down to the table, I wasn't sure how I'd force anything down on account of my nerves. But Carla is a superb cook. I hope he pays her well.

Jace shakes his head and frowns, pushing the remains of his steak around his plate. Our dinner conversation has been far from painful, and it's because I've spent most of it talking about what I do, which helped me forget about that cardboard box in his office, which is too far away from the main powder room for me to use the excuse of a bathroom break to sneak in.

Jace actually seems interested in the business side of my world—understanding how I approve and manage micro loans made by organizations for specific projects. But he clearly still has a hard time understanding why I would ever subject myself to the human side of it. "Couldn't you at least build something more suitable to live in?"

"I could, but I won't. What kind of message would that send to these people? They work so hard for so little. Do you know the average villager walks five to ten miles every day to get to work and back home? And if you knew how little they get paid . . ." I shake my head. "Most of them are lucky to make a dollar a day." I point at his plate. "That hunk of meat you're going to throw in the trash would feed an entire family. *If* they ate meat. Most of the villagers I know live off of grains. And they never leave their bowls unfinished."

His eyes drop to my plate, completely bare. "You seem to have learned a thing or two from them."

"I have. I'm also probably going to be hospitalized for indigestion after eating this. My body isn't used to rich meals anymore."

He chuckles as Carla swoops in to collect the plates. "Dessert, señor?"

"We'll wait on that." He dismisses her with a wave. "Thank you, Carla. You can go home."

"*Sí*, Mr. Everett." She disappears into the kitchen with her arms laden.

He settles his gaze on me, and I see amusement forming. "You can't hide much with your expression, can you? What have I done wrong now?"

I grit my teeth. "She's old enough to be your mother and yet you make her address you so formally."

"I'm sure you've been around enough servants to know how it works."

"She's your *employee*, not your servant." I've always hated that word.

"She's a nice lady who cooks and cleans for me three times a week, and I pay her very well to do that," he corrects. "Reminds me of the nanny I had growing up."

"And have you not grown up yet? You're, what, thirty-one?"

He smirks. "And don't tell me you didn't have your share of nannies."

Perfect segue . . . "Only one that I remember. Her name was Rosa. She came to live with me when I was five years old, with her daughter, Celine. The one who died recently?"

I pause for a reaction. I think I catch a glimpse of something, but I could be wrong. I'm on my third glass of wine now. Not the smartest move to get tipsy, but it helped with my nerves.

"Anyway, we grew up together. And never once has Rosa called me by anything other than my first name."

"To each their own." If I've irritated Jace with my views or concerned him with my reference to Celine, he doesn't let on. "Excuse me for a minute." He saunters down the hall, giving me a reason to grab the last two dishes and bring them into the kitchen. I find Carla stooping in front of the dishwasher.

"*Hola.*"

She peers up and, smiling gently, holds her hands out for the glasses in my hand. "*Gracias.*"

"*La cena fue maravillosa.*" I smile, hoping my Spanish isn't as rusty as I think it is. "The best meal I've had in a long time." I check over my shoulder to make sure Jace isn't standing behind me. I'm pretty sure he disappeared into the bathroom. "One of my very best friends was Mexican. Her name was Celine. Maybe she was here before?" I watch, hoping to see a glimmer of anything that looks like recognition.

"Maybe, señorita." Carla isn't even looking at me, as she continues her duties. Given that Carla's only here three days a week, Celine still could easily have been in the apartment without ever having met "the help." Or maybe Celine never did house calls with Jace. Now that I think about it, I don't recall reading anything about Celine meeting men anywhere other than at hotels.

I fix my smile in place and duck back out to the living room, to find that the lights have dimmed and a low lull of music plays on the surround system. Jace stands by the coffee table with two freshly poured glasses of red wine.

"Anything more to discuss in the office?" If I can just get a look inside that cardboard box . . .

"If you can't see that I'm the best person to handle your money then I don't know what else to say to you." I guess that officially concludes the professional part of the night. But I can't leave yet, because I need to see inside that damn cardboard box.

The tiny pill vial that contains two crushed Ambien weighs heavily in the pocket of my pants. It's now or never, because as soon as Carla leaves, I won't have any excuses to stay without looking like I want a repeat of the elevator, and then some.

But I didn't see him pour my glass and, maybe I'm overly paranoid, but Ruby's warning plays loudly inside my head. "Where's that painting from?" I point toward the large courtyard picture hanging on the wall behind him, forcing him to turn around. I quickly swap our wineglasses.

"Paris. I did an exchange there during my undergrad." He gazes at it admiringly. "I miss it. Have you ever been?" Leaning down, he collects his glass. Bright blue eyes study me through a sip.

"Twice. I prefer the French countryside to the city, though."

His gaze dips to my mouth. "Why doesn't that surprise me?" I sense him leaning forward, and I'm caught in a split second of panic that he's going to kiss me and I'm going to have to let him.

"Mr. Everett," Carla calls from the kitchen doorway. *"Un momento?"*

I stifle my sigh of relief.

"I'll be back in a sec," Jace says, setting his glass down and giving my elbow a light squeeze as he passes by me.

This will be my only chance.

With one eye on them, Jace's back to me as he gives Carla his attention, I unscrew the cap and dump the powder into his glass, swirling it with my finger to help it dissolve. My heart is pounding so hard in my chest that I'm afraid he can hear it.

God, I hope this works.

"So, how long will you be in New York City?" he asks, returning to the living room and his wine. "The last time we talked about it, it sounded like you'd only be here for a few days."

"It's taking longer than I expected to clear out Celine's things." Any chance to use her name, I'll take.

His eyes drift to the Persian rug under our feet. I hold my breath as he brings the glass to his lips. Is that . . . ? A bolt of panic shoots through me as I notice the small particles floating along the surface.

He takes a long sip.

I peel my eyes from his mouth and turn away to wander toward the floor-to-ceiling windows and look out at the night sky, all the while watching his reflection in the glass.

"So, how did your friend die?" he finally asks.

"She killed herself."

"I'm sorry." There's a long pause, as I watch his reflection frown at the floor. "Do you know why she did it?"

"I'm still trying to figure that part out."

He nods slowly, cradling the bowl of his glass within his fingers. "Sometimes there is no answer good enough."

I wonder how long it will take for the Ambien to work. Will it even work? If not, and Jace tries something on me, I'll leave.

And I'll never know if he has Celine's dragon vase in that box.

I need to keep him talking so he doesn't have time to try anything on me before the sleeping pills take effect. "Do you see yourself ever leaving New York?"

"Not anytime soon. Maybe in a few years, when I find the right woman and settle down."

I wonder if he'll still pay for prostitutes when that happens.

"Where will you go?"

He slowly rounds the coffee table, approaching me from behind in a casual stroll. "Oh, probably the Cape. I have an investment property out there right now." As he gets closer to me, I begin moving away.

"Cape Cod? That's nice. Tell me about it." I edge around the space, fingering the large tropical leaves of a philodendron. A thin sheen of sweat coats the back of my neck. I'm not cut out for espionage.

He begins describing the beach house—it sounds lovely—and I pretend to be interested, inserting suitable questions about it whenever there's a second's lull, all the while keeping a comfortable distance from him, until it begins to feel a bit like a game of cat and mouse.

Eventually he must have gotten tired of playing the cat, because he wanders back over to take a seat on the couch.

And yawns. A blip of hope spikes in me.

"What about you? How long do you see yourself saving the world?"

"Until the world doesn't need saving anymore." In truth, I haven't set an expiration date. There may come a time when I want something else more, when I'd rather stay on the sidelines of San Diego's suburbs and help my own children learn how to read and swim. But without a suitable partner, I don't see that happening anytime soon.

He chuckles. "That's quite the commitment."

Another yawn sneaks out as he lifts and stretches his arm along the back of the couch. I can only hope that the Ambien kicks in soon. I do have to give him some credit, though. He hasn't just assumed that the incident in the elevator granted him automatic access to me tonight.

"So tell me about your firm. I read that your father was a founding partner before he retired so he could run for governor?"

"Yeah. He helped build FCM from the ground up. It was bittersweet when he decided to step away, but like he always says, 'When you conquer a challenge, it's time to move on to another one.'" Jace begins talking about the rise of Dale Everett, first as a private sector businessman and then as the most powerful government official in the state. His yawns grow more frequent as he talks.

"I'm so sorry. Red wine sometimes does this to me."

I smile, and it's genuine but for all the wrong reasons.

Rubbing his eyes, he murmurs, "I may have to call an early night on you."

Shit. That's not part of the plan.

Swallowing my pride, I edge over to take a seat on the couch. "Come here." I set a pillow on my lap and then tug his arm.

A sly smile curls his lips, but he doesn't complain, resting his head on the pillow and stretching out along the couch on his back. He closes his eyes as I weave my fingers through hair that is too soft and silky to be on a man's head. "I can't say I've ever done *this* with a client before."

"I guess we've broken a few rules then, haven't we?"

"I can't seem to get a handle on you, Maggie," he murmurs. "One minute you're slamming me over that day in the elevator, the next you're inviting yourself over for dinner at my house."

"I like to be unpredictable."

"Is being nice not an everyday occurrence for you?" His eyelids are becoming heavy, even as he smiles up at me.

"I'm a hard person to win over again if you've pissed me off once. And I'm extremely judgmental at times."

"Yes, I got that, too." His lips are moving, but the words coming out aren't completely coherent. "I have to say, this is not how I saw this night going . . ." He lifts an arm up and over his head, to curl his fingers around my wrist.

And then, as I quietly watch with trepidation, Jace Everett falls asleep on my lap.

I'm afraid to move, so I don't, watching his chest lift and fall in slow, shallow breaths.

I watch the minute hand on the clock across from me until five minutes have passed, then ten, and only then finally do I dare loosen his grip of my wrist and carefully shift out from beneath him, holding my breath the entire time. He doesn't make a sound.

God, I hope I didn't just kill him.

Pushing that worry out of my mind—I didn't give him *that* much, and his chest still rises and falls in a steady, slow rhythm, after all—I head straight for his office.

For that cardboard box.

My stomach is a tight ball of knots; my heart pounds inside my chest. If it's the vase, then it's coming home with me, and I have no idea what I'll do to Jace.

With the lightest touch, I peel the top of the box back and peer inside.

A blue-and-white floral bowl sits inside.

Dammit. I wanted it to be Celine's vase so badly. I wanted it to be Jace who stole it. It would mean I'm on the right track. Instead, it's the death of another wild rabbit that I've been so aggressively chasing.

I spy a birthday card and certificate tucked into the box. It appears that this bowl is an authentic Ming Dynasty gift for his mom, based on the official appraisal document.

From Ling Zhang, aka the Bone Lady.

I snap a picture of the document and the bowl and send it to Doug. Ten seconds later my phone rings.

"That's not it."

"Yeah, I *know*. Thanks." I can't keep the bitterness from my whisper. "Is there anything else I should look for before I get out of here?"

"Where is he? Shower?"

"Shower? Why would he be . . ." I clue in and scowl. "No! What, you thought I would actually *sleep* with him? Are you nuts?"

"Fine, fine . . . sorry."

I roll my eyes. "I slipped two sleeping pills in his wine. He's out cold on the couch."

"Jesus, Maggie. Are *you* nuts?" he yells.

"It was Ruby's idea!" Even I know that's not a good excuse.

"And that makes it acceptable? Okay, just . . ." He's agitated. "Get out of there. Zac's already in his mainframe. I can't help you if he wakes up and figures out what you did to him."

I hang up, my heart still racing and my eyes stealing frequent glances toward the office entrance.

But I'm not ready to leave yet. This is my one and only chance to find out what Jace's secrets are.

Everyone has secrets.

I struggle to stay quiet as I rush through his office, slamming desk drawers shut, fumbling with cupboard doors, searching for anything hidden. I'm aware of each second ticking by like I'm waiting for a guillotine to drop.

But there's nothing but paperwork and more paperwork. A bowl that's not the vase I want. No diary, no iPhone.

A small decorative box.

I nearly pass by it in my frenzy, but then I do a double take, eying the intricate details, the brushed bronze material. It reminds me of the lockbox I bought Celine.

What are the odds . . . ?

Setting it on Jace's desk, I lift the lid to find it empty save for an envelope resting on a pristine velvet interior. With eager fingers, I slide a white note card out of the envelope and open it to read the message in computer print:

Five hundred thousand to this account by November 1 or your home movie will be released online.

I frown. This is a blackmail note. Did Jace get it from someone? Or was he going to give it to someone?

What is this home movie?

It's hard to tell, but the inside base of the box looks slightly too high. I let my fingers probe the grooves and details of the exterior, searching for a latch or a button, something that will release a hidden compartment. I can't find anything.

My phone's ring cuts through the eerie silence, making me jump. I lose my grip and the box goes flying, crashing to the hardwood floor with a loud thump.

The bottom cracks open and something tumbles out.

I fumble with my phone as I drop to my hands and knees, reaching under the desk as far as I can. "Hello?"

"Get the hell out of there, now!" Doug yells. "This is exactly how things turn bad, fast."

My fingers close over a small, smooth rectangular object. I pull it into the light.

And smile. "It's also how we find evidence."

"If you don't walk out the main door within three minutes, I am quitting this case," he threatens.

"Fine! I'm coming!" I scramble to put the box back exactly as I found it, and then, keeping Doug on the phone, I rush down the hall on the balls of my feet, blood rushing through my ears.

I round the corner into the living room that I'll need to cross to get to the foyer, my teeth gritted with the fear that the loud clatter I just made might have woken him up.

Jace's motionless body still lies stretched out on the couch.

"He's still sleeping," I whisper with a sigh of relief.

Still breathing.

It isn't until I'm three steps from the exit that I look up and notice the small white security camera above the front door.

CHAPTER 24

Maggie

"Does *everyone* have a fucking security system these days?" I snap, watching Doug's eyes on the camera hiding in the corner of the overhang.

Jace, Zac . . . even Celine, though hers was stuffed in a drawer. Sure, we had cameras on the perimeter of our property in La Jolla, but given our money and valuables and high-profile lives, we had good reason.

"Puts a damper on your criminal activities, doesn't it?" Doug has barely said two words to me since I jumped into his sedan outside of Jace's building, and the few he has said have been laced with annoyance.

I grip my scarf tighter around my neck as we stand by the side entrance of an unimpressive bungalow in Queens, concealed by an untamed cedar hedge and lit by a motion-detector spotlight. "*This* is where your high-priced hacker lives?"

"Research expert," Doug corrects.

Seconds later, footfalls sound from inside, like someone's running up a set of stairs. The plain beige curtain shielding the small window in the door shifts and eyes peer out at me from the darkness. Then the dead bolt clicks and the footfalls sound again. Someone heading back down the stairs.

"Come on." Doug opens the door and gestures me in. He locks it behind us as I force myself down the narrow set of stairs, through another heavy door decorated with numerous dead bolts, and into a dim basement that smells of greasy fries and dirty socks and is stuffed with industrial shelves of computer equipment. Ahead of us, eight black screens with continuous scrolls of code form a wall. A low buzz of voices and beeps come from a row of police scanners in the corner.

My chest begins to tighten. I close my eyes and remind myself why we're here, hoping that's enough to distract me from the impending panic attack.

"Zac, this is Maggie. Maggie, Zac."

Zac is as average-looking as one could imagine. Mid-thirties, medium-brown hair, maybe two inches taller than me, arms lacking any significant muscle tone, and the beginnings of a belly protruding from his ensemble of T-shirt and sweatpants.

He throws a lazy salute at me before dropping into his computer chair, a can of Coke in hand. "Should I guard my drink?" His voice is deep and gravelly, reminding me of a slovenly version of Philip Seymour Hoffman.

I offer Zac a sour smile in return. Since when did these two take the moral high road? Though, I'd feel a lot better about what I did had I found Celine's vase tonight.

"How bad is it?" Doug mutters.

Zac hits a key, and the inside of Jace's apartment shows up. "Basic security measures, from the looks of it. There's only one feed."

"But look at that line of sight." I heave a sigh. Right into the living room, a narrow sliver that captures the couch area perfectly.

Where Jace still sleeps soundly.

"Okay, so . . ." With a few keystrokes, he's suddenly gone from the couch. "Here's J-Man, answering the door . . ." Zac commentates as Jace appears from the left, likely coming from his office. I realize that this is a replay. "And here's Ms. Evil," he adds as I stroll in.

"What?" He shrugs when I shoot a glare at him. "You *did* drug him."

I'm not sure that Doug's "research expert" and I are going to get along.

He fast-forwards through the video feed—catching us moving

past the camera several times—until the part where I wander over to a waiting Jace to, first, swap out our glasses with his back turned, and then covertly dump the Ambien into his wine while looking over my shoulder.

Oh, the irony.

Doug rubs both hands over his forehead.

"That's not going to look good in court," Zac announces through a mouthful of fries.

"No, it's not," Doug agrees.

"Thanks, guys, for trying to make me feel better."

Shaking his head, Doug shoots a glare my way. "Anything useful in Celine's apartment building video feed yet?"

"Yup." He wipes his greasy fingers on his sweatpants, adding to the dark stains already on his lap, before punching in a few keys. The lobby of Celine's building suddenly appears on one of the screens, frozen on pause, and I see the top of Jace's head as he passes through. It may not be a clear view of his face, but, to me, it's so very obviously him.

Suddenly my anxiety over the close quarters of this basement surveillance lab doesn't matter.

That fucking bastard. My teeth grit together. "He knew her, and he lied. Not 'Maggie' the call girl who shows up at hotels. *Celine*. Now we have proof." There's no longer any doubt in my mind.

"No, we don't. There's no police investigation and we have no warrant for this surveillance and we have the top of a man's head," Doug reminds me. "Even with a positive ID, this at most puts him in the building. But we'd still have to prove that he was coming to visit her. Chester can't do anything with this. You can't say a word to him about it because we've acquired this through illegal means. And I can almost guarantee that if the cops show up on this guy's doorstep, that little movie you just starred in will surface. That, Chester *can* use."

"The door system they're using is ancient. I can't get anything from it," Zac drawls in this low, bored tone, fast-forwarding through the feed. "But let's assume this is J-Man. He was there for about an hour."

Plenty of time to lace someone's drink with a handful of crushed pills.

Jace appears on the screen again, this time on his way out.

With a cardboard box tucked under his arm.

"Freeze it!" I lean over Zac's shoulder to get a better look at the box. It's sizeable and brown and stamped on one side with blue arrows pointing up, and on another side with the word "FRAGILE." The box in Jace's office tonight was stamped the exact same way.

I'm pretty sure it's the same box.

"The vase could be in there! Just because it's not in there *now* doesn't mean it wasn't *here*." I jab the screen.

Out of the corner of my eye, I catch Zac's eyes dipping down the top of my blouse. I stand, pulling my coat shut.

"How far does this video feed go back?" Doug asks.

"It's motion-activated, so I'm hoping for two weeks, at least."

"Keep going back through it. Let's see how many times Jace Everett has come to this address. And who else may have paid her a visit," Doug says, his voice demanding.

"Yep . . . You said you guys found something tonight?" Zac doesn't seem bothered by Doug's brusque tone. He also doesn't seem like the kind of guy who moves too quickly for anyone.

"This." Doug sets the tiny gray jump drive I found at Jace's on the desk in front of Zac, along with the ransom note. "It was hidden well."

Zac doesn't even ask how I found it. "Okay . . . let's see what we've got." He clears whatever he's doing until a black screen appears. After he plugs the jump drive in, his fingers begin moving so fast over the keyboard that I can't even read what he's typing before the words disappear into hacker's oblivion. "There's only one file on here. A video file." He pauses, glances from me to Doug. "This isn't going to be a gory beheading or some shit like that, is it? Because the last time you made me open one of these secret files—"

"Play it, Zac."

My stomach drops. I really have no idea what could be on here, but my gut says it has to do with Celine.

"Okay . . ." With one key stroke, a video begins to play.

I gasp as a chestnut-haired woman on a mauve couch, surrounded by shelves upon shelves of antiques, comes into view. "That's Celine. That's from *inside* her apartment!"

"From her IP camera," Doug answers, as if expecting this. "Recognize that angle?"

She sits cross-legged, a heavy-looking hardcover book in her lap, jotting down notes as she reads. The apartment is dim, the corners occupied by shadows, with the only light coming from the lamp beside her. "It's from one of the shelves beside her desk. But why would she have a security camera in her apartment?"

"Single woman living in New York City, valuable items in her apartment, from what you've said. It's not that surprising, actually. She probably tucked it between her books on the shelf and turned it on when she went out at night. And look at that." Doug's stubby finger touches the bottom of the screen, where the time stamp reads October 8, more than a month before her death.

"Well, she's not out, here."

"You're right, she's not."

I'm struggling to wrap my head around this as I watch Celine on the screen, alive, a painful ball lodging itself in the base of my throat.

"The software for it is still on her computer, but the feed that was being directed to a cloud was wiped clean," Zac explains.

"Celine deleted all of the videos?"

"Not unless she had mad tech skills that you forgot to mention. But someone who knew what they were doing did. They erased all of the metadata to prove any videos ever existed."

"Celine was never a fan of computers." How she even set a camera up is beyond me. She must have had help. "So it's possible to delete camera feeds? Like that one from Jace's camera? Because if you could—"

Doug cuts me off with, "Deleting evidence is illegal."

"So is hacking into computers and camera systems," I counter. "You're having a case of a guilty conscience *now*?"

"Searching for hidden evidence that could lead us to an answer is one thing. But I won't destroy evidence, and no amount of money will change my stance on that."

Doug's tone—the gravity in it—surprises me. I assumed there was nothing he wouldn't do for the right amount of money. While it certainly doesn't benefit me, I think I've found a new level of respect for the PI.

Of course, right now there are bigger issues than my criminal activity. "Someone did destroy evidence here, though, didn't they? What if . . ." My voice trails off as Celine suddenly looks up on the monitor, her attention toward the door. She sets her book down and walks over to the panel on the wall, hitting the "answer" button on the intercom. Her lips move, but there's no sound.

"Can you turn it up?"

"The audio's not set up. She didn't have a microphone on it."

Whoever is coming, I don't think she expected the visitor, because she's quickly pulling her T-shirt over her head as she disappears into her bedroom, out of range of the camera. In less than fifteen seconds she reappears, buttoning her jeans and smoothing a flattering black sweater over her curves. She yanks the elastic out of her hair and has just enough time to finger-comb it before she opens the front door.

Jace steps in.

A second bitter wave of vindication courses through me. This time we can see his face, clearly.

She smiles up at him and steps back to let him in, reaching out to touch his arm. He doesn't lean down to kiss her or hug her or anything that would suggest a romantic relationship, but when she lifts to her tiptoes to lay a quick kiss on his mouth, he doesn't pull away.

I squint. The angle is a bit off, but I can tell they're having a conversation as they walk over to the couch. A casual-looking conversation. Celine moves her book out of the way to allow room for Jace. He tidily folds his jacket and lays it across the arm, just like he did the day he came to get those papers signed.

By her mannerisms—her light giggles, the way she tucks her hair behind her ear, the way she touches his knee several times, though only a quick touch—it's obvious that she cares for him, that she's flirting with him. But I also know Celine well enough to see that she's nervous.

It looks like he's smiling at her as he talks, but it's hard to tell.

And then he must say something to her that isn't friendly or nice or casual, because her face crumbles. Even from this angle, even in the dim light, I can see whatever spark of excitement had surged through her the second he was buzzed in is now extinguished.

She's surprised, she's stammering, she's ducking her head, she's shaking her head in denial. He's calmly answering her, but the hairs on the back of my neck are still standing on end.

This goes on for a good twenty minutes, with her continuously swiping the tears from her cheek. Is this a fight? Were they together? Are they breaking up?

He reaches a hand out for her, beckoning her closer. She hesitates for one . . . two . . . three seconds before she stands. He doesn't get up. He simply sits there and stares up at her. I can see his face clearly. It wears an almost indifferent expression. He's waiting for something.

And then she peels her shirt off.

"Damn . . . it's one of *these* videos," Zac mutters, dumping more mayo onto his half-eaten container of fries, his chair creaking as he leans back as if getting comfortable, watching her unzip and push her jeans down.

When Celine tosses her bra to the floor, I demand, "Shut it off."

"We need to see this. There could be something important in it," Doug explains.

Celine climbs onto Jace's lap and begins unbuttoning his shirt. She leans in to kiss him and he responds, his hands sliding up her bare arms to grip the sides of her head.

I recognize that move. It's the same way he kissed me, that day in the elevator. My stomach turns.

But then his hands slide back down her arms, to her thighs, and he breaks free of her mouth, turning just enough to make it clear that he doesn't want that. He gently pushes her back, farther and farther until she yields and slides off to kneel in front of him. He undoes his belt and zipper, and pulls out his *very* erect dick.

"I'm going to be sick." This is horrifying. I can't watch this, and I hate that *they're* watching this. I turn around and insist, "Can you at least fast-forward through it?"

"Fast-forward? This isn't 1995," Zac says. "If I speed it up, we could skip over key frames."

I want to miss *all* frames, and so I remain with my back to the screen, my eyes glued to the digital clock across from me as it flashes through the seconds and minutes as Doug and Zac watch my best friend perform oral sex on Jace. "Are they done yet?" I demand to know at the four-minute mark.

"The first act, yeah," Zac confirms. "But now they're doing it on the couch. She looks like she's enjoying it, at least. And, damn, is he givin' it to—"

"Shut up, Zac," Doug barks.

Twelve minutes and fourteen seconds later, Doug announces, "All right, they're done."

I turn around in time to see Jace sliding on his pants. Celine isn't on the screen, so I assume she's using the bathroom. The area looks like it's been demolished—books shoved off the table and scattered over the floor, the side lamp leaning against the wall, flickering ever so slightly. Jace tugs on his shirt and jacket and, reaching into an inner pocket for his wallet, he pulls out a wad of cash.

He tosses it onto the table.

And then he slips on his shoes and walks out the door.

"And we have the governor of Illinois's son paying for some hard-core sex on video," Zac muses.

And my sweet childhood friend delivering it to him.

Celine appears again moments later, her pink silk robe tied tight around her, her thick mane of hair mussed. She stops in front of the couch, seemingly surprised as she looks to the door, then checks the bedroom. Did she expect him to stay?

She stops in front of the coffee table again.

Reaches down to pick up the money.

Looks back at the door.

And then crumples onto the couch, pulling her legs to her chest, her arms curled around her knees.

And begins to cry.

I hold my hand out. "Give that back to me. Now." There's no way I'm letting this tech geek beat off to Celine after I'm gone, and by the look of him and this place, that's probably all the action he's getting these days.

Zac glances first at Doug, who's busy pacing laps around the cramped room, before unplugging the drive and handing it to me. "At least you have something to blackmail him with, if you need to," he offers. I guess that's the silver lining, though it doesn't feel like it.

"*Why* would Jace have this video?" I demand to know, my voice shaky.

"We already know it was blackmail," Doug says, kicking a box out of his path.

"So, what are you saying . . . that Jace hired someone to hack into Celine's camera and videotape that whole scene, just so he could blackmail her?"

Doug frowns. "He'd stand to lose more than she would . . . And she doesn't have that kind of money."

"Would *she* blackmail *him* with this?" Zac asks.

"No," I answer without thinking, at the same time that Doug says, "Maybe."

I scowl at him. Would she? If so, it would definitely have given him motive for murder.

Doug shrugs. "She never looked up at the camera though . . . People who know they're being filmed have a tendency to look at the camera. At least once."

That brings me some small comfort.

Doug sighs. "We're missing something here. There's another piece to this puzzle." He begins pacing again.

"Hacker," Zac mutters, shoveling fries into his mouth with one hand while picking up the camera Doug took from Celine's desk with the other. "Standard model. Cheap. Easy to bypass. A monkey with an SDR could do it."

A sick feeling fills my stomach at the very suggestion. "But she took the camera down at some point before she died," I say slowly, stating the obvious. "So she must have found out."

"So she must have found out . . ." Doug drums his stubby fingers across the desk. He stops abruptly. "That someone had been watching her."

CHAPTER 25

Maggie

Even though I've sat on Celine's couch countless times—and slept on it once—I can't bring myself to go anywhere near it right now. Not after that video. Not that it's at all comfortable anymore anyway, surrounded by countless boxes that Hans and I have filled. Every last item of Celine's collection is now ready for storage.

That is, except for the missing vase that I was so sure—so hopeful—I would find in Jace's home but did not.

A part of me is desperate enough to knock on Ruby's door and invite her over for some tea, but it's after one in the morning and she's long since fallen asleep. Another part of me wants to escape up to the roof, but I don't think I can face Grady right now, and it has nothing to do with the fact that I'm still wondering who he had in his apartment yesterday.

So I hide the jump drive in Celine's lockbox and curl up under the heavy duvet in bed.

And stare at my phone.

Doug called to relay a message from Zac that Jace did wake up. I guess the Ambien only kept him down for a few hours. At least I know that I didn't kill him. Though, after seeing what I saw tonight, after seeing how he used Celine, how he left her there to cry, a part of me wishes that I had.

What's nagging me is that she seemed shocked to see that money left on her coffee table. But why? Unless their relationship had evolved into something more. Something that didn't involve cash payments. Then . . . having him throw money at her again after so long would be a slap in the face.

A sudden knock on the window startles me. I bolt upright, staring at the large shadow that looms behind the curtain.

Someone is standing on the fire escape.

I don't know what to do. Do I see who it is? Call the police? I have my phone open, and I'm about to call Doug, when another knock rattles the old glass. "Maggie?"

I recognize Grady's muffled accent through the glass.

Slipping out of bed, I slide open my window. "What are you doing out here?" Taking in his T-shirt and jeans, I surmise, "You locked yourself out."

A sly smile touches his lips. "No. I just . . . You didn't come up to the roof the last few nights."

"I know. I'm sorry. I've been busy with stuff down here."

He nods. "Well, I just wanted to check in." His shoulders hunch in as he digs his hands into his pockets, glancing up the fire escape. "I'm right there. I just thought . . ." Gooseflesh covers his forearms. "I wanted to see you."

He's awkward and cute and shivering from the cold, as am I in my skimpy thigh-length cotton nightshirt. "Get inside. Quick." I step out of the way, making room for him to climb in, and then I quickly shut the window.

He rubs his arms, his gaze rolling over Celine's bedroom, landing on the bed. "How's it going?"

I take a seat. "Shitty."

Cool fingers graze my chin, and as much as I want to turn away from them, they feel nice.

"Have I done something to upset you?" He tilts my head up to meet his sincere hazel eyes. "You seemed pissed yesterday, when you came to my door with your PI."

"Yeah, well you seemed really suspicious . . . like you were hiding something. Or someone."

A slow grin finally stretches his lips. "Is that what this is about? I *did* have someone to hide. Two someones. Betty and Veronica." He reaches into his pocket and pulls out a joint. "They're kind of hard to miss under my grow lamps."

Realization dawns on me and I fall back into bed, suddenly laughing hysterically. "Of course that's what it was. You're growing pot in your apartment."

He chuckles. "Why? What did you think it was?"

I laugh even harder, because I was jealous for no reason. And because I was jealous to begin with. "I thought you had someone over."

"And that would bother you."

"I don't know. I guess it would. I mean, yes, it did." After a moment of silence, I peer over at him, standing at the end of the bed, staring down at me with intensity. I know what that look means because I've seen it several times already, only in thirty-degree temperatures, hidden beneath layers of blankets.

Reaching down, I pull my nightshirt up, over my head, and toss it to the floor. My panties go next.

Grady grins. "No energy for foreplay tonight?"

"Not tonight. And I don't usually need it with you," I admit truthfully.

I watch him kick off his shoes and peel off his shirt, jeans, and boxers in front of me. He kneels on the bed, pushing my thighs apart with his knees until he's nearly shimmied up beneath me. Grabbing me by the wrists, he pulls me up, his hands landing on my ass to press me flush against him. "You have nothing to worry about. Just so you know, I'm a one-woman-at-a-time kind of guy."

I don't want that to mean something to me—we live worlds apart, and I'm leaving soon—but it does, all the same. I stay quiet, though, as he tears the foil wrapper open with his teeth and then rolls the condom over himself with one hand.

Meeting my gaze, he tenderly pushes a strand of hair off my forehead. "I'm so glad I met you," he whispers, leaning in to kiss me.

My back hits the mattress at the same time that he slides into me.

"You don't think we woke Ruby, do you?" I guess having walls around me instead of a rooftop garden and lattice screens weakened my inhibitions.

"Me? Not likely. But you and those screams of yours, I think everyone on the floor will be eying you oddly tomorrow," Grady murmurs, lying on his back. Looking completely sated.

"Shut up. Really?" I feel my face flushing in the dark.

A tiny smirk curls his lips. "No, not really. Ruby takes her hearing aid out at night and Mr. Sherwood over here," he reaches up to knock hard against the wall behind our head, "he sleeps like the dead."

I smack him playfully against his hard stomach. "Jerk. That's not funny."

"On the contrary," he rolls over until he's pressed against my side, his mouth hovering inches from mine, "I think it's hilarious." He yanks the covers over both of our heads, pinning me down beneath him.

And suddenly all the air is sucked out of my lungs.

"Stop, Grady. Stop!" I spurt out between gasps, bucking him off me and working to free my arms so I can tug the duvet down. My chest heaves with the fresh, cool air. "You can't do that to me," I whisper through pants, my heart drumming against my chest.

He turns to stare at me through bewildered, pained eyes. "Jesus, Maggie. What just happened?"

"I'm claustrophobic." I chuckle, more embarrassed than anything right now. "When I can't breathe . . . I tend to get a little bit crazy."

"I see that now." He winces. "You nearly emasculated me with your knee."

"I'm sorry." I reach for him under the covers, my fingers sliding to the sensitive skin. He groans as I cup him gently, but it's not so much a sound of pain anymore.

"I'm going to miss this when you leave," he whispers.

"You're going to miss getting bagged?"

He chuckles. "Maybe not that. But definitely this. And you."

I feel him hardening against my wrist, so I guess the pain has faded. I help it along by wrapping my fist around the base, enjoying the feel of his velvety soft skin. "Are you going home for the holidays?"

"Nah. I don't get enough time off here to make it worthwhile."

"Seriously? What could people need so badly that they can't wait a week or two?"

"This is an old building. I get a call or text almost daily from a tenant in dire need of having something fixed."

"I was wondering what you did all day."

He smiles. "I replace a lot of screws for Ruby."

"I'm serious. Do you actually enjoy being the building super?"

He exhales, thrusting himself against my tightening fist. "It's easy work. Low stress."

"Not exactly ambitious, though. Don't you want to do something *bigger* with your life?"

"Bigger?" He reaches over to hook a hand around the back of my thigh. He rolls, pulling me on top of him, lining us up perfectly. "Like what?"

I lift my body until I'm hovering, daring him to slip in. "I don't know . . . I know I was kidding before, but you really could come to Africa with me when I go. You're so handy; I could use your help."

"You need someone to replace screws down there, too?"

"I could definitely use someone to do some screwing there." My words end with my mouth on his and our tongues tangled again and him reaching for the nightstand to grab another condom.

"See? They know I keep odd hours." Grady holds up his chirping phone, as if that tells me something. "That's Ms. Sanders in 302. She's texting me about her refrigerator making a weird noise. Wants me to come listen to it now, if I'm awake."

"At four a.m." I glare knowingly. "Is Ms. Sanders attractive?"

"For a fifty-nine-year-old, she's smokin' hot." He fishes his clothes off the floor, working at turning them right-side-out in the dim light.

I prop myself up on my elbow and watch Grady get dressed, admiring his nakedness. "That reminds me . . . when did you fix that window for Celine? My PI said that the latch has been replaced recently."

"About a week before she died, I think?" He yanks his pants on. "Look, about the other day. I'm sorry I couldn't help you and your investigator. I would have, if I could."

Mention of Doug brings me back to the jump drive and Celine. And Jace. The temporary relief that Grady afforded me tonight gives way to agitation once again. "That's fine. We got what we needed anyway."

"Oh . . . okay. Good." He sits on the bed to pull his socks and shoes on. "What were you looking for?"

I sigh. "I wanted to see the surveillance on the night that Celine died. To see if she had any visitors."

"A visitor? Why would that matter?" Grady pauses, turning to study my face. Realization dawns on his handsome features. "You seriously don't still think . . . Is that really why you hired that guy?"

"I have a couple of lingering questions and I can't stop until I have my answers, one way or the other." I don't have the energy to bring up the case of the missing vase right now.

He turns to stare at the window.

I sit up and reach out to touch his bare back. "I have to be sure, even if it's only a small chance."

"Yeah . . ." He hangs his head. "Yeah, it's just . . ." He glances over his shoulder at the bed. I assume he's thinking about where they found her.

Where *he* found her.

"Maybe we shouldn't be doing this in here again."

I've gotten good at blocking out the knowledge that Celine died in this very bedroom. Now these are just walls to contain a bed and a dresser, the contents of its previous habitant packed away. New people will move in here. New people will laugh, will love, will have sex within these walls, without any clue of the horrors that have also transpired here.

If I hadn't blocked those horrors out, I wouldn't be able to sleep in this room. Hell, I would never have stayed in this apartment in the first place.

But now that Grady has labeled what we just did in here as wrong, I can't help but feel downright filthy. "You're right. We'll stick to the rooftop. Or your place." Which I still haven't been inside.

He leans down to place a kiss on my nose. "I should get going. I have things to repair in the morning. And that new tenant wants to come by on Sunday. Are you cool with that?"

"Sunday's not good. The movers come at ten to load up the boxes for storage and then I have a big charity ball to get ready for in the afternoon. How about Monday?"

"All right." He tugs his shirt on. "Charity ball . . . that sounds like fun."

"Yeah, Ruby's going to be my date."

"Kind of like bringing your cousin to a dance, isn't it?"

"I guess, but I know it'll make her entire holiday." Just the look on her face when I invited her made my day brighten. "And I figured you wouldn't be interested in that sort of thing." Though I'm also guessing that Grady could clean up really well in a tux.

"You're right . . . I wouldn't," he chuckles.

I crawl out from under the covers and grab hold of his belt to pull him closer.

With one last deep kiss, he slides the window up.

"Just use the front door!" I pull the covers up and around me as the draft chills my naked, spent body.

"But this is more romantic, don't you think?" He winks, and then he's gone.

CHAPTER 26

Maggie

December 13, 2015

"It was 1971 and we were in the Starlight Roof room. Oh, Maggie. You should have heard her. There was nothing like it." Ruby's eyes twinkle as she recounts her last time in the Waldorf Astoria, to see Ella Fitzgerald perform.

"Well, I don't know that tonight will be as glamorous." I lead her into the Grand Ballroom by the arm, my steps extra low and measured. The room's décor of rich tapestries and crystal chandeliers is luxurious enough. Now, though, with the holiday bouquets and silvery linens and additional lighting, and the orchestra set off to one side, it looks pretty damn fabulous. And packed. Too packed for my liking, but with over fourteen hundred tickets sold at a thousand per head, plus some generous contributions, it's certainly going to generate some well-needed money for VU.

"Well, it's certainly more glamorous than what I normally do on a Sunday night," Ruby muses, smiling at a server who floats past.

"Thank you for being my date tonight."

"I'm just lucky this gown still fits, thirty years later!" With her free hand, she smooths the black lace over her hip, adding in a whisper, "With a little help from my friend, Girdle."

I laugh. "I can only hope to look like you in my eighties. You look lovely."

"Not as lovely as you." She nods to the overpriced gold couture dress that Hans threw a fit over when we went shopping earlier in the week, insisting that I buy it or not bother going to the ball at all. "I'm glad you treated yourself to this. There's nothing wrong with doing that every once in a while, especially when you're so good to everyone else."

"Come." I lead her toward the front. "Let's go find our table. You get to meet my parents. Just do me a favor and try not to mention anything about Celine or the investigation, okay?"

"I'll do my best." She pats my arm. "But if I slip, just tell them I'm senile. They'll believe it."

I find my parents sitting next to each other at our customary table, off to a corner near the dance floor, with a prime view of the orchestra. Even after being divorced for fourteen years, they attend functions like this together. "It's good for the company to see the Sparkes as a unit, even if we're not" my mother always says.

"Magpie." My dad stands as we approach. He was in China on business for Celine's funeral. I haven't seen him since last Christmas. He looks different. More trim. He's always been a jogger, but he looks healthier, his complexion clearer. That's a positive, seeing as he's sixty. I can't be sure, but I think his hair has taken on a darker—artificially enhanced—shade of gray than before.

"Daddy." I don't know why I always revert to my five-year-old self when I first see my father, as if I'm still waiting on the front steps for his car to pull through the gate after he'd been away for business somewhere. I'd run to meet him and throw myself into his arms, asking him if he was home for a while. Back then, two weeks felt like an eternity.

He wraps his arms around my shoulders and squeezes me tight, planting a kiss on my cheek. "You look radiant." He pauses, a teasing eyebrow arched. "Who dressed you?"

"Celine's friend, Hans. He has impeccable taste."

"Ahh . . . Yes, I see that. It's nice to see my daughter embracing her beauty every once in a while."

I roll my eyes. "Dad, this is Ruby Cummings. Ruby, this is William Sparkes."

My dad shifts his focus to a grinning Ruby, who reaches out to squeeze both his hands.

"You've raised an inspiring woman, William. You must be so proud."

He smiles. "Her mother and I are. Have you met Melody yet?" Dad has two personas—fearless and to-be-feared Sparkes Energy exec and congenial people-pleaser, when politics and charity are involved. Ruby's getting the latter now, as Dad introduces Ruby to my mom, and I listen to Ruby go through the whole "I lived across the hall from Celine" spiel.

"Your date's a little old for you, isn't she?" Dad quips in a low, teasing tone.

"Funny. When did you get into the city?"

"Just this morning. I have to fly to Bangkok tomorrow."

Disappointment pricks me. "Too bad. I would have liked to have dinner with you, at least."

"I know, dear." He squeezes my wrist. "But I'll be in L.A. for Christmas. Maybe we can actually spend one together. It's been a while, and I think it's going to be tough for you."

"I'd love that." And I love that he's actually aware. This holiday will be my first one without Celine, and likely my last one with Rosa.

A striking blonde approaches Dad's side. He turns to smile at her. "Good, you're back. Maggie, this is Cindy. Cindy, my daughter, Maggie."

All it takes is the sight of his arm hooked around her miniscule waist and I realize what's going on here. My dad's dating someone. I've never seen him with another woman besides my mom, even after this long. And to bring her out to a company event like this . . .

She can't be more than thirty, at most. My father's dating a woman my age. One who, if I had to guess, spends more time at the gym, lying around the pool topless, and in the salon than anywhere else.

My father is sixty and dating a woman half his age.

I try to keep my facial expression even, as I remember Jace's words just the other day, about how I'm easily readable. I don't want to be rude, even as I wonder if this is what other people felt like when meeting Celine on the arm of her much older "companions." If they looked at her and wondered why she would date a man twice her age, unless it was for his money.

So is Cindy after my dad for his money, or is she more like Celine? An escort?

The very idea that my father would feel the need to pay for companionship makes me ill.

But . . . no. William Sparkes would never bring an escort to a charity ball.

"Your father has told me so much about you," Cindy says, offering a slender, manicured hand.

"Has he now." I accept her hand, all the while casting furtive glances over at my mother. Did she know he was seeing someone—someone he planned to introduce to me? If she did, why wouldn't she have warned me over lunch last week? Did she think I wouldn't care?

Dad pulls Cindy's chair out for her and then, turning, pulls the one on the other side of him out for me.

"Isn't your date a little young for you?" I force out through gritted teeth, turning his words from earlier as I slide into my seat and distract myself with my napkin.

Trying to decide what I think of this.

He leans in and whispers, "Be nice, Maggie."

"I'm *always* nice."

"I'm happy."

"I'm sure you are." Now I see why he's in such great shape.

Cindy's preoccupied with conversation on the other side, allowing me to ask, "Seriously, Dad, how old is she?"

"Does it really matter?"

"Is she younger than me?"

"No. She's thirty," he assures me with a patient smile, and a look that says we're not talking about this here anymore.

I've never responded well to that look. "How long have you known her?"

"Almost seven months."

"Are you . . . Is she . . ." I stumble over my confrontational words, dropping my voice to a whisper. "Do you pay her?"

"Jesus, Maggie!" he hisses, shaking his head at me. "No. And if I did, that'd be my business and *not* something I'd discuss with my daughter."

I've definitely pushed him too far.

He sighs. "We get along well, and she's the first woman since your mother to actually challenge me, which is a nice change. And before you ask, she has more than enough of her own money."

I shift my gaze between the two of them again. Yes, there's a huge age difference. No, I don't see the appeal of a man twice my age, but . . .

Reading through Celine's diaries made me sick because I was picturing a certain kind of man hiring Celine, but maybe what's stuck in my head is wrong. Maybe Celine was with guys like my father—fit and well put together, distinguished and charismatic. Men she might have even been attracted to, had the circumstances been different.

"So? You must be almost finished up with the estate. I can't imagine it being that complicated," my dad says through a sip of his drink, changing topics.

You have no idea how complicated it is. "Almost there."

"Good. And you'll be heading back to Ethiopia in January?"

"Didn't Mom tell you about Rosa?"

"Well, yes but . . ." He frowns. "You have an organization to run. You have people who rely on you."

"Rosa needs someone, too."

"She has people. Your mother said that the Mexican community she's a part of down there is close. They'll make sure she gets what she needs. I'm sure one of them will take care of the bills if you send the money through."

"Cut a check from the other side of the world while the woman who raised me dies?" Forget the bimbo next to Dad. Even suggesting such a thing gets my blood boiling and my voice raised. That's the difference between my mother and father—my mother knows there's no point trying to convince me to change my mind. My father still thinks he needs to sculpt me, and it's usually with a hand too focused on business to balance human need. He's not pushing me to go back to Ethiopia because of the poor, needy children.

It's all about being a responsible leader.

"Oh look, I guess I'll take this seat right next to you," Ruby says, interrupting my father's retort, which I'm sure will only make me more angry. "I just love this music. I may have to get up later and dance, if I can find a suitable partner. Maybe we can find you a young man and you can join," she says to me, dousing the heated conversation.

"Yes, that would be nice," my dad agrees, taking a large gulp of his champagne. "Your mother said something about you investing with Dale Everett's son. Anything there?"

My stomach turns sour with mention of him. For a couple who has been divorced for so long, my mother and father talk to each other about personal things far too much. "Absolutely nothing, and there never will be. He's a disgusting human being."

"He's quite handsome, though," Ruby throws in with a sly smile.

I shoot a glare her way, and she shrugs.

"So, he's a disgusting human being and you're investing your money with him. Did I get that right?" my dad asks with a smirk.

I pour the rest of my champagne back in one gulp. "Something like that."

"A Cold-Blooded Ginger," I order from the bartender, breathing in the free-flowing air with deep pulls, my lungs feeling light again. It's my third trip out of that stifling ballroom and into the hotel bar, where the rich mahogany walls are comforting rather than suffocating. The first time I ducked out, I felt bad for abandoning my eighty-one-year-old date. But upon returning to my table, I found a white-haired man in a tuxedo leading her onto the dance floor, and I realized that Ruby makes friends much more easily than I do. She'll be just fine wherever she goes.

She hasn't left the dance floor since dessert.

And *I* may decide to not leave this bar until it's time to go home.

"When in doubt, the Sparkes princess will be at the charity ball."

A shiver runs down my spine, and I can't tell if it's because I'm hearing Jace's voice, period, or because of the contempt that laces it. He left me three voice messages since yesterday morning. Each of them telling me that we needed to speak and urgently.

I never called him back.

But I can't very well ignore him now. So I turn around. "What are you doing here?" He's dressed in a tailored black tux, looking every bit the classy gentleman that I now know he's not.

"Supporting charity, of course." He leans in to place a kiss on my cheek, and I stiffen.

I highly doubt he actually bought a ticket to this, which means he pulled on a tux and walked in like he owned the place for no other reason than to find me.

"I'm sorry. Between clearing out Celine's apartment and getting ready for tonight, I haven't had time to call you back."

He nods slowly, his steely gaze rolling over the area—decked out in traditional gold and red garland—before cutting back to me.

I see it now. The simmering rage—in his hard blue eyes, in his tense jaw.

I wonder if it matches the rage in mine.

"Your drink, miss." The bartender slides my drink to me with a wink.

I grab it, wanting to be as far away from Jace Everett as I can before I blurt out that I know he lied. That I'm on to him, and it's only a matter of time before he screws up. "It was nice to see you, Jace." I begin walking away, heading toward the hotel lobby lounge area, my heels clicking briskly against the tile. I can feel him trailing me. "I'm sorry, but I need to get back to my—"

A vise-like grip grabs hold of my wrist. "I think first we should find a quiet corner and talk for a bit. About what you did on Friday night."

I swallow the panic, school my expression as best I can. "And what did I do on Friday night?"

He steps in, so close that his chest touches mine. I fight not to recoil. Leaning down, he whispers in my ear, "What did you put in my wine?"

I knew this was coming and yet I'm still somehow not prepared. "I don't know what you're talking about," I lie, my wobbly voice traitorous.

"Oh no?" The first smile tonight stretches across his lips, but it's in no way pleasant. "I always wondered if I *really* needed a security camera. Now I guess I know that I do."

Knowing he has my attention, Jace slides his hand down into mine, weaving our fingers together in a tight knot that I so desperately want to shake off. He guides me to a semiprivate seating area with two beige armchairs and a screen of plants.

"So, was I ever supposed to wake up?"

I bite my tongue, deciding whether I should admit to anything. But then I remember that he's not the only one with video evidence. "It was just a bit of Ambien."

He snorts softly. "No wonder I felt so groggy when I came to." He levels me with a glare that I know is meant to disarm me.

I ease back into my chair and cross my legs, letting the slit break apart, feigning calm.

Jace's eyes wander along my exposed thigh. "You must have been looking for something pretty important, to risk ten years in jail. Because that's what you could get if I press charges."

"Why haven't you yet?"

His lips twist with disdain. "Give me back the jump drive that you took and we'll be square."

"What jump drive?"

"Quit playing games, Maggie. It's unbecoming," he snaps. His eyes narrow. "The one that you stole from the box in my desk, when you searched my office."

"Oh . . ." I lean forward and, in a mock whisper, say, "You mean the one where the governor of Illinois's son pays for sex with a girl who ends up dead a month later? That one?"

He pales slightly.

It's my turn to smile now, though it's with bitter satisfaction.

It takes him a moment to compose himself. "Who else saw it?"

I decide not to answer that yet. "Good job, pretending not to know Celine. You actually had me second-guessing myself." I take a long sip of my drink, finally feeling like I have the upper hand here. "But you not only knew her, you've even been to her apartment. All this time, you've been pretending. Why?"

Jace waves a passing server down and orders a Glenlivet, his eyes glued to her shoes as she makes her way to the bar. I can tell he's weighing his options. Give me the truth, or keep lying.

The question is, will I know what I'm getting?

CHAPTER 27

Celine

July 16, 2015

"What do you mean, you can't come? You *have* to come." Hans jerks his pencil tie straight while flashing a client a tight-lipped smile in attempt to hide his irritation. "I've been working on this auction for eighteen months! It's Hollingsworth's pièce de résistance, I'm telling you, people will be waving their blue paddles like zealots. They'll be talking about the Fabergé pieces for years."

I truly do feel bad for missing my friend's shining moment at the coming Russian Works auction—even if *every* moment seems to be a big shining moment for Hans—but the few vacation days I have left are going to be needed for traveling back and forth to San Diego as often as I can, until I can move. "I'm sorry, I want to, but I can't just take a Thursday morning off of work. My boss isn't flexible like that. I was lucky to get this morning off." Under the guise of an urgent doctor's appointment. It's lunch hour now, and I'll have to head in to the office shortly.

"Have you not explained how big a deal this is to that slave driver?" Hans, with his hands settled firmly on his slender hips and his wing-tipped shoe tapping at a furious rate, is dead serious.

Just like that, he makes me smile. He's the only one who shares my exuberant passion for antique treasures—items that many would simply cast away as trash. Of course they wouldn't if they had any idea what some of this "trash" is worth. "Hey, when you have a chance, can you swing by my place and check out something I picked up at a garage sale? I think it's a high-quality Fauxbergé."

"Really . . ." His eyes widen with excitement; he's temporarily distracted from his distress. "I'll see when I can fit a house call into my calendar. It'll have to be after my auction."

The auction is two-and-a-half months away, but that's Hans. He gets so wrapped up in his work that we can go weeks at a time without talking. "If there's any way you can work me in before then, I'd appreciate it. I want to get as much as I can for it."

He gasps, pulling me away from the celadon jade libation cup that I was studying intently and into the corner. "No . . . No, no, no, Celine. We agreed that you are building your collection for your future. You do not sell valuable pieces like that!"

"I am." The admission guts me. "I have to sell a few of them, actually." I may end up selling most of my collection, eventually.

Finally, the self-absorbed fog Hans normally dwells in dissipates, and his brow furrows deeply with concern. "What's going on with you?"

I'm not about to stand here, in the middle of a private pre-auction exhibit in Hollingsworth, and tell him that my mother's cancer has spread to her bones. That she's dying. I just found out on Monday, and I'm still processing the news. I actually have yet to say it out loud to anyone. Just the thought makes my eyes water. "I just need the money."

"Is this about tuition? I thought you had enough."

"No. I need it for something else." I had a meeting with the school administration office this morning. Under the circumstances, they're allowing me to delay my enrollment until next September. It's hard to say where I'll be by then—still with Mom in San Diego.

Or back in New York . . . without her.

I have so much to figure out. Like, how I'm going to keep my apartment so I have something to come back to. My lease expires at the end of January and I want to renew it, but I may not be able to pay the rent. I'll probably ask Dani if she and her fiancé want to sublet from me while they wait for the builders to finish their condo. She mentioned that she's trying to persuade her boyfriend to move out of his parents' place, where they live right now for free. I don't wish ill for Dani, but I'm so happy that her future mother-in-law drives her insane.

I was a week away from handing in my resignation to Vanderpoel so I could start school in a month. Thank God I didn't do that. I'll need the full-time job for the fall.

But I'll have to sell or store all my stuff—storing costs money, so I have to be selective—in order to put my life on pause and take care of my mother. She doesn't know that I'm moving back to San Diego yet. She'll never agree. She's put a gag order on me with Maggie as it is.

A part of me is angry with her about that. I think I'm finally ready to give in and happily accept Maggie's money, because no matter what I do, no matter how hard I work, I can't seem to get ahead.

Maggie—and all her money that she'd so willingly give—could solve so many of our problems. Besides the cancer, of course.

I wouldn't have to sell my collection.

I wouldn't have to do the other things I do for money.

But at least that part of my life will be over by Christmas. Maggie will come back from Africa and find out what we've been hiding from her, and force her money onto us. She'll be pissed, but at least she'll be right there with me, until the end. It'll be kind of like the old days.

"Hans." A stern-sounding British woman with wire-rimmed glasses and a pinched nose sweeps past us. "Can I see you for a moment?"

"A moment, my ass," he hisses, low enough for only me to hear. "The shrew is going to lock me in the dungeon to catalogue again." With a groan and air kisses, he says bye and speeds up to catch the woman, hiding his displeasure behind a polite "Yes, Gwyneth?"

Leaving me to quietly study an antique gold mirror. It's the last day for these items to be on display before next week's auction. I don't think I've missed a single exhibit at Hollingsworth in the past four years. I would never actually bid. But aside from reading books, it's the best way to learn, especially if I can steal a moment of time from one of the appraisers who floats around. They know me by name now.

"I don't know how anyone can focus on themselves when their reflection is surrounded by this gilded brass," a smooth, deep male voice murmurs beside me, his spicy cologne catching my nose.

"Maybe people weren't as vain in the eighteenth century," I quip, turning to acknowledge the speaker.

My heart skips a beat.

"It's you," I blurt out.

He raises a neatly groomed blond brow with curiosity. "It's me?"

"I'm sorry. I just . . ." I feel my face burn bright. The last person I ever expected to be standing next to at Hollingsworth is Jace Everett. Smoothing my plain black pencil skirt as covertly as possible, I say, "I think you work in my office building. I've seen you once or twice . . . maybe." Seven times. I've stood in the lobby or on the steps outside and watched him and his well-cut suit and perfect stride move past me exactly seven times. He's never noticed me, his attention always on his phone, a newspaper, or a client.

His eyes—blue like sapphires in sunlight—take in the mirror again, in a quiet smile touches his lips. "What are you going to bid on?"

The question catches me off-guard. I would think the natural next question would be related to where exactly it is I work. Maybe he doesn't care. Or maybe he knows that he's somewhat of a discussion piece around our office building. "Nothing. I'm just doing research."

He frowns. "On gaudy mirrors?"

I smile. "On antiques. I'll be working here as an appraiser as soon as I'm finished my master's." I never speak so boldly about my future here at Hollingsworth, but I so badly want to impress him.

"Really? I'm intrigued." He pauses. "What can you tell me about this one over here?" He points to the next display—a blue-and-white baluster vase.

"Well, it's funny. I'm actually going to do my thesis on Chinese art, but I feel quite ignorant about it right now. I *can* tell you that this is from the second half of the nineteenth century." I just began a book on Kangxi period antiques last week, so I know at least that much.

He leans forward, closing the distance, but not too much. Just enough for me to hope it's intentionally flirtatious. "But is it *really* worth eighteen to twenty-five thousand dollars?"

"It's worth whatever people are willing to pay."

His gaze rolls over my face as if taking in all of my features. "You sound like an appraiser already."

It makes me blush deeper. I scramble to keep the conversation going. "You wouldn't believe what some people have paid for a piece of art history." Mr. Sparkes's collection was simply exquisite. Even as a little girl, I knew that being in his office was a rare experience to be cherished. But not until I was a lot older did I realize the true dollar value.

"Oh, I can believe it." He chuckles. "My parents are art collectors, so I've heard a story or two."

"Really? And what is it they collect?" I tend to gravitate toward people who appreciate my love of art.

"Chinese art. Mainly Ming Dynasty, though they are all Chinese porcelain. I'm actually shopping for a gift for my mom's sixtieth birthday this December." He taps on the display price. "I love her dearly, but she's going to bankrupt me."

I only smile in response. It's no secret that Jace Everett does very well financially. While I—in my couture outfits bought on consignment—can pretend, there's no pretending on his part. He's not even in a suit today, and he still looks like he was dressed by a professional.

"What about something like this?" I lead him from piece to piece at a slow pace, relishing the seemingly undivided attention he's giving me as I test my own knowledge base and explain the significance of potential purchases.

We're admiring a gold sugar bowl from the early twentieth century—not Chinese in origin but exquisite all the same; estimated at five to seven thousand dollars—when his phone begins ringing.

He glances at the screen. "I'm sorry . . . business." He holds out a hand that I take, the feel of his palm against mine paralyzing. "I appreciate the help . . ."

"Celine."

"Celine. I'm Jace Everett."

"Yeah, I know." I clear my throat, silently cursing myself for adding that last part.

He seems more amused than bothered. "Maybe I'll see you around."

"Maybe." I stand there like an obtuse child, watching him stroll down the hallway of Hollingsworth, unable to pry my eyes away. Hoping he'll give me another look. Some sign that I wasn't simply a five-minute interruption in his day.

With his hand pressed against the glass door, Jace glances over his shoulder and locks eyes with me. It's so brief, but it's enough to steal my breath. Then, he's gone.

Would a guy like Jace even talk to me, if he knew that I also work as an escort? Apparently his father is the governor of Illinois. I'm guessing he wouldn't take too lightly to his son dating a woman who's funding her future on her back in hotel rooms.

I can't even say I hate doing it. I *used* to hate it. Now I've become numb to it, because it has benefited me so much. And, most importantly, no one knows. It's funny how easy it became to shrug off when I started to think of it for what it truly is—meaningless sex that turns my dreams into reality. I may be giving them my body, but they're not getting *me*.

Speaking of which, I'm meeting a new client tonight. All Larissa told me is that he goes by the name "Jay" and he specifically asked for a young, curvy Hispanic woman.

I sigh.

Back to my reality.

July 23, 2015

Today may be the first time in five years that I'm late for work. I keep my head ducked as I step into the elevator, again checking the damp spot on my dress where I so desperately tried to rub out an ink stain earlier this morning. I'm not sure if I'm just paranoid or if I can still see the blue—

"The antiques appraiser."

My head snaps up to find Jace Everett standing next to me, holding a tall, nondescript cup of coffee. Of course he wouldn't drink Starbucks. I'm surprised he actually bought his own on his way into the office. Rumor has it that Natasha does *everything* for him.

"Hi." I clear the nervous shake out of my voice. I didn't even realize he was following me in. "How are you?" It has been seven days.

And I haven't stopped thinking about him.

"Good." He flashes me a pearly white flirtatious smile. "Still hunting for that perfect gift for my mother."

What a sweet guy, to dedicate that much time and effort to a gift for his mother. Family is obviously important to him. "I can understand that. I spend most of my free time hunting for perfect things."

Intense eyes are locked on mine. "And where do you hunt?"

"Garage sales mostly. And estate sales." We have the elevator to ourselves, an impossible occurrence on a Thursday morning at eight a.m., which tells me these few moments with Jace must be kismet. Too bad the elevator is climbing the building so fast. For once, I wish it would just break down. He looks as incredible as usual today, in a tailored suit, his tantalizing cologne wafting through the cramped quarters, drawing me a step closer to him unintentionally. His collar is curled just a touch, and my fingers twitch with the urge to reach out and adjust it for him.

We're not at that stage, yet.

He frowns with doubt. "Garage sales? Really? Isn't that just people's old junk?"

"A lot of it is. But not all of it."

"Huh. I just thought . . ."

"That all antiques are found in auction houses?"

"No, I just thought . . ." He shakes his head at himself and chuckles. "I guess maybe I did think that, which is stupid."

I giggle at the moment of vulnerability. He's one of those guys who gives off an air of confidence that would make you think he knows everything about everything, so to see him laugh at himself is enchanting. "You have to wade through a lot of trash to get to the treasures, but when you do find something, it's worth it. Many people don't realize what they have, and they sell it off for next to nothing. Luckily, I know enough to know a treasure when I see it."

That seems to give him pause. "Well then, I think I ought to get your help."

The elevator opens to my floor. I so badly want to stay on and ride the rest of the way up with him, but I doubt he's into desperate women. "Sure. You name the time." I step off and turn around, to find him smiling at me.

He nods toward the Vanderpoel sign hanging on the wall. "I'll call you. Have a nice day, Celine."

I feel my cheeks flush.

The elevator doors shut, leaving me staring at my reflection in the metal wall before me. At least I wore a dress like this—my black-and-white striped pencil, the one that I have to wear a blazer over because the plunging neckline makes it highly inappropriate for the workplace. Of course the blazer was undone during that entire exchange. I just gave Jace an eyeful of what my mother calls an "ample bosom."

Considering what I'm doing on the side to make ends meet, it shouldn't faze me in the least, and yet it does. I want him to see me as a classy, smart, competent woman. Not just another girl to screw.

Did he actually mean what he said about antique hunting together?

CHAPTER 28

Maggie

December 13, 2015

"I met Celine at a Hollingsworth exhibit in July. I was there for a pre-auction viewing of a private collection. We started talking and she told me she was studying to become an antiques appraiser. I thought that was fortunate because—"

"Your parents are collectors," I say, cutting him off.

"How'd you . . ." He frowns. "Never mind." Accepting his drink from the server and waving her away with a small pile of bills, he takes a sip. He seems more calm than he was a few moments ago. "Anyway, a week after that, I ran into her again at work, and soon after that, we made plans to visit a few shops together to help me look for something."

"Something?"

"A gift, for my mother's upcoming birthday."

"The same gift that's sitting in your office now, in December? You must be a devoted son, spending so many months looking." I don't try to hide my sarcasm. "So you asked her out on a date?"

"I guess you could call it that."

He's lying. Their first "date" was in a hotel room, when he introduced himself as Jay and she introduced herself as Maggie, and he paid to fuck her on the couch with all the lights on. "Then what happened?"

He shrugs. "We really hit it off. She was beautiful, smart, and motivated. Classy. We went out for dinner several times, spent a

Sunday on Long Island, antiquing. That special trick box in my office that you smashed? Celine bought that for me." He shrugs. "I liked her." He stares at the amber liquid in his glass, deep in thought.

"Why do none of her friends know about you two, then?"

"She didn't want to tell them. She didn't want to tell anyone."

That makes no sense. What single twenty-eight-year-old woman lands one of New York's most eligible bachelors and doesn't tell *anyone*?

Then again, Celine was keeping more than one big secret at the time.

"I saw the video, Jace. I've also read some of her diary entries. I know what she was doing for money. So maybe she didn't tell anyone because you two weren't actually 'dating.'"

"Do I look like I need to pay for it?" he snaps. "I wasn't one of her fucking johns, and I had no idea how she was making her money when we met." A hard gaze levels me. "I didn't find out until I was just days away from bringing her to Chicago for a weekend, to meet my parents. My father, the *governor* of Illinois."

I watch him fidget in his chair. He's uncomfortable, but I can't tell if it's because of the subject or because he's lying.

"I was here for drinks with a client one night. Sitting right over there." He juts his chin toward another part of the bar lounge. "And Celine strolled by with some guy, her arm hooked through his. The way she was dressed, her makeup . . ." He shakes his head and sneers. "I'm no idiot. This guy had to be thirty years older than her."

"When was that?"

"Early October."

Larissa said Celine stopped taking customers in July. Obviously that was a lie. But who was lying to whom?

Jace leans forward, resting his elbows on his knees. "You wanted to know why she didn't tell any of her friends about me? It's because she knew that my father would be heading for reelection. I even joked about it on one of our dates, telling her that if she had any skeletons in her closet, she better tell me because his opposition was particularly brutal, and they'd no doubt dig into her, just like they'd dug into me."

And then everyone would know Celine's dirty little secret. *Rosa* could find out. That's certainly reason enough for her to keep quiet. "So that night at her apartment, the night of the video . . ."

He sighs. "We were supposed to be heading to Chicago the next day, to meet my parents. I went there to confront her and she admitted to working as an escort. Told me that she didn't want to do it anymore, and had mostly stopped after our first date, but that her mother was sick and she couldn't get by on just her day salary. She needed the money. The guy I saw her with was an old regular in town, who just wanted a companion. She swore she never fucked him."

His account jives, in theory, with what I saw on the first part of the video. But not the second part. "Funny. When I'm disgusted by someone, I don't drop my pants."

His mouth twists in displeasure. "I'd had a few drinks and I was angry. So I told her to show me exactly what she did for the ones she *did* fuck. And so she did. And then I threw money down because I knew it would hurt her. I wanted nothing to do with her ever again."

"And did you have anything to do with her ever again?" *I dare you to lie to me, Jace.* I have proof—as far as I'm concerned—that he was in Celine's apartment the night that she died. Unfortunately the apartment's stored surveillance footage only retains about a week's worth before it loops over recorded material, so I can't see how many other times he visited Celine in her home.

He sucks back another gulp of his drink. "That jump drive you stole? It showed up in an unmarked envelope on my desk at work, two weeks after that night in her apartment. The video was on there, with the note that you also took."

Jace was being blackmailed. Just like Doug had suggested. "So you're saying that *you* didn't hack into her computer and make a copy?"

"Me? Hack into a computer?" Jace's face screws up. "I may manage hundreds of millions of dollars, but I don't know the first fucking thing about hacking into computers. Plus, I didn't even know she had a hidden camera. Do you think I would have done that, had I known? My face is clearly on it, along with a lot more of me. That video would ruin my father if it got out."

"I wouldn't know . . . I focused more on the before and after," I admit, feeling my cheeks flush as that same sickness churns in my stomach now that did when I first watched Celine undress in front of him. "So when you found the video on your desk . . ."

"I thought Celine was trying to extort money from me. So I went to her place and confronted her. She denied it, of course. She even made a huge production of pulling her hidden camera off her shelf and ripping the cord out, saying that she must have been hacked. I didn't believe her so I called her bluff. I told her to go ahead and leak it."

"There's no way Celine would do that. She'd never risk her mother seeing something like that." I would bet my entire trust fund on it. But what if I'm wrong?

He smirks. "Well, I didn't pay, and nothing ever happened. You know what that means, right?"

"That you had motive to kill her?"

"I . . ." Whatever he was going to say stalls at his lips as first confusion, then shock, then outrage passes over his handsome features. "No! It means that she had no intention of ever leaking it."

I'm done playing this game. "Or it means that you killed her to stop her from releasing the video. And then you stole a Chinese vase potentially worth millions that she had recently found in a garage sale."

"*Killed* her for a *vase*?" He leans forward, glancing for any potential eavesdroppers, and then hisses, "Are you completely insane?"

"Maybe. But that doesn't change the truth."

"I didn't kill *anyone*!"

I study his face for a moment—full of anger and wild panic. I did just accuse him of murder. "Well, someone did."

"Celine killed herself. You just don't want to believe that, so you're trying to pin this on me." He shakes his head. "And before you come back, accusing me of lying again, let me give you all the facts. I was actually at Celine's twice after the night of the video recording on that jump drive. Once, to confront her about the extortion scam. And then again, on November fifteenth. Yes, the same night that she died."

"Why were you there?"

"Because she called to tell me that she had found the perfect gift for my mother. A Ming porcelain *bowl. Not* a vase."

I snort, a very unladylike sound for a woman wearing couture. "You expect me to believe that she would go shopping for your mother after all that?" Even as the words escape my mouth, I know I'm wrong. Celine was very clearly very madly in love with Jace Everett. She'd do anything to get him back. Finding a gift for his mother may have been one of her tactics.

And I did find that bowl in his office.

"You can believe whatever you want, but it's the truth." He sucks his cheeks in with a mouthful of drink. "I felt sorry for her. She was obviously a good girl who had made some bad choices in desperation. Either way, I assumed she still had dirt on me, and I didn't want to make an enemy of her, so I tried to make peace. I even sent her flowers."

I sigh. "Yellow roses and a card that said—"

"That I still cared very much about her. Yes." Jace peers into his glass. "Yellow for friendship. I wanted to leave things on good terms with her. It was an impulsive gesture, an idea that hit me as I walked by a flower shop. In hindsight, maybe I shouldn't have done it."

What did a card like that mean to Celine?

Did she think she still had a chance?

If she had any hope that he was still the man who would save her from having to spend one more night with any of Larissa's clients, she'd go out of her way to help him. To give him a sign that she still cared.

I hate that his account of his relationship with Celine is making more and more sense. This would explain why he left her apartment with that cardboard box that night.

But, then again . . . "You slept with your assistant, and Celine knew that." I remember Dani saying it was sometime in October. So why would Celine still want anything to do with him?

I can literally hear Jace's teeth crack as his jaw clenches. "How the fuck did you find out about that? Who the hell are you working with?"

"That would have crushed Celine," I say, not answering his question.

Jace sighs, rubs his forehead. "I was piss drunk at a work event, we had just split up, and Celine had no right to be upset, given she'd been fucking other men for money while we were together. But, yes . . . She went mental over that. A lot of crying and 'how could you.' She wasn't stable. And then suddenly a blackmail video shows up on my desk, not even two weeks later. But we talked, I called her bluff and told her to post it, and she didn't. I thought she had calmed down. Come to her senses. And then she left a voice mail, telling me she had found something for my mother. I wasn't sure if it was another ploy to see me." His tone says he's quickly losing patience with me. "So I went to her place, thinking I would pick up the piece if she actually had it, make five minutes of small talk, and leave. She was already drinking, and extremely emotional. She did have the gift for my mom. I think she thought it would somehow fix things between us. When she realized that it wouldn't . . ." He shakes his head. "What she did to herself after I left, only she will ever know. And the Ming *bowl* that she *gave* me? It's not worth millions. She gave it to me with an appraisal certificate for four to seven thousand. She paid thirty-five dollars for it, and I reimbursed her for that. It's now mine."

"I don't care about a bowl. I want the vase with the red dragon . . ." I say halfheartedly. I was so sure Jace had it.

If Celine actually tried to blackmail Jace—or he thought she had, at least—it would take a pretty forgiving guy to keep any communication with her going. Is Jace that forgiving? I doubt it. Even if some of what he's telling me is the truth, I'm sure it's balanced by a few choice lies. But until I can poke holes in his statements, I have nothing. I don't even have the video, which is inadmissible, as Doug warned me.

Jace must see my wavering confidence. "Don't keep going down this path, Maggie. It'll never stick, and you'll ruin my life, my father's life, and yours in the process, along with Celine's reputation." He stands. "That was a private night between Celine and me, and no one has any business watching it."

"No one's going to watch it. For now. *Jay*."

He seems unfazed by my use of that name, but he's clearly pissed off. "If that video ever sees the light of day, you're going to jail." He leans over, so close to me that the smell of the scotch on his breath kisses my nostrils. "Just because you had your people erase security footage doesn't mean you'll get away with this."

Erase security footage? Wait. Does that mean . . .

I fail at keeping the surprise from my face, but he doesn't react. "I'm guessing your fingerprints are all over my office. All I have to do is call the police and report a robbery, and I'll have you on theft." Standing tall again, he slams the rest of his drink back. "You also seem to have forgotten that you've entrusted me with a large sum of your money. If you suspected me of all this, why the fuck would you do that?"

"To get closer to you."

I hear "crazy, rich broad" under his breath. "I hope you're at least covering all your bases before you hang yourself."

"What does that mean?"

"I mean, like looking into her clients. All of them. Especially that building super."

Now it's my turn to glare at him like he's insane. "Who, *Grady*? There's no way he was one of her clients."

He snorts. "I guess you haven't been doing your research well after all." He sets his glass down on the side table in one slow, precise movement before marching away.

CHAPTER 29

Maggie

"There you are!" Ruby finds me, her cheeks flushed. "I'm sorry that I abandoned you to dance." She rolls her hips in a slow, stiff motion. "That gentleman had moves."

Normally, that would have made me laugh. But I can't shake Jace's last words long enough to find humor in anything right now.

Grady?

She eases herself into the chair that Jace was just in. "Did I just see that moneyman leave here?"

"Yes, you did."

"And? Trouble?"

"I'm not quite sure." He's right, my fingerprints are all over his desk. But what happened to the incriminating footage of me? Did Doug have a change of heart? Or did he simply say all that as a cover? I heave a sigh. "He knows I drugged him. He's threatening me."

"Oh, dear. That can't be good." Her words are on point, but her tone says she's more curious than concerned. I replay part of the conversation for her. "So you have something concrete on him, though. Something to hold over his head?" She has a devious mind.

"I do. And it involves Jace paying Celine for her 'skills.'" I haven't told Ruby about the jump drive video yet. I wasn't sure that I ever wanted to. To be honest, I'd prefer to destroy it and have no one ever know about or see Celine like that, ever. "Tell me what you know about Grady."

"Grady?" Ruby laughs and smiles, like I just asked her to tell me about her own grandchild. "He's such a kind, funny young man. He's always coming to help me when I need him. Everyone around the building just adores him. And he's so smart. He can fix anything! The lady in apartment 207 has one of those fancy espresso machines. It just up and stopped working one day and Grady fixed it."

"But what else do you know? Like, what's his last name? When did he become the super there? When did he come over from England? What does he do besides smoke pot and fix things?" I fire off question after question. Questions that, frankly, I should already know the answers to about a guy I've been sleeping with. I feel like I'm about to lose my dinner all over this glamorous dress.

"Maggie, what's this about? Are you okay? You've gone pale."

"Jace said that Grady was one of Celine's clients," I admit reluctantly.

"Grady? Oh heavens, no . . ." She chuckles. "That's preposterous. How could he even afford such a thing? Celine wouldn't have been one of those cheap girls and he doesn't make all that much." Shaking her head, she adds, "Don't listen to that fool. He's trying to steer you away from himself. You're on the right track with the moneyman. It always goes back to the money."

Such a simple and quick dismissal from Ruby—a sharp old lady who knows Grady far better than any of us knows Jace Everett—helps quell the nausea inside me.

But far from completely.

I hold the door to our building lobby open for Ruby and she practically floats in, flashing a business card with a phone number written in blue ink. "Theodore asked me out to afternoon tea next week."

"The *Supreme Court judge* Theodore Higgins?"

"Retired now. Still uses his business card, though."

I pull the tail of my gown over the threshold a second before the door would have shut on it. It's already happened to me once, with the limo door. I'm lucky I didn't cause the two-thousand-dollar dress any damage. I plan on offering it up for auction to a charity. "For when he's out on the town, picking up dames?"

Her giggles echo through the cramped, empty foyer. "I haven't gone on a date in nearly twenty years." She pauses. "Maybe I shouldn't have agreed to it."

"You just danced with the man for hours. I think you can handle a cup of tea." I pause. "Unless that's code for something else, in which case I *really* don't want to know."

Ruby titters like a little girl as my eyes drift over the rows of little metal mailboxes to our right, landing on "C. Gonzalez" with a dip in my heartbeat. I haven't collected her mail once. I haven't even thought about it.

Ruby's box, "R. Cummings," is directly below Celine's. Without even thinking, my gaze scans over the other boxes, searching the names, until I find his near the bottom right corner.

"Oh my God." I stare at the sticker. "Did you know?"

"Did I know what, dear?"

The sound of my two-thousand-dollar dress tearing as I catch the hem on the fence barely registers. Neither does the cold December night, my faux fur white stole a beautiful but useless addition to my ensemble.

He didn't answer his apartment door. That's where I marched to first, after ushering Ruby to her place. I stood there and banged on it until someone hollered "go away!" from another apartment.

I figured I would try the roof. Turns out Grady's quite predictable.

He's lying in his hammock, his head covered in a toque, a joint held burning between fingers of one hand. Flames lick the sides of his little fire pit, the glow from it catching his eyes as he watches me approach. I'm not sure if him smoking weed is going to help this confrontation or make it worse.

"Aren't you a sight," he murmurs, his gaze trailing over me as I weave around the chairs and planters, slipping slightly on the snow-coated roof, my heels not meant for outdoor winter wear.

He lifts the heavy wool blanket up to make room for me. "Did you enjoy your charity ball?"

"Were you one of Celine's clients?" I blurt out. I've never been one for subtleties, but I'd like to think I've kept my head through these last few weeks, biding my time and biting my tongue with Jace. Clearly, the situation with Grady is a more emotional one for me, given how intimate we've become in such a short period of time.

His first name isn't even "Grady."

I don't know what his first name is.

But I do know now, thanks to his mailbox, that it starts with a "J," and Celine had a client she called "Jay," and that means that maybe Ruby is wrong and Jace wasn't lying to me tonight at all.

My words seem to hang in the air for a moment—either unreceived or incoherent—until I wonder if I actually really said them out loud.

"What? . . . I mean," Grady's face twists with confusion, then comprehension, and then shock, "what?"

"Were you one of Celine's clients?" I say slowly.

He doesn't answer me right away.

"Did you pay Celine for sex?"

His deep chuckle is not exactly the reaction I expected. When he sees the look on my face, he finally stops. "Oh, you're *serious*?"

"Yes, I am." I take a few steps closer, to get a better look at his face. "Because someone told me that you were."

"Who?"

"It doesn't matter. Just answer the question." The longer this goes on, the more suspicious I become.

"Well, it kind of *does* matter, because some asshole out there is filling your head with lies!"

Finally, a reaction from the always calm and collected Grady.

"So you're saying it's not true?" There's a part of me that's calling "bullshit," but it seems to be battling with something equally loud.

My heart.

Celine was the one to listen to her heart. I've always been better at listening to my head.

"Seriously, who told you something like that?"

I sigh. "The guy that Celine was seeing. You met him. He came by the apartment last week."

"The one with his hand on your knee. Yeah, I remember." It's such a subtle dig. Did he really care about that? I had already forgotten about it. "And he just offered this information to you?"

"No. I accused him of being behind Celine's murder. *Then* he told me about you. It's a long story . . ."

Grady butts his joint into a can of sand to put it out, and then reaches back to tuck his hands behind his head in a relaxed fashion. "Sounds like someone who's trying to misdirect your attention."

"Maybe."

"Not that I want to disparage myself, but I think he looks more like the kind of guy who could afford a high-end hooker than I do."

"Escort," I mutter softly—though, in the end, I know that he's not wrong.

"Frankly, I'm kind of offended that you'd believe that so quickly."

"I didn't. But then I—" I cut myself off. I've divulged many facts to Grady with complete ease in recent weeks. I felt comfortable with him since the first night up here. But suddenly that comfort has been replaced with unbalance and distrust. I need to be a better poker player. And I can't ignore what Jace told me tonight, simply because I don't want it to be true. Especially since so much of what he told me adds up.

So if it's true, and Grady just lied directly to my face about being Celine's client . . . what else could he be lying to me about? Could *he* have been the one to feed Celine enough drugs to make her overdose? Why would he want to kill her? To what end?

For the dragon vase.

That would explain why I didn't find it in Jace's place that night. Maybe Jace didn't take it after all. Maybe Grady did. He has keys to her apartment. He has access. But . . . what the hell does Grady even know about valuable antiques, or what to do with them?

"But then you what?" Grady probes.

I swallow the painful ball forming in my throat. "Nothing. I think this investigation is going to drive me insane." My clutch vibrates in my hand. That has to be Doug. I sent him a text earlier, on the drive back from the Waldorf, to update him on my encounter with Jace.

"Come on. It's cold. And you're beautiful." Grady lifts the end of the blanket up again. Beckoning me to the warmth, and to him.

Had I not seen that "J" on the mailbox, I might have written Jace's words off and accepted the invitation.

Now I merely offer him a tired smile. "Good night, Grady."

I wait until the outside door is shut to dig my phone out and call Doug. I need him to tell me that my gut is wrong and Grady isn't lying to me.

CHAPTER 30

Maggie

"Let's play this out." Doug's fingers strum against Zac's desk, the diary open in his free hand. Zac is busy clicking away at his keyboard, trying to hack into Grady's network. He must have one, given that he has a camera sending a live feed from the rooftop to his apartment.

So far, it's proving a lot more difficult than Zac expected. Which begs the question, why?

"'Jay' as in 'J. Grady' meets up with Celine in a hotel room. Introduces himself as 'Jay' and she's surprised because she knows him only by his last name."

"That's all he's ever gone by. Even Ruby didn't think much of it."

"'And I just spoke with him at the office earlier today,' she wrote in here."

"But Grady has no reason for being there."

"'What if he tells someone what I've been doing to make money? I need that job!'" Doug recites. "There's some sort of connection to work and Grady. There must be."

So far, Doug isn't quashing my worry that the man I've been sleeping with is a filthy liar.

I groan in frustration. If Celine had just outed people in her goddamn diaries like a normal person, we wouldn't be going through all this. "Why wouldn't they admit to knowing each other?"

"Role-playing," Zac pipes up, his eyes scanning over my dress without shame. I highly doubt this living space has seen anything more upscale than a pair of jeans and a button-down flannel shirt before I started coming here. Doug answered on the first ring and demanded that I meet him outside my building right away, so I just kept going on down the stairs from the roof, not bothering to stop at the apartment to change.

"Okay. Fine. So, they decide to stay in character," Doug agrees. "It's easier for her . . . he gets off on it . . . then what? Do they see each other again? How often? At this hotel or somewhere else? Zac, forget that for a minute. Check out the hotel's reservation log. Everett said he saw her at the Waldorf with the old man, right? Start there."

"Date?"

Doug scans the top of the diary page. "July sixteenth."

Zac's thick fingers fly over the keyboard, and what looks to be an internal hotel system pops up. When he looks over and sees my shock, he shrugs. "We do a lot of hotel room checks in this line of work so . . . I already know all the loopholes."

For a moment, I forget why I'm here and try to wrap my head around Zac's level of access. "Aren't you worried about getting caught?"

"I'm the gingerbread man," he sings, smirking. "I've been in their system a hundred times. The trick is to not touch anything. Especially money." A few more clicks and then, "Nothing at the Waldorf."

"Try the other luxuries. Trump, the Plaza, the London, Langham."

"Yeah, yeah. I know the drill."

"I'll be back in five. I need some fresh air." Doug pulls a pack of cigarettes out and runs up the stairs.

Which gives me the opportunity, the few minutes I need. "Zac . . ."

"J-Man said something about the feed from his security camera being missing, didn't he?" Zac says, never lifting his fingers or eyes from the monitor as he jumps from system to system.

"Would you know anything about that?"

"I know absolutely nothing about how a technology genius the likes of which no one has ever seen must have waited for the sleeping baby to wake from his drug-induced nap to ensure that he was not in fact murdered, and then wiped out all traces of Ms. Evil ever being there, not only from J-Man's security video but also from the building's video."

"So all that stuff Doug said, was he just covering his ass?"

"He meant it *and* he was covering his ass." Zac shoots a sideways glance to me. "What Doug doesn't know won't hurt him."

So Zac did this of his own accord. I sigh. "I owe you, big-time."

"You do." His gaze wanders over to the slit in my dress.

"Not happening. *Ever*."

"A simple thank-you would suffice."

"Thank you."

"And maybe some new equipment," he adds, before he's stopped by Doug's pounding feet. A waft of cigarette smoke trails in with him. That wasn't five minutes. That wasn't even one minute.

"I want to know everything there is to know about J. Grady. Where he was born, what he eats, where he shops. The more I think about it, there's something not right with him," Doug demands. I guess nicotine really does help Doug think.

"If I find a reservation, I can pull up his credit card bill," Zac says.

"Seriously, is *nothing* safe online?" I mutter.

"You know what they say about getting on a good hacker's bad side . . . don't."

"Do you have his fingerprints?" Doug looks at me.

"Yeah, in my back pocket."

He rolls his eyes. "In the apartment. Has he touched anything in there?"

The mattress, which was pitched, but he had gloves on. The window, the night he came in . . .

Me.

He's touched me.

I shudder. "I'm not sure."

"I need his fingerprints. I'll see if I can lift some from around the building."

"Okay, hold on. We don't even know if Grady's worth this level of scrutiny yet. Consider our source of informa—"

"Found him."

I turn to see the name "James Grady" on the screen.

My heart sinks.

CHAPTER 31

Celine

July 16, 2015

I inhale deeply, forcing my anxiety down, and then knock on the door.

I've met clients at the Langham twice before. It's one of a handful of high-end hotels that I agree to, as a requirement of Larissa's. No seedy motels, no private homes. No backseats.

It's probably my favorite. The décor is classic, the details are elegant, and the doormen are discreet.

I stick a piece of spearmint gum in my mouth while I listen for the approaching footfalls.

The door finally opens . . .

And I stifle my gasp.

We stare at each other for a few agonizingly long and painful seconds before he steps back to make room for me to enter.

I'm frozen in place. Do I walk in? Do I say there's been a mistake and leave?

Finally he smiles at me, a secretive lopsided smile. "Call me Jay."

"Maggie," I manage to get out, even though we both well know that's not my real name.

I can't believe this is happening. I'm sure this moment is changing his opinion of me. It's *definitely* changing my opinion of him. Is this a complete coincidence? Did he somehow figure out how I make money?

"Well, Maggie . . . Your secret is safe with me."

His words, spoken softly, remind me that I'm standing in the middle of a hotel hallway and anyone in the rooms nearby can hear this conversation. A quick glance out their peephole and they've seen our faces. I have two choices: I either leave or step inside.

If I leave, will my secret stay safe with him?

Taking in a deep breath, I step inside.

And prepare to offer my services to my building super.

CHAPTER 32

Maggie

December 14, 2015

The brakes on Doug's Ford Taurus squeak as he pulls up to the curb outside Celine's apartment building. It's two in the morning.

And I know that Grady lied to me.

On July 16, the same night that Celine met a new client who she was familiar with, and who introduced himself as "Jay," Grady rented a hotel room at the Langham under the name James Grady.

Was it just that night, though?

I watched Zac go through every high-end hotel reservation from July through November. There were no more rooms booked by a James Grady beyond that one.

"No reservations means either he didn't see Celine again, or they weren't meeting at hotels anymore." Doug leans forward to study the fire escape in the alleyway. "Ruby may not have heard any man coming to Celine's door, but that doesn't mean none came to her apartment."

My stomach tightens, the same way it did the first time Doug suggested that Grady and Celine had used the fire escape to maintain discretion and minimize cost, especially if he became a "regular" that Celine knew and trusted.

He used the fire escape when he came to me, claiming he didn't want to disturb Ruby. He had even called it "more romantic" than using the door.

At least he didn't leave any bills on the table for me.

It still doesn't make sense. "Do you really think he could afford her?"

"Not with what Zac found in his bank account, but he could have another one somewhere else. But he'd also have to be making some serious cash outside of this gig," Doug reminds me. "Zac will get into his electric bills to see if he's growing enough marijuana. I'm guessing that'll be a dead end though." Doug purses his lips. "I still think he has a connection to Vanderpoel that we don't know about yet. There's a link and we'll find it."

It's late, and I'm exhausted, and yet I know that I won't be falling asleep anytime soon, so I'm reluctant to leave the warmth of Doug's car. "So, what's the plan going forward?"

"You and I are going to walk into that building as if nothing is out of the ordinary, and then, after we part ways, I'm going to go and lift some prints off his door handle."

"Right now?"

"Zac's busy digging up everything he can remotely," he goes on, dismissing my shock. "And you are going to stay the hell away from that guy. I know you're angry, but don't say another damn word to him about Celine. You've already put the guy on high alert."

"He was definitely on a high when I left him," I mutter sarcastically. "Maybe he'll forget." I'm furious with him for lying to my face.

And disgusted that he would use Celine like that.

And hurt, which is pathetic, given how casual our "relationship" was.

"Don't count on him forgetting that. Not when he was trying to cover up the truth. But is he doing it out of pride, or respect for her, or because he's hiding something else?"

Neither of us have come right out and said it yet. "Do you think he could have had something to do with her death?" Could Grady actually be capable of that?

Doug raps his fingers against the steering wheel in thought. "I've learned never to underestimate anyone and you shouldn't either. And if there are potentially millions of dollars involved . . ."

"But this is *Grady*! He assumed everything she had was old crap. There's no reason he'd think that vase was valuable."

"Unless she told him it was."

"He said he hated money . . . ," I murmur, more to myself.

"Who did? Grady?" Doug lets out a derisive snort, but then he frowns. "When did he say that? How often do you two talk?"

"Not often. I don't know how it came up. So, what now?" The last thing I want Doug finding out is that I've been sleeping with a suspect. Possibly our *prime* suspect.

"Stay away from him. Zac's going to look for any connections between him and Chinese art. And first thing tomorrow, you're going to go down to that firm and find out *exactly* what Celine told Jace about Grady. Word for word."

I groan at the idea of seeing Jace again, now that I know I might have drugged and stolen from an innocent man. Well, "innocent" is a stretch after what I saw on that jump drive. But innocent of murder, most likely. "He wants me charged and put behind bars. He's not going to tell me anything."

"I'm guessing he'd rather have you focused on someone other than him," Doug counters.

He's probably right.

"You know what he's going to want in return though, right?"

"Yeah."

Doug reaches into his console and pulls out a small black kit. "Ready?"

CHAPTER 33

Maggie

"What exactly did she tell you about Grady?"

Jace looks up from his computer, his phone pressed against his ear, the skyline of midtown Manhattan looming behind him, the sky filled with drifting snowflakes. It's much like the first time I stormed into his office, only now I finally have some answers.

But I also have far more questions.

"I'm sorry, Mr. Everett. She must have snuck past the main desk. She *pushed* me out of the way!" Natasha says from behind me. "Can I please call Security?"

"I'll call you back," Jace says and hangs up. "Yes, Miss Sparkes is willing to do just about anything to get what she wants." He's much calmer than when I saw him last night at the gala. Amused, in fact. "No need for Security. Maybe an apology?"

"Sorry, Natasha." I don't even try to make it sound sincere. Jace wouldn't answer any of my calls this morning, and when I called her and asked her to patch me through, she refused.

He nods toward the door. A dismissal.

"So?" I take a seat without being offered.

"Didn't feel like wearing one of Celine's dresses today?" He scans my sweater and leggings. "Yes, I recognized them." He refocuses on his paperwork. "They looked better on her."

I let the dig roll off my back. I don't care about impressing Jace, and he's obviously not a big fan of mine anymore, now that I've accused him of theft and murder. "What exactly did she tell you about Grady?"

"I can't seem to remember . . ."

"And what will help you remember?"

He leans over his desk. "You know exactly what will help me remember, so quit playing games. I don't have time for this. Some of us actually earn our money."

I grit my teeth and count to five slowly. Pretending to stall. Finally, I pull the jump drive out of my purse and toss it onto the desk. "What did she tell you?"

He slides it over, rolling it in his fingers several times, and then tucks it into his coat pocket. "What did she tell me . . . what did she . . . oh, right. It was that night in her apartment, when I confronted her about being a whore." Standing up, he strolls around his desk, the scent of his cologne competing for my attention with his overbearing confidence. "You remember . . . Right before I nailed her on her couch. *And* on that big trunk that you like to set your dainty teacup on."

I know he's trying to get a rise out of me. "What exactly did she say about him?" I ask calmly.

He stares down at me for a long moment, with arms folded over his chest. "That he was paying her to fuck him and only him."

"Bullshit." I can hear Ruby's voice in the back of my head, can see her face squished up with incredulity. Grady can't afford that.

"I'm just relaying what she told me." Jace is acting indifferent to the entire situation, but a vein in his neck is pulsating. Something's definitely got him agitated. "When I confronted her about the old man I saw her with at the hotel, she told me everything and swore she was trying to get out of the business. She said that was a one-off—that the man was a longtime regular who offered to pay her enough to cover a month of rent—and that she was only sleeping with one client. Her super."

"That's a lie." I still can't wrap my head around this.

He shrugs. "Don't believe me then. I don't care."

"Did she say anything else?"

He twists his lips, as if he's deciding whether he wants to help me anymore.

CHAPTER 34

Celine

August 4, 2015

I pace around my living room, chewing my thumbnail and then scolding myself for doing it. First the oven, now my fridge? Within a week of each other? The oven isn't a big deal—I don't bake. But my fridge has to stay cold or I'll lose a week's worth of groceries.

So this time I didn't have a choice.

I had to text him for help.

I've avoided running into Grady—or "Jay"—for three weeks, afraid it's going to be painfully awkward to face him in normal life.

A knock sounds.

Taking a deep breath, I open the door. "Hey."

I have always found his piercing hazel eyes attractive. Actually, he is, in general, a good-looking man. If he put more of an effort into himself—maybe trimmed his hair and shaved the stubbly beard, invested in something besides jeans and sneakers—he'd have a girlfriend, and he wouldn't be paying for sex.

And how can he afford it? I still don't understand. We didn't really talk at all that night, and I didn't think it was appropriate to ask.

"Got your text about the fridge. I'll see if I can fix it."

"Great. Thanks." I feel a blush creep into my cheeks and immediately back up to make room for him. A shadow passing under Ruby's door across the way tells me she's awake and listening. She's always listening.

I shut the door and follow Grady as he heads straight for the galley kitchen at the far end. I catch a glimpse of my reflection in a mirror on the way by, and immediately begin smoothing my hair down. But why? I'm not attracted to Grady; not enough to want more from him. He's nice and smart, and that accent makes me swoony sometimes, but he's not very ambitious. I'm looking for someone driven and successful.

Someone like Jace.

Who I haven't heard from since that day on the elevator. I guess it was all just lip service.

"When did it stop working?" Grady turns the temperature up all the way and, tossing his tool bag onto the floor, grabs the fridge by either side and shimmies it away from the wall.

"Umm . . ." I can't help but spy the muscles straining in his arms. He has a nice upper body—I know, I've seen him naked now. "I'm not sure. I came home from work around five with groceries and thought it wasn't as cold as it should be. But it was still cool."

"Have you heard it running at all?"

Now that he mentions it . . . "No, I don't think so."

With a screwdriver, he adjusts something on the back of the fridge, and stops to listen. "It's got to be your compressor. Lucky for you, we have the same model in every unit here, and I keep a few parts in the basement." He pulls a cylindrical part out of his tool bag and begins working on the metal grate at the bottom of the fridge.

"So it's an easy fix, right?"

"Won't take me long at all." He glances up to meet my eyes, and I'm brought back to the Langham, with him looking up at me then, too. I hate admitting it to myself, but I actually enjoyed that night. A lot.

And I've been forced to replay my night with Grady—or "Jay"—inside my head many times since, if only to try and erase that *other* night the following week, with that disgusting pervert that Larissa set me up with. It was the last client date I've gone on, the one that made me tell her that I'm finished with that line of work.

Even thinking about it now makes me shudder. I should have

known—when the guy told me to get on my hands and knees and face the TV, when I felt the first trickles of lube running down my backside, when the home video came on and girls who were nowhere near eighteen filled the screen, running and laughing in their bathing suits.

Once I realized what was going on, it was too late.

It hurt to sit the next day.

I've spent quite a few nights over the last few weeks thinking about this man now on his knees in my kitchen, just to erase that awful experience.

I can feel my cheeks redden further. I should wait in the living room until he finishes. "All right. Well, I'll leave you to it then."

"How have you been?" he asks, trapping me here in conversation as he works.

"Fine."

"You sure?" His tone, soft and low, carries with it a hint of something else. Like he knows I'm lying.

I hesitate. "Not really. My mom is sick. Dying, actually." My voice cracks with the admission. Only Dani at work and Ruby know so far.

"I'm so sorry to hear that." He doesn't look up, and I appreciate that. It allows me to wipe the stray tear that slips out.

"Yeah, actually I've been meaning to talk to you about it. I'm leaving to go back to San Diego in early December and then I'm going to sublet to my friend and her fiancé beginning in January, until I come back." Once my mother is gone.

He shrugs. "Okay."

"Okay? Doesn't the landlord need to approve it?" Some guy named Dean who I've never met.

"Don't worry, he'll approve it if I tell him to, and I will. I mean, I assume you know and trust your friend to pay rent on time."

"Oh, definitely."

"Then . . . Okay. Great."

God, Grady's so easygoing. I wish I could be that easygoing.

"And how is everything else?" Again, there's that hint, making me wonder if he knows that the last few weeks have been especially rough. But before I can answer—and lie—I hear a motor start running.

"There. That should do it." He sits back on his heels. "Just try not to open the door at all for a few hours."

I sigh. "That's awesome. Thank you. I really can't afford to throw fifty dollars in groceries out."

He climbs to his feet, wiping his hands on a rag. "Money's tight?"

"A little." I blush, realizing what he's insinuating.

He steps closer, forcing me to take a step back until I'm pressed against the counter. "How often do you meet men in hotels, *Maggie*?" His voice is low and calm and unreadable. He can't possibly disapprove given our own encounter, but there's nothing particularly lighthearted about that question.

"How often do you meet women in hotels, *Jay*?" I throw back, but my stomach does a nauseating flip.

A small smile curls his lips. "That was the first time."

He says it so convincingly, I almost believe him. "I'm not doing it anymore."

"Really?" He frowns. "Why did you stop?"

"I had a bad experience recently."

"Not three weeks ago, I hope."

I smile. "It wasn't you. You were fine. Really good."

His eyes trail over my face, settling on my mouth. "Good enough that you'd be willing to do it again?"

"Can you really afford this?" I blurt out.

He chuckles. "I have enough money." He steps in even closer, settling his hands on either side of the counter, caging me in. "And I'd be willing to pay you for a night each week, if you're not going to be with anyone else."

"I'm not," I say quickly, because I'm done with showing up at hotel rooms and wondering what's waiting for me behind closed doors.

Grady runs his fingertips over my arm. "And we can just keep this between the two of us. No need to get your booking agent involved."

"I'm not working with her anymore, anyway."

"Good. Saves you some money. Saves me some money, if I can just come here."

"*Here?*" I drop my voice even more. "What about Ruby and the other tenants?"

He presses his body into mine. I can feel his erection against my belly. "We'll be really careful. I *am* only one apartment above you, and there is a fire escape connecting our apartments."

I glance past him toward my bedroom. How much easier would this be, if he just showed up here, got what he wanted, paid me, and then left? Normally I'd never agree to this, but it's Grady. He's always been respectful and kind. He's attractive.

And having *one* guy to please instead of several each week? One who I know and trust not to ask me to do weird things that I don't want to do? It sounds like he wants to be discreet, too. The last thing I'd want is anyone around the building finding out, or even guessing at it.

"So?" He reaches into a back pocket for his wallet, to pull out a small wad of cash. He lays it on the counter, his warm eyes resting on my face, his breath skating across my cheek. "What do you think?"

I take it he wants to start this arrangement right now.

I eye the bills and smile.

Is Grady the solution to my money worries?

CHAPTER 35

Maggie

December 14, 2015

Jace settles against the edge of his desk. "Celine and I started dating mid-August. She told me that this thing between her and her super started a couple of weeks before that. She wanted to end the arrangement right away, but she needed that money until she left for San Diego."

"And Grady told her he has a lot of money?"

He chuckles at my scowl. "Surprised me, too, especially after I met him that day at the apartment. Doesn't look like a guy who can afford a decent haircut, let alone a girl like Celine at his beck and call. Anyway, the night I confronted her and we broke up, she told me that she was going to end it with him. She wanted a new life away from it all . . . with me."

This man was once my salvation.

Celine saw Jace Everett—successful hedge fund manager and son of the governor of Illinois—as her Prince Charming, her gateway to a new life. The life she always wanted to lead, since growing up in La Jolla with my parents and me.

"But why would Grady pay weekly for an escort? He could go out to any bar, buy a girl a few drinks, and bring her home. Way cheaper."

"How the fuck should I know? And I don't care! He probably didn't want to pick up some average woman at a bar. Or maybe he was in love with her and knew that a chump like him didn't have a shot at a girl like her otherwise." Jace shrugs. "And maybe he didn't take it so well when she dumped him for me . . . *if* she ever did."

I'd like to believe that Jace is feeding me lies to divert me from the trail I've been following, but the more he reveals, the more I'm realizing he may be telling the truth.

"Did she say anything else at all about him?"

"No . . . We didn't talk much after that." Cold eyes pierce mine. "You should have watched the full video. Then you would have seen for yourself." He's helping me here, but he's enjoying my suffering far too much for my liking.

"I still can." My laugh sounds hollow. "Oh, come on. You actually think I wouldn't have a copy made? You're smarter than that."

"Remember what I said," he warns, his jaw clenching. "I wasn't bluffing. I will bury you, and I don't care how much money you have."

I let his threat roll off my back as I stand. "Home surveillance camera systems really aren't safe. I wouldn't recommend one."

"So I'm now realizing." He reaches behind him for a thick legal-sized envelope and thrusts it into my hands. "Thank God I hadn't tied your money up yet. I've already made arrangements to release and return all funds to you and terminate this business arrangement of ours."

I struggle to hide my surprise. I figured he'd be the type of guy to condemn me out of one side of his mouth and recommend investments to make us both a lot of money out of the other.

He stands to his full height and closes the distance to loom over me, his size and height all the more daunting. "I don't want your money. I don't want to see you ever again. I regret the day you ever walked in here. I regret the day I ever met Celine." He delivers each statement in an overly calm voice. "Get out of my office, now."

Judging by his poorly veiled fury, I'd say I've pushed him far enough. "If you honestly had nothing to do with this, then you'll never see me again."

"Then this is good-bye." He rounds his desk and sits.

"Just so you know, I'm not letting this go. I will spend every last dollar I have figuring out what really happened to Celine. And when that stolen vase surfaces—because it will, eventually—I will know about it. It doesn't matter where . . . New York, Chicago, Shanghai—" I reach for the door handle, "*anywhere* . . . I will find out, and whoever tries to sell it will have a lot to answer for."

I leave, feeling a strange mix of relief, vindication, regret.

And fear.

Fear that I've been after the wrong person all along.

CHAPTER 36

Maggie

"By the way, whatever happened to those other cases you had?" I call out, dumping the last of Celine's pots and pans into a box, my gaze wandering over the cupboards and counter. There's nothing left but one cup, one bowl, a set of cutlery, and a drawer full of takeout flyers, none of which I probably even need. I haven't been eating much, and when I do, it's usually takeout on my Seamless account.

Now that Celine's collection is in storage, my assistant has arranged for a Goodwill truck to come tomorrow afternoon and collect everything else that's left.

Soon, all traces of my best friend will be gone.

While that saddens me, I also need something to occupy my hands—and my mind—while I wait for Zac to come back with information on Grady.

"They all wrapped up last week. Lucky for you, I might add, seeing as you're now monopolizing all of my time," Doug says from the living room.

I wonder when Doug will be saying that this case is "wrapped up." Will it ever truly be "wrapped up," with answers that bring me closure?

"What were the cases? Can you tell me?" I debate whether I have it in me to tackle the fridge that I haven't opened since the night I arrived here. No doubt there's a putrid stench of spoiled cheese and rotten fruit waiting to assault my nostrils.

"Cheating husband, an old man who was poisoning the neighborhood cats, and a club owner who was embezzling money from his partner. The usual. Thank God for a world of sinners. I'll never be out of work."

"Well, it's a good thing you've maintained a positive attitude through it all." I lean against the kitchen's entryway and watch him pass a small, rectangular box with a short antenna sticking out from one end along the bottom edges of the couch. He hasn't sat down on it since coming here. I'm guessing that's because of the bright splotches of bodily fluid that his high-powered UV light illuminated. Some of them he assures me are most likely from Jace, based on what he saw of the video that I still refuse to watch. And the others . . . I'm just hoping this couch was a secondhand purchase for Celine.

Either way, I'm never sitting on it again. I don't even feel right giving it to charity.

"Any update on the prints?"

"All partials, and most of them are smudged. I can't call in a favor with NYPD on a partial." I can hear the frustration in his voice, and that's rare. Normally, Doug speaks and carries himself like there's no answer that he can't find.

"I wouldn't have thought getting a fingerprint from a guy who lives in this building would be so difficult." Doug skulked around the building at two a.m. last night, lifting any mark he could find from the fire escape, Grady's mailbox, the door leading to the roof. Unfortunately, Grady's front door handle—the best place to lift his prints—is too grooved and rough.

"It's not as easy as they make it look on TV, is it . . . ?"

I study the big forensics case Doug arrived with this afternoon, sitting open on the floor, full of all kinds of technical things I can't even identify. It's making me realize that I don't know anything about Doug, except that he works nonstop. "Did you learn how to do all that on the police force?"

"Some of it. I specialized in crime scenes so I learned how to do things like fingerprint dusting, photographing, casting. All kinds of evidence collection."

"Why'd you leave?"

"For the exact reason that I'm here now." Doug pulls the old wooden folding chair to the corner and climbs on it to test the vent. "Because I needed to be able to follow my hunches, and sometimes those don't match what the preliminary evidence might suggest."

"So you were going rogue, is what you're saying."

He chuckles. "My superiors sure didn't like it when they'd catch me investigating a case that was already closed. Said that I was insubordinate and argumentative, and unable to follow directions."

I mock-gasp. *"No way."*

He shoots a smirk my way. "What are you complaining about? You always get what you want from me."

"Because I keep writing you checks," I mutter, grabbing a trash bag and making my way over to the bedroom.

"It's a good thing you have a never-ending supply of money then, isn't it?"

"I knew you were trying to hose me." In reality, I don't think he is. I have no explanation for that belief, it's just my gut instinct, which is usually pretty good. "So, are you and that secretary of yours together?"

"Who, Donna?" He snorts. "Are you kidding me?"

I guess they're not. "Have you ever been married?"

"Once, in my twenties. Biggest mistake of my life." He joins me in the bedroom in time to see me roll my eyes. "You need to keep all of her clothes and other things." He gestures to the dresser drawers. He knows what's in there. There isn't a cupboard or drawer that he hasn't poked his head into at some point. "There could be evidence on them. Nothing that would stand up in court on its own, but maybe it'll help build a case."

"I guess I can put it all in the storage locker for now."

"Yes. The couch will need to go into storage, too."

The telltale three knocks sound on the door, saving me from going through Celine's black lace and rubber.

Doug mouths, "Who is it?"

"Ruby. I said she could come over for tea."

"Get rid of her," Doug hisses as I pass him. "Senior citizens talk too much. They're a hazard to investigations."

I ignore him and open the door. Ruby's wide grin meets me, bringing with it a moment of comfort.

"Good afternoon, dear. Ready for a break?"

I take the tea set from her shaking grasp, noting the three cups.

"I thought I heard your detective arrive." She steps inside the apartment. "Oh, yes! There you are. Good. I brought some fresh homemade shortbread for us all to share."

He shoots me a warning glare as he passes, but has no issue snatching a cookie from the tray.

"So? What are you up to?" Ruby murmurs, dragging the folding chair over to the table, eying Doug's case. "Oh, looks like you're collecting evidence?"

When Doug doesn't answer, I pipe in. "We're doing a background check on Grady. I know it sounds crazy, but we need to rule him out."

"Yes, that's probably a good idea. Ease your conscience." The lid of the teapot rattles against its base ever so slightly as Ruby pours three cups of tea. She drops her customary three sugar cubes into hers. "Of course you mean *James* Grady."

Doug stops with whatever he's fumbling with in his case and glares at me. "What part of 'keep it to yourself' did you not understand?"

"She didn't tell me anything." Ruby slowly swirls the silver spoon around her cup and very simply says, "I asked him."

I think Doug's eyes are about to pop out of his head. "See? The elderly and investigations cannot coexist!"

If Ruby's insulted, her tiny smile doesn't let on. "Silly me . . . When I went down this morning to pick up my mail, the key somehow snapped in the lock. Imagine that. It must have been getting weak. So, I called Grady and asked him to see if he could fix it. He came down and fiddled with it for a bit, but couldn't get it to open. Said we'd need to call a locksmith in to replace it." She takes a sip of her tea. "My mailbox just happens to be nine over from his, and I just happened to notice that his says 'J. Grady.' So I asked what the 'J' stands for. He told me 'James.' And then I asked why he doesn't use it, and he said that it's because his father's name is also James." She shrugs. "I had never even noticed it before. I'm so daft in my old age."

Though she plays the role well, Ruby is anything but daft.

I shoot a grin Doug's way, making a mental note to pay for her new lock, because I'm sure it's not cheap. Doug's already on his phone, no doubt texting Zac with the new information about Grady sharing his father's name.

"So, I'm guessing his fingerprints would be helpful, too?" Ruby says.

"A full set would be, yes. Doug hasn't had any luck finding one, though. I'm going to have to meet up with him for coffee, or something. Get his cup." My stomach tightens at the suggestion. I don't know that I can face Grady and pretend everything's okay.

"What about the garden on the roof?"

The roof. That beautiful, peaceful oasis that I found some shred of happiness in, with him, throughout all of this. Now I cringe picturing it. "He has a camera up there." I used to think it was simply a security measure, but now I'm wondering if there's more to it. "It's better that he doesn't know we're on to him."

"You know, Grady stopped by yesterday and returned a cookie tin. The surface is metal and smooth. It probably has a full print or two on it."

"Where is it?" Doug demands, marching toward the door. "Do you still have it?"

"I believe it's still sitting on my kitchen counter where . . ."

He's gone, out the door, across the hall, and into her apartment before she can finish the sentence.

"What was that he was saying, about the elderly not being very helpful in investigations?" she muses, a small, glib smile hiding behind her teacup.

"I'm sorry. Doug doesn't have the best bedside manner." I add a sugar cube into my cup. I'm going to miss this when I'm gone, I realize, as I lift the delicate china to my lips.

My eyes meet Grady's, and I nearly choke on my tea.

He's standing in my open doorway with a young woman next to him. With her long, dark hair, deep olive complexion, and healthy curves, she could almost pass for . . . Celine.

"Hey, Maggie." Unlike me, Grady is all smiles. "This is Jemma. She's here to see the apartment."

"Oh my God. It's Monday." With everything going on, I completely forgot.

"I just live a few blocks away." Jemma gives me a wide smile. "I hope you don't mind."

Grady steps in before I can tell him that this is not a good time. "I can't believe how bare it is in here." His gaze drifts over the emptiness, landing on Doug's forensic case.

"You weren't lying. There are *a lot* of shelves," Jemma exclaims with a giggle, her big brown eyes skating over the room as she steps around a box full of books, the hems of her light blue jeans dragging. She doesn't seem to have picked up on the tension in the room yet. "I don't own enough to fill them." She smiles up at Grady and deep dimples form in her cheeks.

Jemma is pretty. Very pretty.

"I'll help you take those ones down." He waves a hand to the left. "They were all added in. The former tenant needed it for her art collection."

Jemma looks at me, and then at Grady, and I see the question in her eyes. *No, I'm not the former tenant.*

"And this is the bedroom over here." She follows Grady, his arm stretched out behind her, his fingers so close to grazing the small of her back as they stand in the entranceway. "It's small but full of character."

"And bright." She quietly admires the length of the window.

Suddenly, I'm hit with an image of Grady slipping through that window to have sex with another pretty girl in this apartment.

And maybe killing her.

I can't help myself. "I'm the old tenant's friend. I'm just cleaning up. She died right over there." I point to the bedroom. "The police say it was a suicide, but I'm honestly not convinced."

I'm too busy watching the shock on Grady's face to pay attention to hers, which I'm sure is classic. She'll thank me later.

"My name is Ruby. I live next door." Ruby eases out of her chair and offers her hand to Jemma, who takes it, though she looks like someone just slapped her across the face. "It's a wonderful building. Would you like some shortbread?" Ruby holds out the plate, her sweet smile helping lessen the unsettling mood that I just created in the room.

"Sure." Jemma takes a cookie, nibbling the edge like a dainty little mouse.

Doug's heavy boots stomp across the hallway. "I think I should be able to pull a good print—" Doug stops dead still, the royal-blue round metal tin balancing precariously between his hands.

Grady's eyes narrow on it slightly.

"Hi." Doug shoots a glare my way—as if this is my fault, which I guess it is because I'm the one who forgot that Grady was coming by today with the new tenant—and then sets the tin down on one of the empty shelves. "We met a few days ago."

"Right." Grady gives Doug a tight smile. "Jemma, let me give you a quick tour of the kitchen and bathroom, and then we can get out of their hair. Looks like they're busy." He leads her across the living room, his wary gaze touching mine for a split second.

The quick tour is literally that—sixty of the most awkward seconds of Doug, Ruby, and me passing unintelligible warning glares at one another while Grady leads the new tenant through the apartment.

Finally, they're at the front door again.

"It was nice meeting you," Jemma offers, eying me cautiously. She doesn't know what to think of me, I'm sure.

"Thanks for letting us in, Maggie." Grady ducks out behind her without giving me another glance, shutting the door behind him.

"And I thought senior citizens were the dangerous ones," Ruby murmurs with a wry smile, taking a seat with her cup. "I'd say that between the expressions on the two of you, Grady knows all he needs to know now."

"Did you know he was coming?" Doug barks.

"I forgot!" I snap back, but then lower my voice, warning him, "These walls are thin."

Doug's narrow gaze darts from the door to the evidence kit to the tin. "He looked worried. He knows that we're investigating him now, and he's worried about what we might find."

"And did you see that girl? Did you see how he was acting around her? All smiley and touchy-feely." I begin pacing circles around Ruby now. "He's going to crawl through that window for her, the same way he did with Celine. And then God knows what's going to happen. I had to warn her."

"Warn her?"

"Yeah. I told her that the previous tenant killed herself."

Doug heaves a sigh. "Okay. That's fine."

"It was quite uncomfortable, actually," Ruby surmises. "I've never seen Maggie so emotional before."

"Emotional." I watch Doug's analyzing gaze study the window for a long moment, and then my unmade bed, the sheets rumpled in a heap. "So when exactly did you and Grady start . . ." His brows jump. *"You know."*

My cheeks burn. "I don't know what you're talking about."

"Don't forget that I have a forensics kit over there that will tell me anything I need to know," he warns.

Dammit. Knowing him, he'll make me stand here and watch him run that UV light over sheets I haven't washed since Grady was over. How mortifying would that be?

From the corner of my eye, I catch the grin that stretches Ruby's many wrinkles. It's like she's forgotten why we're investigating Grady in the first place. That, or maybe it's just a thickening plot that excites her.

Still, I'm not paying Doug to investigate me. "Can we please just focus on the important stuff here?" Sadness and anger and disappointment erupt inside me. "Like, who the hell is Grady, what exactly happened between him and Celine, and is he the one who stole that vase?"

And could he have killed her?

A soft knock against my window sounds, echoing through the almost empty apartment. It doesn't wake me. I haven't been able to fall asleep, instead staring at the cracks in the plaster ceiling above me.

He came to my door an hour ago and knocked, but I didn't answer then, either.

Though I know I could just confront Grady again, that's probably not the smartest thing to do. The fact that he's already lied to my face once makes possibly antagonizing him now a supremely stupid thing to do.

It could be nothing.

It could be everything.

I hope it's nothing.

I need to know more about James Grady and I need to know right away.

A second soft knock sounds, followed by a "Maggie? I need to talk to you."

I lie still, staring at the thirteen oversized garbage bags that consume every square inch of bedroom floor space, like giant black marshmallows. More fill the living room. Five bags' worth went straight to the Dumpster—all the things I can't donate. Others, I need to store and save for any possible future investigation.

I could let him in, let him tell me what he wants to tell me. But I know myself. I won't believe him. And what if it's not simply a conversation he has in mind?

What if he wants to hurt me?

Maybe like he hurt Celine?

Would he be stupid enough to do that, with Doug on my payroll?

Doug's warning stays my voice and my body. *Never underestimate anyone.*

"Whatever you think I did . . . you're wrong," he says.

I've never really been good at listening to myself.

Scrambling out of bed, I pull the curtain open. He's standing on the landing again, in a T-shirt and jeans, shivering. Just as he was before.

Only this time I have no urge to slide open the window.

This time, I have no reason to invite him in.

My chest aches. Whatever we had vanished so quickly.

"And what exactly is it I think you did that I'm so wrong about?" I snap, folding my arms over my chest, both to ward off the draft and his gaze.

His jaw tenses. "Can you just let me in so we can talk about this?"

A bitter laugh escapes me. "So you can hurt me, too? Maybe make it look like an accident this time, instead of suicide? Not a chance in hell."

He frowns. "Maggie, I would never—"

"I'm not going to believe *anything* you have to say. You looked into my eyes and you lied." I lean in to the glass, to get a close look at his face as I say, "I know you were one of Celine's clients. I know you were paying her for sex, and you were coming in through this window, just like you did with me the other night."

His Adam's apple bobs with his hard swallow.

But he doesn't deny it.

My eyes begin to burn. I can't believe I'm about to cry in front of this asshole. I'm *not* going to cry in front of this asshole. "I'm sure that's not the end of it, either. I'm sure I'm going to discover all kinds of other disgusting things about you. Stay the hell away from me." I pull the curtain closed before the first tear slips, burning hot against my cool skin.

I hear the subtle creaks of the fire escape as James Grady climbs back up without another word.

CHAPTER 37

Maggie

December 15, 2015

"More my style," Zac notes, eying the track pants and sweatshirt I threw on this morning before the donation truck came to collect Celine's things. Aside from the antiques, the couch, and potential evidence going into storage, and a box of Celine's personal items—her old diaries, the lockbox, pictures that I want to keep—the apartment is ready to be rented.

"Did you find anything good on Grady?" I was in a cab and on my way to Zac's within two minutes of getting a call from Doug.

"Oh . . . I'd say so. But let's wait for Doug. He'll be here in five. He likes to do the grand reveals."

"Okay. Five minutes." I hug my body tight and focus my energy on what Doug may have found, and not on the dust particles caught in the beam of daylight shining in through the tiny basement window. A window that I doubt I could fit through, should I ever need to escape.

I much prefer Zac's dungeon in the dark of night, I decide, taking deep breaths to quell the rising panic. I haven't had an attack since the day in that elevator with Jace. That day . . . I guess I have a few secrets to take to my grave, too. I can't very well judge Celine for her decisions, especially when they were borne out of financial desperation, and the only excuse I have for what happened that day is insanity.

And what's my excuse for carrying on as I did with Grady?

"You know, if you're meeting clients here, you should probably hire a cleaning lady."

Zac snorts. "No one comes in here except Doug."

I frown. "*I'm* not Doug."

"You're right. You're taller, and slightly less bossy." He reaches into his bag of Cheetos—breakfast of champions—and grabs a handful. "I did some research on you."

I glare at him, suddenly on high alert. "What kind of research?"

"The legal kind." He grins. "I already did the other kind earlier, for Doug. You know, you *could* be using your money and power and beauty for evil."

"Yeah. I guess?"

He licks the cheesy powder off his fingers. "It's nice to see that you aren't. It's rare."

I smile. This is Zac's way of paying me a compliment. "Why do you do this, anyway? Sit in this dirty little tech cave all day as Doug's monkey."

Through a mouthful, he explains, "Because I'm good at it and he pays me well."

I grab the nearby stool and take a seat. "You mean *I* pay you well."

He merely smirks in response.

"I'm sure you could be doing this kind of stuff somewhere brighter? More social?"

"Yeah, well . . . My mom's blind and getting up there in age. At least this way I'm around when she needs me." He says it almost reluctantly, as if he doesn't want to admit that he has a human side to him.

I study the wall of monitors in front of us. "It really is scary what you can do in this room of yours."

His eyes watch a series of code churning on the far top screen. A jumble of letters and numbers and symbols that mean nothing to me but I'm sure do to him. "All I'm doing is finding the weakness. There's always at least one. Humans, usually. Humans and their inherent stupidity, using passwords that a ten-year-old following a hacker's script can guess, humans clicking on emails from people they don't recognize, humans not doing their research and loading malware into their computer. Sure, it's not all that. I spend hours, or days—or even weeks sometimes—writing code and breaking systems."

"Why?"

"Because it's fun. It's a challenge."

"But at least you do all that with good intentions, right? I'm sure you *could* be using that big brain for pure evil."

"If it weren't for Doug, I might be. He keeps me too busy to get into trouble."

"Say his name and he shall appear," I joke, spotting Doug's bald head in the camera a second before the loud buzz of the doorbell.

Zac climbs out of his chair and jogs up the stairs to unlock the door, moving surprisingly fast for his size.

Two sets of feet stomp back down.

"You're here. Good." Doug—with heavy bags lining his eyes, as if he hasn't slept all night—shoves a tall caramel latte into my hand. It's the only beverage I buy at Starbucks.

I frown. "How did you know I like—"

"My connection at the precinct came back to me on the prints we pulled from that tin."

My concern over the coffee is quickly forgotten. "So he has a criminal record?"

"No. The prints came back clean."

My shoulders sag with relief, even as my disappointment swells. Finding a criminal record would have felt like a step closer to proving that Celine didn't kill herself, but I'd prefer it be someone other than Grady who did it. "Then why are we here?"

"Because of sheep." Doug kicks the stool I was just sitting on, and it rolls across the dingy gray concrete toward me. "Get comfortable. Zac?"

Zac wipes his hands on his pants—they're streaked in orange by now—and then begins punching in keys. The monitors flip to new screens, one by one. The last one fills with a student ID card from MIT and a much younger picture of Grady—maybe in his early twenties.

"You found him."

"James Grady Hartford Sr. runs Hartford Wool, a small but successful wool textiles business in Ipswich, England."

"Sheep." Now I understand. The name "Hartford" rings a bell. That wool blanket that Grady uses on the rooftop is one of his family's products. He said his family was into sheep farming. They're obviously into much more than that.

"He married an American by the name of Dorothy Haynes, and together they had two children. Their oldest, James Grady Hartford Junior, was born February 2nd, 1985 in New Jersey, where he lived with his mother for the first six months of his life, until they both moved back to Ipswich."

So Grady's last name isn't even Grady. "What about the other child?"

"Another son, who died of a drug overdose in 2009."

At least he wasn't lying to me about that.

"James Grady Hartford Jr. spent his childhood in England and then, using his dual citizenship, moved to America. He attended MIT for two years before dropping out, and moving back to England."

"MIT?" I frown. "That's one of the top universities in the world." How did Grady end up fixing toilets and replacing screws in Little Italy?

"Your super has a big brain," Zac murmurs, waggling his eyebrows knowingly at me.

And another lightbulb goes off. "And *he* uses it for evil."

"I called a connection in London and found out that James Grady Hartford Jr. was once under investigation for cybercrimes, back when he was just twenty," Doug says. "They suspected him of building a back door into a government system and then exposing it to prove their vulnerability. They were never able to make it stick."

"So he's a hacker."

Zac chuckles. "A hacker? No. *I'm* a hacker. James Hartford is a fucking god. He goes by the name GenerationInvasion online. I've heard him speak at Def Con—that's a hacker convention. He's broken some of the biggest—"

"Yes. He's a hacker." Doug glares at Zac. "He enjoys breaching company networks and charging them big money to redesign and fortify their systems. He runs a business under his online name."

Another monitor changes to a simple—and unimaginative—website. "Kind of basic, isn't it?" Villages United's website has more personality than this. I'd expect someone with his technical prowess to do better.

"It's a me-myself-and-I operation. Some people have accused him of attacking systems anonymously and then strolling in to save the day, setting it up so companies feel it necessary to hire him. Either way, he's made himself quite a name for solving security issues. A name he doesn't seem to go by in everyday life for whatever reason, seeing as he's adopted the name 'James Grady' and even has a credit card registered in that name."

"That's why I didn't make the connection between his screen name and who he is right away," Zac adds.

Thank God I'm sitting, because my knees are shaking. "So, he would probably know how to hack into Celine's camera."

Zac snorts. "In his sleep. Her camera, her computer. Everything."

"You said she wasn't very tech-saavy. She could have asked him to help set the camera up in the first place. Makes it even easier for him to get into the system," Doug says.

Zac's heavy almost-unibrow arches. "He could have been watching her for months, for all we know."

Which means Grady could have been the one watching the night Jace came over, somehow figured out who he was, and seen an opportunity for blackmail.

My stomach sinks. "But why be a building super when he has this company? And why would he watch her like that? Who does these things?"

"Someone who had serious affection for the pretty tenant downstairs?" Doug must see the distress in my face—he's figured out what kind of relationship I had going with Grady—because his harsh tone softens just slightly. "But we're just spitballing here. We need to play out all the possible scenarios. Zac can't get into his system remotely."

"Fort Knox," Zac confirms. "Ain't happening from the outside."

"But it got me thinking about Grady and Celine and the connection to Vanderpoel, from her diary. Zac started doing his thing."

"I thought to myself, if I were stalking a chick . . ."

I cringe at Zac's verb choice. Though, if Grady was monitoring Celine through her camera, then there isn't a better word for it than that.

". . . I'd be looking to run into her every chance I could, and make her think all these coincidences must add up to the universe's grand scheme for me and her. I've already got the perfect connection at home—she's only a floor below me, I can watch her in her apartment, I have keys to get into her apartment if I need to—but I need more. So I find a reason to be in her building. A legit reason, because I *want* her to know that I'm there. And what am I good at? Breaking into company systems." Zac blows up the testimonial page of Grady's website.

My heart sinks.

There's the missing connection.

There's the reason Celine wrote about running into Grady in her office building the same day she ended up sleeping with him for the first time.

CHAPTER 38

Celine

July 16, 2015

I smile at the middle-aged lady and take my place on the other side of the elevator, hiding my disappointment that it's not Jace riding with me. I've gone months at a time without seeing him around the building. Of course I'm not going to share an elevator with him a mere hour after running into him at Hollingsworth.

We travel up in silence, stopping several times to let people off on their floors. I keep my eyes ahead, feeling the glances from men as they get on. Although it's something I've become used to, I'm still not comfortable being stared at like that.

The doors open on my floor and I step out.

And I stop short, in surprise.

It takes me a moment of gawking at him—his typical jeans and T-shirt replaced by a suit, his scruff trimmed and his hair gelled back in a dark, loose wave—to accept that I'm not mistaken and this is in fact Grady, the same guy who I run into in the hallways of my apartment building on a semi-regular basis. We seem to have the same mail pickup and laundry schedule, and he's always fixing something for Ruby. "Hey. What are you doing here?" At *my* place of work.

His hazel eyes crinkle with his smile. "Fixing your computer system. You guys were hacked a couple weeks ago."

I frown. "Really? You know how to do that?"

Grady chuckles. "Yeah. It's kind of a side business for me."

"Wow, that's . . ." My eyes trail over his appearance again.

He looks really different in a suit. Really attractive. It feels like I'm actually *seeing* him for the first time.

And if a company like Vanderpoel has hired him to fix their system, he must be really good at it. "That's impressive. Do you do this for a lot of companies?"

"Just a few, here and there . . ." He sighs. "I'm not really into the corporate world."

"But you could do really well. You wouldn't have to—" I cut myself off before I say, *fix toilets and trap mice.*

He knows what I was getting at. "I like doing the building management stuff. It's easy, low-stress, lets me work with my hands. That's what I like. This is just easy money for me."

My disappointment swells. *Not very motivated* is more like it.

The elevator doors open again and Vanderpoel employees filter out, forcing me to step closer to Grady. He doesn't back up. "So, how long will you be here?"

"Just the afternoon. But do me a favor and don't mention it to Ruby, or anyone else in our building. The owner's weird about me working another job. I kind of promised him that I wouldn't."

I wink. "Your secret is safe with me."

CHAPTER 39

Maggie

December 15, 2015

"I think it's safe to say we have enough proof that Grady was paying Celine for sex," I mutter. And she enjoyed it, based on her diary, so it makes sense that she'd agree to it on a regular basis. Hell, *I* was doing it on a regular basis—for free—because I enjoyed it with him. Now the very idea makes me want to vomit. "But do we think he took the vase, too?" Where does that play into this? It *has* to play in, somewhere.

"Well, I did find this." Zac scrolls through the company info page. "See this engineering company here? It's based in Beijing and owned by Jin Chou, one of the richest men in China. Grady did some contract work for Chou's company back in 2011, and then again in 2013, only that was for Chou's private home. The guy obviously trusts him."

"So the guy is Chinese. Not exactly a smoking gun for art theft," I say.

Zac waves a dismissive hand. "What's interesting about Chou is that it's rumored he's involved in black market trade. Mainly iPhone rip-offs that are sold to India and Thailand. If I were a guy like Grady, who got his hands on a major Chinese art find like this and was afraid to sell it out in the open in case someone started asking questions, the first thing I'd do is call up my rich Chinese buddy who likes to make money and probably doesn't care about going through regular channels to do it, and say, 'Hey Jin Chou, how should I sell this thing? I'll split the money with you.'"

I open my mouth, but he cuts me off. "And Jin Chou would say, 'Holy shit, sell it to me because then I can turn around and taunt Li Jie with it.'" Zac hits a few keys and a face shows up on another monitor, of an unsmiling Asian man in a charcoal-gray suit. "This is the guy who bought the twin vase with the phoenix on it, back in ninety-six. Another obscenely rich Chinese guy, who owns a communications company. *And* both Chou and Jie are members of the same private member's club in Beijing."

"Huh." Maybe it's just me wanting it to be true, but that definitely is a connection. I look to Doug for his opinion and find him giving me that knowing nod. "Two degrees of separation between Grady and the man who, arguably, would want that vase the most. Of anyone in the world. That's something."

Jesus. What if Celine *did* tell Grady about the vase—about how valuable it could be—and he decided to get rid of her so he could take it? Or maybe she didn't need to tell him. He probably was monitoring her computer—like everything else to do with her—and read her blog post.

While I ponder this, Doug drags a whiteboard easel over and turns it around to unveil a mess of scribbled handwriting in orange and blue markers. A vertical line splits the board into two, the larger half marked "Prime Suspect" across the top, the narrow half labeled "Other Suspects" with names, possible motives, and question marks in boxes. They're there because a good investigator doesn't entirely dismiss them until he knows he can.

But if we're being honest, this board is all about Grady.

"So here's the best possible scenario, based on what the diary and Jace told us, and what we think we know about Grady. Plus a little bit of conjecture." He starts at the top, where it says "July." "Jace and Celine meet at Hollingsworth, by chance. Celine also meets James Grady in the Langham, for paid sex. We are going to assume, based on Grady's technical abilities, and the fact that he was very likely invading Celine's personal life on multiple levels, that this meeting wasn't a coincidence. If the eighty-one-year-old neighbor pegged her moonlighting career, you can bet he did, too. He's likely been watching her for months, monitoring her phone backup and her computer, spying on her through that lobby camera. Maybe he knew about her mother's health situation, and how desperate Celine was getting for money. He figured out who Larissa Savoy was and called her, asking for a pretty Hispanic woman. Maybe he even hacked into Larissa's life, just enough to have a client referral name to throw out."

"He's that good," Zac confirms, his face showing his awe.

"Based on Celine's written records, escorting was a part-time thing, only once or twice a week, mainly on weekends. She had a bad experience near the end of July and quit working for Larissa entirely. Maybe she wrote about it in the diary that's missing. Maybe Grady read it while she was out. He doesn't want to share her anyway, so he offers her a chance to still make money while feeling safe, and of course she takes it, because she's a young, beautiful woman and he's a young, attractive man and she'd rather be sucking his dick than that of some sweaty sixty-year-old stranger. Okay, fine, that was a bit harsh—" Doug holds a hand up to silence me before I chastise him.

"But why would he want to pay for it? He's attractive. He'd have no issues finding someone else." I know that for a fact.

Doug's eyebrows spike and he says nothing, as if waiting for my wits to start working.

"Because he doesn't want anyone else. And because he couldn't catch her interest otherwise. He probably already tried." Jace's guess isn't so crazy after all.

"Bingo. She doesn't want the blue-collar apartment super."

"He also isn't blond," I mumble to myself, though I'm guessing it had nothing to do with that and everything to do with his perceived earning potential and future ambitions. Celine dreamed of a life of financial comfort, and she admired men with drive and goals.

A guy who changes the lightbulbs doesn't fit any of that. But . . . "If he's doing this tech stuff, then he's not exactly blue collar. He must be getting paid really well." Which must be how he'd been able to afford Celine.

"Still looking for an account to verify that, but yeah, he'd definitely be making some good dough with these gigs," Zac says. "Thing is, he's known for being hard to nail down. He was supposed to speak at another conference I was at and just didn't show up. No reason. He tends to disappear off the radar for months at a time and then reappear to break something or fix something."

"So, not very reliable." And, oddly enough, he's the exact opposite when it comes to his job in the apartment building.

"Okay," Doug says, tapping on the whiteboard with a capped marker. "So Celine and Grady have their arrangement, and then not a couple weeks later she begins dating Jace Everett—the man she obviously wants to be with. But she doesn't end things with Grady."

"And Grady gets jealous? Angry?" I can't picture him angry.

But I also can't picture him paying Celine for sex.

"Maybe. We don't know that," Doug says. "But Jace said that Grady wanted exclusivity and here she is dating another man."

"She bangin' Everett?" Zac asks.

"Don't know. Do we know?" Doug frowns at me in question.

"He never said. I never asked." If I had to guess, I'd say yes. Jace doesn't seem like the kind of guy to last too many dates without one of them ending with breakfast.

"So, she's dating Everett, getting paid to screw Grady, and then fast-forward almost two months, and with her mother's medical bills mounting and the last-minute travel she's booking, Celine decides to meet with an old client at a hotel to make some extra money. Everett sees her while she's out with the client and ends it with her, that night we saw on tape. Everett screws his assistant not long after, and Celine finds out about it. Two weeks later, he finds the jump drive and blackmail note on his desk. He goes to her apartment and accuses her of it. She denies it. Assuming she's telling the truth, then the question is, who would do that? Out of everyone in Celine's life, only Grady has the skill to hack into her computer and her camera to watch her. And if he expected to have her all to himself, he wouldn't have liked what he saw on that video. So he decided to blackmail Jace Everett with it."

I frown. "Why not blackmail Celine, though? She's the one he's angry at."

"Because she doesn't have any money. Because he still cares about her. Because he wants to end any chance of Everett ever coming back. Plenty of reasons."

"But she may have already ended their arrangement, like she told Jace she would the night they broke up."

"If the guy's been stalking her for the past however many months, it's not over just because she says it is," Zac says.

I guess that's true. "How would Grady even get into Jace's office at FCM?"

"Probably replicated a visitor pass card and got into the building security mainframe." Zac waves it away, as if it's all child's play. "I'm working on the camera feed playback for FCM. It's not as easy."

"Okay. Fine. But then Jace doesn't pay up, and nothing happens."

"Maybe Grady has a change of heart," Doug says. "Or maybe Celine knew enough about Grady's computer skills by then to figure out that it was him who hacked her computer. Jace told you that he went to her apartment to confront her about the blackmail, right?"

I think back to the night of the charity ball, the night this entire case shifted. "Yes."

"Maybe Celine questioned Grady about it and he panicked. Blackmail and invasion of privacy are serious offenses. He'd earn jail time if Celine went to the police. And with that, we could have our motive for killing her."

I scan the board again. We have a lot of solid information, but it's trailing off in too many maybes. My eyes settle on the bottom right corner of the whiteboard, a boxed-off section that reads "vase." It's an outlier, with no direct connection to the other sequence of events, but with dollar signs and a large question mark above it. "So where does this vase come in?"

"Celine bought it on November eighth, based on her records. That's a week before she died. But there's no mention of that bowl—the gift for Everett's mother that you saw in his apartment—anywhere."

True. I chew the inside of my mouth in thought. Why wouldn't she document it, like she had everything else? A thought strikes me. "Because her records are for her collection. That bowl was always meant to be a gift."

Doug pauses. "That would make sense. So she found the dragon vase, started researching it that week, got excited by what she thought she had found. Was ready to post about it on her blog. Was probably typing up the post when Jace Everett came over that night to pick up the gift."

"He said she was drunk and emotional."

"I can see why," Zac mutters more to himself, shaking his head.

"So if what Jace says is true, and she was fine—albeit 'drunk and emotional,' but alive—when he left, then Grady could have used the window to slip in." He says he fixed that lock a week before Celine died, but maybe he didn't fix it until after, to hide his method of access. I have to question everything Grady's ever told me. "But there were no signs of a struggle, no screaming or fighting that anyone reported."

"Anyone being the two senior citizens with hearing aids?" Zac reminds us. "She's got Ruby across the hall and Mr. Sherwood next door. Plus, she was drunk. Maybe they 'reconciled,'" Zac air quotes, earning my frown.

Doug quickly dismisses it. "Autopsy says there was no evidence of sexual intercourse that night."

"So Grady slipped the drugs into her drink without her knowing. And then took her phone and diary, to hide anything that might connect the two of them."

"They were talking, and she tells him about the vase—she would have been excited, how could she not tell somebody?—and then she passes out and he can't help but take it."

"Or maybe Jace somehow smuggled it out in that box when she wasn't paying attention, and Grady killed her out of anger and fear, and it has nothing to do with the vase."

Doug sighs. "Maybe." He sets the marker down. "Or maybe no

one killed her. Maybe that part happened just like the police report said it did."

I still refuse to believe that, even though the logical side of me says I should at least consider it. That there was much more going on in Celine's world than I had any idea of, and in a moment of weakness, it might have felt like too much for her to bear.

How much of what we're conjuring is true? All of it? None of it? While these revelations about Grady make me sick, I feel like we're getting closer than ever to the truth.

My ringing phone cuts into the sudden quiet in the basement. I don't want to answer it, but I could also use the distraction.

"It's Hans," I mutter, looking at the screen before I answer. "Hey."

"I just got a call from my friend over at an auction house in the Garment District. You are not going to believe this!" He's practically stumbling over his words, he's talking so fast. "A man by the name of James just left a message for him on his voice mail, asking him to call him back about a vase that he would like to have appraised. He left a phone number and everything."

"Are you kidding me?" I stare at Doug and Zac in shock.

This seems far too easy.

CHAPTER 40

Maggie

"He doesn't know that we know about the vase, right?" Doug's eyebrows spike.

"I didn't say anything."

"What about her?" He jerks his head in the direction of the door, and Ruby beyond.

"She knows. She's good at keeping secrets."

"So then there's no reason for him *not* to call up an appraiser," Doug surmises, pacing the empty floors of Celine's apartment. He holds his phone to his ear, squinting with concentration, and I know that he's listening to Grady's message again. The appraiser sent over an audio recording after Doug demanded it.

I've heard it twice already, and I don't need to hear it again. Even with all the competing background noise, there's no doubt that it's Grady.

"I thought he wouldn't go through an appraiser if he stole the vase and has these Chinese connections of his," I say.

"All speculation. He's obviously near a train station. I wish I knew which one. Zac could tap into their security feeds and . . ."

I let Doug's voice drift off as I try to come to terms with this turn of events. As I wallow in regret for ever trusting a guy like Grady, I can certainly see why Celine did. He may be a crazy stalker, but he wears a convincing cloak of a nice, totally normal guy. All these sickos probably do.

And I fell for the act.

". . . He'll call me as soon as he's made the appointment with Grady." Doug's voice drifts backs into my consciousness. "In the meantime," he marches over to the bathroom and begins stuffing my toiletries into my bag, "you're packing up your things and staying at a hotel. I don't want you in this building anymore. Plus"—he casts an arm around the vacant apartment—"it's your dead friend's empty apartment. It can't be good for your mental state. I'll do surveillance outside. He's not leaving the building without me knowing it. Please don't fight me, Maggie."

"Fine."

He stops. "Fine? Seriously?"

I don't want to be in here anymore either. "Let me just pack my things and let Ruby know."

His stubby finger comes up.

"I know." I roll my eyes. "Don't say anything about the investigation."

December 18, 2015

"What do you mean, he bolted?" I sit up in my hotel bed, frowning at my reflection. The rooms in this boutique hotel are standard New York issue—closet-sized. I guess the designer figured that putting a floor-to-ceiling mirror opposite the bed would trick patrons into thinking the three-hundred-dollar-per-night room wasn't a jail cell.

I hear Doug take a sip of his coffee.

"He couldn't have. Why bother phoning the appraiser then?" I argue.

"Maybe the appraiser tipped him off. Someone must have."

It's been three days since "James" called the appraiser. Three days of waiting for him to return the message that the appraiser—with a carefully worded script from Doug—left on his voice mail. Three days since Grady used his cell phone, according to Zac, who has been monitoring activity on that number through a hack into the phone company. Three days of Doug sitting outside Celine's old building and not seeing a single hint of Grady.

"But when would they have tipped him off?"

"Had to be before I started surveillance."

"Or he waited until you were going to the bathroom or sleeping to slip out."

"I've got cameras angled at both the door and the fire exit, and Zac's watching those while I step away. I haven't missed him. This isn't my first stakeout," Doug snaps. "But guess who *did* come out about twenty minutes ago, with a plate of shortbread?" His tone is thick with accusation.

"She called me yesterday morning, but I did *not* tell her you were there. I swear."

"I know, because Zac's monitoring your calls. She said she saw me yesterday when she was getting her mail."

Part of me wants to yell at him for the invasion of privacy, but I find more satisfaction in needling him than reprimanding him. "So the eighty-one-year-old woman with Coke bottle glasses busted your cover? You sure it's not your first stakeout?"

He ignores my dig. "She came down to express her concern over Grady. Apparently she called him two days ago to fix her drain and he hasn't called back or stopped by. Normally she gets an answer within three or four hours." There's a long pause, and then a rushed "Gotta go."

Anxious flutters erupt in my stomach. "Is he there? Do you see him?"

"Nope." The phone cuts off.

And I'm left glaring at my reflection, trying to figure out what the hell Doug is up to now.

Six hours later, with a phone call from Ruby, I finally find out.

CHAPTER 41

Maggie

"Do you live on this floor, ma'am?"

"No, but I—"

"Then I'll have to ask that you go back to your apartment and let us run our investigation." The police officer ushers me backward, toward the stairwell. Another officer stands outside Grady's open door, on guard. I can't see inside, but it's not hard to spot the yellow caution tape at the door.

"Can you at least tell me what happened to him?"

"Are you family?"

"Yes!" I exclaim without thinking.

"No, she isn't. Maggie, don't get in their way," Doug's stern voice calls out from behind me. I turn to find him and Detective Childs walking side by side down the hallway.

Childs's dark but kind eyes land on me. "Miss Sparkes. You're still here."

"I am. And now, so are you." Turning to Doug, I add, "But I thought we didn't have enough evidence for the police to get involved?"

"It's a Missing Persons case. Of course the police have to get involved."

I glance back at the door with a frown. "Grady's *missing*?"

"Yeah. Several tenants were concerned about his safety, so Ruby Cummings, down on the third floor, reported it to NYPD this morning." Doug's wide-eyed glare stalls my tongue. I have no clue what angle he's playing at here, but I hope it works. I guess in one way it already has.

We're now in his apartment.

Well, the police are.

"I didn't think you were Missing Persons, Detective Childs."

He shrugs. "I was just finishing up on a case nearby and heard about this one. Recognized the address, so I thought I'd stop by." His gaze drifts past me, to the open door. "Sounds like there could be some things of interest in there. If you'll excuse me now." He steps past me and makes his way toward the apartment door and a middle-aged white man who must have arrived from another direction. He greets him with a handshake and a "Good to see you, Detective Patterson."

"What is going on?" I hiss.

"Exactly what I just said. Tenants called in reporting their super missing, and the police have to respond."

"By breaking in? They can do that?"

"After checking all the local hospitals and contacting his next-of-kin without luck . . . yes. They will check a person's place of residence and use whatever force is necessary to get in. Given the guy is the super and the owner is out of the country, this was the only way."

"But Grady's not here." At least I assume he's not. "What happens now?"

Doug takes a long, drawn-out sip from his coffee cup, but I can feel the excitement radiating from him. "Normally, if the person isn't in the apartment, they'd just walk right back out and continue their search elsewhere. But if they were to find something suspicious or criminal sitting in plain sight, then they'd have to act on it. Probably launch an investigation into the individual, while trying to find him. Which means they'll have to get a search warrant to inspect his personal belongings."

It finally clicks. "The marijuana plants." I turn around to watch the officers milling about the hall. "They're waiting for the search warrant to go back in."

"Should be here soon." Doug links his arm through mine, pulling me toward the stairwell, but not before a single nod toward Childs—a silent acknowledgment that I can't decipher but also don't miss.

"I know it has been under the most unpleasant of circumstances, but I've really enjoyed this time with you," Ruby offers, her spoon clanging against the china. She didn't bat an eye at my suggestion that I drag her kitchen chairs and TV tray over to Celine's empty apartment, so that she could join me for a cup of tea. It was a smart idea on my part. Even thirty seconds inside her apartment caused me tunnel vision.

I smile from my spot on the floor, with the wall acting as my backrest.

My attention is split between the door and my phone, waiting to hear from Doug or Childs, or both. Doug's phone rang an hour ago, and he disappeared immediately after, insisting that I stay put and not get involved because it would be a risk to the investigation. I complied, and now I'm going to go crazy.

"Same here, Ruby. Are you sure I can't persuade you to come to San Diego with me for the holidays?" I mentioned it to her last week, when Taryn was booking my flight home for me. I would gladly book a ticket for her, too.

"Oh, you're too kind. I'm sure San Diego is lovely, but I think I'll stay. Theodore has invited me over for dinner. He has a large family."

"Wow. From dancing to tea to an invitation to Christmas dinner with family in, what . . . five days?"

"You have to move fast at my age. Never know when you're not going to wake up one morning."

"I have a feeling you'll outlive all of us, Ruby."

She chuckles. "And besides, I don't know that any airline would let someone my age fly across the country."

I roll my eyes. "Don't be ridiculous."

"So when are you leaving, again?"

"I have a one-way ticket booked for the morning of the twenty-third. The charity auction is on the twenty-second." We'll see when I need to book a ticket back.

"Well, won't that be nice." Deafening silence falls over the apartment as Ruby sips her tea, until I'm forced to my feet to pace around the old woman perched in her chair. I wonder if I could just sit in the stairwell and listen. Maybe I could catch—

"If Doug said not to go up there, then I think you should listen to him," Ruby warns, somehow reading my mind.

"I'm going crazy. I need a distraction. Do you have a TV in your place?" I can't believe I'm considering even stepping in there.

"Heavens no. I don't waste time with that sort of thing. I'd rather spend my time reading. Or writing, lately."

"You're still writing?" I size up those small, wrinkled old hands.

"Oh, yes!" Her eyes sparkle. "In fact, I've gotten further in this story that I'm working on than any other one in the last twenty years. It's a page-turner. A mystery thriller."

She's very obviously excited. "So tell me about it."

"Not yet." She grins secretly. "It's not finished."

I smile. "I'd like to read it when it is. In fact I'm going to buy all your books when I'm in San Diego."

"Well, that will certainly help with my royalty checks."

Doug's telltale stomps sound seconds before he barges through the door.

Ruby and I both stare at him expectantly.

"They found a vase matching the description of the one stolen from Celine's collection. It was tucked away in the hallway closet. They're dusting for fingerprints right now."

My mouth drops open. Wait. It's been in Grady's apartment the entire time? "He just left it there?"

"Looks like it. They also found an iPhone 6 with a pink sparkly case—"

"Celine had a pink sparkly case!" Ruby confirms eagerly.

Doug nods. "And a shoe box with several pairs of women's panties, a red lipstick, and a few candid shots of Celine."

I take a deep, shaky breath. "Candid, like walking across the street?"

Doug twists his mouth. "More like she's lying in her bed, asleep."

"Oh my God," I whisper, shivers running down my spine. Grady was a bona fide fucking weirdo. And I was sleeping with him.

"I think they call those 'trophy boxes'?" Ruby offers.

"Or a shrine. He clearly felt something strong for her. But we haven't seen anything that indicates he ever meant her any harm."

"You mean like Celine's dead body?" I glare pointedly at Doug.

Doug ignores my sarcasm. "He has a serious network of computers in there. They've seized them and are taking them back to their tech experts."

Hope sparks. "So if they find videos of Celine on there—"

"Then Childs will have enough to reopen Celine's investigation. I've just now filled him in on what we know. Both on and off the record."

I grab hold of his forearm, suddenly remembering. "What about the missing diary? Did they find it? We *need* that. I need to see it." As hard as it will be, I need to read Celine's last thoughts. I need to know what went on. Did she suspect Grady of anything? Was she afraid of Grady at all?

Doug shakes his head. "Nothing like that yet."

"Dammit." I release my grip on him.

"But this is all still good, isn't it?" Ruby asks, nodding her encouragement toward me. "It looks like we were right."

A slight frown touches Doug's brow. "Yeah. Maybe."

CHAPTER 42

Celine

August 20, 2015

"You don't think Ruby heard us, do you?" She's like a grandmother to me. Having her know what I'm doing to pay my bills would be almost as bad as my mother finding out.

Grady settles back, tucking his arm behind his head. "Nah. She's usually asleep at this time. Plus this bed's quiet." He pauses. "Why? Has she mentioned anything to you?"

"She's not going to come right out and say it." I pull the sheet up to cover my nakedness, but Grady promptly yanks it down, his brow arched, his smile devilish. That's one of his requirements: that my body is on display for him whenever he's paying for it.

His eyes trail over my breasts and stomach, and I see the excitement in them. I figure he'll be ready for another round in about ten minutes. That's another requirement—the special five-hundred-dollar rate I'm giving him is for the full night, until he's ready to climb back up the fire escape, to whatever it is he does in that apartment of his that apparently no one has ever stepped foot inside.

That's usually not for a few hours, as I learned after the first paid night here, nearly three weeks ago now.

"How is that security camera working out for you?" he asks, as if we're two lovers having a casual conversation.

"It's great. Thank you. I feel safer already."

"Good."

"You think I'm nuts, don't you?" Every once in a while, I've come home to this eerie sense that someone has been in my apartment. A shifted clock. A drawer that's open a crack. A slightly rumpled duvet. Things that a normal person probably wouldn't notice but because of my need for tidiness and order, I do. Then I tell myself that I'm crazy, that it's just nerves over living alone in this giant city.

But I've been coming home to that eerie sense more and more lately.

I mentioned it to Grady last week. He chuckled a little, but then recommended I install a discreet camera just for peace of mind. He even offered to get one for me and set it up.

"Maybe a little." He rolls to face me, reaching out to push a strand of hair off my face. "But that's okay. We're all a little bit nuts, aren't we?"

"Yeah. I guess."

I'm used to putting on a sexy dress and a mask of makeup and heading out to an impersonal hotel to spend an hour or two—depending on how much the client is paying for—and then parting ways.

I'm not used to lying in bed on Thursday night in a tank top and boxers, my face washed clean of mascara and lipstick, only to have a client tap on my window. And I'm definitely not used to lying around in bed and talking with ease afterward.

This is beginning to feel like a relationship.

"I don't get it, Grady," I finally blurt out. "You're a really attractive guy. You don't need to spend five hundred dollars a week for sex. You could find someone amazing out there."

His finger trails along the length of my arm, giving me goose bumps. "You don't want my money?"

"I didn't say *that*." The first round of Mom's medical bills have come through, putting a dent in my bank account. I don't have a choice. I *need* this. "I just . . . I'm trying to understand."

"I'm not big on relationships. They take a lot of work and commitment."

And Grady doesn't seem too eager for either. Which is why he'll never be the guy for me.

But Jace Everett is.

And Jace Everett finally called my direct line at the office and asked that I take him out on one of my "treasure hunts."

I've stopped going on them, seeing as I'll be packing or selling my collection. But for a man like Jace Everett, I'll gladly plan a route. Maybe I can persuade him to take the train with me out to Hudson, to hit up the antique shops. Or better yet, we could drive upstate, to Bloomfield Antique Country Mile. Of course, that would be an overnight thing . . .

"What are you smiling about?" Grady asks.

I press my lips tight because I'm getting ahead of myself. It's just one date. A date I haven't even told Dani about, because Dani and Marnie are close, and it'll get back to Jace's assistant, Natasha. We all know she has a thing for her boss. Plus, it could be nothing. Maybe he really does just want my help with finding a gift for his mother. Maybe this is just a friendly outing.

"Nothing. I'm just happy."

"Yeah . . . me too," he says with a wry smile, reaching over to slide his hand up my inner thigh, pushing my legs apart.

September 5, 2015

I am in love with this man.

It's only taken two dates to know this for a fact. Now I can simply enjoy gazing at him as he discusses the sommelier's bottle of wine with the grace of a man born and bred into a world of high expectations, his perfect features cast under the dim light.

Because I know that I have found the man I have been looking for. He's handsome and educated and driven—God, is he ever driven—and, best of all, he appreciates my own career interests.

With glasses poured—our second pricey bottle—and alone once again, Jace turns back to me. "All right. Where was I . . . Why are you smiling?"

"Because I'm having a good time." I don't want him to know that I'm in love with him just yet. That might scare him away.

His head falls back with his laugh. "Talking politics is enjoyable to you? Or is it the wine?"

"I will gladly listen to you talk politics all night long, as long as you remember it when I'm neck deep in Chinese dynasty research and need to tell somebody about it."

"Deal." He reaches across the table and takes my hand, and my stomach instantly does a flip. He kissed me goodnight after our first date, which was only supposed to last the afternoon and ended up dragging well into the evening. I've been waiting desperately for him to do it again today, but he's been a perfect gentleman. "You know, you're something else, Celine. I had a feeling about you, from the moment I started talking to you at that auction house."

"What do you mean?"

With a light squeeze, he releases my fingers to lift his glass. I meet it in a toast, his eyes twinkling as he watches me through a measured sip. "You have this perfect balance to you. You appreciate the finer things, but I can tell you also value the little things; things money can't buy. And you're obviously working hard for this career of yours. I grew up around spoiled brats who don't know how to sacrifice for something they want, and who've had everything handed to them. That's not you. You don't take anything for granted."

My cheeks flush with his compliments.

"I wish we'd started this sooner. Sometimes I get so wrapped up in work that weeks can go by before I let any part of my personal life in."

"You're not completely to blame. Lately, my weekends have been tied up." I've flown back to California twice since we met at Hollingsworth; two red-eye flights for the weekend, to see my mother.

Sympathy overtakes his handsome features. "How are you doing with all of that?"

I force a brave smile. "She started her radiation treatments. We'll see how much it helps." I'm trying not to dwell on the fact that there's no hope; it's only a matter of time now.

He scoops up my hand again, only this time he pulls my knuckles to his mouth, and kisses them so softly, making my stomach flutter. God, not only is my mother dying, but now I have to face moving across the country and leaving this beautiful man behind. We just only found each other. Will these next three months with me be enough to hold his attention until I come back?

As if reading my mind, he says, "San Diego is just a plane ride away. And it's only temporary."

He's already thinking about long term, too.

I force down the bubble of excitement. Still, he must be able to hear it in my voice when I push. "So . . . your dad . . ." I want to know everything there is to know about Jace Everett.

"Yes, to answer your question about my dad, he never truly stops campaigning. He's always rubbing shoulders with this person or another, looking for support. He has a bit of a break now, though, since winning the election last year."

"Is he going to run again in 2018?"

"I think so, but we'll see. He loves the politics, but can't stand the opposition. They've been vicious through both elections, especially in this last one, last year. The initial front runner was ruthless; he had no qualms about hitting below the belt. Three days after my dad announced that he was running again, they dragged my mother into the spotlight with some story about her abusing our housekeepers. It was fucking ridiculous. When you meet my mom, you'll see that it is. She's the sweetest woman alive."

He wants me to meet his mother.

"They've gone after me, too. First with some bogus story that I was embezzling investors' money, and when they couldn't make that one stick with public opinion, they got hold of a story about a female coworker that I dated for a short time."

"What about her?" I've heard this story. It was the talk of the building.

He hesitates. "She was still technically married, but very much separated from her husband," he quickly adds. "They spun it to make it look like I was some home-wrecking womanizer who doesn't value the sanctity of marriage, and that she was trying to sleep her way to the top. It wrecked her reputation and her career. She left soon after."

"That's horrible. Can't you sue them for that?" I ask out loud, but inside the worry is already churning. What would happen if the media started digging into me? Could they uncover my secret? It would be a lot juicier than what he's describing. Just the thought of it . . . It'd be blasted all over the place. All over the state of Illinois, at least. That means the Sparkes would find out, and Maggie would find out. Oh my God, Maggie would flip! And my mother . . .

The last thing she needs to hear about on her deathbed is this.

"No, they use anonymous mouthpieces on social media to blast rumors out there, so it can never be tied back to them." He takes another sip. "So, if you have any skeletons in your closet, you should probably warn me about them now."

I force a smile and shake my head.

And hope that it's believable.

"You look worried," he notes with a frown.

"I'm just . . ." I scramble to explain what he obviously sees. "I don't know how I'd feel about someone delving into my life like that. I'm a very private person."

He reaches over to take my hand again. "We just won't let them find out about you. For now, anyway."

"I like that idea." That could work. Keep this quiet until I'm back from San Diego. Until he's fallen in love with me, and will forgive me, should my past ever come out. Because it'll all be in the past by then. "Maybe we should set some ground rules then."

His eyebrow spikes with amusement. "Ground rules?"

"Yes. Especially for at work. There's a lot of water cooler talk around there." I add with a blush, "And you're a hot topic." So far we've somehow avoided notice, but if Jace starts calling my work line or we start meeting in the lobby or anything like that, everyone's going to know within a day.

"Whatever makes you comfortable," he says easily. "I don't want you to worry. I'll take good care of you."

I smile.

And believe him.

October 26, 2015

I throw the door open on the second knock.

"Hey." Grady frowns when he sees my face, eyes puffy and skin splotchy from hours of crying. "Your text said that your toilet's not working?"

"That's right." My voice is barely higher than a whisper. I step back to make room for him and his tool bag. As soon as the door shuts, he heads for my cramped bathroom without another word. It's been radio silence between us for more than two weeks, since I told him our arrangement was over.

That was the day after Jace came here to pulverize my heart.

I should have said no when I ran into Raymond. He was my very first client, back when a date was just that—a friendly casual outing, with no hotel rooms involved. But he had a company function the next night and no date, and I had just found out that day that Dani and her fiancé can't move in until February which meant I'd have to cover another month of rent, and my savings were almost gone. So I said yes.

I'm so stupid for saying yes.

I deserve what happened. I deserve that Jace found out and came here to confront me the night before we were supposed to fly to Chicago to meet his parents.

I deserve being treated like a whore.

But what I don't deserve is what Grady is doing.

"What exactly is wrong with the toilet?" he calls from the bathroom. When I don't answer, he finally emerges. That's when I throw the computer camera at his head.

"You're the one who's blackmailing him, aren't you!" Even in anger, I'm careful not to yell. This building is full of gossips.

He stares at me, cool and calm. "What are you talking about, Celine?"

I hate his accent when he's like this. He sounds so goddamn condescending. "Someone has been spying on me, using this camera that *you* installed."

"Well, I'm sorry, but those cameras aren't completely hack-proof. So . . . I assume there's nothing wrong with your toilet then?" He heads for the door.

I grab his arm to stop him. "It was you. Admit it. You've been watching me. You didn't like that I was seeing someone else, did you?"

"Did he know that you were fucking me, too?" he asks without missing a beat, a flare of anger in his voice.

"He knows now." I can no longer hold the tears in. And here, I thought I was done crying. "And he wants nothing to do with me."

Grady sets his bag down on the coffee table and wraps his arms around my back, pulling me into his chest. His hand strokes my hair soothingly. "Maybe he wasn't the right guy for you then."

"He was! He's the perfect man for me. He's everything that I want, and now he thinks I'm blackmailing him. And that video . . ." I'm barely coherent through my sobs. "If that gets out and my mother finds out, I'll kill myself."

"Don't talk like that."

"It's true!" I stopped taking my Xanax in August, even though I knew that I shouldn't. My depression tends to creep in quietly, unnoticed, until it's already taken up residence in my brain. But the pills cost me money and make my limbs swell, and I was feeling better. *And* I normally have eight or nine months before I have to restart. But with my mother's illness, and now this devastating breakup, the depression is marching in behind a ticker tape parade, not even three months later.

"It's not. Don't be stupid. You were seeing him for, what . . . not even two months," he mutters, his tone turning angry. "That's not long enough to mean anything."

"Time doesn't matter when the connection is that strong." I pause and frown. "So you knew I was dating someone?" He never said a thing. He kept crawling through my window once a week to screw me, sometimes staying in my bed until morning, only to leave a wad of money on my nightstand.

And how does he know how long I've been seeing Jace?

Has Grady been watching me all this time?

His body stiffens against me.

I push away to see the momentary panic flash before he veils it. And we're back to where we started. "Why are you doing this to me?"

"I'm not doing anything to you." His scruff-covered jaw tightens. "And I'd be very careful about accusing me of anything. Otherwise, who knows what'll end up on the Internet."

I'm left staring at the back of my door long after he's gone, his threat heard loud and clear.

CHAPTER 43

Maggie

December 22, 2015

"I want you and Zac to keep looking for him, until you find him. Find out what hole he's run scared to. He's not getting away with this." The doorman holds the heavy glass door open for Doug and me to pass through.

Inside, a low hum of voices mix with the solo pianist playing from the far corner. The exhibit hall in Hollingsworth—exquisite on its own, in soothing grays and warm wood and crystal chandeliers—is decked out for the holidays, with evergreen bows and bronzed urns overflowing with white poinsettias. They've dimmed the lights throughout, making each piece of Celine's collection in its individual glass case truly shine under the spotlights.

"Having Childs onboard with getting this investigation reopened helps, but I have to warn you, Maggie, a guy like Grady knows how to disappear in the wind."

He's already been "in the wind" for seven days, four since the police invaded his apartment. It took NYPD's technical experts thirty-six hours to break into Grady's "Fort Knox" computer system. While they have enough secured and encrypted files to keep them busy for months, they were able to get into the video files—including the hidden ones.

Grady has been watching Celine in her apartment since August. The police won't tell us exactly how much footage there is—they won't tell us much of anything—but they did say that there was plenty of evidence to suggest they had an intimate relationship.

Translation: The sick fuck recorded them having sex and saved it to watch later.

But that wasn't the biggest shocker.

Apparently, there have been others. Specifically, two women that Grady has, at minimum, spied on in the past. Police are trying to identify them, to confirm whether anything untoward happened.

"You have to find him."

Doug squeezes my shoulder. "And you have to get on that plane tomorrow morning and spend whatever time you have left with Celine's mother. There's nothing more you can do here."

"You're right." Soon, I'll be away from this city and this never-ending fucking nightmare. As much as I want the police to find Grady, I've done what I intended to do, which was get them to reopen the investigation.

Now it's time for me to be home with Rosa. I still haven't decided what I'm going to tell her. There's really no good news yet. No *your daughter didn't kill herself* announcement. But there's at least doubt now in everyone's mind, and enough motive pointing toward Grady. Doug no longer looks at me with that sympathetic smile.

Hans storms toward us, his steps swift and purposeful, his suit plum-colored and stylish. "Finally!" He blows air kisses before I know what's happening, and then turns his attention to Doug, eying him up and down with the same look of disdain that he gave me that first day we met at Celine's.

"And on that note," Doug glances around a sea of formal wear—Hans insisted on a black tie event in Celine's honor—and smooths his bomber jacket over his chest. "Enjoy the warmth of California. I'll be in touch with any updates."

I smile. "Thanks for everything, Doug." Watching him leave, I call out, "And tell Zac to stay out of my business. It's not right what he can do."

A backward wave answers me and then Doug is gone, and Hans is thrusting a champagne flute into my hand and linking arms with me. He pulls us into the fray of antique lovers and partygoers and people who generally have too much time and money on their hands. There are quite a few of them.

"Celine would have loved this," I murmur, a lump forming in my throat. I wash it down with three sizeable gulps of my drink.

"Can you believe she had enough to fill the entire gallery, and then some?"

"Yes, I can." I laugh, taking a sip of my champagne. "I packed it all, remember?"

"It's a shame about that vase. I was so sure that if she thought it was something, then it definitely was . . . She always kept her expectations low when it came to her treasure hunts, and I don't know how she could have mistaken cookie-cutter shit." He tsks. "She had a better eye than that. She must not have been thinking straight."

"I know."

Much to our disappointment, the vase found in Grady's closet was a reproduction of the famous Qing Dynasty twin vase.

And not a very good one, at that.

But the pieces that are here tonight are stunning. Hans obviously spent a lot of time going through Celine's collection and hand-selecting the best ones to include. Now, as we move past each and every display, Hans gives me the CliffsNotes version of its history as I polish off two more glasses of champagne.

"Her collection belongs in one of the top auction houses in New York, doesn't it?" I murmur.

"*The* top auction house," he corrects me, "and yes. It does. She always had a special eye. You could see it, just by walking into her apartment. It was like walking into an art studio. Trust me, I've gone into plenty of antique shops, and with that many pieces, it usually feels like walking into a shed of random castaways that I want to run screaming from. But with Celine, she managed to amass a collection of a thousand pieces, each one hand-selected for its historical value and beauty, and then turn her apartment into a masterpiece that you could sit back and enjoy. She wasn't just a collector, she was a curator."

He's right. I hadn't thought of it that way, but Celine's apartment was a piece of art in and of itself.

Hans gestures toward the middle of the gallery, drawing my attention to the elderly couple arm-in-arm. Ruby spots me and grins, patting the hand of the white-haired man I recognize from the ball. They slowly shuffle over.

"Hans, you've outdone yourself! Celine would love this," she exclaims, grabbing Hans by the arms until he leans in for a kiss on her cheek.

"How long have you been here?"

"Oh, awhile, but you two looked like you were having so much fun, we didn't want to disturb you." She gestures to her date. "This is the Honorable Theodore Higgins."

"Just Teddy," the man chuckles, shaking our hands.

"We're going to head out now. Theodore needs his rest, and I'm quite tired after all the excitement we've had going on recently."

"Yes, Ruby filled me in," Theodore says, frowning deeply. "If there's anything at all I can help with, let me know. I may be retired, but I still have plenty of connections."

I smile. "Thank you. I'll keep that in mind."

Theodore makes his way to the coat check, while Ruby takes both my hands in hers. "So? I suppose this is it?"

"Until I fly out here for some afternoon tea," I promise, wrapping my arms around the tiny, frail woman, a sheen of tears forming over my eyes that I quickly try to blink away.

She has a surprising grip and squeezes me tight. "You are quite the character, Maggie Sparkes," she whispers, winking at me as she goes to join her date.

"Oh shit." Hans groans, pulling my attention back to him and the sharp-looking middle-aged woman in a suit waving him down from across the room. "I've gotta go, too. That's the boss. I need to kiss her ass for letting us do this."

"And she can kiss *my* ass for paying for it," I mumble under my breath, earning that high-pitched, awkward laughter of his. "Listen,

I'm probably going to head back to my hotel now. My flight in the morning is early, and I'm practically asleep on my feet. And drunk, I think."

"Oh." He turns his bottom lip in an exaggerated pout. "So this is it for us, too?"

"I know you're not the hugging type. Neither am I." I wrap my arms around him anyway. "Thank you for everything." When he pulls away, I'm surprised to see his eyes are shining.

"I'll call you," he promises.

I laugh. "No you won't."

"Fine. But I'll text. Maybe. Once in a while."

I smile and wave good-bye as he trots off to answer the director's request, abandoning me in front of Celine's doll collection.

"It doesn't matter where you are, it feels like they're watching you, doesn't it?" a deep male voice says beside me.

I turn to find Jace standing there. He doesn't even need a tux; his high-end suit and wool overcoat fit the bill for a black tie affair.

"What are you doing here?"

His blue eyes gaze over the mingling crowd. "I was invited, remember?"

"Under the circumstances, I figured you'd decline."

"Yeah, I know. But I thought I'd stop by on my way home from a work event. Pay my respects, in a way." It does sort of feel like that's what Jace is doing. He's solemn tonight, and the way he's standing with his hands clasped in front of a glass case—it reminds me of how people stand at gravesites.

"But after everything . . ."

His Adam's apple bobs with a hard swallow. "I'm sorry about how things ended for her. And for how I treated her that night." His gaze dips down to my red-painted lips. "And for how I treated you."

A shocked laugh escapes me. "I'm the one who owes you an apology. I accused you of murdering her."

"Oh, yeah. You did." A tiny smile curls his lips, but it doesn't reach his eyes. "Is the witch hunt finally over?"

I sigh. "Not exactly, but you're not the witch anymore. You were right about the super." It stings to admit that.

He nods grimly. "I'm sorry that I was." Awkward silence hangs between us. "Although I'm surprised he had it in him."

"We're still not exactly sure *what* he had in him, but he definitely looks guilty of a lot of things right now. They found Celine's stolen vase in his apartment, at the very least. The cops are onto him now. They're reopening her case."

"The infamous vase." He glances around. "Where is it? I'd love to see it."

"In evidence" is all I say.

"Ah, yes. Of course." A pause. "You're not still staying in her apartment, are you?"

"No. I'm at a hotel now. I'm actually leaving for San Diego in the morning."

"What about the super?"

"Don't know. Looks like he ran the second he sensed that we were onto him. Left everything behind, including a lot of incriminating evidence." As I say this, I realize something. Given what I put Jace through, I probably owe him a warning. "Listen, they've seized his computer, and it's very likely they're going to find that video of you and Celine on there."

His eyes widen. "So he's the one who tried to blackmail me."

"Yeah. Most likely. I don't think Celine had anything to do with it. And if it comes out, it wasn't me who told them. I swear."

He chews the inside of his mouth. "I guess I'll just have to deal with that if and when it comes up then." He sighs. "One way or another, I just hope this brings you and her mother the peace you need."

"So do I." Another lump is forming in my throat, and I take a sip of my champagne to keep it down. I really should stop drinking.

Jace's eyes skate over my simple black gown. "You look stunning tonight."

"Thanks." I feel my cheeks flush. From the moment I first laid eyes on Jace, I was sizing him up for a crime. This is the first time I'm seeing him without outright animosity and suspicion. I'm seeing him as just a man. The man my best friend was pining over and banking all her future dreams on.

"In another time, and another place, I think this could have worked," he says, and I know he's not talking about our business relationship.

"If you stopped counting money."

"And you stopped trying to save the world."

In reality, Jace and I would mix together like oil and water, but it's a nice amicable way of leaving things.

He does a quick scan of the room. "I'm going to head out now. I have an early flight in the morning, too."

"Heading to Chicago?"

"For an entire two weeks. Can you believe it? First time ever, I think. But my mother's birthday is just after Christmas. We have a big party planned."

"Right. You need to give her that Ming bowl."

He purses his lips tight, in a worried way. "Take care of yourself, Maggie. I hope we can wish only the best for each other."

"Yes, definitely."

He leans in to place a soft kiss on my cheek, and then Jace Everett is gone, out the door.

Out of my life.

I last another ten minutes and then head for the coat check to retrieve my stole—which is a ridiculous article of clothing to wear now that the temperatures have dropped to single digits—and leave. The entrance to the auction house is on a narrow side street, and while I know that cabs will make the turn down here every once in a while, I won't last a minute in this cold standing still.

About fifty yards up, I spot Jace leaning against a sleek black car—presumably his—his phone pressed to his ear. He looks up, likely at the sound of my heels on a metal sidewalk grate. "Yeah . . . okay . . . listen, I'll call tomorrow after I land . . . Okay. Talk to ya." Hanging up, he stands. "Maggie, get in. I'll give you a ride."

"It's only a few blocks away. I can grab a taxi."

"Come on." He opens the door rather abruptly. "Get in. I promise, my car smells way cleaner than any taxi."

I'm relieved. On a night like this, with the holidays, it could take me time to hail a cab. "Thanks." I climb in, tucking the hem of my dress under my legs, brushing fresh, fluffy flakes off the material. It's pretty outside, the trees lining the street covered in snow and sparkling with tiny white lights. He shuts the door for me and then rounds the car quickly. "You're right. It does smell better." It smells like Jace's cologne.

"See?" He presses the ignition button and the car comes alive. Cracking a bottle of water, he takes a sip. "Thirsty?"

"Yes, actually. I think I had a few too many glasses of champagne, and flying hungover all the way to San Diego is going to suck."

"Here." He pulls another bottle out from the console and twists the cap to open it before handing it to me. "So, do you think everything will sell tonight?"

I chug back a large gulp as he pulls out onto the street. "I hope so. Hans said there was a lot of interest expressed. I guess I'll find out tomorrow."

His fingers tap over the steering wheel at a fast, almost nervous, rhythm, and he makes a right-hand turn.

"I'm sorry, I think my hotel is the other way, just a few blocks."

"Right, sorry. I don't know why I assumed you were staying close to Park Avenue. I should have asked. I'll go around."

"No worries." Silence fills the car. "What happened to your knuckles?" I ask, spying scrapes and bruising across his right hand.

"Just some boxing. It's my way of relieving stress." He shrugs it off.

I focus my attention on the pretty brownstones on this street, covered in wreaths and lit with festive lights. "I hate to admit it, but the city is pretty during the holidays."

"It is. When were you here last over Christmas?"

"It's been forever."

"Let me take you around a bit then." He makes a left, and suddenly we're driving past a row of horses and carriages outside Central Park, the horses wearing red coats, the carriages decked out in festive bows and baubles, waiting for tourists. Jace changes lanes to avoid an asshole taxi driver who is going so fast that the taillights blur in my eyes.

"I don't know how you drive in this city. I think I'd go crazy."

His chuckle—sounding deeper than normal—fills the car. "I try not to, unless I have to." Even his voice sounds deeper than usual. "Hey, what do you think will happen with this police investigation?"

"I don't know, honestly. They better do their jobs this time around, though." I guess I can't blame them, really. The official autopsy report arrived just yesterday, confirming that Celine died from a lethal combination of narcotics, ingested. To anyone looking at the facts, her case looks like a suicide. Thankfully we all know better now.

My body is beginning to sink into the comfortable passenger seat, exhausted. I let my head fall back against the headrest, and I close my eyes for just a moment. Thank God I left the auction house when I did. The frenetic pace of the past few days is catching up to me. "I'm keeping Doug and Zac on retainer until Grady's found."

"Won't that be something if the real vase turns up, after all the media attention this story will generate?"

He makes a right-hand turn, and I'm pretty sure we're driving in the opposite direction of my hotel, but I figure he's taking me on the scenic route. "The media's not getting hold of this story, if I have anything to do with it." At least, not until Rosa is gone and safe from the secrets it may reveal. *But wait* . . . "How do you know the vase isn't real? I didn't tell you, did I?" My words sound muffled and slurred in my ears, my tongue feeling thick and tangled.

He reaches over and slips the water bottle out of my hand. "The media will definitely be getting hold of this story."

The water bottle.

I never heard the plastic seal crack when he opened the water bottle for me.

"Celine never noticed anything in her drink either," he says in a voice that sends chills down my spine. "And there were big chunks of Oxy and Xanax in there. I mean, I tried to crush them up as fine as possible, to make it easier on her. But in the end, it didn't matter. She would have drunk anything I gave her. She was a fucking head case over the breakup."

Jace.

Oh my God.

It was Jace all along.

CHAPTER 44

Maggie

December 23, 2015

It's the bitter cold I feel first. I can't say that it's what wakes me up, but it's the first thing I feel.

The second is the consuming darkness.

And then my fuzzy mind sorts everything else out at around the same time: the constant jolts and the loud whirl of tires; the ache in my shoulders, arms, and my wrists, which are tied behind my back; the laced water Jace handed me, that I so willingly took.

I scream. Until my throat stings and my voice doesn't work anymore.

My wrists burn.

Hours of trying to break free of the rope that binds my hands behind my back have left them raw, the rough cord scrubbing away my skin and cutting into my flesh. I'm sure I'll have unsightly scars.

Not that it will matter when I'm dead.

I resigned myself to that reality around the time that I finally let go of my bladder. Now I simply lie here, in a pool of urine and vomit, my teeth numb from knocking with each bump in the road, my body frozen by the cold.

Trying to ignore the darkness as I fight against the panic that consumes me. I could suffocate from the anxiety alone.

He knows that.

Now he's exploiting it. That must be what he does—he uncovers your secrets, your fears, your flaws—and he uses them against you. He did it to Celine.

And now he's doing it to me.

That's why I'm in a cramped trunk, my lungs working overtime against a limited supply of oxygen while my imagination runs wild with what may be waiting for me at the end of this ride.

My racing heart ready to explode.

The car hits an especially deep pothole, rattling my bones. I've been trapped in here for so long. Hours. Days. I have no idea. Long enough to run through every mistake that I made.

How I trusted him, how I fell for his charm, how I believed his lies. How I made it so easy for him to do this to me.

How Celine made it so easy for him, by letting him get close.

Before he killed her.

Just like he's going to kill me.

I'm a collection of frozen bones and numb terror when the car finally comes to a squeaking halt. The trunk pops open.

"Come on. Get up," Jace demands. I don't know how I never picked up on that harsh undertone in his voice before. His looks must have masked it.

I couldn't even move if I wanted to, so I simply remain curled in an awkward fetal position, until he seizes my underarms and yanks me out. I drop to the ground, the bite of the snow barely registering against my naked legs.

Stars shine above me. It's still deep in the night. The same night or another one, I can't say.

"Get up or freeze out here." As he heads toward a small cabin built into a hill, the snow crunches beneath his boots, the only sound that reaches my ears. We're nestled within a peaceful forest, Celine's killer and me. The only things I can see are thickets of trees and a beautiful expansive sky and a Cutlass with New York State plates that's bordering on vintage status. Definitely not the car I climbed into tonight.

I don't even scream. Without even trying, I know that my voice is long gone.

Is this his place?

Picking up a loose brick, Jace breaks the panel of glass in the door and reaches through with gloved hands to unlock it. He disappears inside.

I guess it's not his place.

I stay where I am, pondering how this could have gone so differently had I not let my guard down. It was a beautiful setup, really. Cameras at Hollingsworth would have captured nothing more than a five-minute conversation and then an amicable farewell, with Jace leaving before me.

That side street was dark and empty and, I'm certain, void of any security cameras. Of course he couldn't know for sure that I'd accept his offer, that I'd be thirsty enough to take the water he had prepared especially for me. He could only hope for it.

And it paid off.

Boots crunching against snow announces his return. "You're a stubborn bitch, right to the end." He hoists me to my feet by my arms. I struggle to stand, and so he ends up half-dragging me through the snow and in through the door. It leads into the cabin's unfinished basement, nothing but concrete-block walls with exposed joists above and two naked bulbs to give some light. A furnace sits in the far right corner, a flight of wooden stairs ahead.

He shoves me at the stairs. "Climb, now."

"I can't. My wrists," I manage, my voice a hoarse whisper.

He grabs the binding, and I wince in pain and expectation, thinking he'll drag me. But after a few sharp tugs and the sound of cord being cut, my arms flop to the stairs, freed.

And now I know that he has a knife.

"Get upstairs."

Slowly, and painfully, I crawl each of the soft steps that still smell of fresh pine, like they were recently built. When I reach the main floor of what looks like a small but homey A-frame cabin, Jace forces me to the left, toward a blindingly bright light and a tub of running water.

He pushes the bathroom door open and a wall of steam hits my face. "No, no . . ." My head shakes and I try to take steps back but I'm too weak, too numb.

"Get in." A violent tug and tearing sound, and the next thing I know my dress is on the floor and I'm down to my soiled undergarments and Jace is lifting me into the bathtub.

I'm stabbed by thousands of sharp prickles as the hot water touches my frozen skin. My mouth opens, but I find no relief in my soundless screams, as he stands there and watches me suffer.

I begin to cry.

CHAPTER 45

Maggie

Even though I suspected Jace at one point, being in this situation now is surreal. I look up at him, hovering over me with arms crossed, waiting for—I assume—my body to thaw, and I still can't believe this is happening.

That he is capable of this kind of cruelty.

"Don't bother fighting back," Jace warns, his voice hollow and deathly calm. He grabs hold of the plug with gloved hands and releases it. The now-cool bath water begins draining quickly.

"Why are you doing this?" I ask, and my throat burns with the question.

"Because you wouldn't fucking stop. You just kept pushing and pushing and—" Anger slips into his tone and he abruptly cuts himself off. When he speaks again, it's back to that eerie calm. "If you'd just left it alone, this wouldn't be happening. I wouldn't have to do this. You brought this on yourself. You did. This is your fault. No one else's fault but yours."

"Are you trying to convince me or yourself?"

He glares at me, but in his eyes, I see a wild mix of panic and fear burning bright. "She was going to destroy my life."

"No, she wasn't. She wasn't the one blackmailing you. Grady was!" I'm waiting for Childs to confirm that, but I'm sure of it. "It wasn't her fault."

"Wasn't it?" He bites the inside of his lip. "If she hadn't been a whore, then none of this would have happened. But because she was a whore, she invited that sick fuck into our lives to try and ruin me."

The water is receding quickly, exposing my pink, raw skin to the cool air, making me shiver uncontrollably. I curl my limbs around my body to ward off his icy blue eyes as they travel over me.

His lips twist in an unpleasant smirk. "Where is that confident Maggie Sparkes who liked to dress up and tease me in my office?"

I glare at him. "She's been kidnapped. It doesn't suit her."

"There she is . . . Don't worry. There's nothing about you right now that turns me on."

Then why throw me into the bath? I assumed it was because I pissed and vomited all over myself, and he wanted me clean before he violated me.

Even with the shock of the hot water, I still feel groggy. "What did you give me?"

"It doesn't feel good, waking up after someone has drugged you, does it?"

I glare at him.

"I wasn't sure how well the Ambien would work on its own so I added a Percocet. You went down faster than I expected. I'm guessing the champagne helped."

And here I was, worried about a hangover.

His voice turns icy again. "Get up."

I use the sides of the tub to brace myself as I stand, every inch of my body sore. There's no point in refusing him, because I'm guessing it'll just cause me pain.

That doesn't mean that I won't fight back.

Jace takes several steps back, as if he can read my thoughts. "Don't try anything because it'll only end badly for you." As if to prove how badly, he retrieves the serrated hunting knife from the leather holder attached to his hip, and a gleam of light catching the sharp blade stalls my plan of attack.

He changed at some point, exchanging the suit from the auction house for a simple black crewneck and black pants. I don't know what he has planned for me, but the black leather gloves tell me it's something that requires covering his tracks.

I need to be smart. Injuries will make it harder to run.

And I still don't have my full strength. Even after soaking in a hot bath, my bones ache and my body shakes uncontrollably. I've never felt cold like this before in my life, right to my core, as if I'll never fully thaw. "Can I have a towel?"

"No. Walk."

With wariness, I do, catching my reflection in the mirror—a hideous version of myself, the little makeup I wore to the auction streaking my cheeks. Dark bruises have already formed around my arms.

I catch Jace's icy gaze in the mirror and I hold it defiantly, refusing to show the fear he wants to see, even as a sharp point pricks my hip.

"Here." He throws a bath towel at me, holding it by the very edge with his gloved hand. "I can't stand the sound of chattering teeth. Now move."

I hug the towel around myself and stumble to keep up as he uses the edge of the knife to herd me left and down the hall, toward a faint glow of light, never laying so much as a finger on me. I think that's intentional. Now I understand why he forced me into the bath—hoping to rid my body of all evidence that he ever touched it. That brings me some small comfort that rape isn't on the agenda.

"In there."

I find myself in a small, simple bedroom with a double bed adorned by a quilted blanket. A clunky wooden nightstand sits on the far side, decorated with a picture of two small children smiling out at me, and a sizeable granite rock with a clock embedded in its face, telling me that it's nearly four a.m. Resting next to the picture and the rock clock are a set of handcuffs, a glass with clear liquid in it, and two plastic ziplock bags with contents I can't see from here.

That's his plan.

He's going to bind my wrists and pump me full of drugs. That's how I'm going to die. An overdose, just like Celine. Quick, clean, the least risk of leaving evidence of himself in a struggle. "Coward," I whisper.

"Why? Because I'm smart? Because I'm not stupid enough to use a gun that could somehow be traced back to me? Because I'm not animalistic enough to carve you into pieces with this knife? Anyone can buy Oxy; no one will ever be able to connect those dots. Not even your overpriced PI."

"Like I said . . . coward."

"Get on the bed," he demands. He doesn't even sound like himself anymore.

He sounds like someone who's preparing himself for murder.

But I refuse to prepare myself for dying.

My instincts tell me to run, and so I try, spinning on my heels, ready to claw, punch, knee my way to safety. Because I *am* going to die here if I don't.

He's ready for it, though. Pain explodes in my cheek as his fist connects with it. I stumble back and lose my balance, falling onto the mattress.

"You never listen, do you?" he snaps. He sets the knife down on the nightstand—at least he didn't stab me—and, seizing my ankles with rough hands, he hoists my legs onto the bed until I'm lying on my back. I'm still so dazed, I don't realize that he's bound my wrists at the front with the handcuffs until after the metal click sounds.

"You don't have to do this," I say, stalling, struggling to breathe through the pain. I need to keep him talking. Just long enough to stall that lethal cocktail from sliding down my throat.

"Yes, I do. You won't stop. You said so yourself, that day in my office. You're like a dog on a bone with that fucking vase. I guess I can understand, given the value of it." He shakes his head. "Celine and all her note-taking. Who keeps paper records still? I'm glad I was at her apartment that day when you handed those books over to that friend of hers. I thought I'd covered my ass when I deleted her pictures and that post she was writing."

Realization hits me like a hard slap to the face. "You did take it, after all . . ." I was right the first time around. It wasn't Grady. But then . . . why was that vase in Grady's closet?

"Of course I did. I'm not going to leave millions of dollars behind." He dumps the crushed contents of a pill bottle into the glass, tapping the bottom of it once . . . twice . . . I'm guessing he's not going to stage this as a suicide, seeing as there's no reason for me being out here, in the middle of nowhere. "I had already decided to sit on it for a while before I got it appraised, to see if Celine was right. But once I learned you guys were inventorying everything she owned, and I realized that she also kept written catalogues, I just knew that little friend of hers would find a record of it. And with my luck, he'd start thinking the same thing she did—that this was a real find—and then he'd notice it was missing. And, lo and behold, I was right."

"So you killed Celine for money?"

He scoffs. "What kind of a bottom feeder do you take me for, Maggie?"

And now he's coming at me, grabbing the back of my neck and hoisting me into a sitting position. He lifts the lethal cocktail.

He's not going to put that in my body. I'm not going to let him.

He must see the unspoken determination in my eyes because he picks up the knife. I gasp with panic as he approaches me, aiming the edge at my neck until I feel a sharp pinch. "So here's how it's going to work. You're going to drink every last drop and not move, because if you move, this knife will slice open your throat and you'll bleed out quickly."

I close my eyes as tears slip down my cheeks. As much as I'd like to defy him and fight, my survival instincts keep my body frozen in place. Maybe there's not enough Oxy in this drink to kill me. Maybe someone will rescue me in this isolated part of the woods.

He presses the glass to my lips. "Open!" I do, and he pours the liquid down my throat. I struggle to swallow against the chunks of too many pills and the burn of alcohol.

I'm going to die here tonight.

I wonder how long it will take.

I glare at him, waiting for him to pull the glass away. His eyes flicker to mine once but then shift away quickly as he does. As if he can't actually face what he's about to do to me.

Good. At least he feels guilt.

"You shouldn't have killed her," I mumble bitterly. "If you hadn't killed her, I wouldn't be here now. So this is all your fault. You have no one to blame but yourself."

He shakes his head, tucking the knife back into the holder hanging from his belt. "She would have turned on me eventually. Do you even have any idea what your friend's mental state was that night?"

I wince against the gritty pill residue left on my tongue. "No, I don't. Why don't you tell me?"

CHAPTER 46

Celine

November 15, 2015

I can still fix this. I know I can.

I smear the tears from my cheek with my palm as I gaze at his picture.

It's been weeks since I found out that Jace slept with his assistant and I still can't shake the hurt. That day, when my phone beeped with a group text from Marnie to Dani and me, saying "Guess who's banging her boss! Shhhh . . . ," followed by an image of Jace lying asleep in his bed, it was like someone punched me in the gut.

I bolted from my desk and ran for the office restrooms, but not before several people saw the tears streaming down my face and sent Dani in to check on me. Of course I used my dying mother as the excuse. How horrible am I! But I had no choice. I couldn't tell her the truth.

It was wrong of Natasha to take this of him—he would hate it if he knew. It was probably also wrong of me to print it out, but I couldn't help myself.

Natasha shouldn't have taken it and Marnie shouldn't have forwarded it, but I'm glad she did. It proves how easily personal, private information can spread. I'm glad we kept our relationship under wraps. Now there's no one to question why we broke up.

I deleted all record of the photo from my possession, except for this printed copy. It's helped ease my anxiety, helped me drift off to sleep. Almost more than the alcohol.

What if I can't fix this, though?

I trace my finger over his image, sleeping so peacefully. "You are going to ruin me," I whisper. God, I'm such a fucking mess.

I fold up the picture and tuck it into the secret compartment of the lockbox that Maggie got me for my birthday years ago—the most thoughtful present she's ever given me—next to the wad of cash I've managed to set aside. It's enough to cover rent and bills for December and January. After that . . . well, Maggie will come in and save the day, and there's nothing Mom will be able to do to stop her.

I need to get ahold of myself. I'm usually pretty good outside the comfort of my apartment, forcing smiles with Ruby and Dani. But the depression has bowled me over. I reach for the full bottle, a new prescription that I filled this morning at the drugstore. I told my doctor that I needed a stronger dose, that this time it was bad.

But it won't be forever, I promise myself. It's going to get much better, soon, because I have made the discovery of a lifetime with this vase.

At least, I'm pretty sure that I have.

Cracking the top of the pill bottle, I pop one and wash it down with the vodka, even though I know I shouldn't. It's kind of like water for me anyway now.

The yellow rose petals and card that Jace sent me last week sit at the top of the box. I pull the note out and smile, reading the message. He still cares about me.

Yes, there's still hope.

The buzzer rings, and I frown. I'm not expecting anyone tonight, and no one I know ever just drops by. Shutting the box, I force myself out of bed and hit the "answer" button on the wall.

"Hey, Celine. It's me."

My heart skips at the sound of Jace's muffled voice. It's late. Ten thirty on a Sunday night. "Come on up!" I slam the door lock release to let him through. And then I panic, checking my reflection to confirm that my face is indeed as puffy as I think it is.

There's not much I can do about the puffiness or my bloodshot eyes or the fact that I've already had two too many drinks, but the tank top and sweatpants can be improved upon. I have just enough time to swap them for a cute nightshirt and my silk robe before I hear his knock.

I throw open the door.

He smiles, but it's off. It's the same smile he gave me the night he came here to confront me. Then, I was none the wiser. Now, it's like I'm on eggshells. I won't let it sway my determination, though. "Hey, come in." I usher him in, not wanting to answer any questions from Ruby tomorrow about the man in my apartment. But she's likely asleep at this point anyway.

"I got your message." His gaze drifts over the apartment, settling on the far shelf next to my desk. I know why. It's where my camera used to be hidden, back when I didn't know Grady had used it to spy on me. Grady still hasn't admitted to it, of course, and I haven't gone to the police because then they'd see the video and I'd have to explain why Jace threw cash down on the table. It won't end well for anyone.

"There's no camera. I swear. It was just the one and it's disconnected. You can check if you want; it's in my desk drawer."

Nodding, he turns to look at me, his eyes drifting down to where my robe sits parted slightly. "How are you doing?"

"I'm okay. Do you want a drink?" I gesture at the bottle of vodka sitting out, my half-finished glass next to it.

"No. Thank you."

I reach out to graze his forearm lightly, because I can't help myself. "I got your flowers. They were beautiful. Thank you." I already told him as much in a voice mail that he never responded to.

A frown flickers over his face, but he says nothing. "What is this Ming bowl you were talking about on your voice message?"

"Here. Come." I hook my arm through his—because I need to touch him, I want him to remember how good this felt, how good this can feel again—and pull him over to the couch, where it sits in a box, waiting. I carefully pull the blue-and-white floral bowl out to show him. "I found it last weekend. It's perfect for your mother. She's going to love it." I've never even met her and I know.

He turns it over to study the seal. "Is this authentic?"

I show him the certificate that Ling gave me, pressing my lips together to keep from grinning too proudly. "I would have had my friend at Hollingsworth appraise it, but I couldn't get hold of him in time." Hans would lose his mind if he knew I was going to that "hack shop" for appraisals.

I can't read the look on Jace's face. "Where'd you find this?"

"An estate sale in Queens. It was only thirty-five bucks."

"This is . . . I don't know what to say."

That you've forgiven me. That you realize we're too perfect together to let my past get in the way.

"You want to see something really amazing? Look what else I found." I grab his hand and pull him to my desk, where the twin vase sits. "There's this well-known story of a missing Qing Dynasty vase with a red dragon on it. Everyone believes that it's been lost forever." I tell him the story of the emperor's twin boy and girl, and the phoenix and the dragon vases made in memory of them. "And these markings?" I use the excuse to hold his hand so I can trace his finger over the script. "I really think this is legit, Jace. I think I've made an insane discovery!" I can't keep the excitement from my voice.

It must be infectious because I can feel his excitement now, too. "What would something like this be worth?"

I hit the space bar on my keyboard, and the blog post I've been working on for days opens up. "Look at all of these . . ." I scroll through the list of articles I found on other authentic Qing Dynasty items. At the lowest, they're worth tens of thousands. "Chinese businessmen are snapping these up as soon as they hit the market, wanting to bring their heritage back home. Look at this one." My stomach does a flip. "It went at auction for equivalent to eighty-five million dollars. And that's not nearly as valuable as this twin vase. I honestly don't even know what someone might pay for a famous missing piece like this. I'd gladly take one million, but I know that if this proves to be authentic, it's going to be more than that. This is life-altering for me."

"You said this is a twin? Who has the one with the phoenix?" Jace asks.

"It's in a private collection, but I haven't confirmed exactly who has it just yet." That's where I'll definitely need Hans's help.

Jace nods slowly, peering down at me through those gorgeous blue eyes. "This is quite the find."

"Isn't it?"

His gaze skates over my lips. "Am I the first person you've told?"

"Yes. You're the first. The only." I lean into him.

Hoping he'll close the distance.

Praying.

He takes a step back.

My heart falters. "Don't you get it? It means I'll never have to worry about money again. I'll never have to do that other stuff again! I've already stopped," I'm quick to say. "I'm done. A hundred percent. I swear. I'm sorry I lied to you like that. And that video is never going to surface. I promise."

His jaw tenses. He was so angry the day he came here with that jump drive and note in his hand to ask me what the hell I was doing. Like *I* was the one blackmailing him.

When he plugged it in and showed it to me, I made it to the bathroom just in time to lose my dinner. I thought that alone would have been enough to convince him that it wasn't me.

"I swear, I had no idea that Grady was capable of that. I ended it with him right after I said I would." *Right after you dumped me.*

But I'm going to get you back. I am.

He opens his mouth, hesitates. "That's good because you shouldn't be selling yourself like that. You're far too smart and beautiful to let just anyone have you."

"I'm not letting *anyone* have me. Ever again. I'm yours and only yours." I grab hold of his hand, the tears already beginning. I can't seem to keep them at bay lately. "*Please* let me have another chance. I will make it up to you, I promise."

"You have to stop this, Celine," he says, his voice icy calm. "The calls. The visits. Notes, like this one." He pulls from his back pocket the envelope that I sent through the internal building mail service. "People are going to figure it out."

"No, they won't. Not from that." All it said was that I'm sorry.

Because I am. *So very* sorry.

"Natasha opened it. You don't think a woman's handwriting on a note like this would make her start asking questions?"

"Why? Because you're sleeping with her?" I snap. I didn't mean to snap.

"I . . ." His mouth drops open. "Where did you hear that?"

I should tell him what she did. But I don't want to drag Dani or Marnie into this. "It doesn't matter how I know. It's bad enough that I know. And only a week after we broke up?"

"You're kidding me, right? It was one night—one mistake. You've been whoring yourself out for months and you have the nerve to even say a single word to me about that?" He's angry now.

And he's right.

"You're right. I'm sorry, I shouldn't have said anything. Please, can we just start over? I promise I won't say anything."

He heaves a sigh, like he's exhausted. "Celine . . . come on. I can't keep having this conversation with you. We were together for a couple of months. It was nothing."

"Do you take all your girlfriends to see your mother?"

He grits his teeth. "Okay, fine. It was more than just a casual thing."

"And we can have it back." I press myself up against him in an attempt to convince him.

"No. We can't."

Tear. More tears pour out, unbidden. "Please don't say that. I can't take that."

"It's over, Celine. I don't know how else to explain it."

I start to sob uncontrollably, my face falling into his chest. "Then why did you bother coming tonight?" There's nothing comforting in the feel of his body under my cheek anymore. It's tense and unwelcoming, and why oh why am I begging and pleading like this?

"Honestly? I looked into that Grady guy, and he's not hurting for money. Plus, he never followed through with the blackmail threat. Why?"

"Because I asked him not to?" I honestly don't know why he didn't. I want nothing more to do with Grady, or Jay.

Jace's well-groomed eyebrow arches. "So he's willing to go to the trouble of blackmail but doesn't actually go through with it because you *asked* him not to? Doesn't make sense, Celine. But what *does* make sense is that the one person who's willing to do just about anything for money and is obviously feeling unstable right now would do something irrational and then feel guilty about it after."

"What?" I pull back to look at him. Now I see it. The question in his eyes. "You don't still believe that I had anything to do with it, do you?" Anger flares deep within me. I hate that he thinks I could do something so vile and cruel. "Well then maybe I should just go and leak it then!" I don't even have a copy. "Maybe I'll wait until my mother dies and then I won't give a shit who sees!" As soon as the words are out, I gasp and slap a hand over my mouth. I can't believe I just said that. "I'm sorry. I didn't mean it. I'm just going through a really hard time with my mom and stress with work and now this."

He closes his eyes and rubs the frown lines out of his forehead. "I don't think you're okay at all."

I laugh through my sobs and I sound even more pathetic. "You're only just realizing that now? I'm heartbroken! I'm madly in love with you!"

"Okay, shhh . . ." He holds his hands up. "Calm down!" I hear a whisper of "Jesus" before "Have you slept lately?"

I shake my head, trying to stop crying. I can't. "I just took a pill, though. It should help. If not, I'll take another."

"Sleeping pills?"

"Yes. And a Xanax. I went off them for a while, but I'm getting back on them now. I'll be fine soon, trust me."

He eyes the vodka, and I know what he's thinking. Stupid. Yes, I know.

"Okay . . ." He heaves a big sigh. I've shaken him up. He just wants to get the hell away from me.

"Please don't leave." I reach for him, rope my arms around his waist. "Please stay awhile. I'm having a really tough night."

For so long, he keeps his eyes closed. Thinking.

Fighting his feelings for me, I'm sure.

He knows we're perfect together.

When his eyes finally open, they trail down the front of my nightshirt. And his fingertips . . . they twirl the spaghetti strap, as if he's tempted to slip it off. "I want you to go lie down in bed," he says softly. "I'll get you another sleeping pill."

My heart jumps with hope. Is it possible? Has he changed his mind, at least for tonight? I'll start with just tonight. He's not ready to walk away from me yet, no matter what he says. He's just afraid. I have to convince him that I won't ever hurt him. I won't ever betray him like I did.

And I won't, because I'm going to make millions of dollars off the sale of that vase and live how I'm meant to live, and even though I can't do anything about my dying mother, at least I have that.

Everything is going to work out.

"Okay," I agree, making my way over to slip into my double bed that he and I haven't slept in together yet. I want to. I want to erase the last time we were together, on my couch—and I want to do it tonight.

I've learned a thing or two in my time trying to please men who pay for me, and so I lie down on top of my sheets, letting my gown slide high up my thigh without giving too much away. Jace did say that he likes my muscular thighs and my curvy figure.

Finally he returns, with a clear glass in hand, and chunks of ice floating inside. He has one for himself, too. "Figured one drink wouldn't hurt." His eyes trail over my body and I see something unreadable in them. Something cold.

I push the thought away.

He'll change his mind.

"I crushed the pill and dumped it in for you. That's what I do sometimes, when I can't sleep. Works every time."

I take the glass, even though I know it's stupid to take a sleeping pill with vodka, but Jace does it and he says it's fine and he'd never hurt me. He cares about me. I know he does. I wince as tiny chunks of pill coat my tongue.

"I know, it tastes weird, but it works. Trust me."

"I do trust you." I smile and take another large sip, forcing back the granular bits. "An Ambien, right?" I should have made sure he didn't take the pill from the unmarked bottle on the left in the medicine cabinet. I don't even know how old that Oxy is. Six months at least. A client gave them to me one night. I never took any, but I also never flushed them.

He smiles gently. "Right. Drink up."

By the time I've finished my drink—straight vodka's an acquired taste that I have mastered in the last year—my tongue has gone numb.

"Talk to me."

He smiles, but it's a bit strained. "About what?"

I nod to his drink. "Aren't you going to have yours?"

He swirls it around. "I don't know. I like watching you more." His gaze crawls over my body, stalling on my panties, where I've let my nightshirt slide up. "Here. How about you drink mine." He hands it to me and then, with his now free hand, strokes the side of my face, pushing my hair away. "Go on. Drink up."

I do, happy to please him in any way I can. He's so gentle, so slow, it's almost like he's not even touching me. Or maybe it's the sleeping pill taking effect. I can feel the weight of it in my stomach almost instantly, the potency beginning to radiate out into my limbs.

He continues stroking my face as I force down the drink, telling myself that this is the last one. In fact, this is the last vodka I'm ever drinking. I'm going to have to call in sick to work tomorrow, but I don't care. I've already given my notice. Those assholes know my mother's dying and they can't give me more than three months off? Fuck them.

Everything tastes gritty now, like it's chalky with pills, but that must just be the residue on my tongue from my drink. This is Jace's drink.

"Can you lie down with me?" I ask, my lids beginning to feel heavy, my body sinking into the mattress. It's not the most relaxing feeling, to be honest, but I guess that means the pill is working and I'll be asleep soon.

Tomorrow will be better.

"Jace?" It takes some effort to say his name.

I crack my eyes open to see him flipping through my diary left on the nightstand. "Oh, God. No . . . ," I say, and I intended that to be more vehement than I think it is when it comes out. There's all kinds of things in there, about how much I love him, and about Grady—I don't want him reading about me sleeping with another man.

"It's okay. It's good for me to read this," he whispers, his face a sorrowful mask. "It makes me feel better about doing this. You weren't going to stop, were you?"

Trying to win you back? I smile with my eyes closed now, because everything's spinning. "No. I wasn't. I love you too much," I whisper, and I can't be sure I even moved my mouth. "I think I'm going to fall asleep now." I force my eyes open. Jace isn't beside me anymore. Where did he go so fast? Movement catches my eye, and I strain to focus farther. He's still here. He's at the door now, with a cardboard box in his hand.

I knew buying that bowl for his mother was a good idea.

Swallowing is so hard right now.

Why is it so hard?

I'm so tired.

I'll sleep well tonight. I can feel it.

CHAPTER 47

Maggie

December 23, 2015

"She was fucking *obsessed* with me," Jace mutters. "Pages and pages of diary entries about me, about how much she loved me, about how perfect I am for her, about how I'm the one."

"I knew there was another diary," I whisper in triumph, even though it seems silly now to be so happy about that. My limbs are beginning to feel tingly, like I might not have complete control of them if I try to move. At least it's taking longer than I expected for these drugs to sink in.

I'm not dead yet.

"And it told me everything I needed to know. She had turned our short relationship into some fairy tale with a happily ever after. We were already getting married, in her eyes. And then when we broke up . . ." He shakes his head. "She completely lost it. Between the phone calls and the constant crying . . . You should see what she wrote in there about me, about never giving me up. And every time I told her that it was over, she'd start bawling her eyes out. It was only a matter of time before that turned into anger and revenge. Plenty of other women like that have brought down powerful men before. They're the irrational ones who turn bitter and call up the media to try and destroy your reputation when they finally realize they're not going to get what they want."

"Celine would never hurt someone she loved. Or thought she loved."

"Bullshit. She threatened me that night."

"She didn't mean it."

"Stop protecting her," he snaps. "You didn't see her. You didn't have her crying her eyes out all over your shirt. The woman was insane. Next thing I know, she'd be tag-teaming with that British asshole and blackmailing me again. She was a whore, nothing more. And I wasn't going to let her destroy my life. Or my family's life. She should have been honest from the start."

"So, when you went there that night, did you plan on killing her?"

"No!" He shakes his head. "I was going there to get the Ming bowl that she phoned me about and keep the peace. You think I'm some kind of cold-blooded murderer. I'm not." He takes his time capping the empty pill bottle and dumping it into a bag. "I just did what she was going to do anyway, and then made sure I didn't leave my fingerprints. Her medicine cabinet was full of drugs. She had probably already taken enough to kill herself that night."

"Just like I was going to do this?" I lift my arm to point at the empty glass, but my movements are sluggish.

"You should have just minded your own business. Just like that sick fuck Grady. He deserves to be punished, even if it's not for the right crime."

"They're going to catch Grady eventually. Aren't you worried what he's going to tell them when they accuse him of murder?"

Jace looms over me, pausing to watch. I'm sure he's gauging how far off I am. How long before he can leave me and be sure, just like he did with Celine.

I open and shut my eyes slowly a few times for impact.

He turns his attention back to the nightstand, now opening up the other ziplock bag. "Grady won't be talking to anyone, anymore."

The meaning behind his words hits me like a punch to the chest. I gasp. "Oh my God." Grady isn't in the wind. He isn't using his technical prowess to escape any nets.

He's dead.

"You killed him, too?" My chest feels like it's collapsing in on itself.

"What do you care? If he hadn't videotaped and blackmailed me, your best friend would probably still be alive."

I don't know why I care, but I do. The last time I saw him, it was through a window, when I told him to go to hell. I wouldn't give him a chance to explain. Maybe he would have admitted to everything, and I would have turned my attention back to Jace. Maybe this wouldn't be happening right now.

"You set him up. Everything in his apartment."

"Just her phone and the vase. The creepy 'Celine' box of pictures and panties was all him."

"And the phone call?"

"People will agree to do just about anything when they think it may save their life. You wouldn't believe how many of those manufactured fake dragon vases are out there. I started looking for one as soon as I realized you had Celine's paper records, just in case I needed a decoy. And now, when this story hits the news, everyone is going to be checking their mother's closet for a fifty-million-dollar vase."

Fifty million dollars. "Is that what you think it's worth?"

"That's what the private collector who has the other one is willing to pay me, in cash, if we avoid auction houses. That Asian appraiser friend of Celine's helped me locate him. Of course now I'll have to wait awhile, and use an anonymous front man for media purposes, and give that person a cut, too. I can't have my name tied to this after you've had your PI all over me. It'll raise too many questions."

"Where's the vase now?"

"In a hidden safe in my office."

I missed that entirely. "So you knew it was Grady who blackmailed you all along?" Where the hell is Grady right now? Did Jace pump him full of drugs, too? My eyes graze over his knuckles, bruised and raw. He said that was from boxing. I'm guessing that was a lie.

We've fallen into a strange, calm conversation now, like two friends in the dark and quiet night, as the drugs course through me.

He seems almost relieved. It probably has something to do with confessing all of his crimes to a soon-to-be dead woman. “Not until I read Celine’s diary. I was waiting for him to come back to me, to threaten me again. I wasn’t going to do anything otherwise. With Celine dying, if something happened to him, it might raise suspicions. So I kept my distance and hoped it would all dissipate. Then you came along and ruined everything.

“I used you as an excuse to meet with him. I told him that I had information for him.” He smiles as he reaches into the ziplock bag and pulls out a few hairs. Holding them up to the light, I see the dark brown color.

Grady’s hair color.

Jace releases them and they float onto the floor next to the bed.

He’s planting evidence.

“That’s not going to be enough,” I argue, though I have no clue.

“Maybe not. But then there’s also his car, which has a soiled trunk full of your DNA—thank you for that. They’ll find that abandoned, twenty or so miles away from here.”

“They’ll find his body.” My heart is starting to beat harder in my chest, working against the toxins.

“Not soon, anyway.” He sounds so confident. Do I even want to know what he did with Grady?

I want more information, but I can’t let this drag on much longer. I’m beginning to feel the heavy pull of what he put into my body, and I don’t know how much longer I have. Playing dead may be my only option.

And so I do, staying as still as possible, closing my eyes for longer periods of time, until I’m afraid that I’m not pretending anymore.

And then the chance that I’d assumed I wouldn’t have happens.

“Shit,” I hear him mutter.

A small plastic container from the bag of Grady’s DNA slips out of Jace’s hand to land on the floor. It must have rolled under the bed because he curses somewhere below, as if he has turned and stooped to get it.

Summoning all the energy I can, I seize the rock clock from the table. It's heavier than I'd imagined, and I have to struggle to maintain my grip. Swinging my bound hands as high as possible, I slam it down, hard, on the top of his head.

And then what's left of my conscious brain screams at me to run.

I slither off the end of the bed and bolt out the door and down the hall, expecting hands to seize me at any moment and pull me back. I don't stop, though, using the stair rail to keep me from falling as I stumble down into the basement. I don't stop even when the snow bites into my bare feet.

I run and run, tripping up the driveway, my balance off either because of my bound hands or my panic or the drugs.

I dare to check over my shoulder only once. I don't see Jace, but he's there, I know it. I can hear his feet, pounding into the ground. Or maybe that's just my heart that I hear, pounding in my ears as I run.

I reach the road and don't know whether to go left or right. It all looks the same—dark and empty—but I have to choose one and hope that I'm not guaranteeing my own death. "Which way . . . which way . . . which way . . ." I close my eyes and try to remember which direction he turned in from, when I was trapped in that trunk, but I can't.

I choose right, and hope that it truly is right, even as I struggle to stay on my feet, struggle to focus.

The frigid cold keeps my body going, but I'm so tired. I don't know that I can go any farther. But I think I see something. Far in the distance. Beams of light. A beacon for me, maybe.

I just need to . . .

My knees buckle and sink into the snow, but I barely feel the cold anymore.

I guess that means I'm not going to make it.

A door slams somewhere, my ears catch muffled voices. "Jesus . . . Call 9-1-1!"

CHAPTER 48

Maggie

January 4, 2016

Detective Childs exhales loudly as he sops the runny egg yolks up with a piece of rye toast.

"Is now the right time to say I told you so?" I murmur, my voice still raspy, not fully recovered. They can't be sure which caused more damage—the screaming that injured my vocal cords or the tubes thrust down my throat to try and pump the lethal dose of Oxy out of my stomach.

But I'm alive, so I don't care.

"Where do you see this going, Chester?" Doug asks from his seat next to me. He was there when I woke up in the Ellenville Regional Hospital, two hours north of New York City, near the Catskill Mountains, where Jace had taken me.

"A lot of different departments involved now. Us, local sheriff, state." His chocolate eyes drift over the sidewalk on the other side of the glass, and the pedestrians rushing past on their way back to work after the holiday season. "He's got some fancy lawyers, but the bastard sure looks guilty."

Jace wasn't two steps behind me that night. He was unconscious on the floor of that bedroom with a deep gash in his head. Not enough to kill him, but the corner of the clock made for a sharp weapon, and I hit him hard. I must have stepped on the broken glass by the door on my way out. The police followed the trail of blood from my foot up the driveway and found him there, along with the bag of evidence he was in the process of planting.

"I knew I didn't like Grady for murder," Doug mutters, shaking his head. "Too many things didn't add up."

Grady. I don't know what to feel about Grady, and what happened to him. On the one hand, he was a sick guy with a perverted fascination for Celine. He violated her privacy, manipulated her weaknesses, and lied to me about everything.

On the other hand, he was the guy who kept me warm on the rooftop, who gave me a few moments of respite amid what was probably the hardest time of my life.

Did he really deserve what Jace did to him?

His body hasn't turned up anywhere. We may never know exactly what Jace did to him. He vehemently denies any involvement with Grady's disappearance, even though they found him with Grady's hair.

Childs's laugh booms in the fifties diner. It's the same place where I met him the day he handed me Doug's business card. To think, had I not hired him, had I let this go, both Grady and Jace would have gotten away with their crimes. "Easy to say now, Dougie."

Doug scoffs. "Hey, who's the one who bugged Maggie's phone?"

"Illegally," I mutter, but I don't care that my PI had the sixth sense to stick a tracking device into the back of my cell phone as soon as we realized Grady was missing.

"Told you, things didn't add up. A guy like Grady would know that he can't just delete files on her computer and be done with it. On the day she died, no less. And the vase . . . No way your friend would mistake that for an authentic."

I smile. Doug didn't even know Celine and he had faith in her talent.

Thanks to that tracker in my phone, which Zac was monitoring they knew that I left Celine's auction but never made it back to the hotel. They found my purse—with my phone inside—tossed on the side of the freeway, heading north.

But had that lovely couple not been heading to the airport at that ungodly early hour, no one would have found me on the side of that lonely old road until it was much too late.

"Well, Jace looks guilty *and* he admitted everything to me."

"And his lawyers will argue that you were 'not of right state of mind,' pumped full of drugs. Best thing the prosecution can do now is build a strong enough case that Jace finally accepts that he's not getting away with it and confesses."

"Do you think that's possible?"

"I do." Childs pushes his plate away and leans back in his typical relaxed demeanor that used to anger me. Now I get that it's how he has to be to face these kinds of things day in, day out. "It sounds like he killed Celine out of fear and opportunity. He's not a psychopath. He's still human. Soon that side of him will prevail, when he sees how much he's hurting his parents. When he realizes that his life as he's known it is over. Until then, we'll keep building a case. We've got Ling Zhang cooperating with us now."

The Bone Lady. Another piece of the puzzle that didn't add up in Doug's eyes, so he had Zac dig deeper into her. She may not be a high-end auction house, but she sure has connections with black market art trade in China.

From what she told the police, Jace showed up one day with a cardboard box containing the blue-and-white Ming bowl that she had already appraised for Celine and a vase with a red dragon on it— and a shockingly authentic-looking seal. He wouldn't tell her where he got the vase from, and he wouldn't allow her to contact anyone about it yet for additional appraisals, to authenticate what she already believed might be the real deal. He simply asked her to track down the collector who owned the other one, and to not say a word about the vase, or he'd be taking his business elsewhere and she could kiss a sizeable dealer's cut good-bye.

She wasn't stupid. She knew how much it could be worth.

When we went in there on the very same day and asked about a red dragon vase, she began to suspect something might not be right.

"Where is Jace now?" I ask.

"Out on a ten-million-dollar bail."

While the fact that he's out doesn't make me feel great, I'm not worried that he's going to come after me. He was only a killer when he needed to cover his tracks. Now that those tracks are exposed, I'm confident he'll lay low. He doesn't need anything else to incriminate him.

I take a long draw of my tea—it doesn't taste as good from the diner's porcelain mug as it does coming from Ruby's dainty china cups. "So, now what?"

Childs levels me with a rare solemn look. "Now you let us do our jobs and close this case the right way. And you go back to helping people who are still alive."

Doug clears his throat.

"And let me guess . . ." I don't hide my sarcasm from my voice, though in truth I owe the overpriced PI and his basement-dwelling hacker for my life. "I need to write some more checks?"

EPILOGUE

Maggie

August 9, 2016

"Where's Hakeem?"

"It's me!" The little boy runs to me, squealing, carrying a fistful of wildflowers.

"No . . . Hakeem is only this tall." I measure against my thigh.

He giggles hysterically. "I grow. I am big now!"

I drop my duffel bag and reach down to wrap my arms around the gangly little boy's body, his skin slick from playing in the warm sun. "And your English has improved."

Hakeem's mother calls him from the doorway of their little home, one of several I helped build with my own hands almost a year ago now. She waves hello to me with a smile, and then herds him back with a string of Amharic. I was just beginning to learn enough of the language to communicate before I left.

"Soccer, later?" he asks, a hopeful look on his adorable little face.

"Definitely. As soon as I'm settled."

He scurries off to his mother, and I continue on, appreciating the changes and growth in the village since the last time I was here.

I sling my duffel bag over my shoulder, groaning under the weight of the four-hundred-page manuscript that arrived in San Diego just before I left, care of Ruby. I should have expected she would be hammering away at the keys on her typewriter, capturing the mystery of Celine's death as it unfolded. As soon as I found out, I bought her a computer with a twenty-inch monitor to make it easier on her eyes.

I'm equal parts petrified and curious to see how the shrewd old lady translated the recounting I gave to her over tea, on several trips back to New York since December.

She already has a publisher signed on. Given that the book is based on a true story, it can't be published until after the court case against Jace is over. The murder trial doesn't start until next year, so it'll be years before this book ever sees a store. I'm sure when it does, it'll be a big seller. I just hope Ruby's alive to see the day.

With each day that passes, I'm more and more confident that Jace will be punished for his crimes. He has fancy lawyers, but I have one of the best private investigators, working alongside the NYPD, state police, as well as the FBI, who got involved because of the value of the vase and because this is such a high-profile case. His lawyers will try to dismiss my testimony about the night in the Catskill Mountains when Jace tried to kill me—I was heavily drugged, after all—but they can't dismiss the stolen dragon vase and Celine's missing diary, which were found in Jace's hidden safe. Which I pointed the police toward before any search warrants were procured.

Doug said that the diary is apparently chockful of details that will help the prosecution piece together the truth. He warned that it's also the daily ramblings of an emotionally distraught and psychologically ill woman and it's not an easy read for anyone. I equally dread and long for the day that the trial is over and the diary is returned to me, her benefactor.

And then there's Grady's body, which washed up along the Hudson River in the spring. I'd be lying if I said that, hiding somewhere beneath my overall shock and disgust for the building super, I didn't feel a slight pang of sorrow the day Doug phoned to tell me.

Unfortunately, there was no evidence left to secure from it, but the bit of chain still wrapped around his legs suggested that someone had weighed him down. Childs won't tell me what they've found on that side of the investigation, but Doug has hinted that there are video surveillance cameras near one of the bridges that may help tie Jace to the death.

Ironic, if it's Grady's favorite criminal pastime that will help bring some closure to his death.

The police confirmed that the two other women in videos found on Grady's computer are alive and well and oblivious to their admirer's intrusions, only emphasizing that, while Grady's proclivities may have been deplorable, a death sentence was far too harsh.

The police also had a lot of questions for me about my relationship with him, thanks to the video feed from the apartment building's rooftop. Obviously I wasn't too concerned about that motion-activated camera when we were up there together.

I'm sure that the media and the courts aren't going to look too fondly at me once they secure details of my relationships with both men, but there's nothing I can do about that now. I'm not going to try to hide it.

I'm just going to enjoy the peace of this village while I have it, knowing that Jace is going to be punished for his crimes.

I round the corner to find the VU employee huts where we'll all be staying for the next two months while we get the solar panel power system up and running. And I smile. It's good to be back, even if my time away marked a very sad period in my life.

Rosa's passing.

She finally succumbed to her cancer in early June, and I think she was ready to go by the end of it. She tried to chase me off several times, but I refused, holding her hand as she slipped into unconsciousness that she never awoke from.

Kind of like her daughter.

Given the ongoing investigation, there was no way to keep Rosa from discovering the truth about Celine's demise, and her past, though I made it seem like she was mostly a paid companion. She handled it quite well, and in the end, she was just happy that Celine didn't make the choice to kill herself. If she didn't take her own life, that meant Rosa would be with her daughter in the afterlife.

Rosa's last dying wish was that I use my money and my connections to stop other young women from falling into the same trap that

Celine did. I had planned on it anyway, but to have Rosa ask me to do that—when she had asked for so little—only made it that much more important. I have every intention of making sure that vase is returned to Celine's estate after the trial against Jace is over, and the sale of it—through Hollingsworth rather than some back-alley Chinatown dealer—will get as many young women out of prostitution as possible.

I push the bittersweet thoughts aside as I wave at Graham from across the way. He's my right-hand man and the guy I've relied on for the past nine months to keep VU's mission going. He said he hired three new people for this project. I don't know much about them, but I trust his judgment.

Still, when I see the male figure lounging in the hammock, in the shade of one of a few trees, avoiding the midday heat, my stomach lurches. Not until I'm five feet away does he roll his head lazily toward me, opening one eye to size me up.

"Hey. You must be Maggie. They said you'd be getting in today." He reaches out to offer a hand. "I'm Sam."

I take it, hyper-aware of the way my name sounds in his Australian accent, and of his thick, wavy brown hair, damp and curling at the nape of his neck, and his lean but muscular body, on display without a T-shirt.

"Hi, Sam. You are here to . . ."

He grins. "I'm your electrician. I run a small solar panel installation business back home, outside Perth."

I fold my arms over my chest, drawing his golden eyes to my breasts for a second before they snap back to my face. "What made you leave your business and come out here, then?"

He shrugs. "Thought it'd be something different."

"Right. I'm sure it will be. Well, it was good to meet you, Sam . . ."

"Jacobs. Sam Jacobs. A lot of people just call me Jacobs."

"Of course they do," I mumble, giving him a half wave as I continue on to where I'll be staying. Feeling his eyes on me the entire way.

I slip my cell phone out of my pocket and dial.

A groggy Doug answers.

"Are you actually sleeping?"

"God forbid," he mutters. "What's up?"

I glance over my shoulder to watch the Australian electrician rest in his hammock. "I need a full background check done on someone."

ACKNOWLEDGMENTS

I have many people to thank for helping me get this book into readers' hands. Thank you to my amazing team at Atria Books. I say time and time again that the stars aligned when Sarah Cantin came into my (writing) life. Sarah, I sense your blood and sweat (and probably tears) within these pages, almost as much as my own. I guess multiple drafts along with working on two other books with me at the same time will do that. Let's not do that again, maybe? Judith Curr, for continuing to believe in me and for suggesting such a unique and perfect title. Suzanne Donahue, Ariele Fredman, Tory Lowy, Kimberly Goldstein, Jin Yu, Albert Tang, and Alysha Bullock (the brains and muscle behind the curtain)—thank you for being a part of the publishing house that I have come to know and love.

Stacey Donaghy, my super Type A agent who meshes so well with my own Type A tendencies. You work hard for me, you make me laugh, and I truly appreciate both those things.

Kelly Simmon of Inkslinger PR, who is always available to me, even with this pesky new time zone difference.

My two best cop friends (who shall remain nameless in print) for tolerating my random and likely inappropriate law enforcement–related texts at all hours of the day and night.

My readers—without you, I would not be sitting here, writing these acknowledgments right now. I know this is a slight departure from what I have given you in the past. I hope you loved reading it as much as I loved writing it.

My family—for always being in my corner through the lengthy, exhilarating, emotional, and sometimes painful process of writing novels.